THE UGLY BUREAUCRAT

A Novel

H. J. Lassek

Riverhaven Books

www.RiverhavenBooks.com

The Ugly Bureaucrat is a work of fiction. While some of the settings are actual, any similarity regarding names, characters, or incidents is entirely coincidental.

Published in the United States
by Riverhaven Books,
www.RiverhavenBooks.com

ISBN : 978-1-937588-41-0

Printed in the United States of America
by Country Press, Lakeville, Massachusetts

Edited by Bob Haskell

Designed by Stephanie Lynn Blackman

Cover Picture ©iStock.com/ChrisBoswell

Advanced praise for *The Ugly Bureaucrat*

...three men, along with their wives and various associates, make up the core of the novel. Deception, manipulation, lies and corruption become the norm and these characteristics make and destroy careers and relationships. It all comes across as being too close to the reality of bureaucracy and politics. Author H.J. Lassek has also woven into *The Ugly Bureaucrat* a number of social realities and these fit beautifully with the story...flashbacks of Vietnam and ...the plight of the American Indians and the abuse they suffer within the welfare system are covered in some detail. *The Ugly Bureaucrat* will hold your attention to the end.

Reviewed By Jeffrey Brooke-Stewart for Readers' Favorite

The Ugly Bureaucrat is a political drama but H.J. Lassek wrote it in a way that a layman, like me, understood the entire thing easily. It all sounded very authentic, as if the author really knew and experienced what he was talking about. It was excellent. The characters were interesting, credible and with good dynamics...It was kind of painful how it concluded but I still loved the whole thing and would rate this with five stars. The struggles and hardships of being in a bureaucracy were all new to me and it was enjoyable to read.

Reviewed By Lorena Sanqui for Readers' Favorite

You will be pushed right into the deep end of action and government machinations when you leap into this well written story by H.J. Lassek. It has been a while since I truly enjoyed a political action novel like this one. The characters are well written and have depth to them that you don't always get in action novels. I was able to read through and enjoy this book from start to finish in relatively fast order. There are no points that drag and nothing that feels like it is going too fast. I could find a lot of corresponding parts of this book that match with current themes and I think most readers will do so as well. I would recommend this book for those who like political action.

Reviewed By Kathryn Bennett for Readers' Favorite

...H.J. Lassek's knack for character development entices you to keep reading...the work highlights the inherent prejudices against the American Indian at the time. There is something very disturbing about reading a book of this nature, because the attitudes portrayed are so convincing that it becomes hard to tell if they are satirical or truthful, blurring the lines between entertaining fiction and thought-provoking fact. Either way, fans of political dramas and strong, character-based storytelling are sure to find *The Ugly Bureaucrat* to be a challenging and rewarding read.

Reviewed By K.C. Finn for Readers' Favorite

This book is dedicated to my two children.

I wish to acknowledge the StoryTellers of Cape Cod,
especially Elaine Brennan and Jo Ann Kelley,
for their friendship, their encouragement, their candor.

My gratitude to
Loretta Kucera, Pam Emery, Forrest Beam, and Jim Breagy
for laboring through the manuscript early on,
offering insights and encouragement.

And my thanks to Susan Truitt
for sustaining me through my self-doubts,
being tolerant of my intolerance,
and not forgoing the often painful but necessary honesty.

Bob Haskell did the editing.   He was masterful.
His injection of syntactic order, grammatical analysis,
and common sense were critical to the finished product.
Further, Bob captured the story's essence,
giving it greater depth.
His patience, persistence, and unfailing judgment are
appreciated beyond my ability to express.

To these good people, I offer my sincere thanks.

CHAPTER ONE

Bob Elam experienced a nagging but understandable fear of the unknown as he contemplated his future.

He surveyed the sprawl of his lumberyard from his second-floor office while he waited, noting how the long rows of stacked lumber produced the optic effect of converging upon a distant point.

What the hell, he mused. No matter what the report says, this is all mine. Nothing's going to change that.

He thought of the work that had taken him from a fledgling businessman to the owner of the state's largest lumber company. This enterprise is real, tangible, touchable, he assured himself. And this business of the state legislature would be but a sideline, a part-time job. It would offer perks and prestige, those pleasant but meaningless trappings.

Placing this item in its proper perspective, he sipped at his coffee, his eyes still fixed on that distant point.

His telephone briefly distracted him before someone else picked it up after two rings and apparently dealt with the caller. Elam resumed staring out his window, this time focusing on a small shed in the center of the lumberyard. Although seldom used, he allowed it to stand as a reminder of more humble, more modest days.

He sat in his comfortable, high-backed chair, placing his coffee cup on the desk, taking pride in his orderly office. It was relatively quiet up here, connected to the yard but away from its noise and dust.

He should have torn down that shed years ago. But it served its purpose, pinpointing his origins. It was close to ten o'clock. Just a few minutes more.

Elam decided not to receive Bill Sergent in his office. He took off his suit coat and walked along the paneled and carpeted corridor, then downstairs to the lumberyard, to the shed. Minutes later, he was comfortably situated in his old office, again aware of who he was and how far he had come. Even so, a queasy sensation stirred his stomach at the sound of a double rap on the door. He knew the next few minutes would determine if he'd continue his successful but rather routine work here at the lumberyard or if he'd venture into a new, more challenging endeavor.

He assessed Bill Sergent as he shook his hand, exchanged pleasantries, and gestured for him to take a seat. He noticed how Sergent's premature balding contrasted with his youthful, almost cherubic face. He also noticed Bill grimace as he sat down on the dusty chair.

Elam spoke first to avoid the usual, meaningless amenities. "Well, what you got?"

"It looks promising. It really does."

"Good. Let's hear it."

"Yeah. You asked us to look over the political horizon, assess the popularity of a bunch of incumbents and those waiting in the wings, gauge the mood of the people, find a place for you in the political system, and," he smiled, "determine your viability."

"Generally that was the chore I gave your boss. Incidentally, you guys were recommended to me by some party pros. And I've known Herb for years."

"We did a thorough job for you. You got your money's worth."

"Let's get to it."

"Sure." The window air conditioner hummed to life and they edged closer to one other. "We checked you out real good. You're okay."

Elam nodded, impatient to know what else they found. He drew on his pipe.

"Your father was active in the party, a two-term legislator. You've been active; central committee member, state chairman, national committeeman. You've been hardworking, unassuming. Your class action suit on that superfund won't hurt, may even help. You're okay. But we got problems."

"What are they?"

"The Democratic Party is at a low ebb, given Vietnam, LBJ's not seeking reelection, Humphrey's loss to Nixon. It'll pick up with time, but right now, the Democratic Party ain't the best party to be aligned with."

Elam's eyes sharpened. What the hell do I have to do with national politics? I just want to reclaim dad's seat in the state legislature. Elam's brow furrowed a bit despite his attempt to mask his confusion. *Damn, they've got something else in mind. Secretary of state? Attorney general? No, dammit, I'm not a lawyer. Christ, I told Herb what office I had in mind, didn't I?*

"But like they say, 'all politics is local'," Sergent continued. "So we'll have to energize the available cadre within the party. We're really gonna need that band of supporters to mount a major campaign."

Elam stared at his visitor. Sergent's words weighed on him. *To mount a major campaign.* Things were losing their context. *What in the hell is he talking about?*

Sergent seemed comfortable with the silence that settled over the shed. For him it was just a routine job of assessing a client's future. He'd seen this reaction before.

"Mr. Elam, we're talking about the office of the governor."

Heavy, heady moments passed as Elam processed those words.

"It's not what you had in mind, but we think it can be done. You might have to lose one to win one," Sergent went on. "But if you do all the right things, you could win the first time out."

Elam tried to hold his emotions in check because he couldn't believe what he was hearing. It was much more than he was expecting. He wanted to hear more. *So what if this was only a dream that would be crushed by the reality of politics.* Bob returned his attention to the man Herb Chandler had assigned to chart the future course of Robert Temple Elam, lumberman.

"We talked with a lot of folks, very informally. They had no idea why your name was included in the conversation. We kept our cover."

Bob nodded, pleased with the firm he had chosen.

"You came off as a liberal, at least in this state. You've spoken positively about LBJ's Great Society. Not too many people but enough for us to know where you stand." He paused. "Your opposition will probably be the incumbent, but the GOP could run a conservative against their own moderate governor. To win, you're gonna have to out-Republican your opponent, be a helluva lot more conservative. It's the only way. It's the mood of the electorate."

Elam's face reddened. "I'm no goddamned radical or bleeding heart. I'm a hardnosed businessman. And I'm a yellow-dog Democrat! And I'm not about to abandon those principles the party stands for, those programs it's fought for. Without them, there'd be no middle class, only the rich and the poor. There'd be no minimum wage, no forty-hour weeks, nothing but sweatshops."

Sergent had little personal interest in political spectrums. He remained impassive as Elam went on lecturing his visitor. "Dammit, it's against everything we stand for to let hopelessness enter the American psyche. We've got to help those who are losing hope, whose self-esteem is destroyed because their spirit's destroyed. I don't intend to badmouth these programs. I want them run better, maybe expand them." Elam sat back. Then he said quietly, "That's who I am, dammit."

Silent minutes ticked away as the two men stared at one another, refusing to look away. The standoff, the test of wills, became overpowering.

Sergent finally looked at the floor. "Well, that's it for now. Call me when you want to talk further. I'll look forward to your call." He got up and left.

Elam wanted to tell him to wait, but now the shed was suddenly empty except for himself. He slumped in his chair.

Elam remembered hearing the bell when had it signaled the lunch hour. Then, later, it rang again. The workday was over. He had done very little since Sergent's departure. The stack of invoices was left untouched. He vaguely remembered canceling appointments with several builders. His entire day had been consumed by a brief visit with an obscure, behind-the-scenes peddler of dreams.

Elam stepped into the heat of the lumberyard. He thought of Truman's advice about staying out of the kitchen. "Christ," he muttered to himself, "I was thinking legislative this morning, gubernatorial this afternoon - now presidential. Ridiculous! I've got to get back to the legislature."

Nodding to his employees, he walked to his car, sitting in it for several minutes before turning the key and pulling onto the street. The old Plymouth dutifully responded. Elam checked the odometer. It read 86,327. Three years ago, when the car hit a hundred thousand miles, Elam was ready to trade. But as the months and then years went by, it became a challenge to see how many miles the car would go.

Elam was only faintly aware of the radio but turned up the volume when the evening news came on. NBC was still reporting on the vice president's Des Moines speech. A voice he couldn't identify accused Agnew of a frontal attack on the First Amendment. U.S. imports remained high, rising two percent in the past month. Representative Myles of California spoke of the forthcoming peace dividend as the war in Vietnam wound down; the local temperature remained at 96 degrees Fahrenheit, 36 degrees Celsius; Senator Hammond was going to testify against the governor's reorganization bill...

Elam then realized how little he knew about the machinery of government, how absurd his gubernatorial candidacy would be. To hell with it, he decided. I'm going after my father's seat in the legislature.

He arrived home twenty minutes later. His wife, Pam, was standing at the kitchen counter. In heels, she stood almost as tall, as statuesque, as his six-foot frame. But now, in stocking feet, she appeared strangely vulnerable.

She turned her face toward him and smiled, continuing to prepare the salad. Bob walked up behind her, placing his hands on her well-defined hips. "Uh huh," she said.

He kissed the nape of her neck, his hands encompassing her waist, his libido slightly stirring. He wondered how she had retained her enduring feminine mystique during their twenty-three years of marriage. Regardless of the many times they had made love and that he had examined and caressed her, he would still lie awake watching her, having the inexhaustible urge to touch her, to feel her closeness, to experience her again.

His hands slowly moved up her rib cage. He cupped her breasts. He kissed her neck.

"Uh huh!" she feigned shock.

Bob lied to his wife in a soft voice. "Herb Chandler's boy thinks I can reclaim dad's legislative seat."

CHAPTER TWO

Enjoying the morning's warmth, Jeff Vinton walked the four-block area around the state capitol. Pausing occasionally, he surveyed the architectural beauty of the building. The gold-leaf dome contrasting with the blue sky gave the structure a sense of majesty. Approaching the west entrance, Vinton read the words inscribed on the pale stone: THE SCRUTINY OF THE CITIZEN REPRESENTS THE SECURITY OF THE STATE.

A healthy dose of cynicism was needed back then, he thought, but now things are more orderly and predictable. Governance is pretty unexciting. Yet, public service appealed to him, a part of his makeup. Nowhere within twenty-seven-year-old Jeff Vinton was there a desire for personal gain. Profit, material acquisitions, wealth, the motivations of the private sector were remote values.

Having just been discharged from the army, it made sense that he would want a job in the welfare department.

Before entering the capitol, he studied its uncomplicated design. There was, he thought, a sense of order to the tidy structure and, by extension, the business conducted within.

At that moment, the upper house of the legislature was debating a bill sponsored by Senator Patrick Sloane. At the request of the governor, Sloane had introduced the Governmental Reorganization Act. The bill had routinely worked its way through the committees and was now before the full chamber.

Sloane sat as Senator Jake Hammond expounded on the flaws in the bill. Hammond, an orator comparable to a La Follette or Bryan, was enjoying the verbal combat. Affording himself full advantage of his deep resonant voice, he projected his thoughts and eloquence into every corner of the chamber.

"I stand not opposed to progressive reform nor wish to perpetuate the inanities of our present structure; not being satisfied - no, being enraged - at the farrago of agencies, departments, boards, and commissions which we, I repeat, we the legislators have created. But, my esteemed colleagues, this is not the bill to remedy the sins of our past. This is not the tool our governor needs." Pausing to ensure the proper timing, he continued in a lowered voice. "Even if the Honorable Mr. Norman, God bless him, and help him, thinks differently."

Muted chuckles filled the gallery and the senate floor. Hammond looked to Sloane and smiled. Then with his flair for inflated and abstruse verbiage: "The concatenation of state governmental units that my normally able colleague proposes will, I deeply believe - and do so with some insight - only exacerbate the disorder, the duplication, the non-system of government we have imposed on our constituents. An example: May I direct your attention to line five hundred thirty-nine of the bill? Here it proposes to merge the Commission of Native Americans with the Department of Natural Resources. My distinguished colleagues, this makes as much sense as, where is it? Here, on line eight hundred twenty-three, merging the Commission of Revenue with the Department of Administrative Services."

As Hammond continued his ridicule, Sloane organized his rebuttal. His first point would come from the governor's message to the legislature, then extracts from the State of the State address in which the plan was proposed, then bits of testimony from the elderly and poor. He had even persuaded a few bureaucrats to ridicule the number of independent boards and commissions. When two were fired following their testimony, the media had paid greater attention to the bill.

The power of bureau heads to openly militate against the governor disturbed Sloane. Although not with Hammond's flair, he felt he could defend the technical aspects of the bill. Further, he was willing to compromise on a number of issues to ensure passage. What he and his governor wanted was an initial restructuring that other governors and legislatures could further refine.

Sloane noticed the change in the inflection of Hammond's voice. He listened more closely, sensing Hammond was ending his remarks. "I know we should change our governmental structure. This chamber and our distinguished friends across the rotunda know we need to change our governmental structure. The governor knows we must change our governmental structure. And the good Lord knows we must change our system of governing." Hammond paused, his expression tightening. When all eyes were upon him, he feigned a troubled expression. "I hope my sequential listing of those concerned about the structure of this sovereign state's government will not be interpreted as being in the order of the importance I personally rank them. Indeed, a more astute and less biased observer might have listed them inversely."

Waiting for the laughter to subside, Hammond stacked his papers, his eyes scanning the senate floor. "Now I haven't entered this debate for just the sake of recalcitrance, although I confess I'm enjoying myself a bit. I grant you, the motivations of this bill are sound. We all concur to the exigent need of reform. The difficulty lies with the bill's style, not its intent. The Lord God too, saw the need to change the imperfect world He created. But did He do it with a single act? No, my esteemed colleagues. His style is more subtle, yet deliberate; better planned, more effectively achieved. Not with a devastatingly broad, even radical realignment of the forces of the universe. No! The Lord God chose to effect change differently. We call His system evolution. Senator Sloane calls for widespread change to be implemented by the signing of a single bill. My dear colleagues, I propose we more deliberatively, less radically, change our system of governance. I propose we not presumptuously try to eclipse the good Lord, but that we learn from Him. I propose we accomplish an evolutionary approach: one more God-like."

Hammond ignored the chuckles throughout the chamber. "Further, it is the intent of the committee I chair to bring to this chamber such a deliberative and evolutionary bill during our next session. I will not vote for this bill, and I urge my able colleagues to thoughtfully consider what I have said. Agree with me! Return this bill to committee!"

***

Jeff Vinton walked past the portraits of the state's twenty-six governors that lined the corridor leading to the rotunda as Senator Hammond ended his remarks and acknowledged the applause from the floor and gallery. As Jeff walked past the entrance to the senate chamber, Patrick Sloane rose to address the body. Before Vinton entered the elevator, Sloane began speaking on behalf of what the full chamber knew was a lost cause.

Jeff stepped from the elevator and entered the state welfare office. After speaking to the receptionist, he was ushered to an office in the personnel division. A man rose to acknowledge Vinton, invited him to sit. "Your letter inquired about work in this department. You cited casework experience while in the army."

Christ, Jeff thought, he talks like a robot. He nodded.

"Well that's not much to go on," the man said as if to himself. "We could begin you as an intake worker. You know, asking applicants a few questions. Mundane stuff. You'd quickly get bored."

Vinton didn't know if he should agree with or challenge this assessment. Instead, he sat silently.

"Your work with Army Emergency Relief could be considered as welfare work."

Vinton nodded again.

"Well there is a situation that might interest you, might challenge you." The interviewer reached for a manila folder. After leafing through it, he looked up again. "Under Civil Service regulations, you might be eligible for a county directorship. Interested?"

"Yes, sir."

"Now the county runs things. It hires and fires staff, calls the shots. You'll have to travel out there to meet with them. They've been looking real hard for a director, and you might fit the bill. They'll be meeting next Tuesday. If you want to go out there and chat with them, I'll let them know."

Only minutes had passed since Vinton had entered the office. He was surprised by the sudden course of events. "Tell me a little bit about the local situation."

"It's a long story. I promise a challenge if you get the job. You want to go out there?"

Vinton thought for a second. The title "Director" appealed to him; not a bad place to start. But he considered the absurdity of it. He knew nothing about welfare. But, not a bad place to start, a directorship. "Which county is it?"

"Harney. Way out west."

"They've obviously got some problems. If I go out there, I oughta know what's going on."

"They ain't looking for someone with a Phi Beta Kappa key, just a warm body." The interviewer dropped his friendly manner. "I've got another appointment. If you get the job, come back and see me. I'll go over the situation with you. I have time to tell you this. The director's been there eighteen years. She's tough as nails, uncaring, punitive. She routinely disregards regulations and runs a county welfare office with little concern for the welfare of the county. If you get past the interview, we'll talk more. Good luck."

"Tell the board I'll be there Tuesday morning."

Vinton thanked the receptionist as he left the office. In the elevator he considered what to do next. His first stop was the legislative library where he got a book about the state's counties.

COUNTY OF HARNEY (HAR knee) County seat: Union. Seventy-fifth county organized by legislative act in 1910. Land mass: 662 sq. miles. Population: 28,016 ('60 Census). Named after Colonel (Brevet General) Lawrence T. Harney, U.S. Army (Cavalry). Born July 3, 1828, Bridgeport, Conn. Served under General William Tecumseh Sherman. As foragers during Sherman's March to the Sea, Harney's troopers saw action at the sieges of Atlanta and Savannah. After the Civil War, Harney was transferred to the High Plains. In 1873, Harney commanded a detachment of cavalry that defeated a band of Oglala Sioux at the battle of Dismal Creek. Colonel Harney authored several manuals on cavalry tactics. He received several awards for valor and meritorious service. Ran for U.S. Senate from the State of Connecticut: defeated. Died in Washington, D.C., November 18, 1899. Buried at Arlington National Cemetery.

Christ. An honest-to-God Indian fighter! Vinton was acquiring a positive feeling about the county and the job. He decided he should visit with the local welfare director.

On the main floor he took some time to look at the portraits lining the corridor. Staring at one, he bumped into Senator Sloane who had just left the senate chamber. Depressed over his debate with Senator Hammond, Sloane was as remiss as Vinton. The awkwardness of the incident was compounded by Sloane spilling the papers tucked under his arm. Both stooped to gather up the documents. The papers were again in Sloane's hands who apologized and hurried to the governor's suite.

Governor Charles Norman was pacing in his office when his secretary announced Sloane. Norman sat at his desk, shuffled some documents, and asked to have Senator Sloane shown in.

His papers in disarray, Sloane entered the governor's office. Norman rose, gesturing for him to sit. The chatter from the senate floor was the only sound. Norman, pointing to the encased speaker on his desk, signaled that he had heard the debate.

"Then you know as well as me."

Norman walked to the artfully concealed liquor cabinet. "I normally bring this stuff out to celebrate," he said, pouring Napoleon Brandy into two snifters. "But what the hell. My term's drawing short, and I've some left." Offering one to Sloane, he returned to his desk and motioned for Sloane to begin the discussion.

After a brief silence, Sloane muttered, "Hammond's a worthy opponent. But why? He knows the need for structural reform as well as we do. It doesn't make sense."

"Yeah, it does. Hammond's looking ahead to when his party takes over this office. New jobs - patronage - come with restructuring."

"Risky. Everyone knows we need this bill to manage those God-almighty bureaucrats." Sloane halted. Then with renewed energy: "If there's a mistake putting the bureaucrat in, how the hell do you get him out? You don't elect a bureaucrat, so you can't impeach or recall a bureaucrat. Obviously, you can't vote him out. You and I go before the voters who use our every act, personal and public, as a touchstone to judge if we've met their personal values. One wrong vote in the eyes of a special interest group can switch three percent of the vote. We have to submit to a litmus test that the bureaucrat is exempt from."

Governor Norman swirled the brandy. "Yeah, a bureaucrat's like a headless nail. Once you put him in you can't get him out."

"But they exist, and I'm a realist," Sloane interjected. "Two-thirds of them make a goddamned liar out of Descartes. Dammit, they exist - and can have as much power as elected officials."

"And," Norman joined in, "because they hang around longer, they magnify that power, 'cause they know the rules better than any first-term governor or freshman legislator."

The two men were enjoying their diatribe aimed at the faceless bureaucracy, each preempting the other.

"The thing I resent most is their anonymous arrogance," Sloane continued. "They damn well exercise power but take none of the heat for their decisions. We're the dumb bunnies who put our jobs, our reputations, our asses on the line every election while they sit back, building their retirement. At least some are subject to the control of the governor. But in this state we've got so goddamn many commissions, boards, authorities, councils - Jesus Christ!"

Sloane continued. "And those bureaucrats in the autonomous units are impervious to any elected official. It's insulting to our form of government! Those damned boards and commissions - they're constitutional anomalies. But try to change this structure and there's hell to pay. Those units have developed constituencies, folks dependent on them for services. Like if you merge the Aging Commission with the Department of Human Services, the old folks will be calling you a sonofabitch. What you proposed required guts. An act of a statesman, not a politician," Sloane said, returning to the realities of the moment. "You might lose the election because of this, but if a Democratic governor-to-be thinks he can make political points off an ineffective reorganization, he's not very bright."

"I suppose you're right, should I lose," Norman acknowledged. "But if he's bright, and I suspect he will be, he'll come up with a cosmetic reorganization that'll just rearrange the boxes. It won't solve anything, but it'll look nice."

"I made two mistakes," Sloane admitted. "I believed this issue to be nonpartisan, that the votes wouldn't be subject to party discipline. And I felt Hammond would set a precedent and do something honorable."

"And I screwed up," Norman admitted. "I didn't realize how lazy our legislative friends are. Most legislators, and Patrick, I exclude you, have never accepted the basic responsibility of oversight. Instead of determining how effective the programs and agencies are, they create more programs and agencies. The tough but necessary task of oversight and evaluation is a thankless job. There's no glamour, no headlines. They go where the headlines are, not where the work is. And by God, they can't admit to the errors of their ways, not with elections always coming up. I suppose I don't blame them, human nature being what it is, but dammit, I resent them."

Norman looked at Sloane, his fatigue and disappointment obvious. Then, as if struck by a bolt of lightning, he jumped up and began pacing. "You know, as he and I walked down the hall for my swearing-in and his departure from office - I mean Governor Dawson - he took

12

my arm and told me not to forget one thing. I don't suppose you know what that was, do you, Patrick?"

Sloane shook his head.

"Dawson told me - let me put it in his own words. He told me, 'Two bedrock values permeate government. To leave this office a winner, never forget them.' I remember now. His exact words were 'The two forces no politician can overcome are the absolute indifference of the people and the practiced inertia of the bureaucrats. You can achieve anything you want in government, except change.' "

Sloane slipped into a deeper depression. He realized that the former governor actually had said those words and that the current governor now believed them.

Norman noted his friend's despondency. He swirled, sniffed, and sipped his brandy. Then in an effort to lighten the mood, he smiled at Sloane. "Ol' Phil Dawson. You know what he's doing now? He bought a cathouse ranch in Nevada. I hear he's making a fortune. You know, there's a politician who's providing a service!"

CHAPTER THREE

Vinton's interview lasted forty minutes. When it ended, he was the Harney County welfare director-designate. The only awkward moment was when his request to be reimbursed for his travel expenses was denied. Nonetheless, Jeff left the county courthouse with positive feelings about his new job and his new home in the city of Union, county of Harney.

The drive back to the capital was uneventful. The High Plains and ranch country gave way to rolling hills, then the flatlands of the eastern part of the state. Vinton called the welfare office the following morning. He was told to report Friday to process the necessary paperwork.

Replacing the telephone, he surveyed the confines of his small apartment. He began packing his books and papers into cardboard boxes. As he emptied a shelf of books and moved to the next, he saw the photograph of Andrea. He looked at her soft eyes, high cheekbones, demure smile. The anguish of her being so far away replaced the pleasure the photograph had brought him. He cleared the table before him.

He wrote her that he had a job, that he was a county welfare director. He told her about the low pay for social workers. He questioned if he could support her and her children. He inferred that he could not. But he told her to keep hoping. And he told her that he loved her.

Looking again at her picture, sadness engulfed him. He hadn't seen her in months. Their romance was sustained primarily by telephone and mail. Yet it persisted.

During the year he was in Vietnam, she wrote faithfully, he not so dutifully.

They had not been together that often during the past three years. Yet, she was always in his thoughts, always at home when he called. Somehow, the long-distance romance endured. Different people with different lifestyles, committed to each other.

Jeff slept soundly that night, rose early, showered, and dressed. At nine o'clock he reported to his benefactor, the nondescript bureaucrat who had suggested he become a welfare director.

He accepted the congratulations graciously as he was introduced throughout the department. After these amenities, his resume was reworked. In a few minutes, Vinton's duties as an Army Emergency Relief officer were transformed into those of an experienced social worker. The benefactor worked his pencil. "Interview" was changed to "counsel," "dispense emergency assistance" to "comprehensively assess client's short and long-term needs and capabilities, jointly preparing a realistic budget and systematic debt liquidation schedule." In twenty minutes, Vinton was transformed from an army sinecurist to an expertly qualified social worker, one fully deserving the responsibility of directing federal, state, and local assistance programs.

The revised resume was presented to Vinton for his inspection. After reading it, he was convinced his qualifications were appropriate for any position in the welfare bureaucracy. Then, as previously arranged, his resume was sent to an individual in the state's Civil Service Commission who was waiting to review it. Minutes later he learned that it met the minimum requirements for the position. His test was scheduled for Monday morning.

Vinton was impressed by how rapidly the bureaucracy moved in this case. He wanted to mention this, but the benefactor was briefing him on the examination. Vinton interrupted him. "What if I fail?"

"No problem. We'll make you acting director and schedule another try. Regardless, you'll be on the job a week from next Monday. Now listen to some of the questions."

Vinton left the capitol an hour later, knowing that anything is bureaucratically possible. You just have to know how.

CHAPTER FOUR

Andrea had grown up as a typical army brat, the daughter of a career officer. Living her critically formative years on numerous military posts had taught her about the transitory nature of life. Each time her father was transferred, she was reminded of the sharp and distinctive beginnings and endings that defined her own life. Her personal relationships began and ended in eighteen-month cycles. Nothing lasted forever; it was always too finite. Therefore, to protect herself from the pain of breaking off friendships, she developed none.

As with many military families, her mother dominated the household because her father was frequently absent. The occasional presence and authority of her father could be ignored or humored because he would inevitably be transferred to an outpost without his family. Therefore, most decisions were made by Andrea's mother and only begrudgingly shared during her father's times at home. Andrea's mother was the only element that embodied permanence and stability.

Her youth was a confusing period although she never understood why. While sensing the absence of an essential part of her life, she never identified or understood the missing component. To Andrea, life was more disjointed than it was a systematic development of one's essence.

Her sixteenth year brought forth a relationship defined more by lust than by love and resulted in the conception of a child, a marriage, and the child's birth. Her seventeenth year produced a second child and a divorce. Interspersed among fleeting moments of joy were endless hours of sarcasm, criticism, and the emergence of an abiding hatred for her husband and, by extension, those who shared his characteristics. Rather than remember the little joy and happiness of the experience, she disciplined herself to only recall the pain and anguish.

After the divorce, she returned with her children to the home of her parents and her truncated youth. Although she tried briefly to live the life of a carefree young woman, the reality that she was the primary source of warmth, affection, and security for her children forced her to accept the loss of her girlhood.

Andrea's days, weeks, and life were devoted to caring for her children, indulging their every whim, warding off every intrusion. At first she felt the need to protect the children when her father was home; then, eventually, to protect them from her mother. She daily enlarged the parameters of control, sometimes through subtlety and guile, sometimes with confrontation and hostility. Her father accepted her emergence as a domineering, protective mother with little resistance. Her mother did so more reluctantly. Her children looked to her for direction and guidance. All others were to be ignored or humored.

After her position was firmly established and her children's security assured, Andrea expanded her world. Initially it was just to help her mother entertain. Her innate poise and composure was an asset to the colonel who took pride in his lovely, blonde-haired daughter. He watched her attract the junior officers and mesmerize them with her ready smile. But he never understood why she remained home every night. He never realized that Andrea equated those qualities of assertiveness, aggressiveness, the "can do, sir" mentality imbued in the officer corps, with the perceived arrogance and viciousness of her former husband.

The colonel gave up on Andrea, no longer bringing the bright young men home for dinner, resigned to the housing and feeding of his daughter and grandchildren.

Then Andrea began to engage in activities outside her parents' home. Seeking satisfaction in volunteer work, she could often be found at military day care, army relief, Red Cross, and USO facilities. Each organization required a uniform. Within a year, her father had purchased more than a half-dozen dresses, each with a patch designating Red Cross Volunteer, WOFGO (Wives of Field Grade Officers), Army Emergency Relief Volunteer. The list of uniforms went on.

Andrea spent a lot of time with WOFGO, which allowed the members' adult daughters to participate. Andrea enjoyed and exploited her youth and stood out among the cosmetically-masked older members. She pitied those desperately clinging to lost years. She used less makeup to emphasize her youth. In contrast to those who used too much perfume, she chose a scent so subtle that a man had to dance with her closely to detect it. However, she still spent virtually all her evenings with her children, in her parent's home, to her father's vexation.

Then, suddenly, Andrea was away at night. That left her parents pondering which was worse, her being home every night with no prospect of establishing her own home, or her being away each evening, and they relegated to babysitting.

The change in Andrea's life was brought on by a tall, almost scholarly-looking officer she met while volunteering for Army Emergency Relief. She saw in Lt. Jeffery Vinton none of the arrogance characteristic of the other young men and of her former husband. Vinton, although at times firm and unyielding, was soft-spoken, empathetic to the difficulties of others, and prone to use his abilities and office to aid and not to hinder. Although he wore the crossed rifles of infantry, Andrea couldn't picture him carrying a rifle, leading men to kill and be killed.

She set her sights on Lt. Vinton. Having previously used her beauty and charm to entice, this time she used them to entrap. She soon realized that she was in love for the first time.

Vinton, attentive when she volunteered at his office and eager to be with her each evening, nonetheless remained aloof, never making the commitment Andrea wanted. Still, the romance flourished for eight wondrous months until it was interrupted by the demands of military duty.

Andrea had called him at his office to firm up their evening. Vinton was with a soldier whose wife had filed for divorce, who was near emotional collapse. Unable to take her call, Vinton focused his attention on the soldier whose dreams for the future, whose faith and trust in his spouse were irreparably destroyed by the legal paper crumpled in his hand.

The lieutenant who answered Andrea's call idly chatted with her while waiting for Vinton. When finally Vinton picked up the phone, the officer was telling her that Jeff had received orders for Vietnam. Jeff heard her begin to cry, then looked to the tearful soldier, then felt tears form in his own eyes. Suddenly he was ashamed he had not spoken, that he was eavesdropping on his own call. He quietly replaced the receiver.

He later called Andrea to tell her about his orders. She was composed by then. They met that night and she wept softly.

After Vinton departed for Vietnam, Andrea stopped her volunteering. Her parents had their evenings free. Andrea spent her time with her children.

She easily accepted Vinton's absence as a part of life. She knew he would return safely. In the meantime, she would reinforce her position as family matriarch.

CHAPTER FIVE

As Senator Jake Hammond charged into his office, his secretary could tell he had enjoyed the morning's committee meeting. She never saw the senator walk anywhere leisurely. He always walked with a sense of urgency, as if he had not enough time, as if he was on an errand from God.

Once in his office, like a windup toy soldier that had worn down, Hammond sat at his desk. He leaned back, his feet on the polished desktop, his thoughts on the meeting, his contribution to it. He felt unsettled. He didn't know why.

The Military Affairs Committee had been reviewing the preparedness of National Guard units. Hammond shamelessly castigated the commander of a brigade whose members resided outside his Fifty-Third District, accusing him of "not even a modicum of mediocrity." He toyed with that phrase, thinking it could be improved.

He looked at the stack of incoming calls, most from lobbyists. One was from Bob Elam. Hammond recognized the name but couldn't connect it to an interest group. He picked up the phone.

"Ms. Sara, whereas I'm fully cognizant of all these fine gentlepeople who graciously seek my advice on matters of state, I regret to inform you that I don't remember who the hell this guy Elam is."

Accustomed to the Senator's indirect requests, Sara brought him Elam's three-by-five card.

ELAM, ROBERT TEMPLE Central Committeeman 59-60. State chair '62...

"Hot damn. I'm getting too old for this racket, forgetting ol' Bobby-boy," Hammond said to himself.

His eyes returned to the card...married, straight arrow; wife Pam, nee Hoyt; two children, Robert Jr., senior at State Univ., Elaine, married, one child. Father John deceased, was two-term senator, 3d Dist, '41-49. Bus: owns lumberyard. Veteran: US Army. Hobbies: Unk. Memberships: BPOE, Rotary, country club. Drink: bourbon (light drinker). Conversational topics: Unk. Weaknesses: None noted.

Contributions: '61- $75 '65 - $50 '69 - $65 '71- $75.

Hammond rang Sara and melodiously intoned: "Please get my dear and faithful friend Bob Elam on the phone - in about ten minutes - and Sara, let's change 'weaknesses' to 'foibles'. Sounds a bit softer, less accusatory, don't you think?" He replaced the telephone before she could answer.

Hammond wondered why Elam had called. After some thought, he realized he knew no more about Elam than the three-by-five told him. He sat back, awaiting the call.

Minutes later when the call came through, Hammond didn't recognize Elam's voice. "Bobby, Bobby, how are you boy? I can't remember the last opportunity I had to chat with you." Not allowing Elam to respond, Hammond asked about Pam, Bob Jr., and Elaine. He spoke of everything, of nothing, but with a flair that was inimitably his own.

Elam finally interrupted. "Jake, before we go on, I have a favor."

"You want lumber exempted from the sales tax. Well, you got it."

"Of course - that - but something more difficult to arrange." Elam told Hammond he wanted to meet with him.

Hammond eyed the contributions section. He computed two hundred sixty-five dollars. And, Bob lived outside his district. The money wasn't that much, but this was the first time Elam had ever called him. It might be important. "Of course. When are you free?"

"Tomorrow night," came the quick response.

"Can't do it, Bobby-boy." He noted Elam's urgency. "How about Thursday, about eight at the Enterprize Club?"

"Sounds good."

"See you then, Bobby-boy. Say 'Hi' to that lovely wife."

"Will do, Jake," Elam responded, replacing the receiver. He wondered where Hammond had come up with "Bobby-boy." They had never spoken informally before.

Hammond couldn't dismiss Elam's call as routine. Perhaps it was a premonition or just the firmness of Elam's voice. Regardless, he felt uneasy about calling him "Bobby-boy."

During the next few days he asked his associates about Elam. Many knew Bob but added little to Hammond's three-by-five. Phrases like "family man," "supports the party," "minds his own business," "solid

21

sort of guy" did little to satisfy him. What's he really made of? Hammond wondered. What does he want? What are his weaknesses? Hammond had no compunction using that word in reference to Robert Temple Elam.

***

Unsure he would recognize Elam, Hammond arrived at the Enterprize at seven thirty, leaving instructions to the headwaiter to escort Elam to his table. Rather than one of his flamboyant blazers, Hammond wore a business suit.

Seated in the lounge, he surveyed the expanse of the city below him. Traffic on the streets was heavy; he noted a backup caused by an accident. The waitress brought him his customary gin and tonic with lime wedge. Lobbyists were awed by Hammond's redoubtable capacity. He would begin drinking early and continue throughout the night. No one suspected that he had an arrangement with the club ensuring his gin and tonics would actually be club sodas.

Embracing the drink with both hands, he observed the erratic comings and goings far below him. The sun was low in the sky and a reddish hue through the clouds was enveloping the city. Hammond looked north to the capitol, noting how the sunset affected its pale colored stone. He was interrupted by Elam who had been escorted to his table and feigned a cough to attract his attention.

Hammond quickly stood, extending his hand. "Bob Elam. By golly, you're looking great and, darn, it's good to see you."

Elam shook Hammond's hand, sat, and ordered a drink.

Hammond looked at Elam, attempting to quickly size him up while maintaining his usual banter. "Gosh damn, Bob, you know I think this is the first chance we've had to just sit and relax. It's good to be with a guy who works for a living. Political life operates in such an artificial world. You won't believe this, but I was with a friend at a little get-together one evening and some God-awful lobbyist came over and asked how we were. He had on a silly looking zoot suit - lapels as wide as my outstretched hand - and the minute he joined us he began looking for someone more important. My friend, a bit naive to the ways of the capital, took him seriously and began responding. Well by then the guy

22

with the zoot suit had seen the minority leader come in and thought he was more prestigious than we were. As my friend mentioned his wife's car accident and injuries, the lobbyist in the zoot suit grabbed his hand, shook it firmly - conveying much sincerity - and said, 'Couldn't have happened to a nicer guy. I've got to run now.' "

Hammond's soft chuckling caused Bob to smile.

"Well, Bob Elam, I don't know what in tarnation he said to the minority leader, but I know my friend voted against the zoot suit every time a vote came up. God, it's a zany business! I knew a freshman who stayed here all the time - never got back to his district, never missed a roll call, made all the right votes, lost in a landslide the next election. And the junkets. You know, Bob, that's not just a Washington perk; we got them, too."

Elam thought he had a chance to change the subject when Hammond stopped to reorder his drink and another for Elam. It was not to be. Hammond gave the impression he could continue the monologue indefinitely. Elam gently refused additional rounds. Hammond continued to sip and consume his, once asking the waitress, "You sure you're using Beefeaters, hon?"

Then Hammond stopped in midsentence, looked at Elam, and humbly lowered his head. "But you don't want to hear an old man ramble on about old times."

Elam felt guilty. Perhaps he hadn't been attentive enough or hadn't laughed heartily enough. He nearly told Hammond to go on, to continue his stories.

Hammond noted Elam's discomfort. If Elam's request was unreasonable or simply unachievable, he could feign injured pride, tacitly blame Elam's untoward conduct, and deny the request. The meeting would end. In a humble voice he asked, "How may I be of service to you, my good friend?"

Bob felt uncomfortable. Good God, he thought, I'm glad I'm not asking him to sponsor a bill or get my son a job.

"I just wish," he began, "I had more time to listen to stories about this town and that big building across the way. But I've another need. I understand you're against the reorganization bill."

Hammond's eyes matched Elam's. Then Hammond nodded, encouraging Bob to go on.

"I'd like to know why."

"Why, my good friend, do you want to know why?"

Bob set his drink down and dipped his pipe into his tobacco pouch. "Well, life's been good. I've a fine and beautiful wife, a couple of good kids. My business is okay; it damn near runs itself. My health is good. I'm thinking of getting more active in the party, in government."

"How much more active?"

"Don't know."

Hammond allowed moments to pass as he studied Elam's face, then the politician leaned back to better assess the businessman.

Elam, feeling more confident, broke the silence. "Jake, I've a layman's view of government. I passed my poli-sci courses years ago, but I need a practical view. Tell me about the reorganization bill."

"Okay. But with one caveat - that our chat be off the record."

"My word, Jake."

Hammond leaned back in the captain's chair, stretched his legs, and crossed them at the ankles to get more comfortable.

Encouraged, Elam leaned forward, elbows on knees, hands clasped.

When Hammond spoke, it wasn't with the empty verbosity for which he was known. Instead, his thoughts touched the bedrock of governance.

"Bob, nowadays there is nothing clear and self-evident in government. Jefferson's words were relevant back then. People didn't fight wars and get killed over a monarch who was sixty-one percent evil. The sonofabitch had to be a hundred percent evil! There were polarities then, but not now. Now the only question is 'Who gets hurt?' and more importantly, 'Who benefits?' Sloane's bill was the governor's bill, and the governor is an alright-sort of a guy except that he sits on the wrong side of the aisle. But this issue transcends Norman, Sloane, and me. It gets back to Jefferson."

Hammond paused to observe Elam, then continued. "The worst thing we can do is make government efficient. Efficiency denotes well-oiled gears easily meshing together. It connotes one person pushing all the buttons. Norman's bill would have achieved an efficient and cost-effective government. And that's bad."

Elam looked at Hammond as if he was drunk or crazy.

"You look perplexed," Hammond said.

"Hell yes. These are my tax dollars paying for this inefficiency you're promoting."

"I know, Bob, but have you ever thought of the alternative?"

"The alternative to inefficiency is efficiency."

"Look at it another way. The alternative to diffused power is concentrated power. Now we get back to Jefferson. A strong man on a white charger can be one dangerous sonofabitch. That's the reason we set up all those autonomous units of government, units impervious to the change of administrators, to the will of one man."

Bob sat back, confused. This designed inefficiency, this bureaucratic never-never land, was alien to his sense of order, of basic values, of cost-effectiveness. He was stunned.

Hammond was relaxed, feeling no need to justify his philosophy, his legislative actions. Elam, silent, tried to make sense of this governmental design to which Hammond so unabashedly adhered.

Then Elam tried to summarize Hammond's basic concept of government. "Although we are a nation of laws, with a constitution, judicial review, legislative monetary control, recall and impeachment powers, with all these things within the hands of the people..."

Hammond interrupted. "Bob, if you get more involved in politics, you'll learn one word that replaces everything you've said. From now on just say 'notwithstanding'. Now, finish your sentence."

Elam smiled. "Jake, your use of words is as economic as your concept of government. Your advice is totally out of character."

Hammond, comfortably self-satisfied, smiled.

"Nonetheless, and 'notwithstanding' constitutional safeguards," Elam continued, "you, an experienced lawmaker, are scared to death of creeping despotism, preferring instead competitive duplication, uncoordinated effort, and wasted tax dollars."

The two reached an impasse.

Finally, Hammond spoke. "It isn't that I'm distrustful of Norman or of the next sonofabitch who's going to sit in his chair. What I am afraid of is anyone with that much power. It just ain't worth it. Good men sometimes come to think they're messiahs. Others are just born sonsabitches. The governing of a people is too great a responsibility to take a chance. That's why I killed the reorganization bill."

"I don't know. It doesn't make sense, designing inefficiency."

"No it doesn't, at least in a practical sense. But, Bob, over the long haul it does make sense."

Elam couldn't respond. His frustration was mounting. He wondered if Hammond's colleagues were knowingly co-conspirators. Then he began to play with this notion. How does one calibrate inefficiency? Can a mechanism be a hundred percent inefficient? A thousand percent? How much inefficiency is tolerable? What positive values lie with a negative? At what point does negation become affirmation? Elam could no longer pursue this madness.

He thought of all the jokes about red tape, bureaucracies, and government, and how he had dismissed them so easily. Were the jokes closer to reality than he had thought?

Elam recalled his frustration while in the military: the inane busy work, the purposeless tasks, the absolute futility of it all. He could justify the idleness of a standing army during peacetime. But how do you justify idleness when the poor, the aged, and the unemployed are clamoring for help?

Hammond grew tired while watching Elam. Silence was the one thing he couldn't tolerate for long. He waved his hand to catch Elam's eye, to bring him back to the role of attentive listener.

Elam looked at Hammond. He had no idea how long he had been isolated in thought. "I've been thinking about what you said. I, too, think this issue transcends a basic philosophy. How do you think your average state employee deals with this designed lack of purpose? At what point and where and to whom does he vent his frustration?"

Hammond had never considered that element. It disturbed him. "Don't know, Bob."

Elam's expression let Hammond know his response was not adequate.

Hammond, used to winning wars of words, had a new appreciation for Bob Elam. Bob had come up with a commodity that politicians rarely consider: the goddamned individual. Hammond became angry. Why's this guy concerned with a bureaucrat's goddamned pursuit of happiness? "Who the hell are you," he retorted, "the champion, the patron saint of the bureaucrat?"

Elam smiled, saying nothing.

Hammond realized he had allowed anger to unmask his discomfort.

He quickly recovered, slapping Bob on the knee and laughing a bit too loudly. "No, Bob, these bureaucrats are a breed apart. They all fit in. They go along, get along. You know, we got a pretty healthy retirement plan for them."

"I suppose a few get frustrated," he conceded. "As a matter of fact, one or two have gotten a bit ugly; you know, appearing before legislative committees, going to the press. You know. But we get rid of them, one way or another."

Elam stared incredulously at Hammond. Then his newly acquired political acumen took control. He softened his glare. Regardless of Hammond's zany views of government, he was a political presence, a powerhouse in his district and across the state. If Elam were to enter the race for governor, he would need the Hammonds of the state. No need to alienate anyone over a principle at this point. "Well Jake, I may not agree with your theory of government, but my God, it got me thinking, something I've got a lot of to do."

Hammond was thankful for Bob's accommodation. "You know, I believe about forty-one percent of what I've said. But it's a good topic: efficiency and the police state versus inefficiency and democracy. Where the hell do you draw the line? You know, you're a good adversary. Why didn't you ever become a lawyer?"

"Christ, I don't know. Never thought of it. But I well may need some sound legal and political advice. Can I count on you?"

"Of course, Bob, anytime."

CHAPTER SIX

Union, the seat of Harney County, was in the northwest corner of the state. Back east, Union would only be a small town. Here it was a banking, transportation, and agricultural center. Three-fourths of the town was laid out in an orderly manner, streets running on true north-south grids. The northwest section stood in contrast. Railroad tracks disrupted the orderly pattern. Paved streets became dirt roads when one ventured into that part of town. The area was primarily consumed by a rail yard with intersecting tracks and maintenance buildings. Warehouses and livestock pens along with loading facilities were there. Small manufacturing plants were located beyond the rail yard. Clusters of houses were beyond the plants.

It was here where several hundred American Indians lived. Most were Oglala Sioux who had worked at an army training base west of town and remained after the war. Their living quarters during those critical days would have been categorized as subhuman had anyone bothered to appraise them. Some lived in abandoned freight cars. Others put up shanties. Families frequently lived in tepees until an adequate supply of scrap lumber could be found to erect a hut.

Now twenty-five years later, the tepees were gone. The jerrybuilt shacks proved more structurally sound than imagined. They still housed families of American Indians.

The hoeing season doubled their number. Because few farmers provided housing for the migrant workers, most moved in with family members, exacerbating their level of misery. After the arduous labor was completed, the workers and their families returned to the dismal reservation, relieving the imposition.

Located on the High Plains, the area enjoyed a diverse climate with seasonal variables. Unlike the hot and humid summers to the east, the High Plains featured warm days and cool evenings. The winters, although harsh, would generate Chinook winds that rushed down the slopes of the mountains, giving recurring respite from the subzero cold.

The land was rich and spacious, fenced off by cattle and wheat ranches but uncluttered by cities. It was a place to take root, to start anew with a sense of permanence. And Vinton wanted what this land offered to be a gift for Andrea.

The gift of love is the most amorphous of life's experiences. Always subject to change, yet constant, to grow at times, to diminish at others, to cascade into bitterness and disappointment, to escalate into unbridled joy and expectation, but above all to be shared; the sharing of moments, of lifetimes.

Vinton, driving through the scenic beauty of the rolling hills, catching the scent of the pine forests, following the uneven ridgeline of buttes and mesas, wanted to share that captured beauty.

Traversing almost the entire diagonal distance of the state, Vinton arrived in Union late in the evening.

Vinton's first day as the Harney County welfare director was uneventful. It was early when Commissioner Brian Scott, chairman of the board, and a reporter visited Vinton. The newsman took notes as he interviewed Vinton. Vinton then stood with Scott behind Agnes Moore, the outgoing director, for the obligatory photo. Moore, tight-lipped as she had been tight-fisted, said good-bye to the staff.

Vinton surveyed his office. It was small, compact, efficient. He sat and reflected. He knew nothing of welfare procedures, eligibility criteria, which forms effected which actions. The nondescript bureaucrat had enticed him, reworked his resume, prompted him for the interview, and briefed him about the exam. He had effectively placed Vinton in the chair he now occupied. Vinton looked to the phone, hoping the man would call to tell him what to do next. The telephone remained silent. Vinton was left to his own devices.

Minutes passed, Vinton sitting behind the closed door of his office doing nothing, wondering what he should be doing. He finally stepped into the outer office. "Have we any coffee here?"

Evelyn Pearce, the secretary, rose and went to a cubicle hidden among the partitioned offices. "Black okay?"

"Fine." Vinton looked over his employees, catching and holding their eyes as he went from person to person. He thanked Evelyn for the coffee, assessing her. "Could you guys grab some chairs and join me?"

Good God, they're all clones of the former director! He pushed his desk against the wall, freeing up space. He reviewed his assessment of the staff. Evelyn, tight-lipped, smug, and priggish, was the first person an applicant would see. A caseworker in her early sixties smiled when Vinton looked at her, then looked away. The only man was overweight, baldheaded, and somber. A bland looking woman in her mid-thirties made no impression.

The chairs were in a semicircle, the staff seated. Vinton leaned against his desk. "I want you to know there'll be no staff changes. As we go along, we'll restructure, move some desks, change some assignments, resolve any problems." He stared at the tile floor, then looked at each staff member long enough to assert himself. "There will be policy changes and changes in philosophy. We're going to be more sensitive to the needs of our clients, not use technicalities to keep folks off welfare. Let's find reasons to help them. How many applicants did we have last month?"

Evelyn quickly responded. "None."

"How many inquiries?"

"A few," she said, "but after seeing Mrs. Moore, they didn't apply."

"What's the present caseload?"

"Forty-one cases."

Vinton was familiar with the term ADC. "How many ADC cases?"

"Six."

"How about the rest?"

"They're AABD. Two are MA."

Jeff figured that AABD was Aid to the Aged, Blind and Disabled. He noticed that only Evelyn was responding. She's got more clout than the caseworkers, he surmised. It figures that Moore would delegate authority to the person who most resembled her. Unsure how to go on, he spoke to the male caseworker. "Bring me your last five cases. I'd like to go over them."

Looking to the other caseworkers, he said he would see their cases later. They removed their chairs and returned to their cubicles. Vinton resituated his desk, refilled his cup, and waited.

Jerry Milner rapped on his door and entered.

"Draw up a chair. Let's look them over."

Milner stacked the cases on Vinton's desk and sat.

"Take me through the entire process. Start with the entry forms and carry me through to the final decision. If you've got any observations, insights, or thoughts, let me know."

Milner looked at Vinton. "We'll take them step-by-step and I'll show you the county's way of doing things." Milner moved a file to the space between them, leaving it unopened. "Look, Mr. Vinton, I don't know how much you know about this office. My degree is in education, and I've applied for some teaching positions. I've received an offer, so I'll probably be leaving. The point is, do you want to know about the unheeded needs of this county or do you want to know how we keep folks off welfare?"

The sonofabitch's backing me into a corner, Vinton realized. I can't allow that. I can't give in the first time I'm confronted, but what will the county board say if I have a resignation the first week? Jeff faked a confident smile. "Do me a favor, Milner, call me Jeff. Now, let's go by the numbers. What's step one?"

"Okay. Step one is Evelyn. She keeps half the clients from getting past her desk. Step two was the director. She effectively discouraged another twenty percent from seeing a caseworker..."

"How?" Vinton interrupted.

"Through intimidation, coldness. Hell, I don't know. She has a flair for it."

"Go on. How about those who get through?"

"Well, once they sign an application, we got a living document. That's why three-fourths are dissuaded from getting that far. Once they sign it, the bureaucracy must move. But our movement never equals the speed of continental drift. The applicant is told her appointment will be in two weeks. That's a rule, never move the first week. Then we give them a list of items to bring in; stuff required by regulations, but twice what we need. For example, we need to know the person is who she says she is. That's okay. A number of documents indicate that, birth certificate, driver's license, diploma, and so on. One would be enough. We require three."

Milner opened a file, pointed to the color-coded application form. "The state gets the white copy, we retain the blue. We give the applicant - guess which? Give up? The pinko one of course!" Thinking aloud he said, "I'm sure it's coincidental."

Milner looked at Vinton and shook his head. "Since I've come here - it's over a year now - well, my mild skepticism has turned into one helluva case of jaded cynicism. We pass laws in this country; the bureaucrats negate them. In all candor, I've become really adept at denying assistance." He thumbed through the case file. "I got this gal on a technicality. But things were getting uncomfortable. I approved two cases last month."

Jeff wanted to use these sessions to learn the welfare regulations. It bothered him to hear about the punitive policies of the office, but the state bureaucrat had warned him, and dammit, he still had his need to know. He asked some other questions, but Milner was unresponsive.

After effectively sparring with Vinton, Milner picked up his files and returned them to his desk, then refilled his cup and looked out the window onto the courtyard square. The tree branches were swaying in the northerly breeze. Yesterday the wind was warm, from the south. Everything in nature has its balance, he thought. Directions, dichotomies, diversities; for each night, a day; for each winter, a summer. Why can't government be like that, he wondered. Instead, he forced the analogy. The displacement of one bureaucrat with another isn't noteworthy, and it sure as hell doesn't signal a shift in policy. There's no diversity, no polarities in bureaucracies. Machines are interchangeable as are their component parts. The products of the same mold remain the same. This guy was hired by the county because he's an interchangeable part from the warehouse of interchangeable parts.

Milner returned to his cubicle: "Please accept this letter as my resignation."

Vinton next saw the younger caseworker. She knew the regulations and used the manual to justify her decisions. The older caseworker went through the same procedure of familiarizing Jeff with more obscure rules used against the applicants.

Jeff left the office shortly after five. Except for Milner's resignation, he was pleased with the day's events. He had learned some of the procedures while his staff assumed he was testing their competence. Now he knew where to look in the manual for eligibility criteria. Too bad about Milner, but not a bad start.

He walked from the courthouse square to the hotel lounge, ordering a beer. The barmaid looked at him as if she knew him. Vinton returned her glance, sipped his beer. Finishing it, he rose to leave. As he opened the door to the lobby, she said, "Thank you, Mr. Vinton."

Jeff looked back, "Sure thing, see you." He went to the restaurant and ordered dinner. Bored, he looked around the nearly empty dining area. He walked to the counter to buy a newspaper. The headline stunned him: WELFARE'S NEW BOSS IN UNION. Below the headline was the photograph of him, Scott, and Moore. Moore looked as harsh as her tenure in the office had been. Scott looked reasonable. Vinton stared at his own image. Damn, he thought.

He placed a quarter on the counter and returned to his table, hoping no one noticed his excitement. He quickly ate his meal and left. Outside, he looked for a coin-operated newsstand. Seeing one across the street, he walked to it, placed a quarter in the slot and withdrew three newspapers.

Back at his motel, he went to the desk looking for stationery. There was none. He took a yellow pad from his briefcase.

Hi Andrea, This is my first day as welfare's new boss in Union. Note the enclosed news article! A problem exists! I don't know a damn thing about this business. The town looks nice. I've no idea what the housing situation is. In fact, I've got to get an apartment tonight. Being in a strange town makes me lonely. I thought of you a lot today. I know it's impractical, but maybe we could afford to live here. But I warn you, I didn't see one backyard swimming pool in the whole damn town. Love you but things might end in a disaster given the pay I'm getting. Hey, I'm getting too serious. How's things? How's the kids? How are you? Wish you were here, a Harney County person. Hurry and send me a letter. Be good. Jeff

He mailed the letter before looking for an apartment, renting the third one he saw. He returned to the motel room and reread the news article.

The next thirty days were more of a montage than separate entities. Days flowed into weeks. Weekends were used to consolidate and codify disjointed notes into bureaucratically acceptable case files.

The news article was the catalyst to increased activity. Word spread throughout the community that a new director was on board. A few people worked up the courage to come in and discovered they were treated with courtesy. Applications were taken, and it was assumed they would be processed. Changes were even occurring among the staff. But

33

luckily for Vinton, human nature changes slowly.

Evelyn's condescending manner became a positive factor. Jeff postponed his decision to distance her from the reception area. He appreciated her aloofness. The icy stare still discouraged some applicants from making their personal tragedies into public problems. Thanks in part to Vinton's encouragement, Evelyn did soften her heart enough to let those suffering most severely see a caseworker.

The office was soon soiled with the untidiness and disorder of the poor. The reception area was filled with the aged, young mothers, the disabled, and those wheezing with emphysema. The wailing of children, their stomachs empty of nourishment, became a routine the staff learned to ignore. The biggest difficulty was adjusting to the peculiar and pervasive stench of poverty. Although indescribable, it blended the odors of sweat, mildew, urine, soiled clothes, and so many more. It defied description but was instantly recognizable.

Evelyn was most vulnerable, her desk abutting the reception area. Office windows were opened and fans displaced the foulness with outside air. But the stench was never completely removed.

Jeff realized that for each case that was completed, more were opened. His staff engaged in endless labor. Vinton was confined to his office during those long days. When caseworkers brought him a completed case, he had them go through the process, associating eligibility checkpoints to the manual. At night he concentrated on regulations governing ADC cases. They were politically sensitive, ones the county commissioners scrutinized. The staff was surprised when he had those cases referred to him.

Past policies had precluded virtually all the ADC inquiries from resulting in signed applications. Now Vinton was quietly welcoming the applicants into his office. He saw six cases before his first meeting with the commissioners. By his actions alone, the ADC population of the county was increased by sixteen - four mothers and twelve children.

Vinton put the applicants at ease. Those whose claims were rejected were told why. Those Vinton approved were willing to indulge in his idle questions. He initially caught them off guard, but after a few moments they easily responded.

"What happened to your marriage?"

"So help me God, I don't know. To this day, I don't know. He just left." Too bad, Vinton thought.

"You wanna know why my old man ain't no part of mah family no more? 'Cause I threw his black ass out. That's why! Three times I get a dose from that man. And he was 'posed to be working all those nights. He just couldn't leave those jiggly young niggers alone. And here's I sit with three kids and no money to buy food or even see a doctor. That man was simply no good. Many a night me next to him, he sleeping off his cheap booze, I just wanted to tie that damn thing in one helluva big knot." Adultery, Vinton thought.

"He drank a lot, used to gamble. I'd wait on payday each Friday and not see him until Saturday afternoon. Sometimes he'd win and he'd be so proud. And he'd give me all his winnings. But mostly he lost. He hocked my wedding ring, our appliances, his shotgun, and he kept on gambling and kept on losing. One Saturday afternoon he never came home. I haven't seen him since." Gambling, Vinton made a mental note.

"I really don't know. Neither of us had an education. I got pregnant while in high school. He wanted to do the right thing. He got a job in a garage but wasn't happy. Jack's a bright guy, but without a high school diploma…anyway in two and a half years we had three kids. I guess the pressure got too great. I don't know where he is." Pregnant, married too young, no education.

One afternoon he had time to drive to the northwestern part of Union.

Seeing the American Indians in his office and hearing their plight hadn't prepared him for what he saw out there. He drove past the railroad yard, warehouses, and factories, then saw a shack in an open area. From the road, he judged its living area was about six hundred square feet. Four children were playing outside. Observing the adults' clothing hanging on the clothesline along with the children's, he figured that six people lived there.

Driving past other shacks, he saw most had junked vehicles near them. On an impulse, he pulled off the dirt road and approached one of the shacks. He stopped his car twenty feet short and walked toward it. A small puppy, its tail wagging, cautiously circled him. He rapped on the door, noticing several small children peeking out the windows. After several moments, a bent old lady slightly opened the door.

In spite of the brisk wind, Vinton was nearly overwhelmed by the odor emanating from the door that was opened just a few inches. "Hi, I'm with welfare. Can I come in and talk?"

"What about?"

"Just see how you're doing; if I'm able to help."

The old lady, nonplussed, briefly glanced at Vinton. He was the first wasicu to ever come to their door. "Where you from?"

"The welfare office."

The woman kept looking at the ground, then to a point beyond Vinton, but not at him. She stood there a minute or two, saying nothing. Vinton heard the laughter of the children from within. The old lady said something in Lakota. The laughter stopped.

"Are they your grandchildren?"

"We take good care of them, our little ones."

He realized that she was afraid he would take the kids and place them under the court's jurisdiction. "You seem like a nice lady. I bet the kids love you."

She looked directly at Vinton, suspicious but surprised by the words of this stranger. "You don't want to take my grandchildren?"

"No," Vinton quickly said.

"Then what do you want?"

"To talk with you."

She spoke in Lakota to someone inside the home. A male voice responded.

"Come in," she said.

Vinton stooped to get through the door. He lit a cigarette to surround himself with smoke, but it didn't neutralize the familiar stench he knew from his office. To his left was a tiny kitchen area. He saw a hand pump next to the sink, a small work counter, and shelves for food. There was no refrigerator. The main room was about eighty square feet. A woodstove in the center filled the room with too much warmth.

The shack had two bedrooms, one opposite the kitchen, the other perpendicular and jutting out perhaps twenty feet. Vinton counted the people as the old woman spoke in Lakota to her husband: the grandparents, a daughter, four small children. He saw a boy peeking from a bedroom. Eight people, four fully grown, maybe seven hundred square feet. He drew heavily on his cigarette. He introduced himself to the young woman, assuming she was the children's mother. Leaning over, he patted the heads of two of the children.

Then he spoke to the old woman. "These youngsters your grandchildren?"

The old woman nodded. "Of my adopted daughter Dee."

Vinton looked to Dee. She shyly returned his smile. "Is your husband home?"

"No."

"Do you and your kids live here with your adopted parents?"

"Yeah."

"Kind of crowded."

Dee kept smiling but blushed.

Vinton continued. "Do you work anywhere?"

She shook her head and nearly inaudibly said, "No."

"How do you get food around here?"

No one responded.

"Dee, you'd better come see me. Maybe I can help."

He went to the old man who remained seated. Jeff extended his hand. "What's your name?" The old man remained silent. Vinton turned to his wife. "Is he deaf?"

"He speaks no English. Our name is Red Shirt. He's Horace, I'm Annie."

"Annie, there are programs that can help Dee. Have her come see me in the courthouse. We'll try to get a home for her family. Give you some more room."

No one spoke. Jeff needed some fresh air. He had tried. He looked at the old lady. "Annie, it's good to meet you, I'll be going now. 'Bye."

The old woman looked at Vinton, saying nothing, her mouth vaguely assuming the configuration of a frown.

Jeff left that part of Union, returning to where he and the town could disregard the shanties and misery. As the workday was over, he drove to his apartment. Making coffee, he considered his upcoming meeting with the county board. He would have twenty-one cases to submit, all developed and finalized during his first month on the job, thereby causing a substantial increase in the county's caseload. He wondered about the board's reaction. No! He knew the reaction. And for God's sake, today he was out recruiting Dee and her four kids. He had noticed Dee's decaying teeth. Surely the kids would have dental needs as well. And the county's share of MA was twenty percent.

The cost of caring for human needs required exacting money from those who are employed and transferring it to those who aren't. Not really fair, he judged. He thought of the kids, the innocents, the pain and deprivation they endure. Ain't their fault. That's not fair either. They're here, they exist, realities to be dealt by either his office's involvement or its disregard. And each kid is going to mature, copulate and reproduce in his or hers and God's image. It was a dilemma. Should he favor those who are productive and contribute to the community? Or should he be partial to those with needs. On whose side would the angels fall? He reached a resolution that was simple, foolish and naive. He would comply with the law.

Vinton would come to dread the fourth Tuesday of each month. That's when he met with the county board to seek their approval for the growing welfare rolls of Harney County. This would be his first meeting.

Actually, the board's approval was pro forma. If the county accepted state and federal funds, it had to comply with state and federal regulations. It was a thorny legal question whether a county could refuse that assistance and thereby ignore its regulations. The question was never raised.

It was the staff that had the leverage. They had the manual. They could tell the commissioners what may or may not be legally accomplished, and they could tell the poor what could or could not be granted.

Vinton paced the hallway outside the board's conference room. The stack of approved case files were on the chair beside him.

The county attorney was discussing a legislative bill the Senate Committee on Local Jurisdictions was considering. He had just returned from the capital to report to the board. The bill, LB192, placed a ceiling on the counties' mill levies, their share of the assessed tax revenue. If it became law, Harney County would have to substantially reduce its budget. Its current mill levy exceeded the bill's limit.

Vinton had to report on additional county outlays immediately after the board was briefed on LB192. It was bad timing.

Phil Maenner, the county attorney, left the boardroom. He smiled at

Vinton while passing him. A smug smile, Jeff thought.

The table stretched the length of the room. The commissioners sat three on each side, the chair at the head. The men were in their late forties to mix-sixties: ranchers and businessmen, pillars of conservatism in their communities and churches.

Vinton steeled himself. "Good morning gentlemen." He sat at the vacant end of the table, placing his files before him.

"Good morning, Jeff," Commissioner Scott quickly responded. "The courthouse chatter tells us you had a rough first month."

"Busy. It's been busy."

"What do you have for us?

"How many goddamned Indians?" asked Commissioner Hank Oldfield, chewing on an unlit cigar.

"I've twenty-one cases." Jeff ignored Oldfield. "Each worked by me or my staff and approved by me. Each is eligible. I recommend your approval."

"Can you give us an overview, Jeff?" Scott asked.

"There are eleven ADC, nine AABD, and one MA. I've referred the ADC cases to the county attorney. We know where most of the runaway pappies are; they're right here in town. The county attorney should bring these men to court, citing them with desertion or contempt. I'll work with him to get those dads to support their kids. When the judge acts on the petitions, some cases may be closed. The other dads left the county. So dependent on the county attorneys to where they moved, the ADC cases shouldn't last that long. The AABD ones may be with us for a while."

"How many goddamn Indians?" Oldfield asked again.

"I don't know," Jeff lied.

"Give me the files, and I'll tell ya."

Commissioner Scott interrupted. "Jeff, are these cases legitimate? Are they really eligible?"

"Yes, sir."

Scott nodded to Jeff. "I move we accept the cases, move their approval."

Oldfield felt he should contest the chair making the motion. But he didn't. "Second," another commissioner said.

"Call the question," the chair moved. Counting the ayes, Scott ruled that the motion had carried.

Vinton noted Oldfield was the lone dissenter. He thanked the board and left.

Walking to his office, Vinton felt good about his first month on the job. He had gotten through his first board meeting and had become conversant about office operations. Milner had withdrawn his resignation, the staff was responding to his direction, and he was helping a lot of kids and old folks. He was impacting his environment.

He walked into his office, feeling good.

16 Jun 67

The staccato sound of the engine and the two main rotor blades was deafening as the helicopter flew through the heavy air. The excessive humidity acted as a solid wall, reverberating the Huey's monotonous cacophony. The blare drowned out the sound of the eleven other helicopters that were grouped in combat formation.

Vinton sensed the rapid descent of the aircraft. He stood. Looking over the pilot's shoulder, he could see the landing zone before him. His eyes followed a small and muddy stream until it disappeared into the rain forest. He looked to the north and south of the stream, noting that the forest formed a V, closing in on the small marshland of the landing zone. The stream disappeared into the jungle about seven hundred meters southeast of the LZ.

Turning, he saw his men were ready. They had sensed the LZ was directly ahead. The helicopters approaching from the east were approximately four meters above the flat marshland, traveling at about forty knots. As he looked to the north, the jungle blurred past him. He estimated where the LZ would be and tapped the gunner on the shoulder, pointing to an area he wanted fire laid down. The gunner, without turning, nodded. The helicopter rapidly decreased its speed but didn't touch down, hovering awkwardly.

"Go! Go!" Vinton yelled, his men jumping the three feet to the ground, sinking into the several inches of water that covered the marshland. The helicopter gunner had been firing the M60 for about a minute now, raking the area. Seconds later, before Vinton jumped from the aircraft, his men were taking small arms fire from the jungle to the north.

Vinton was last to leave the chopper. Ejected shell casings from the M60 hit his helmet and the side of his face as he made the short jump. For a moment, he thought he was hit by hostile fire. Then he realized it was just spent shells. The hot brass began blistering the left side of his face. Before he hit the ground, he saw that two of his men had been hit. He ran toward them, yelling for his radioman. Reaching the first, Vinton quickly turned him on to his back so he wouldn't drown. It was a futile effort. The soldier's chest had been completely opened up. Vinton moved in the direction of the other fallen man, still yelling for his radioman. Damn! We're committed, we're here; the other helicopters were discharging their cargo of infantrymen.

Still looking for the other man, he pulled a canister from his belt, pulled the pin, and threw it between his men and the rain forest. The red smoke, indicating a hot LZ, slowly obscured his men from the hostile fire.

He couldn't find the second fallen man. His platoon was returning the fire from the jungle. His radioman. He needed him! "Where the hell's Pruitt?" he screamed.

"Over here, Lieutenant," someone yelled. "He's hit!"

Vinton changed direction, now running toward the voice he had just heard, firing in the direction of the red smoke. The elephant grass, about five feet high, nettled and cut his arms as he ran through it. A mortar shell exploded a few meters to his left, spraying him with water. He heard the other platoons returning fire to the west; one of his men yelling for a medic. Running hard through the tall grass, he suddenly and luckily tripped and fell over one of his men who had taken a single round that had penetrated his helmet and now rested in his forehead. A few feet away lay Pruitt, also hit. Vinton crawled toward the radioman. Once there, he grabbed the receiver, yelling into it - "Red Striker, Red Striker, this is Little Wedge. We're taking small arms and mortar fire. Hot zone! This is a hot LZ! Do you read?"

"Ah ... Roger ... read you, Little Wedge. What are your losses? Over."

"Don't know. Got some. Need an air strike! Do you read?"

"This is Red Striker ... ah ... Roger, Little Wedge, we'll get air support on its way. Over." The voice was efficient, aloof, dispassionate.

"Willie peter, then napalm and HE," Vinton yelled into the receiver.

"Have them strike due north, I say again, north of the tree line; approach on an east-west axis or south to north."

"Ah ... Roger, Little Wedge, we'll patch you into them. You'll be in contact with them shortly. Over."

Vinton, crouching, scanned the sky. Nothing. His men, continuing to return fire, were blindly pointing their weapons in the general area of the jungle to where he had earlier pointed. The Hueys, after unloading the infantrymen, had made several passes over the area, firing their M60s. But now they were gone.

"Air strike on the way," Vinton yelled. "Stay put! Keep firing!" From the sounds of battle, he estimated only half his men were returning the fire. He threw out another canister of red smoke. Then running from area to area, he located most of his men and individually repositioned them until they formed a skirmish line. He tried to remember where the dead and badly wounded were relative to those still firing.

He looked again to the sky.

Nothing!

Running low and with erratic patterns, Vinton returned to his wounded radioman. "Red Striker, Red Striker, this is Little Wedge. What's the status of our air support?"

"Ah ... this is Red Striker ... ETA four minutes, I'm advised. Over."

"Roger." He looked now to his radioman. Pruitt's belly had taken one or two rounds. But his fatigue jacket was wet with the muddy water of the marshland and his sweat and blood. The soaked shirt would keep any exposed organs moist. He searched the black radioman's eyes, tapped his helmet, and smiled as assuredly as he could. The medic had covered the wound with a field dressing and given him a shot of morphine. There was nothing more to do. The wounds were in critical areas; the kidney, the liver, the pancreas.

Vinton wished he could magically touch the radioman, could harness the power to heal the wounds. But knowing he couldn't, he had an intense urge to leave Pruitt rather than remain and be reminded of his powerlessness. But he knew even greater pain would be caused if he rolled Pruitt over onto his belly to remove the radio.

He lay beside Pruitt, blindly, futilely firing into the rain forest.

CHAPTER SEVEN

Herb Chandler wasn't impatient. The primary was ten months away, still plenty of time to accomplish the many things necessary to conduct a major political campaign. But dammit, he was curious. He had known Bob Elam's father, a bright man filled with integrity, as was his son. But the father had ambition, once confiding his interest in the U.S. Senate. So what was the matter with his son?

Chandler had assigned his brightest lad to the task of testing the waters on Elam's behalf. The kid had done a top-notch job. Herb disciplined himself not to force the issue, but he had twice redirected the format to test his intuitive judgment that Elam could become the next governor. The results of the survey were valid. Elam could capture the moment, and the office.

Chandler called his secretary. "Tell the kid to get the Elam file and get his ass in here."

Chandler went to his liquor cabinet, poured some bourbon and returned to his desk, sipping from the glass. He lit a cigar and leaned back in his chair. Bill Sergent opened the door to the large office and approached Chandler.

Making a sweeping motion with his cigar, Chandler signaled him to sit. "It's been over a month. Elam hasn't called me. What the hell's going on?"

"I don't know. I thought he would."

"Let's go over those results again," Chandler's creased forehead indicating he hadn't finished. Moments later he added, "For Christ's sake."

Only then did Sergent feel comfortable in responding. "Well, as you know, the project had three facets to it. Let's go over the first. We initially polled 1,012 people, allowing for a margin of error of less than three percent. We excluded Elam from the list. The results were Sorenson 8, Malek 20, Shannon 15, Dubisky 16, None of the above 22, No opinion 19.

Well, Sorenson moved to Idaho a year ago. Shannon is having marital problems and is in no condition for a major venture. And

Dubisky ain't gonna leave his law practice for the governor's wages. That leaves Malek. Now Malek just ain't gubernatorial timber!"

He paused. "The next poll was taken three weeks later, this time just among Democrats, using the same list but including Elam this time. It broke out Sorenson 5, Elam 10, Malek 11, Shannon 13, Dubisky 17, None of the above 29, No opinion 15.

"Now this ain't bad considering our assessment of the other four. Elam, a behind-the-scenes sort of guy, polled a solid ten percent. That's amazing considering that some of the smart money's backing Malek. The truth is the Democrats have been out of office so long there's nobody groomed for the job. You know, media accessibility, responsible public position, all those things incumbency allows. There just hasn't been that opportunity for the minority party these past years. The critical element here is there's no competition."

Chandler nodded.

"Okay. The second part of the survey was to determine Governor Norman's vulnerability. We found the governor's in deep trouble. Among Republicans, he broke out Excellent 6, Good 24, Fair 33, Poor 23, No opinion 14.

"In other words, among Republicans, only thirty percent consider him favorably. The Democrats, amazingly, came out 4, 32, 28, 18, with eighteen percent having no opinion. The Democrats - now listen to this - view him thirty-six percent positive, six points higher than his own party. The guy is too moderate for his party and this state.

"Now the third aspect was the issues questionnaire. It's a damn classic conservative litany - less attention to the poor, the aged, the unemployed, minorities. Generally speaking, people want fewer services for the poor and more tax relief. Now the background stuff we did on Elam came up with a few surprises - all positive..." Sergent hesitated. He hadn't been interrupted by any words or gestures, only by some vibes he picked up. He stopped and looked at Chandler whose eyes met his.

"Yeah, I know about Bob's strengths. What's your analysis?"

"With financial backing, he'll win the primary," Sergent predicted. "If Norman is the GOP candidate, he'll win the general."

"You sound confident."

"Yeah."

"Okay. I'm gonna see Elam. You know, there's a time for everything. It's time Elam gets off his ass."

"What do you think he's gonna do?"

Chandler sipped at his bourbon. "I suspect he's still a bit overwhelmed, that he's toyed with the idea, even been bitten a bit by the little bug. He's fantasizing about the power and the prestige of the whole thing, and he's a little afraid right now. You knew he was only thinking of running for the legislature, didn't you?"

"No. But he was overwhelmed when I told him the governor's office was a possibility."

"What was his exact reaction?"

"Initially shock, then complete incredibility," Sergent recalled. "Then he went off the deep end, getting emotional. But I don't think he ever got past the point of disbelief. But by now, the bug should have bitten hard."

"It's time I go see our next governor. You do whatever polishing needs to be done. Make it look good. Concentrate on those last pages where we make our judgment, and the critique. Make sure the language is clear, uncluttered, and snappy. Okay?"

"How promising should I indicate his chances are?" Sergent asked.

"Say it's a piece of cake."

"You sure you want me to say that?"

"Yeah. If you shape events before they happen so that they happen, you ain't lying. You're just predicting the future. Get it ready,"

Sergent nodded and smiled. In response, Chandler looked up sternly, then allowed himself to smile. Sergent picked up his papers and returned to his office.

Chandler drew on his cigar. The operatives, he thought, are within the Democratic Party; labor, educators, civil servants, minorities, some farm and ranch associations. And the activists of any party tend to lean to its extreme. He recalled the old joke; the motorist asking JFK for directions to Washington. The response: "Go to Harvard, then turn left."

In a memorandum for file, Sergent had detailed Elam's spirited defense of Democratic programs. So Chandler knew Elam would have no problem during the primary. He would then just need to turn right.

In Cook County, Elam's liberalism would earn him a C-minus. In this state, he was close to the lunatic fringe. How to align him with the political realities after the primary? Would he resist? How much integrity did he really have? How deep were his convictions? Sergent perceived them to touch bedrock. But just how solid was the mantle?

Chandler again sipped at the warm bourbon. Then he listed the critical elements of the campaign on a yellow pad. He began with the premise that Elam would win the general election. He listed the steps necessary to achieve that objective. Chandler often toyed with this method he called his reverse-logic system. He simply did things backwards. Instead of logically beginning at step one, the first item to be achieved, and systematically progress from that point, he would begin at the last step then work back.

Chandler spent the next few hours laboring at his desk, filling sheets of his legal-size pad. He was exhausted when he finished. He examined the matrix he had designed.

To a casual observer, it was just a series of diagonal and horizontal lines, emanating from one large square at the left side of the paper, each going through an intertwined maze, with critical benchmarks identified by a series of symbols and numbers beside each. Then all the lines converged on their final destination. To Chandler, this was the critical outcome: the election of Robert Temple Elam as the next governor of the state.

▼-95 was the mobilization of labor's support (Higgins - AFL-CIO, Ryman —Teamsters, White - public employees).). ▌-120 was the development of agricultural position papers (Evans - National Farmers Organization, Rutherford - Farmers Union, Hartner - Cattleman's Association, Larsen - Ag College, State University). ♣-90 was the critical element to be quickly acted upon: secure commitment of $180,000.

Chandler sat back, sipping at his bourbon. It can be done, he told himself.

The meeting occurred three days later. Sergent packaged the survey, Chandler had his graphics staff produce the matrix.

Chandler initiated the call. He and Elam idly chatted for several minutes before agreeing to meet. Oddly, neither spoke about the reason for the call. Both men knew why they were meeting.

When Pam asked what he wanted, Elam explained that Herb

wanted to discuss his meeting with Sergent. Elam hadn't spoken to Pam or anyone about the possible gubernatorial race. Granted, it was important to make the announcement at the proper time to maximize the impact. Furthermore, a premature announcement could adversely affect one's chances, and Elam knew there's no such thing as a political secret. Tell one person, anyone, and the word gets out. But if you intend to run for office, you have let the voters know sooner or later. Bob hadn't even told his wife. Why? Because the whole thing was preposterous! But he couldn't shake the thought. He began fantasizing. The inauguration ... the Lincoln Continental ... the state aircraft ... the governors' conference at Hilton Head ... he and Pam invited to the White House... He snapped out of it. Knotting his tie, putting on his suit coat, kissing Pam lightly on the lips, he left to go to the Enterprize.

The Enterprize Club catered to the executives of government. Elected officials received gratis memberships and would spend long hours there. Lobbyists ran up sizeable tabs. Nongovernment types joined just to vicariously enjoy the ambience. It was as much a political institution in the state capital as the branches of government; an arena in which deals were struck, tradeoffs were accomplished, and souls were purchased.

Entering, Bob looked over the crowd. He didn't see Chandler. He ordered a drink and then wondered how to pay for it. Should he start a tab? Could he, considering he wasn't a member? He was beginning to feel a bit awkward when Herb tapped him on the shoulder.

"Herb, how are you?"

"Fine. I've a little room for us." Chandler extended his arm in its general direction."

Walking through the crowded bar, Bob sensed that inquiring eyes were following him. He felt strange, not being accustomed to attracting attention. He knew that Chandler had the reputation as a powerbroker, but what the hell, he thought, I've been with Herb in other places and never gotten a second look. He didn't know whether to be annoyed or flattered.

Herb negotiated them through the maze to a corridor. He opened the door to a room, allowing Bob to enter.

"Here we are. I thought we might want a quiet place to chat."

The room was dimly lit, with large overstuffed chairs around a table. In a corner of the room was a small wet bar and a bottle of Old Fitzgerald. Chandler refreshed Bob's drink and poured himself one.

"Well, Bob, we got a lot to talk about."

"Where the hell does one begin?" Elam asked.

"A lot depends on you. Where you are, what you want, how much you want it."

Elam hesitated. "Herb, I'm not sure I've got any answers for you." He thought a bit longer. Chandler waited. "There's no question I want to be the next governor. I suspect there are few who wouldn't be honored by what you suggest. But there's this business of practicality." Elam paused, not knowing if he should admit how fearful the concept was.

This fear had operated on two levels. Initially he was concerned about his ability to perform well should he win. But he had gotten through that impasse. He was confident he could effectively bring his managerial skills to the job, could attract competent executives to the cabinet posts, could expose and correct the unwholesome structure of government that Hammond and his ilk had foisted upon the state. He could not, however, shake the trepidation that surfaced the moment he resolved the first apprehension. How serious, or using Sergent's parlance, how viable a candidate would he be? What would happen if he announced and no one cared? If he rented a hall and no one came? If he printed twenty thousand bumper stickers, and nobody wanted any? How ignominious would the defeat be if someone as equally unknown beat him in a landslide? How could he and his family live with that humiliation? What if a smart-ass reporter asked: "Okay, Mr. Elam, why should I or anyone vote for you?" What would he say?

His biggest concern was that he might damn well make a fool of himself. And if he did, after giving this endeavor his best effort, could he live with the defeat? It's easy to become a candidate. But how do you become a "viable candidate?" How do you persuade the opinion makers, the press, the county chairmen, and precinct workers that you're "viable"? How do you look like a winner when you've never won anything? Elam had searched for the answers long enough to know he had no answers.

"Should I give this effort my best, and assuming my son isn't arrested in a drug bust or my daughter doesn't run off with Agnew's son, what are my chances of getting through the primary?"

"We can't guarantee anything. But given the givens, you're beyond that point. You'll win the primary. It's the general election my staff is working on," replied Chandler before going over the surveys, explaining in detail those subtleties revealed in the polls. He listed Governor Norman's vulnerabilities, the possibility of bloodletting in the GOP primary, the reality that the Democrats have no one in the wings, how the party desperately needs a new personality, how Elam's background, family, appearance, personal resources, and availability could catapult him into filling that void. "There's no question it's a chance, and it's gonna take your total commitment. It's going to take a lot of money, too, and I'm gonna send a bill next December whether you win or lose. But, Bob, it's a rare moment in the political life of this state. The people want a change, but they don't know it yet. The GOP may shed some of its own blood, and the Democrats could walk away with the prize if they select the right man - if the right man offers himself. You want my judgment? I feel a lot more confident about your chances than I did about Phil Dawson's."

Bob looked up, surprised.

"Sure, Bob, we work both sides of the aisle. It's a business. Hell, I'd work for a WCTU candidate if she'd pay the bill," said Chandler, raising his glass in a mock salute. "But we restrict our services to those with a good chance of winning. We can't stay in business by overseeing our clients' defeats. We're friends, Bob, but this is a business. We think you're a winner. We want to help you win, thereby enhancing our reputation as a firm that produces winners. That way we stay in business."

Elam was impressed. To hell with friendships, philosophies, partisan leanings. It's a business with Herb, and Chandler & Associates thinks he's a winner. And they're the pros. "How about fundraising? And how much will I have to throw in?"

"We're pretty good at fundraising, but we want you to invest twenty grand to get the ball rolling. Can you afford that?"

It was then that Elam knew he had been caught up in the vortex of ambition, the power and trappings of high political office. He nodded weakly, committing himself. As an afterthought he said, "I'd better let Pam in on it."

Herb smiled. "You'd better let her know, and before you make that final commitment, make sure she's with you. The days ahead are going to be tough, physically and emotionally demanding. You're gonna need Pam like never before. If she's reluctant, we'd better drop it." Chandler paused, looked hard at Elam. "I mean that, Bob."

Elam nodded, wondering what Pam would say, wondering how to tell her.

"If you throw in the first twenty thousand, we'll get the other $160,000 to get things going. We'll be in the background. We'll make the arrangements, do the work behind the scenes, advise you about the best courses of action. But, Bob, you'll have to do the rest. It's important that you come off as the man in charge of his campaign, and you will be. But we'll always be in the next room, meeting with you every night, drafting your speeches, preparing your press releases, allocating your time, scheduling your appearances, formulating your position papers. But out of sight. You'll be the front person. And, Bob, let me tell you something else. You're gonna enjoy it, and you're probably gonna win."

"Herb, I've got to talk to Pam about this. I can't commit until we both have time to think about it. It may be a week or so before I get back to you. I hope you understand."

"Sure. There's still plenty of time."

Elam looked out the large window at the seat of government. The capitol was illuminated by floodlights on the outside and by office lights on the inside. The custodians were removing the debris from the offices. Considering that nothing happens in government without a piece of paper preceding the event, paper is the critical element. The forms and plans and projections and surveys, cost analyses and computer printouts, memoranda, their courtesy copies and responses were all eventually consigned to the fleet of trucks that appeared each evening to haul the paperwork away. But no matter what or how much was discarded, photocopies and microfilms were always filed somewhere. No document was ever completely destroyed. A copy always existed somewhere, assuming the importance of the original, and photocopies were routinely made of surviving photocopies.

Elam watched a truck enter the bowels of the great building, reappearing in a few minutes, headed for the city dump.

He turned from the window and faced Chandler. "Herb, you've done a lot of work for me. I appreciate it. You know I want to go for it. And I don't think Pam will have any reservations. But I'd better make sure. You've proven to be a good friend - and business associate. Thanks." They shook hands. Herb opened the door. They left the quiet of the room and briefly became a part of the crowded club.

It was after eleven when he got home. Surprised Pam was still up, he went to her. He extended his hands but stood far enough away to force her to rise. She looked into his eyes, not losing contact as she rose. Rather than grasp his extended hands, she slipped between them, hugging him with her full body. She held him for a minute, saying nothing, then relaxed her embrace. She drew back her head and again looked into his eyes.

"Bob, you've been behaving strangely for over a month now. What's going on? You can tell me."

"Yeah, Pam, it's time I shared something crazy with you." He wondered where to begin, how to tell his wife something that even he couldn't fully comprehend. He looked again at Pam, noting her troubled expression.

"Pam, you know how important you are to me, how much I love you. You know nothing will ever change that."

Her eyes sparkled, small tears forming. She smiled and lightly kissed him.

"Now let's talk about our little problem. Make some coffee, would you?" Pam walked to the kitchen, Bob following her, watching her. As she prepared the coffee, her back to him, Bob quietly said, "Herb Chandler wants me to run for governor."

Pam froze, then raised her head slightly, her eyes level with the window. She stared into the darkness of the night.

Bob watched her for a minute, she not moving. "Hey lady, how's our coffee coming?" She turned, walked to him, hugged him, patted his buttocks. "To hell with the coffee. Pour us a couple of stiff drinks."

"Of course." Bob left to make the drinks, once going back to the kitchen to get ice. Pam still stared into the darkness through the window. He said nothing, leaving her to her thoughts.

Minutes passed before Pam came to the living room. She picked up her drink, gulped it, her forehead creasing from its sharpness. Bob watched her, waited for her to speak. She leaned back on the couch, closing her eyes for a few seconds. Then, smiling at her husband, she looked him differently. Bob sat on the edge of the chair opposite the couch, holding the drink he hadn't tasted.

Pam looked intently at her husband, seeing this different person. Damn, she thought, he does look like a governor. "What did you tell Herb?"

"I told him I was flattered, and interested. Let me start from the top: when I asked about dad's legislative seat. Remember that night at the country club? Well, that was the extent of my political ambition. Then, a month ago, Herb sent Bill Sergent to chat with me. Remember the evening I told you I might be able to win dad's seat?"

Pam thought for a moment, then remembered his telling her, how he held her breasts. Her face reddened. She felt flushed.

God, she admitted to herself, I'm blushing. This is Bob I'm talking to, my husband of twenty years. But she knew at this moment she was viewing someone else. He was taking on a different identity right before her eyes. Pam shifted, feeling an arousal within her. She nodded, acknowledging that she remembered that evening.

"Well, that's when it - my candidacy for governor - was first mentioned. Pam, it didn't make sense then, and it doesn't make sense now. But tonight Herb showed me the surveys, the polls, his action plan for the campaign. Somehow it makes sense. Norman is going to lose. The only question is to whom. Herb's convinced I can beat him."

"But, Bob, you've never run for elected office."

"I know."

"We don't even know what we have to do."

Bob noted the collective "we." He smiled. "Herb will set the whole thing up."

"What about the business?"

"It runs itself. I'll promote Kreiger to general manager."

"You want to do it, to run, don't you?"

"Let's invite Herb for dinner next week. Give you a chance to chat with him."

Pam sensed he wanted to end the conversation. No way, she told herself. I want to savor this moment, to fully experience it, to share it totally with Bob. She tried to think of ways to continue the conversation. "Who knows about this?"

"Just us, Herb, and his staff. They're a disciplined lot, used to this sort of thing. They won't tip our hand. So really, it's just you and me."

"They think you can pull it off?"

"This is Chandler's business, a substantial amount of the work his firm does. No guarantees, but he's confident."

"Shouldn't you see a doctor? To make sure that you're physically fit for the rigors of a campaign?"

"Yeah. Good idea! Can you get me an appointment?"

"Sure." Pam was at an impasse again. "What role would I have in the campaign?"

"Pam, I will need your total support; I will be putting demands on you like never before."

She felt pleased and again felt her face flush. She sipped at her drink, then gulped the rest of it, feeling shivers throughout her body. Bob had indeed made her a strong drink. She extended her hand to him. "If you want to go for it, then dammit, let's go."

Bob reached out to hold her hand. Pam again felt shivers, possibly an aftershock from her drink. No, she told herself, it's not the bourbon; it's not even Bob. It's this other man before me. The next governor of the state. Pam was excited, sexually aroused. She wanted Bob very much. "Another drink," she said, handing him the empty glass, her fingers lingering as they touched his. "Bring it to me in the bedroom."

When Bob brought her the drink, she was in bed, her eyes sparkling as she looked into his. He stirred, sensing her need. She drank nearly half the bourbon and water as she watched him undress. Long minutes later, at the moment of orgasm, she was only thinking "the governor of the state," her body shuddering throughout with elements of love, fear, excitement, and the newly found strangeness of the man she had solely and faithfully loved her entire adult life.

CHAPTER EIGHT

The Chevrolet gained speed as it neared the bottom of the hill but now needed to climb the next one. The speedometer read forty-five mph. George Iron Rope pushed in the clutch and reengaged the gear, depressing the accelerator. The car surged forward. After it climbed and crested the hill, George shifted into neutral and turned off the motor. The car coasted down the long decline. It passed the Flying Hawk Inn, a bar situated less than a mile from the reservation. The discarded beer cans and liquor bottles covering the shoulders of the road reflected the sun, the shimmering radiance nearly blinding George. The car reached the bottom of the hill, its speed near fifty. Now he simply had to negotiate the flattened highway. George was confident he had the momentum to get to the USDA's commodity distribution station.

He chatted with the clerk and signed the forms acknowledging he was a resident of the reservation, an enrolled member of the tribe. He had no compunction about signing these forms even though he and his family lived in Union. He never claimed to live here except when he signed the documents. On a reservation even as large as this, everyone knew everyone's predicaments. With extended families, informal adoptions, and the concept of the clan tying nearly everyone together, it would have been useless to lie. Signing the forms to feed his family had nothing to do with falsification, only survival. And George had signed the forms each month for the last six years. He no longer recalled the statements to which his signature attested.

George had brought boxes for packing the food. He and the clerk then carried them to his car. Powdered milk and eggs, peanut butter, a few cans of boned chicken, bulgur, some cornmeal, and several bags of beans and rice. He thanked the clerk, started his car, and eased it onto the road for the return trip. The commodities would feed his family for the next month, and he would have some for his adopted grandparents, Annie and Horace.

The car sluggishly overcame the flat ground and long incline it had earlier coasted down. George saw he was leaving a heavier trail of smoke. He had brought along two jars of oil. He would allow the car to slow to a halt once he reached the flats, then check and, if necessary, add oil.

George had risen early in the morning, leaving Union before sunrise to avoid the midday heat. It was still relatively cool, the temperature in the lower eighties. The car, however, was running hotter than normal. He wondered how many more trips it could make. Best not to think of such things. George forced his mind from the road before him and the smoke behind, thinking of Mary and his sons. But even that brought concern. His older son, who was seven, had a harelip, a pronounced cleft to his upper lip. George didn't know what to do about it. He had tried to check his son into the Public Health Service hospital for corrective surgery. The PHS administrator was fussier about details than the surplus commodity clerk. Since George lived off the reservation, his family was ineligible for medical care. The deformity would be with his son for the rest of his life.

Feeling guilty, George sometimes ignored him to avoid more pain. He knew Junior felt the pain of his father's aloofness without understanding the reason. So George would compensate, bringing Junior a soda or a toy even though he couldn't afford a second one for his other son. And sometimes he would hug Junior so tightly the little boy would grimace with pain.

While thinking of the joys in his life - his wife Mary; the gentleness, kindness, and wisdom of Annie and Horace - the car's steering wheel tugged sharply to the left. George heard the familiar thumping. He steered the car to the shoulder of the highway to replace one bald tire with another.

The remainder of the trip was filled with apprehension about what he'd do if he had another flat. He drove past several service stations because the tire wasn't worth repairing and because he had no money.

He breathed a sigh of relief when he finally made it to Union and his home. His sons ran to him as he got out of the car. George knelt, holding his arms to catch them. His tried not to notice Junior's face.

He unloaded the car, a month's supply of food securely at home. Mary sidestepped to avoid him as he brought the food into the small kitchen. "Can I help put these away?" he asked.

"Thanks, I'll get them. Relax. You've had a tough trip."

"How'd it go with you today?"

"Fine."

"You know, you're a beautiful woman, and I'm a lucky man."

Mary didn't know what to say. She smiled and looked at the floor, her foot thoughtlessly scraping the hardened dirt. "Oh, Pat walked over. He was looking for you."

"Did he say what he wanted?" George was planning to see Pat about a serious issue.

"No, he just wanted to see you."

"Dammit," George muttered, "the damn wasicus pick up a telephone if they want to talk to their brother. I've got to walk over a mile to talk to mine. It just ain't fair." He looked to Mary. She could only sadly look back. "But what the hell," he reflected. "If I had a phone I still couldn't call him. Pat would need one too."

Mary noted his despondency. "I'm sure it's nothing serious. Why don't you play with the boys?"

George went outside and called his sons. They ran to him, sweat forming on their foreheads and mixing with the fine dust, creating a gritty residue. "Let's go inside and have a man-to-man talk," George said, wiping the perspiration from their faces. Entering the home, George sat on a chair, his sons on the cool floor. George tapped Junior's head. "What's your name, young man?"

"I'm George Iron Rope Junior," the older son said, giggling.

"And who are you named after?"

"My daddy."

"And who are you, young man?"

His other son, age six, also giggled. "I'm Patton Iron Rope."

"And who are you named after?"

"My uncle Pat."

"And who are your daddy and uncle named after?"

"George Patton," they said, laughing together.

"And who was this guy Patton?"

"A great American general," they said in unison, familiar with the game they often played with their father. But this time, George asked another question, one he hadn't asked before. "Now think real hard. Who was the bravest and smartest and best general America has ever produced?"

The boys looked at each other. Junior smiled, his face contorting more severely. "We don't know," he said. "Who was it, Daddy?"

"The smartest and bravest and best general America ever produced was a man named Crazy Horse."

"I know who he was," Junior responded.

"He was one of our people, and he was a great American. But what's your last name?" George kidded his sons.

"Iron Rope!" they shouted.

"Is that a German name?"

"Nooo!"

"What kind of name is that?"

"An Indian name," they shouted.

"Right," George softly said, patting his sons' heads. Despite the joy of being with his children, hearing their laughter, feeling their closeness, George couldn't shake the concern he had for Dee and her kids and, by extension, his and Mary's. He sat troubled. The boys looked at their father's distressed expression, wondering what was wrong. But not knowing any better, they entrusted their security and safety to him.

George was distracted by the touch of Mary's hand. She had seen the children watch their father and needed to shake him from his mood. She did so by touching him, looking at him, then the children. George nodded, forced a smile, and patted his youngsters' heads.

They smiled, assuming again the innocence of their years. "Let's go outside," George said. With his sons holding his hands, they stepped out of the shack.

The sun was past its zenith, beginning to create shadows. The boys, taking their cues from their father, were silent. They walked to the dirt street. George stirred up the dust along the edge of the road, his sons soon imitating his movements. They walked leisurely past the church, the Head Start center, to where the Kills Crow Indian family lived, then beyond to the end of the road. George and his sons stood for a moment, looking toward the rich farmland on the flats before them. Beyond this land, on the distant horizon, was a ridgeline that continued until it was dwarfed by and lost its identity to the mountains eighty miles to the west.

George and his sons, looking to the horizon, took in the beauty of the land. In the foreground was the golden stubble of a wheat field that giant combines had cut a few weeks earlier. Beyond the stubble lay green pastures where fattened cattle fed, then a river which sometimes was a quarter-mile wide but seldom more than a foot deep. It was this river that provided the wasicus the pathway through this country, this land of the Oglala. And George, sensing the magnificence of the land his people had fought for and lost, returned his gaze to the ugly gully between the golden field and the dusty road. It was filled with trash; discarded paper and boxes, ruptured tires, the ubiquitous beer cans and wine bottles.

Disgusted, George turned to his sons who should have been heirs to this land. "Let's go back." George directed his boys a block north in order to pass Annie and Horace's home. George had been concerned about Dee and her kids ever since he had seen the wasicu's car in front of their home. He had asked them what the man wanted, but no one answered to his satisfaction. "He wanted to see if there was anything he could do," Annie said.

"He told me to come to the welfare office," Dee said.

"He seemed different than the other wasicus," Horace, speaking in Lakota, supported Annie and Dee.

George had muttered obscenities to each response.

Weeks had passed; the wasicu hadn't returned. George assumed he was preparing the necessary paperwork to take Dee's children, to place them under the court's authority, to put them in strange homes, houses with different food, a different language; houses that would purge from them the essence of their blood, their culture, their traditions. Accepting the assumed intention of the wasicu as reality, he prepared himself for the inevitable. He had no knowledge of the judicial procedures necessary for taking children from their families, but he knew it was common practice in the nearby counties. He had spoken with fathers who wept over their children's absence, fathers who wanted to hug, to touch, to see their children.

The American Indian families in Harney County hadn't been subjected to this legalized abduction of their youngsters. So far, the children, either to their advantage or detriment, remained with their families, blood, and traditions. It was as if the children didn't exist.

Now the county had a new welfare director. Now the county would be involved. Maybe the kids would be better off with the wasicus.

They'd be in a home with carpeted floors, not dirt, an inside toilet and sink and bathtub, screens on windows to keep out flying insects, a refrigerator to keep their milk cold.

What's the matter with us Indians? George asked himself. Why can't we offer our young real homes like the wasicus? George knew some of the reasons: chronic and pandemic alcoholism, lack of education, lack of pride of self and culture.

Although unable to articulate, to use the correct words, he knew most of those elements were symptoms, not the cause of the American Indians' conditions. Alcohol was a means to escape the hopelessness of their reality for a few hours at a time. The absence of education could be attributed to many factors: not having an alarm clock, not having clean clothes, the isolation of prejudice, the feeling your people are intellectually inferior. George tried but was unable to grasp the reality of the American Indian in Harney County. Perhaps Dee's children would be better off, but an elemental wrong would be committed if the wasicu has his way.

How do we fight this man, he with his paper and words, we with nothing? He with his courts, we who suffer from the rulings? It's wrong, but what can we do to counter this wrong? How can anyone take small children from their parents, destroy families, and wash away bloodlines? No one should have such authority!

Perplexed by their father's silence, the boys tried to capture his attention. George held their hands so tightly they cried out, jerking him from his thoughts. He knelt to comfort them, wiping away their tiny tears.

He looked beyond his children to Horace and Annie's house. He sensed something was wrong, but he was afraid to find out what. Pat and I will see them tonight, he reasoned. Still kneeling beside his sons, he forced a smile. "I'll race you home!" The boys began running, their little legs churning the dust. How small and helpless they are, George thought. How innocent but damned.

He walked to Pat's home after supper. Rather than go in and worry his pregnant wife, George asked his brother to come outside. Minutes later, Pat told her that he and George were going to see Horace and Annie.

Walking the dusty roads, George more fully spoke of his fears. He told Pat about the wasicu's appearance at their adopted grandparents' door; about this guy seeing Dee and all of her kids in the small house. He was from the welfare office! And welfare takes kids away from parents. And the wasicu came in from the capital a few weeks ago. And when he takes Dee's kids, will he stop there, or will he eventually get around to Pat's child and to his sons? "We've got to stop this guy, Pat, before he takes Dee's kids."

"How?" Patton asked.

"I don't know. I've no idea."

They walked in silence, feeling the northerly breeze at their backs. "It's a legal matter. Dee is gonna have to get a lawyer," Pat finally said.

"Lawyers cost bucks," George replied. "Hell, I can barely afford to feed my kids, let alone hire an attorney to keep them."

Pat kicked an empty beer can into the ditch. The sun was low in the sky, the temperature moderating when they arrived. They were greeted by Donny, the sixteen-year-old boy living with Horace, Annie, and Dee's family. Dee was bedding down the children for the evening, so George suggested they take chairs outside for Annie and Horace. George and Patton sat on the ground before their grandparents.

"Has the wasicu come back?"

"No," Annie answered.

"Did Dee go see him?"

"No."

"Good."

George remained silent for a few minutes. Horace and Annie were too much a part of the past; meriting and expecting the respect of those younger than they, still viewing the family as the elemental unit, still pampering the little ones. Could they grasp the possibility of children being taken away because their mother was poor?

George obliquely approached the subject. "You know the white man has never really understood us. How we care for ourselves, our own, without the government. How we have our own welfare program. How each of our children will always have a parent. The system worked throughout the years, and though it's breaking down it's still better than what the wasicus have." George paused, reorganizing his thoughts. "You see, Grandpa," he said in Lakota, "the white man doesn't understand our clan. Sadly, we're forgetting it, too. But in our culture, there's the family, the extended family, the clan, and the tribe. And that's all we need. Our family provides basic support; and you and Annie, my adopted grandparents, are secondary support, like the wasicus' godparents."

Horace's expression conveyed his confusion over the word 'godparent'.

George tried to think of the Lakota work for godparent. There was none. "Remember in the old days when a brave got killed?"

Horace looked at him passively.

"Well, if the father was killed fighting the Crow, his child had another father. A member of the clan would step in and serve as the father to the fallen warrior's child. And since they lived and worked together, and the kids knew all the clan members as family, the loss was kind of filled. Well, the white man uses a godparent. But it's not the same." George was losing his train of thought. Impatiently he continued. "Our adopted parents and grandparents and the clan system are like the wasicu's godparents. Only we take our roles more personally, more seriously."

Horace nodded.

"The wasicu doesn't rely on family like we do. They rely on government, on welfare, on courts, on judges. And the entire system relies on paper, the written word. Saying things, speaking the truth means nothing unless it's written. And we don't know how to write things. But that welfare worker does. And we don't understand his system, his way of doing things. So, we got to be very careful. Do you understand, Grandfather?"

Horace was tormented by what George was saying.

"We got to talk to Dee about this. Let her know what she's up against. And tell her not to see him. Do you agree?"

Horace nodded slowly. "We got to find out more about this wasicu. But we can't believe he's bad," Horace's eyes twinkled, "'til we know he's bad."

George felt uneasy. Maybe he was assuming too much. He was making judgments without the benefit of facts, just his bias and fear. He had once considered the possibility that he was just looking for trouble, that the American Indian children of Harney County weren't in harm's way. He quickly rejected that possibility, ashamed that he would even think about trusting a wasicu.

Something had to done – right now. "Dee, come out here," George commanded.

Dee opened the door moments later and joined her adopted grandparents and their adopted sons. Diffidently she stood behind Horace, her hands grasping the back of his chair.

"Grandpa says you haven't seen the wasicu."

Dee nodded.

"Pat and I think it best you don't."

Dee again nodded. She hadn't given any thought to Vinton's suggestion, had no interest in going to the courthouse. It was alien turf to her. In fact, there was a mental barrier between northwest Union and the rest of the community. She couldn't remember the last time she had left her part of town.

George maintained his steady glare, wanting more than a nod. "Dee, this is important. We don't know anything about this wasicu. But to us, to our people, he is powerful. He has the power to take our children from us, to send them to boarding schools and foster homes hundreds of miles away. Your kids, Pat's kid, my kids, as many of our kids as he wants. We got to stay in the background, far away from his eyes. We don't want him to think about us, let alone see us. Do you understand, Dee? This is important. This is damned important. We've just got to stay away from him and his kind."

Dee nodded and smiled.

Exasperated, he remained calm. He looked firmly at her. "Dee, say after me. I will not see the wasicu. He's not our friend. He's our enemy."

Dee repeated the pledge.

"Good," George said, knowing now she would not see the wasicu.

Satisfied that she had said and done what George wanted, Dee retreated into the house to tend to her children. The three youngest had already fallen asleep on mattresses laid on the floor. Flies buzzed and hovered above them, frequently lighting on their exposed skin. The children, accustomed to this irritation, slept soundly. Dee took a fly swatter and drove away the files. But as she walked away, the flies returned to the faces of the children.

CHAPTER NINE

The bill placing a statutory limit on county taxation had sailed through the legislature and was awaiting Governor Charles Norman's signature. After conferring with his aides, Norman knew he had no choice. The taxpayer revolt had begun. Years later, Proposition 13 in California would attract the national media. But it was here, in this state, that the revolt first occurred. At the request of the County Officials Association, Senator Patrick Sloane had attached an amendment which read "…the effective date shall be concurrent with the State's forthcoming fiscal year." This allowed county governments a little over a year to adjust their services and expenditures.

In the governor's office, Sloane and Norman were discussing the bill's impact.

"There are many problems presented by LB192, not the least of which is the assessment angle," Sloane cautioned.

"What do you mean?" Norman asked.

Sloane was surprised by the question. The guy must be slipping, he thought. He didn't wish to appear patronizing, but he had to make sure the governor was fully aware of the repercussions of the bill.

"Norm, let's take it from the top, even going over some of the obvious things to ensure we don't miss anything. LB192 limits the mill levy counties can assess. That limit is already exceeded by fourteen counties. So, at the very least, those counties will have to decrease expenditures and services. Eleven counties are so close to the limit that they're virtually there, too. Now the simple thing to do is to reassess property values at a higher rate. Well, goddammit, the state constitution says we can do that only at the turn of the decade. So the counties have over seven years before they can up the evaluations. That's the catch twenty-two. The legislators were really pressured, real heavy threatening sort of stuff. So, obviously, they passed it and passed the buck to you. The escape clause - the only one - is here in line six hundred nine. The voters can increase the mill levy's limit by a simple majority after the initiative is approved by the county board. Well, you and I know that ain't gonna happen. In other words, we're stuck with this damned bill."

Norman pondered Sloane's words. "It's a dumb bill and, unfortunately, a done thing. Damn few legislators had the guts to vote against it. Well, it's the wish and wisdom of the people now. There's no way I can veto the bill. It'd be suicidal."

"You've no choice, knowing full well it's gonna play havoc with the counties. Christ, they at least could have put a hold-harmless clause in the bill."

"Sloane, you've been in contact with the county association's lobbyist. How bad will it hurt? What functions of county governments need to be eliminated?"

Sloane sat in one of the leather-covered chairs semi-circling Norman's massive desk. "There's obviously fat in county government like any level of government, so there'll be some trimming. The rural counties have less population and more roads, especially out west. And if those counties have lots of poor folks, they're in trouble. There's gonna be lobbying by the counties to get the state to pay more welfare costs. If that doesn't occur, some counties may become insolvent. Then we have a constitutional question. The counties are creatures of the state. Thereby, is the state ultimately responsible for them? The state is probably going to have a more active role in the next few years with such things as insolvencies, receiverships, that whole gamut. We better have the AG look into that."

"You think it's that bad?"

"Not now, but soon."

"Then perhaps I should veto LB192."

"You're not serious?"

Norman returned Sloane's gaze. There was no answer. Where does politics end and honor begin? Is the goal of a politician to win the next election or to govern capably? Norman spoke to Sloane's question. "What is it our favorite adversary would say in times like this?"

Sloane's expression was blank.

Norman paused for rhetorical effect, then he intoned: "My friends, I can assure you that in days of crisis, there are no truths which are clear and self-evident..."

Sloane, smiling, slowly shook his head. "Jake Hammond."

The governor also smiled and said, "Jake Hammond."

***

Chairman Scott was reviewing the agenda. "It appears the tough issues this go-round are, and I'll number them as I see their importance, first, this God-awful LB192. I'll never know what happens to a person after we elect him and he heads back east. We'll have the county attorney in on this. Remember, he briefed us several months ago. I'll allot forty-five minutes. Secondly, and we better have Maenner in on this, too, is our damned jail. I got a letter from the state fire marshal. He visited us a while back and says we're not in compliance with fire codes. I have a list of the violations he cited. And he's gonna ask the state health commissioner to check us over too. Not enough exercise room for the prisoners and something about air circulation. We'll give that thirty minutes. Then we have to approve the transfer of some general fund monies to welfare's line item." Scott paused, looking at Oldfield.

"Any comment, Commissioner Oldfield?"

"Nope. Maybe later."

"Okay, I'll allot five minutes. Fourth is the mental health line item. We got lots of patients in the state hospitals. At four hundred a month apiece, it's costing big bucks. The police tell me public drunkenness is on the rise. One can assume alcoholism is also increasing. Since the County Health Board keeps committing this type of patient to state hospitals, and because most are penniless, the county is stuck with the bill."

"Scotty," Commissioner Ryan interrupted, "I can't believe alcoholism is the problem here. As I understand it, after they're committed, the sheriff hauls them to whatever hospital has an open bed. The hospital just dries them out for thirty days and releases them. Care for this type of patient shouldn't cost a million-plus a year. The problem just can't be that great. Who do we have to look into this?"

"It's in the clerk of the district court's budget, but she just pays the bills," Scott said. "I don't know. Let's think about it. Fifth is the approval of county warrants. We can look at the bills during the meeting. As usual, we'll give each department head about thirty minutes. That's how I see it, gentlemen. Any questions?"

"What's the total on human services?" Oldfield asked.

"You mean welfare costs?"

"Yeah, that and mental health."

"We know the patient costs: over a million dollars. The welfare costs are hard to project. They're rising each month. I can get an estimate from Vinton, but he's obviously overspending his budget. It appears he'll triple the projection Agnes gave us."

"Her projection was sixty thousand dollars county money?"

"Yeah, and change," Scott replied.

"Scotty, we can't spend well over a million for these items, especially with this new law."

"I know," Scott looked to Oldfield. "Christ, I know what's happening to the welfare costs, but that's because Moore wasn't doing her job."

"What's the answer?"

"Christ, I don't know. We can't raise taxes. We're already over the limit."

"Where can we cut?" Ryan asked.

"We'll ask for revised budgets from each office," Scott said, trying not to think what Vinton's revision would be.

"Let's send the goddamn Indians back to the reservation," Oldfield offered.

"How's the new judge doing?" Scott asked, ignoring Oldfield.

"Staroski's doing a good job," Commissioner Reisner said.

"For a Polack," Oldfield added.

"I hear he's left-handed, too," Ryan said.

All but Scott laughed. He rapped his pipe against his coffee cup. "Give me a break, you guys. Let's convene at one o'clock."

"Hear, hear," Ryan contributed.

Seeing they had forty minutes, Scott went to see the clerk of the district court, Reisner to see Maenner, three to the hotel for coffee. Oldfield and Ryan walked across the street to the Elks Club.

Oldfield got out his member's key to open the club's door. Entering the bar, he saw a few lawyers and businessmen, some drinking coffee, others clear liquor.

"Vodka tonic," Oldfield ordered.

"Gin on the rocks," Ryan said.

66

Taking their drinks, they walked to a booth. "You look troubled," Ryan noted. "Jack and Lisa still having problems?"

"Lisa's going to file," Oldfield said. He took off his glasses to wipe away a tear. "Damned kids, I love them both. I don't even know who's right or what's wrong. I worry about my grandkids."

"How's the ranch?"

"Okay, but I can't get any help since Vinton came to town. Not for what I can pay when they can go on welfare and get just as much."

"It's that bad?"

"Well, I can still hire those goddamned Indians. But they're just no good. Hired two of them to do some fence work. Three hours later, I went looking for them. I had to kick them in the ass to wake them up. All in all, though, I guess things aren't so bad. They just seem that way."

"What are we gonna do about Vinton?"

"I don't know. Vinton's probably a good guy," Oldfield conceded. "It's just that he doesn't belong in Harney County. He oughta be back east, where everybody's on welfare. 'Course, give him a few years and he'll have half of this county on assistance. He wants to bring the food stamp program in."

"He does?"

"Yep."

"We going to let him?"

"Probably."

"Christ," Ryan said, finishing his drink, signaling for another.

***

Commissioner Scott, noting all the commissioners were present, called the meeting to order. He asked the county clerk if notice had been published pursuant to the Sunshine Act. The clerk nodded. Scott declared the meeting open. "First item of business, LB192. Will the clerk ask Mr. Maenner to join us?"

The county attorney, seated outside the conference room, entered and sat facing the chairman.

"Good morning, Phil. Good to see you," Scott said. "Now tell us, how big is the problem?"

"If you mean either Vinton or LB192, the problem is big, really big," Maenner replied.

Scott rapped his pipe against the table to inhibit laughter. "I'm speaking specifically of LB192."

"LB192 is a blockbuster, as you know. It overwhelmingly passed both houses and is on the governor's desk. I don't have a pipeline into that office, but he'll sign it. He's up for reelection, so it's a *fait accompli*."

"A what?" Ryan asked.

"A done thing," Maenner said. "It sets the statutory maximum of fifteen mills on county government. We're currently well above that. We're talking tens of thousands in reductions. A state senator, forget his name, tacked an amendment onto the bill. If the governor delays his signature for the thirty days he's allowed, we won't have to adhere to it until next fiscal year. So you gentlemen have a whole year to hack away at fat."

"Perhaps if I sent the governor a nude picture of me, he'd see I'm just skin and bones," Commissioner Abbott offered.

"We can't blame the governor. He knows it's a lousy bill. It was his people in the senate who tacked on the amendment."

"How do we proceed?" Scott asked.

"We need major cuts. Look to the big-ticket items. Cut there."

"Then we're talking roads, welfare, and mental health," Scott stated. "Of course, welfare wasn't that big last year. It will be this year."

"The farmers and ranchers need roads, and need them in good repair," Oldfield stated. "I won't allow cuts there."

"Too early to talk absolutes," Scott replied. "Let's not lock ourselves into anything. Could the county officials' lobby get a constitutional change? I'm talking about the assessments."

"Just not practical. The procedure to amend was designed to make it difficult. And it'd just be an obvious circumvention of the intent of LB192," Maenner said. "To complicate things, I understand we need to build a new jail."

"One thing at a time, Phil."

"Okay, Scotty."

"So you think we got a year after the governor signs it?"

"Right."

"I'll entertain a motion to charge the chair with convening a special meeting for department heads regarding LB192," Scott suggested.

"So moved."

"Second."

"Call the question."

"How many ayes are out there?" Scott asked.

The clerk counted six.

"Motion passed. We're not resolving anything," Scott said to Commissioner Abbott, "but we're sure as hell moving the agenda."

Vinton was seated outside the conference room. He had overheard Maenner discuss LB192 and the sheriff discuss the fire marshal's report. Vinton had eighteen new cases for the board's approval. He had denied two, and one was being closed: a net gain of seventeen. He wanted to discuss the food stamp program, but after hearing the board's problems, he ruled that out.

The county clerk approached Vinton. "Commissioner Scott wants to have lunch with you and have you to sit in on the mental health discussion. Go on back to your office and relax. Scotty will join you there."

Vinton was reviewing the new cases when Scott walked in. Jeff felt uneasy because of the increasing costs of his office. But dammit, he had a job to do. He was doing it and doing it well. He had no reason to apologize. "Howdy," he said, as upbeat as possible.

Scott nodded. "It's been a tough morning. Okay if we skip lunch?" Acknowledging Vinton's agreement, he continued. "I assume you heard our discussions while you were waiting outside the conference room."

"Yes, sir."

"Then you know you and I have got some problems."

"Yeah."

"Jeff, I've no difficulty with what you're doing. In fact, I couldn't wait to get rid of Moore. We must have interviewed a dozen people for the job. We made offers to half of them. They didn't accept. The pay was too low, I'm sure of that. The problems too many, I'm sure of that. And you've done your job quietly and well. But now we need to cut other departments' budgets while increasing yours, not because we want to but because we've no choice. Jeff, you've opened the floodgates. The poor have become aware of their rights. There's no way to go back to the old days, regardless of what you or I want. But those forces at play make our problem worse."

Scott paused. "You heard about the mental health costs to the county? The million bucks?"

"Part of it, toward the end," Vinton acknowledged.

"Enough to know what I'm talking about?"

Vinton nodded.

"It seems to me your office could help."

"How?"

"I don't know. It's your job to find out. I'm not even sure who the hell the patients are. I just know they're costing this county a lot of money. I want you to see if you can help through whatever resources your office has."

"I really don't know what we can do about it," Vinton said.

***

It was three thirty before Commissioner Oldfield left the courthouse. He and his wife had gotten little sleep the night before. Their son, Jack, had stopped by to tell them of Lisa's intent to end the marriage. Jack had then left, declining his parents' offer to spend the night.

Tired, disheartened, Oldfield got in his pickup. Driving north from Union, he noted how the gray November sky reflected his mood. The trees stood barren, the land covered with dormant brown prairie grass. Only the occasional yucca plants kept their green. To the west, the high mesas with their stands of ponderosa pine also provided a departure from the gloomy gray and brown of the day.

Oldfield thought of the county's predicament. Scott, damn him, would step down from the chair next June. And he was to succeed Scott. And when the crunch came, he'd have to explain why things went to hell. And the ranchers would ignore his explanations when the roads fell into disrepair. It ain't my fault, but sure as hell, I'll get the blame. Just ain't fair.

His ranch was forty miles north of Union, and Oldfield was in no hurry to get home. There's nothing I can do for Jack, he reasoned. Once this thing is over, I'll help get him out of debt. But anything I do now won't do any good. Oldfield left the highway and drove along the county road to his ranch. Driving through the gate, he looked up to see his brand swaying in the northerly breeze. He remembered how, years ago, he and Jack, just a lad then, had made the brand from a tough old ponderosa.

The passage of time and what it brings, he lamented.

His home was a mile from the gate. Oldfield drove his pickup over the macadamized road, seeing Jack's car parked in the driveway of his house that stood on a rise of land. He walked to the door in no hurry to see his wife and son. For a moment, he wanted to turn back, to drive around the ranch for a while. Realizing that to be silly, he entered his home.

In the living room, the fireplace was alive with dancing flames. Sitting in front of the flames and bathed in their light were Jack and a young woman Oldfield didn't know.

"Hi, Dad," Jack said, rising to greet his father. "Dad, I want you to meet your new daughter-in-law. Well, as soon as the divorce is final. Barbara, this is my dad."

Oldfield was stunned. His thoughts had been with Jack all day; how he might somehow comfort his son, ease the pain.

Barbara rose to acknowledge Oldfield.

Oldfield was speechless. He walked to the kitchen, saying nothing, not even looking at Barbara.

His wife was at the kitchen table, a coffee cup in her hands. He saw she had been crying. He touched her, his massive hands slowly kneading her shoulders. "I'm sorry, Kay." He stood by his wife, deep in thought, for a few minutes before going to the phone. The call was answered after the first ring.

"Jack, is that you?"

"No, Lisa, this is your dad. How are you and the kids?"

"I'm sorry Dad, I thought - I hoped it might be Jack. We're okay, I guess."

"Lisa, I had no idea."

"What do you mean?"

"About Jack and his, his girlfriend."

"You know," Lisa said.

"Yes."

"I tried to keep it from you in spite of the hurt. I knew it would hurt you more."

"Do you have a..." Oldfield could not finish the sentence.

"A boyfriend?"

"Yeah, that's what I mean."

"No, Dad, only Jack."

Oldfield didn't hesitate. "Lisa, you are my grandchildren's mother, therefore my daughter. I want you to come to the ranch as often as you can. And I want you to bring the kids. You understand? Kay and I love you very much. We don't want to lose you. As far as Jack is concerned, you'll get over him, as will we."

"The kids and I love you."

Oldfield hung up the phone. He turned and looked to Kay. Keeping eye contact, he sat at the table and took her hand into his. He maintained the intense visual contact, his forehead furrowing, his eyes searching. For minutes, no words passed between them. Kay kept concentrating on his last words to Lisa. "...as will we...as will we..." Finally, Kay painfully nodded her head. She sobbed again, this time more violently.

Oldfield walked into the living room. Jack and Barbara were sitting on the davenport. Jack stood. "Dammit, Dad, I bring my wife-to-be over to introduce her to my family, and you don't say a damn thing, not even a simple 'Hi'."

"You done, Jack?" His voice betrayed his anger. He looked at his son then turned away in disgust. He sat, looking at the flames in the fireplace. Staring for several minutes, he considered what he was to do. With absolute despondency, he thought: Damn me! Goddamn me! Why can't I take in the entire spectrum? Why only the extremes? Seeing only black and white limits one's perspective; limits one's options; forces one to do damnable things, irrevocable things.

But he was, he realized, an absolutist. He could not change. He knew he could not stop what he was about to do. He looked at Jack, then to Barbara. A handsome woman, he thought. "Jack, I just spoke to your wife. I told her that your mother and I are sorry. I told her we love her and that she and our grandchildren would always be welcome in our house." He stopped, again considering his next words. Slowly, deliberately, he spoke to his only son. "Unfortunately, my message to you is quite different. I want you and my daughter-in-law-to-be to leave my house."

Jack began to protest but was cut off by Oldfield's firm voice.

"And Jack, my son, I don't want to see you again. Good-bye." He walked to the kitchen to rejoin his wife. Tears flowed down his face.

***

The following Monday, Vinton called Evelyn Pearce to his office. She appeared tired, older than when Vinton had met her.

"How you bearing up?"

She looked at him. "It seems like ages, an eternity ago, but I used to dread coming to work. It was so boring, just sitting, trying to look busy. I still dread coming to work, but for a different reason. At least now I'm getting satisfaction out of it, my job, I mean. You've changed this office, Jeff. A lot of people think for the better."

"A lot of people think for the worse," Jeff added.

They both laughed.

"You want to take some vacation, Evelyn? You've got a lot accrued. Just to rest up?"

"Maybe next month, around Christmas."

"Sure."

Silence replaced the conversation.

Tired, her legs outstretched, she stared at the floor.

"Evelyn, you know the county board's got some problems, money-wise I mean."

"You mean the new law? Yeah, the whole courthouse is talking about it. Folks are worried about their jobs."

"I suppose they resent us, the way we're increasing the cost of county government."

"That has come up, more than once," she said with a tired but supportive smile.

"I've felt some coldness, too. Last week more than before," Jeff agreed. "We've got to help the county out."

"How? We don't take money in. We just hand it out."

"Maybe by handing more out, we can keep more in," Jeff ventured.

73

Dumbfounded, she stared at Jeff. He mischievously returned her stare.

"What in God's name are you talking about?"

"I haven't the slightest."

"That's obvious," she warmly responded.

"What do you know about the county's mental health bill?"

"That's not our program."

"I know."

"I don't know anything about it."

"Who does?"

"I suppose the mental health board."

"Who are they?"

"Milner represents this office on it."

"He does?"

"I guess we didn't have time to tell you."

"Ask him to come in."

"I'll see if he's free." Minutes later, she and Milner walked into Jeff's office.

"Good morning, Jerry. I hear you're our expert on mental health."

"You say that only because I'm approaching a total breakdown."

"That, and because you sit on the county's board."

"Oh, that."

"Tell me about it."

"Well, the last three we sent to state hospitals were all suffering from severe alcoholism. Really in bad shape. Didn't know what day or month it was. One didn't even know who the president is. 'Course, I try to forget that too."

Jeff smiled. "Who sits with you?"

"The clerk of the district court, a physician, usually Dr. Hall, the county judge, and me."

"Who appointed you?"

"Moore. Two years ago. I represent this office."

"Have you committed anyone whose problem wasn't alcoholism?"

"A while ago."

"What was the story?"

"Kind of sad. He was retarded, about seventeen. Anyway, his mom had a stroke a year earlier. She had cared for him up until that time. His dad passed on years ago. The point is, she obviously couldn't care for him anymore, he couldn't care for himself, so we committed him for custodial care."

"Where is he now?"

"Still there, I guess."

"But he's not mentally ill?" Vinton asked.

"No. Technically he's retarded."

"Technically hell! He's simply not crazy."

"You're technically correct, Mr. Director."

"So where's that put us?"

"What do you mean?" Milner asked.

Vinton relayed the county's predicament.

"I see possibilities," Milner said. "Let me explain. A couple of times a year we get letters from the hospitals. The letters say some patients have received - they use a term, let me think - 'maximum therapeutic benefit' from the treatment there - that they're ready to go home. Then a long list of names."

"That's right!" Evelyn joined in. "Mrs. Moore told me to toss those letters. How did you see them?"

Milner ignored her. "I suppose the difficulty is that they're so used to the hospital regimen, they wouldn't fit into a normal lifestyle. They've had all their decisions made for them. They're probably completely institutionalized. Hmm." His facial expression changed. "I don't think I see possibilities anymore."

Vinton thought for a moment. "Let's get a handle on this." He turned to Evelyn. "Who gets the bills from the hospitals?"

"The clerk of the district court."

"Do me a favor, Evelyn. Go to the clerk's office. Get copies of last month's bills from the hospitals, then get the bills from five years ago. Use whoever you need to check the patients' names with our files. Some were probably once on welfare. Remember, we're not interested in the sixty-day patients. Look for those who've been there a while. Okay?"

"Right."

"Get this as soon as possible."

Evelyn and Jerry began to get up. "Milner, stay for a moment."

He nodded.

"If he has any appointments, shoot them to someone else," Vinton instructed Evelyn.

"Sure," she said, closing the door behind her.

Milner was perplexed. "What's going on?"

"I'm not sure. The county is paying over a million bucks a year, but nobody knows which office has oversight. It goes without saying that the clerk of the court behaves like a clerk. She gets the bill, she pays the bill. It's probably not her purview anyway. The county board has the ultimate responsibility, but it doesn't know what's going on. I'll bet this thing just grew like Topsy with all the bureaucrats dutifully processing the paperwork, not looking for any resolution, not even realizing there's a problem."

"Where are you leading me?" Milner asked.

"I don't know, but hear me out."

"Sure." Milner sat for several minutes as Jeff paced.

"Let's take the case you mentioned, the retarded kid."

"Okay."

"The county committed him. Someone, some office I assume, investigated his family's ability to pay. Hell, I'll bet that's our responsibility. Anyway, it figured the family couldn't pay the bill. Come to think of it, I'll bet we don't even check on the families anymore. Anyway, the hospital bills the county 'cause the county committed the patient. It follows. It makes perfect sense."

"And the dumb-ass county just pays the bill. Right?"

"I'll bet it's that simple," Vinton said.

"Okay. What's your answer? See if the family can pay the bill?"

"Of course. But is that all you can come up with?" Jeff asked.

"What do you have in mind?"

Jeff was interrupted by the telephone. Milner sipped at his coffee, watching him. After a couple of minutes Vinton hung up and broke out in a smile. "That was Evelyn. She's already found some patients who've been in the hospitals for years, folks listed on a statement ten years ago and on last month's bill. I think that's good news."

Milner, not understanding the significance, waited to hear Jeff out.

"Now, where were we? Oh yeah, the retarded kid. Now let me run this by you. The kid's reached majority. The county is paying for a 'totally and permanently' disabled person. You with me?"

"Yeah."

"Jerry, if a disabled adult walked into our office and asked for help, what would you do?"

"Take an application for AD."

"Aid to the disabled. How much does the county pay of that?"

"Twenty percent of the medical costs."

"And right now the county's paying a hundred percent of everything. Right? I heard it averages four hundred a month for each client." Jeff turned away from Jerry and stared out the window, seeing nothing. He turned again to Milner. "You know, it's time the federal and state governments help Harney County with about eight hundred thou."

It took a while for Milner to do the math, but then he shouted, "God, it's simple, but it might work."

"What do we need for an AD application?"

"The critical document is a medical statement attesting to the disability."

"If a hospital kept someone for ten years, would they dare say he wasn't disabled? I don't think the statement will be a problem. It's just gonna cost a postage stamp. The attending physician will sign it."

"But where will these people go? Most don't have a family or home. According to federal regs, they're ineligible for assistance if they're in a state facility."

"Is that right?" Vinton asked soberly.

"Yeah, that's right."

"Where can we put them? I guess that's your question, isn't it?"

"Yeah," Milner said, "and I know where. In a goddamn nursing home."

"Will they take them?"

"That's how these outfits make their bucks. That's what they do. We may have to shop around a bit, but we'll sure as hell find one or two damned glad to take them."

"Hell yes! We'll pay top dollar to the nursing home and still save the county bucks because nursing care is a Medicaid expense. We'll pay the nursing home six hundred a month. The county pays twenty percent or a hundred twenty dollars, a net loss to all levels of government of two hundred: a net savings to Harney County of two eighty a month. And they're the ones paying our wages, Jerry."

"Let's do it!" Milner said excitedly, then upon reflection, added, "It's strange. We're saving tax dollars by spending more."

"Strange? It's wonderfully bizarre. It's something only a bureaucrat could appreciate. And from your, mine and the county's perspective, there is a perfect symmetry, a perfect logic to its beauty."

CHAPTER TEN

The sedan pulled up before the Plainsmen Hotel. Bill Sergent, Herb Chandler, and Bob Elam were out of the vehicle and walking toward the lobby before the doorman could get to the car. Chandler, speaking softly, shared last-minute bits of advice, underscoring the critical attributes he wanted Elam to project. "Be a little coy, a little overwhelmed. But while you're doing so, ensure they leave this little get-together knowing you're one tough sonofabitch. And, for God's sake, forget the bleeding-heart stuff. These guys would prefer a bit of ruthlessness. Now we've gone through this. You're good. You're ready. These guys need you. This state needs you. Stay loose!"

Chandler and Sergent led him through the large lobby, up a series of stairs, and into a large banquet room. It happened so quickly. One moment Elam was ensconced in the security of the large sedan. Minutes later he was the focal point of a room filled with strangers whose idle chatter faded to silence moments after Elam's party entered the large room. For a moment, Elam wondered how they had recognized him. He had met or seen only a few of them. Then he realized it was Chandler they recognized.

Everyone was standing, ignoring the chairs that had been placed along the walls. Most were men in their fifties, wearing pinstripe suits, white shirts, and subdued ties. The individuals, and therefore the entire group, emitted an aura of confidence, of people who have to answer to no one, who have power and know how to use it. They were, or represented, the elite of the capital city, and by extension, the state.

Elam was uneasy. He glanced at Chandler and Sergent. Sergent was uncomfortable, too, but Chandler was in his element, more here than on a golf course, as he led them to a small podium purposely set on the floor in front of the raised dais. Chandler wanted Elam standing among the people, not above them, during this get-acquainted meeting.

"Ladies, gentlemen," Chandler easily addressed the hushed gathering after picking up the microphone. "I've got a fella here I want you to meet. He's a man we're all going to want to know better as time goes on, and he's a man who knows and remembers his friends. Some of us have known Bob Elam for a lifetime. For others, this is the first meeting. But regardless, he's a man whose presence we all need. God, we all know that, don't we?"

A few people, then more, applauded in response to Chandler's question.

"Bob, these folks want to meet you."

It was Elam's turn. He took the microphone from Chandler. "I'm Bob Elam. I appreciate this chance to meet you," he said, remembering Chandler's instructions about holding the microphone so it would pick up his voice without screeching or whining. "It's always good to be with good people."

Elam changed his inflection as he had while rehearsing these comments. "But unfortunately, these are not good times. And I know it's not Bob Elam who brought you here. It's that other guy who brought you and me here. It's that guy over there." Bob pointed in the direction of the governor's mansion. "The fact is, Governor Charles Norman brought us together."

Bob's voice deepened, emphasizing his level of seriousness. "And we're here because we're troubled, because we have serious problems. And in difficult times it's citizens like you who come forth to offer leadership to set us back on a proper course. Whether we admit it or not, it is this group and groups like us to whom the state looks when difficulties arise." Then he vowed, "And we will not disappoint those who turn to us."

Chandler, who had moved to a corner of the large room, observed Elam closely. He had a pleased look on his face.

"Now there's nothing that you alone can do about the direction of our state government, it's unresponsiveness to the business community of our state. And I admit there's nothing that I alone can do about the attitudes in the governor's suite." Elam paused for effect, then continued robustly. "But you," he pointed to a man in a dark suit whose bald head nearly shone, "and I together, we can begin to make a difference." Bob walked toward the man, maintaining eye contact. "And if you and I and the other good people in this room unite toward a common and needed goal, then surely we can make a difference!"

Bob turned smartly, walked back to the podium, and turned to again face the crowd. Then, in a lowered voice, he said, "And that's why we're here. Not for ourselves, and certainly not for Bob Elam, but for our state, our communities, our families, and for all those who depend on us to provide jobs and products and services."

He paused again to let that thought sink in.

"That's why we're here today. That's why I'm here, and that's why you're here. It's because Charles Norman is over there. And as much as we may like Charles Norman as a man, we know we don't like him as our governor. At this time, at this period, we're gonna have to forget party labels and look to the type of person we want, the policies we all want, and the need we feel to get this state moving again.

"My good friends, I want you to know something. If you will help me, I'm willing to carry our thoughts into every city and town of this state. I will do these things, but only as long as I have your support.

"If you believe as I do that we must change this administration, that we must change the person of the governor, then we are beginning to find common ground. And if you believe as I do that there are more effective and efficient ways our government can operate, then our mutual interests will attract others to where before only we stood. And if we are willing to invest ourselves, our time, and our energies, talents, and resources, then by God, we can effect necessary change.

"Gentlemen, ladies, if you will join me, individually and collectively, we can return integrity to government."

A few applauded.

"And if you will join me, individually and collectively, we can bring back a business approach to government."

More applause.

"And if you will join me, we'll bring efficiency back to government!"

Greater applause.

"And if you will join me, we will take government back, away from the bureaucrats, and return its control to its rightful place, with the people."

A cascading ovation lasted for nearly a minute. After it subsided, Bob flashed a toothy grin. "I got an idea. Let's you and me get together on this thing!"

Gentle laughter, then loud applause filled the room. The patrician and normally reserved executives and bankers and chairmen of the boards were crowding, bumping into each other to shake Bob's hand.

Chandler and Sergent situated themselves at the door leading to the foyer. Both were surprised that few people were leaving. They looked at each other in amazement, then turned again to watch this gathering press in on Elam, each person hoping to speak with him, to congratulate him and pledge their support. A few small groups reconstituted themselves, speaking quietly, but, Chandler noted, in a way they could continue watching Bob.

Then, as people began trickling away from the crowd, Chandler addressed each one by name, asking about their families, their businesses, gently chastising one for his golf game last autumn. Sergent noted that his boss spent considerable time with one man, asking about his daughter Amy. As they left, many of them handed Chandler small envelopes. Noting the enthusiasm of the group, Chandler expected a sixty percent return. That would translate into $35,000. The suggested amount was five hundred apiece.

They left the hotel an hour later. No one spoke as they waited for the sedan. "Here he comes," Sergent said, pointing to the Cadillac.

"Good," Elam responded. "I'm exhausted." He hadn't realized that his shirt was wet with nervous perspiration until he'd stepped outside.

It was shortly after seven. "Take us to the office, then take the night off," Chandler told the driver. Then to Sergent and Elam, "We could all use a drink."

Bob was pleased with how the group had responded to him, with how well he had done. He had maintained his composure, had acquitted himself damned well. But neither Chandler nor Sergent said a word, either in praise or criticism. He tried remembering what had transpired, wondering if they had detected something he hadn't. Surprisingly, he didn't feel sufficiently at ease to broach the subject. He sat back waiting for Herb to say something. Instead, Chandler stared out the window. A light snow was falling. But soon it would be spring. Summer would bring the primary; late autumn, the general election.

The car pulled into the enclosed parking lot, stopping at the elevator that would take them to Herb's suite. Soon they were sitting in his large office, each in an overstuffed chair, each sipping a highball.

Finally Herb spoke. "You done good, Robert. You pulled it off real well. But I still sensed a bit of nervousness when you began. Generally, though, I thought it went damned well. What did you pick up, Sergent?"

"I was watching their faces while Bob was talking. A few grimaced when Bob said that whether or not they like Norman they should support us. Obviously, some of these guys know Norman and felt guilty being where they were. We may have reinforced that guilt, to Bob's detriment."

"Good point." Herb was writing on a legal-size tablet. "What else?"

"I think our general approach is good so far. We keep attacking Norman and of course keep standing foursquare for things like integrity, efficiency, and the American way. Before long we'll have to deal with specifics, but generalities should continue serving us well for a bit longer," Sergent elaborated.

"Yeah," Chandler said. "Norman is our biggest advantage. He's a helluva nice guy, but no one likes him as governor. I don't know why. Maybe it's that inexplicable thing called charisma."

"His vetoing LB192 effectively killed any chance he had," Sergent speculated.

"What did you say?" Chandler nearly shouted.

"Norman vetoed LB192," Sergent said. "Didn't you hear?"

"Christ, no! Hot damn!" Chandler broke into a big grin.

Elam, who had been thinking to himself, turned to them, his curiosity aroused by their raised voices. "Forgive me. I wasn't listening. What happened?"

Sergent quickly responded. "LB192, Bob. Norman vetoed it."

Chandler, ebullient a moment ago, was now subdued. "So Norman vetoed One Ninety-Two. That's the bill that limits county mill levies, Bob." Then he reflected, "That single act will be recorded by statehouse pundits as the *coup de grace* for Norman. The poor bastard sealed his own political fate. He's dead in the water. Congratulations, Bob. Unless you or Norman get some opposition in the primary, you're the next governor."

Bob noted Herb's somber mood. "You like him, don't you?"

"Like him? Hell, no. I barely know him. But goddammit, I respect that quixotic sonofabitch. Come hell or high water, he did the right thing. That bill was as lousy as any piece of legislation I've ever seen. It would have wiped out county government. And the damned legislators knew it. But being the self-serving, politically expedient, worthless bastards they are, they passed the damned thing on to the governor, letting him take the heat. Those pusillanimous sonsabitches."

"Hold up a minute, Herb," Sergent said. "The legislature will have another chance to prove its manhood."

"What do you mean?" Elam asked, intent on being part of the discussion.

"The override attempt," Sergent continued. "The bill passed with a veto-proof majority. The question is will the ranks hold? And a more immediate problem is what's Bob's stand on this? Damn, we're lucky the press didn't catch us at the hotel. What the hell's our candidate's position vis-à-vis LB192?"

Chandler thought for a moment. "Well, because of Norman's display of courage, we can't lose. If we come out for the veto's override, we probably will come out ahead. Or, if we support the governor, we can't lose any ground unless a new candidate comes out of the wings."

"The trick is to be on the winning side," Elam interjected. "And if there is a point of morality to the issue, then by God we should use our strength, as candidate and titular head of the minority party, to posture ourselves and the party on the side of the goddamn angels."

"Right on!" Sergent chuckled.

"Hear, hear!" piped in Chandler, laughing.

"Okay, we got work to do," Sergent said. "Let's get started. Bob's right. We got to be on the side of the goddamn angels. Now, assuming that *Gott ist mit uns,* how the hell do we prove it to the people of the goddamn state?"

It was a watershed moment: the time for a critical policy decision. Elam and Sergent sat back, deferring to Herb.

Chandler sat thinking. Elam filled his pipe bowl and soon was puffing vigorously, filling the room with smoke. Sergent rose and started pacing.

"Okay, these are the elements," Chandler began. "Legislators are normally closer to the pulse of the people than governors. We'll assume they reflected the wishes of their constituents by passing One Ninety-Two. Okay? The bill is more opportunistic than substantive. It won't work, and anyone who knows anything about government knows it won't. Next, we gotta find out how and why such an outlandish bill got through the legislature in the first place. Who and what are the forces behind the bill? Bob, you can get with Hammond on that. Then, gentlemen, we must arrive at a moment of truth. We have three options. First, we support the bill, letting local governments squirm. Second, we support the governor, clearly identifying Norman as a courageous individual who will do the right thing despite its unpopularity. Third, we can do our damnedest to just sit on the fence, coming up with statements that sound mighty sage but say nothing. Tough choices. I personally think the last one stinks."

"We should decide before we leave here tonight," Sergent said. "The press may be trying to get hold of Bob at his home. Let's work it out now."

"Christ. You're right," Chandler said, exasperated. "Well, we can say he's studying the issue and that he'll soon issue a statement. Buy us some time."

"I think we're overreacting. But I think I should support the governor," Elam said.

Chandler, surprised by his assertiveness, looked sharply at Elam, then turned away. "I don't know. This is really a profound issue. All kinds of things can flow from it. Something like this can turn a campaign around. From a strictly practical viewpoint, we should line up behind the bill, and thus the override. That's the practical, not the proper thing to do. And in this instance, the two poles are miles apart."

"Any chance public opinion might turn around on this thing?" Elam asked.

"I don't think so," Chandler said. "I hate to say it, but my advice is to draft a press release castigating the governor for being unresponsive to the wishes of the people. Unfortunately, I think that's the only way to go." He sadly shook his head and looked at Sergent. "Bill?"

"I guess so."

"Bob, you're gonna have to live with our recommendation. Do you agree?"

"I'm like you, Herb. I really admire the guy. From what I've heard, he did a gutsy thing. Right now, he's standing alone, and I'm inclined to stand with him. But I suppose I should wait until I talk with Hammond to learn if the ranks in the senate will hold. He can give us a good idea about the house, too. You realize if I support the passage of the bill, deride its veto, and the veto is sustained, I won't be looking all that astute."

"Good thinking, Bob. Sergent, we need an 'I'm looking the situation over' reply in case Bob's asked."

"I'll have it in a few minutes. Then let's go home. It's been a long day."

***

Pam was awake when Bob got home at a little past ten. "Long day, huh?" she said, "You look tired."

"Yeah." Bob sat. Pam went to fix him a highball.

He was leaning back in the chair, his eyes closed, when she returned. She set down the drink so it touched his hand. Feeling its coldness, he grasped the glass. His eyes remained closed.

She sat, saying nothing.

Bob sipped his drink, then looked to Pam. "From what I can tell, this guy Norman is one helluva guy. He's decent; his Governmental Reorganization Bill was farsighted, his veto of LB192 was courageous. He is, in essence, the kind of governor I want to be. I almost wish I wasn't running against him."

Pam listened silently.

"I guess if you take a cold, hard look at the guy, he does everything right, but succeeds at nothing. He's good, but ineffective. Does that make sense, Pam?"

"You, Bob, will be good, and you'll be effective. Don't look back, only forward."

***

The next morning, after his first cup of coffee, Bob went to the telephone. Jake Hammond answered after several rings. Bob identified himself.

"Yeah, I recognized your voice. I was just out checking my Herefords."

"Jake, remember that night I said I might need some savvy political

86

advice?"

"Sure, Bob."

"That's why I'm calling."

"What can I do to help?"

"Well, last time we spoke, I wanted to know about the reorganization bill. This time it's LB192."

"Yeah, Norman vetoed it yesterday."

"Will there be an override attempt? And if so, will it succeed?"

"I can count heads in the senate pretty well. We'll give the bill the two-thirds it needs, so the house doesn't matter."

"You know my status?"

"Sure, Bobby, damn near everyone in the capital knows. When you gonna formally announce?"

"Soon, I think."

"Good. You got my support, you know that."

"Thanks. I appreciate that. But tell me. What is an astute political position on One Ninety-Two?"

"Bob, the senate will override the veto. I'm sure of that. So the winning side is with the legislature."

"What adverse things will follow?"

"Tough question. A lot. I'll need to think about how much."

"When will you be back in town?"

"We're on a two-week recess. I'll be back in the capital a week from Sunday."

"Too long. How about my driving out to see you?"

"That'd be good. I'd like to see you. When?"

"I'll ask Pam. I'll get back to you."

"I'll be waiting, Bobby. Good-bye."

Bob replaced the receiver and went to wake up his wife.

Knowing it would be useless to talk before her first cup of coffee, he wished her good morning and returned to the kitchen. Moments later, he was sitting on their bed while she sipped the coffee.

"Would you like to drive out to Jake Hammond's place in Burke County?"

"What for?"

"I need to talk with him. And, since I've been on this gubernatorial thing, we haven't seen much of each other. It's about a three-hour drive.

We'll be there about an hour. We can stop for dinner on the way home."

"When do you want to leave?"

"About noon if I can confirm it."

"Sounds good."

"I'll call to see if it's okay. I don't know anything about Mrs. Hammond. You can work that out."

Through her sleepy eyes she was again mystified by this man sitting before her, the man she envisioned as the next governor.

"Now get up and fix us some breakfast." Bob grabbed her thigh through the covers and affectionately squeezed.

Bob called Hammond while eating the sausage and eggs Pam had prepared.

"Today?" Hammond asked, surprised.

"Well, if we can."

"Well sure you can. About what time?"

"We'll be there about three. Now, how do I find that spread of yours?"

Elam wrote down Hammond's detailed instructions, thanked the senator, and hung up.

He explained to Pam the purpose of the trip; the governor's unexpected veto, the need for a response, the perplexing question about where he should stand on the issue. Describing his options, he said, "The honorable position would be to support the veto. The opportunistic option would be to back the bill."

Pam was stunned. "If those are the options, what's the problem?"

Bob tried to explain the dilemma. Each explanation had expediency as its basis. Frustrated, he finally said, "Pam, I'm afraid that nothing is simple. There are no obvious answers. Nothing is clear and self-evident in government." He then remembered where he had heard those words – from Jake Hammond. For some reason, that bothered him.

The drive to Hammond's ranch was pleasant. The sun shone brilliantly, its brightness amplified by the freshly fallen snow. The highways had been cleared, allowing them to arrive earlier than expected.

Jake and his wife, alerted to the Elams' arrival by their German shepherds, came out to greet them.

Walking to the house, Jake suddenly stopped. "Bob, would you like to take a look at my prize Herefords?"

"Sure."

While Pam and Adele continued to the house, the men got into Jake's pickup. Jake drove to his west pasture where some fifty head were grazing. "I just wanted to chat with you away from the ladies." Then he looked at Bob. "That night at the Enterprize, why didn't you tell me you were running for governor?"

"Jake, I really didn't know then. Of course I had thought about it. It just seemed presumptuous at the time." He paused. "Now things are different. I'm trying to get organized, money lined up. Those sorts of things."

"Things don't seem so presumptuous now, huh?" Hammond gently chided Bob. "Chandler's running your campaign," he said matter-of-factly.

Bob nodded.

"He's good, the best in this state." Hammond paused, reflected, and slowly asked, "How do we stand?"

"We stand as members of the loyal opposition."

"And?"

"And I obviously need your help. Today, astute advice. Tomorrow, alongside me in your district."

"The reason I ask, Bob, well, I was a little tipsy that night. Gosh damn, I just can't drink like I used to. I want you to know I'm mad as hell about this state's service delivery system and its inefficiencies. When you get in, I'll want to get together with you and your aides to reorganize the government's structure. Okay?"

Bob quickly responded in the affirmative. But he wondered about Jake's sincerity. He had spoken so smugly that August evening about diffused power and the mechanically automated bureaucrats.

Hammond sensed Bob's skepticism. "You know, I haven't had an original thought in twenty years. So I get together with as many folks as I can and chat with them. I suppose psychologists would call me one derivative sonofabitch."

Elam smiled. He sensed that Hammond was trying to put him on the defensive. It won't work this time, he promised himself.

Returning to the house, Jake invited Bob to the living room. Annoyed, Pam continued making small talk with Adele in the kitchen.

She attempted several times to persuade Adele to join Bob and Jake. She wanted to be an active part of the political discussions. She wanted to share these moments with Bob. But Adele had been taught better, so they remained in the kitchen.

Jake set his cup on the coffee table. "I've been thinking about your question. The politically astute thing would be to lambaste the governor for his veto, indicate you'd be more responsive to the wisdom and wishes of the sovereign people of this great state. You and I could have a great time drafting a press release." He paused. "You know, I'm surprised they haven't contacted you yet. Or is that why you're hiding here in Burke County?"

Elam chuckled but didn't reply.

"Yep, that would be the logical thing to do - lambaste our honorable governor. But it's a long time before the election, and a lot can happen. Your best bet is to praise Norman for being so damned ballsy, support him by saying you're sure he did what he felt was in the state's best interest. But then say that it's too bad he doesn't understand the resentment pent up within the taxpayers, too bad he can't see the anger directed at government and its senseless bureaucracy." Jake paused, organizing his thoughts. "What you'd be doing is complimenting the governor for his guts, suggesting he's out of touch with the people, editorializing that taxes are too high, plus you take a cheap shot at the bureaucrats. It's the best of all possible worlds, Bobby-boy."

"Sounds damned good. Would the press let me off that easily?"

"I'm sure Chandler is working on that. But if you ask me, first of all, you'd do this sort of thing with a release. Have your aides hand it out. But more importantly, and remember this, if you say anything forcefully enough, you are recognized as a wise statesman and an orator." Then Hammond said, "You, of course, have to dress up your equivocation with many a profound word and phrase, but I'm sure you can handle that. If not, you're entering the wrong profession."

"I could never eclipse your wisdom, statesmanship, and oratory," Bob smiled.

Jake returned the smile. "Seriously, there's an art to sidestepping an issue and doing so with some credibility. It takes a lot of work and, more importantly, a certain flair. Your advisers need to rehearse you, ask every off-the-wall question they can think of, then examine your every response, tell you where the hard spots are, then do it all over again. And as the campaign heats up, you'll have more meetings with the press and less preparation time. Have you had any press conferences yet?"

"Nope. None yet."

"Have them now while no one's listening, while you have time to polish yourself and your positions. Get your feet wet now." Hammond continued imparting ways to neutralize the press. Bob kept nodding deferentially.

"You're right," Elam replied. He was being distracted by Pam. "I suppose I should have one or two right after I announce, probably out in the state, away from the capital, just to get used to them." He stared beyond Hammond to give the impression that he was pondering a weighty issue. In fact, he was looking at Pam. He could see that she was annoyed to the point of anger. Every time that Adele looked down at her hands or to her cup, or got up to get more coffee, Pam would intently stare at Bob, silently expressing annoyance at being excluded. Bob was puzzled over Jake's insistence that they not involve their wives in the discussion. Worse, he didn't know how to deal with the situation; allow Pam to become more annoyed, invite her to join them, or leave after being with Hammond for less than an hour. Bob returned his attention to Hammond.

"... and the press conference deteriorated from that point on. Well, after everyone quit laughing and things settled down, the guy from UPI asked Phil Dawson why there shouldn't be a sales tax on the services of a prostitute. Well, ol' Phil Dawson thought for a split second, then said, 'I think it's inherently unfair for a man to get screwed twice in the same transaction.'" Jake pounded his knee, laughing loudly. Bob responded with a subdued laugh. "Well, the story has two ironic twists to it. First, UPI put Dawson's quote on the newswires. And, secondly, and some say it's because of Phil's spontaneous wit, and that it was on the wires, he now runs a brothel in Nevada."

Bob hadn't heard of Governor Dawson since he left the state. He was taken aback by Hammond's revelation. "Are you serious?"

"Yep."

"I'll be damned. So that's the next career step for a governor."

"I suppose."

Bob looked beyond Jake to the kitchen where Pam and Adele were. "Pam, have you any idea what Governor Dawson's doing these days?"

In a matter of seconds, Pam rose from her chair, excused herself from Adele, and was standing beside Bob. "What, dear?"

"Jake tells me he's running a bordello."

Pam looked squarely at Jake. "You see, there is a role for women in this world. Phil Dawson obviously recognizes our value in the workplace!"

Bob was surprised by Pam's remark and saw that Jake was flustered. Now it was his turn to laugh. Standing, still laughing, he put his arm around Pam's waist. "Jake, I suppose it's time we let you get back to your Herefords. Really enjoyed our visit and your advice. It's always invaluable. Can I call on you again?"

By now, Jake had recovered. "Sure, Bob." Then looking to his wife, he said, "Adele, our good friends have to get back to the capital." She joined him as he walked the Elams to their car.

Bob had driven several miles before Pam spoke. "Now I know what a male supremacist looks like."

Bob couldn't suppress his smile. "It was unbelievable, but you came down damned hard, left him speechless at least for a couple of seconds. That's more than I've been able to do."

"He deserved it."

"I suppose so. But until the election is over, let's be nice to the Jake Hammonds of the world." He smiled to let her know he wasn't angry, but his voice was firm.

She passively accepted his words. "I haven't seen much of you lately."

"I was going to ask, how are the kids doing?"

"They're fine."

"How are you?" he asked almost suggestively.

"I'll be glad when it's over. I liked it better when you were home every evening."

"Well, we're committed. Can't pull out now. We've invested too much time, money, and, I guess, our self-respect."

"Yeah, we're committed," she said, almost sadly. Then she smiled, reached for his hand and gently squeezed it.

***

After conferring with Chandler and Sergent, Bob dutifully followed the astute political advice of Senator Jake Hammond.

CHAPTER ELEVEN

Spring comes slowly to the High Plains. The rivers fed by mountain streams run clear and cold, then at night an icy film forms along their banks. As they carry the melted snow that had fallen on the mountains to the west, their banks become full, their current strong. Downstream, their swiftness and clearness are transformed as the rivers widen and straighten. Nature has fulfilled is annual ritual; the residue of autumn has been turned into rich and fruitful soil. The earth is reborn.

For those who are young, it is a time when all thoughts are projected forward. It is a time of optimism, a season of promise. All things are possible. It is a time for action.

Jeff Vinton took one final, lingering look at the vista before him. The mesa on which he had stood for so long cast its shadow over the prairie below, signaling the end of day. Jeff walked to his automobile. He had reached a decision during these past few hours of solitary reflection. He would not be alone again.

He drove from the buttes, negotiating the switchbacks. At their base he continued slowly until he reached the highway. Only then did he reaffirm his course of action. His life was about to be irrevocably changed, his self merged with another, his time no longer his alone. Jeff felt good as he sped toward Union.

Jeff arrived at his apartment and sat at the table. He began to write to Andrea, to tell her of his plans for them, to speak of their future with confidence and optimism, to ask for her commitment to be his wife.

He realized he hadn't written in over a month. He explained why he hadn't answered her letters. He wrote that he intended to travel to Galveston in midsummer; that he would call to make plans; that he loved and missed her.

But then the unthinkable surfaced. She had divorced once. Would she again? He thought for a few moments. He judged not. She was young then. She and Jeff were older, more mature, and he could make her happy. Her terrible failure would not recur. Confident, Jeff went to bed. As he slept, he had both troubled and joyful dreams. But the moment he awoke he knew he had made the right decision.

***

Vinton was in his office when Jerry Milner rushed in.

"You move fast for a fat man," Jeff remarked.

"Yeah, but usually not on company time."

"Gosh damn! You're right. Whatcha got?"

"I got the hospital bills from the district court."

"We making an impact yet?"

"Here's December's bill. It'll be our baseline. In December the county was billed eighty-seven thousand dollars," his finger pointing to the line item. "Now here's the February bill." He placed it beside the December bill. "It's eighty-three thousand. In just two months we saved the county four thousand dollars minus our mileage and the Medicaid costs. Let's see, we made six trips at about forty dollars per trip. That's two hundred forty dollars, and we placed ten clients in nursing homes at about five hundred dollars apiece. Twenty percent of five hundred times ten is a thousand bucks. So last month we saved the county $2,760. Each month from now on it will be three thousand. That comes to thirty-six grand a year.

"Still a long way from a million," Jeff said.

"That was only our first month. So far this month we've relocated six patients. It's gonna add up, Jeff. It's working."

"How about the folks we relocated. How'd they feel about it?"

"Three were severely retarded. They were nice, docile, oblivious to the change. The other two were pretty old, but so help me God, I don't know why they were in the hospital. There wasn't a damn thing wrong with them. We chatted all the way back. They were happy as hell to get out of the damned place. They kept thanking me like I was the cavalry that had come to rescue them."

"How long had those two been in there?"

"One six years, the other eight."

"And they seemed normal?"

"Completely."

"For Christ's sake. That's scary. Why were they committed?"

"The findings of the mental health board aren't in our files."

Vinton leaned back, "What do you think?"

"The nursing homes we're putting them in ain't the best, but they're sure as hell an improvement over the hospital. Let's keep going."

"But what about the people?"

"What do you mean?"

"Jerry, you're telling me that perfectly normal people are vegetating in this state's mental hospitals. And they were put there by the county."

"Yeah."

"Christ, until we get a handle on this, don't mention it to anyone. It's one helluva can of worms. You see what I mean?"

"You're saying the county could be sued for millions."

"If those patients were normal when committed, or if they responded to treatment and regained sound mental health years ago, a terrible wrong has been committed by the county. And you're right. We could be sued for big bucks."

"What do we do?" Milner asked, now troubled.

"I don't know. What is the right thing to do?"

"Keep relocating them."

"Yeah. And what else?"

"I don't know."

"Christ. Were those who appeared to be normal at different hospitals?"

"Both were at Keokuk."

"I'll call the social worker there. See what he's got to say."

"That's a start," Milner said.

"Let's hope it's an end, too. I can't believe the state would force people to stay in a hospital if they're not sick, unless the bureaucrats just screwed up again. I'll call this afternoon. You got anything else?"

"You know we got a crippled children's clinic next week."

"Oh yeah, that's right. How many cases we gonna have?"

"About sixty. Some new ones."

"What's wrong with the new ones?"

"Two with spina bifida, a Down syndrome, a CP, one or two with foot problems."

"Big day at the clinic. Anything else?"

"Nope."

After lunch, Jeff sat at his desk. He looked at the pad he had doodled on and saw the word "Keokuk" underlined several times. He called Evelyn, asking her to get the hospital's social worker on the phone and have Milner come to his office. Jerry was standing before his desk a few minutes later.

"I'm getting Keokuk on the line. Get whatever files we have on those two patients, then come back and have a seat. Stay close in case I need some information."

Evelyn rang. She had Keokuk on the line.

"Hi, there. This is Jeff Vinton, calling from Harney County. Who do I have?"

"Yes, Mr. Vinton, I'm Nancy Shields. How can I help?"

"My caseworker brought two patients back to Union. He drove over a hundred miles, and during the trip he didn't notice any problems; at least none severe enough to keep them hospitalized. I have him here if you want to talk with him. But first I should tell you we've relocated some others. They were mentally handicapped. Although I have questions about their being there, I simply don't understand the two we just took out."

"If you're from Harney County, I don't have to ask their names. You folks must have a helluva hospital bill."

Jeff sighed. "We sure do."

"Well, it could take some time to explain, but in a nutshell, most of the patients committed by your county were ready for release years ago. But those who are still here have no family to claim them, and we don't know what to do with them. So we contact your office to get them out. Well, you folks just leave them here, and we're not going to throw them out on the street, so we keep them, and keep billing you. It's that simple."

"For Christ's sake."

"Yeah."

"How many Harney County wards do you have ready for discharge?"

"About twenty-five."

A long silence followed. Then Vinton said, "For Christ's sake, that's well over a hundred thou a year!"

"Whatever."

"Okay, Nancy, it's time we started moving on this. A question, though. How will it affect you folks if we move them out? Job-wise, I mean."

"No problem. We're booked solid. We have to turn away some sad cases 'cause there aren't any beds."

"Nancy, I'll be in touch. Send me a list of those eligible for release, their social reports and medical prognoses. Okay?"

"Sure, Mr. Vinton."

"Another question. Do we have we any liability here? I mean the patients suing us?"

"No idea. See your county attorney."

"Okay. Hope to meet you soon. See ya." Jeff replaced the receiver. "Jerry, there's a bunch at Keokuk ready to get out. If each hospital is the same, that's over a hundred and fifty people."

"Excuse me! I'm gonna buy a lot of stock in some nursing homes."

"No kidding," Jeff said. "Seriously, we're talking about quite a migration. Are we forgetting anything?"

"Can't think of anything.

"Do you want to continue handling this chore?"

"Sure, as long as my car holds out. We're talking a lot of trips, a lot of miles. Our line item for travel is gonna be overspent in the worst way."

"Let's do it,"

"Okay," Milburn said. "If this projection holds, it's gonna mean over a half million in savings."

"Christ," Jeff thought aloud.

"Jerry, take care of the stuff you've got to do. Then let's knock off early and get a beer. We're in the process of saving the county big bucks. It can afford to give us a little time off."

***

Jeff felt the dull throb of a headache as he woke up. His mouth was dry. He was hung over. He and Milner had begun at three o'clock and, except for dinner, had continued drinking late into the night. It had been a happy time. Both men were elated about saving the county a lot of money. Jeff tried to remember their conversation. He recalled that, at some point, he had vowed that not all the savings would be returned to the taxpayers. He would channel some of the money to the tax users.

Dee and her kids were about to receive ADC. He just needed to recruit them.

Because of his discomfort, he decided to spend the morning in northwest Union. He took two aspirins, showered, and drank some milk. He drove to the office and told them his plans. He was parked in front of Horace and Annie's house within a half hour.

From his yard, George Iron Rope saw the wasicu enter the home of his adopted grandparents. Rage consumed him. After so many weeks had passed, George thought the welfare worker had forgotten about Dee and her children. Now, dammit, there he was again. And Annie had let him in. George hurried to the house, dragging Junior by the hand because the little boy couldn't keep up with his angry father. He barged in without bothering to knock. He looked at Vinton, hatred filling his eyes; then at Dee and his grandparents, nodding his head in disapproval.

Vinton stopped talking, taken aback by the intrusion. Then, recovering, he extended his hand and introduced himself. Now George was caught off guard, not knowing if he should even acknowledge the wasicu. He shook Vinton's hand limply, muttering his name.

"What's your son's name?" Jeff asked, looking at the little boy. He crouched down, extending his hand. The boy shied behind his father and away from the stranger.

"We call him Junior."

"Hello, Junior," Jeff said, reaching to pat his head. He didn't know how to gauge George. He made a physical assessment of him. Short, stocky, handsome face, a full crop of black hair. He noted that George made Dee uneasy. He didn't know who to address, George or Dee. Everyone was awkwardly silent.

Jeff noticed Junior's harelip. "I was telling Dee it's time we give her some assistance, George. I'm with welfare, and Dee could get some money to care for her children."

George looked to the dirt floor.

"It would be enough for her to get an apartment and set up a household. Give Horace and Annie some room around here. What do you think?"

"No one bothered us before."

"Bother? I'm here to help."

"How about her kids?"

"Well, we'll fix their teeth, and Dee needs some dental work, too." He turned to her. "When did you last see a dentist?"

Dee smiled, embarrassed and fearful of George.

"Why will you do these things?" George asked.

Jeff was at a loss for words. He looked at the floor. Finally he said, "Well, to help her kids get a better start in life."

"It's not your concern," George retorted.

Jeff was frustrated. "It's my job, what I do for a living."

George was clearly perplexed. "But we're Indians," he said, exasperated.

"Yeah, I noticed." Vinton looked squarely at George.

George began to speak, hesitated, then forcefully asked, "Why should we trust you?"

"Trust me with what?"

"Our children."

"What in the hell are you talking about?"

George didn't know what to say. Dee was trying to follow their conversation. Horace and Annie looked on passively. No one said anything. Finally Vinton spoke. "Where do you live, George?"

"Just up the street."

"Let's leave Dee alone. Let's go outside and talk."

"Okay."

They walked into the fresh air. Jeff needed to gain George's confidence. He decided to use the little boy.

They walked for several minutes before Jeff spoke. "Fine looking boy you got there."

"Quit making fun of my son."

Jeff turned to George, "You mean his harelip?"

George said nothing, kept on walking, sadness overwhelming him.

"Let's get that fixed," Jeff said.

George was startled. "How?"

"Surgery."

"I don't have any money."

"I ain't got much either," Jeff responded. They kept on walking. Soon they were at George's shack. "This your home?"

Vinton took several more steps, saying nothing. George stopped, hatred in his eyes. "Quit toying with me."

"I'm not."

"Yes, this shack is my home. Yes, my son has a harelip. Yes, we're Indians."

"A home's a home. About Junior. You and I and some doctors can repair his mouth. And I don't give a damn if you're Indian or Swiss or German. I couldn't care less."

"Where you from?"

"Eastern part of the state."

"Any Indians there?"

"Some."

"There's a lot of us here."

"Who cares?"

"I care, dammit!"

"Good. Now how about that cleft palate?"

"You mean the harelip?"

"Yeah."

"What if I trust you?"

"What if?"

"What will you do?"

"Not a helluva lot."

"You'll leave us alone?"

"I don't understand the question."

"You won't interfere with our kids?"

"Why should I?"

"You shouldn't."

"I know."

George was confused. He decided to go along; to see what would happen next. "Now what?"

"Bring Junior to the high school gym at noon Saturday. Let's get that mouth fixed," Jeff said.

"I told you, we don't have any money."

"George, there's a program for that. It won't cost you anything."

"Are you serious?"

"Yes."

George was bewildered. All the pain he and Mary had been through. And now this guy was going to fix it, just like that. No matter what he does, if he can make Junior right, I won't care, he thought. "I'll bring Junior."

"Good. Now how about Dee and her kids?"

"Let me think about that."

Now who's interfering with whose kids? Jeff thought. But he decided to proceed at George's pace. "Okay, I'll see you Saturday." Jeff again extended his hand. This time George shook it firmly.

Jeff walked across the empty lot, crapulously noting the wine and beer bottles that made him more aware of his hangover. He stopped again in front of the shack where Dee and her children lived. He decided not to pursue the issue. He walked to his car.

George grasped his son's hand, wondering about this strange wasicu. He knelt until his eyes were at Junior's level. His finger traced the deformed upper lip. Tears again came to his eyes, but this time there was hope.

Jeff stopped at the drug store and bought some aspirins. He grimaced as he swallowed three of them without water and then headed for his office. Evelyn told him that Commissioner Scott was waiting for him. Jeff walked into his office. "Hello, Mr. Scott."

"Hi, Jeff. How you doing?" Scott looked preoccupied.

"Okay. Have you heard about the mental health situation?"

"I've picked up some scuttlebutt. Why don't you fill me in."

Jeff showed him the bills, told him six more patients had been relocated this month, and mentioned his conversation with Nancy Shields. He felt a bit smug.

Scott's expression didn't change. He looked grim.

Jeff expected Scott to be elated over the reduced hospital costs. Scott's expression was thereby troubling. Jeff asked him if anything was wrong.

"No, not really. But I've got a favor to ask you."

"Sure thing."

"It's kind of difficult to bring up."

"Yeah?"

"I want Lisa Oldfield to be placed on ADC. Very quietly. No one is to know."

"Who the hell is Lisa Oldfield? Is she any relation to the commissioner?"

"His daughter-in-law."

"If she's eligible, we'll put her on. Where's Oldfield's son?"

"Here in town."

"I'll have to notify the county attorney. Is she divorced?"

"Not yet."

"Is there a temporary support adjudication?"

"I don't think so."

"Why not?"

"Hell, I don't know."

"Does she want to go on welfare?"

"Only if Commissioner Oldfield doesn't find out."

"It's gotta go before the board."

"Even if I sign it?"

"Okay. But I still gotta notify the county attorney. Not that he'll do anything."

"Why do you have to involve Maenner?"

"It's the law."

"What if you forget? Or it gets lost in transmittal?"

"That could happen, I suppose. Oldfield's the problem. He's not to know?" The obvious question was purposefully asked.

"Right," Scott said, annoyed.

"How about a quid pro quo?"

"What the hell's that?"

"Something for something."

"What do you want?"

"The food stamp program."

"Not a raise?"

"Look, Mr. Scott, you pay me less than what some ADC mothers get. But if I get a raise, I want it because I deserve it."

"You deserve one, of course."

"Then I want a raise."

"Lisa is a good gal. Will you help?"

"Will I get the food stamp program? And someone to run it?"

"A deal. You quietly help out Lisa, and you'll get your program."

"Good."

"Put together a presentation for the board. I'll start lining up the votes."

Vinton sat, watching Scott walk out, reflecting on the events of the past few days. Things were happening quickly. And all for the good. The patient relocations; Dee, George and his son; and now the food stamp program. And he would soon call Andrea.

He spent the rest of the day doing the things bureaucrats do - signing forms, drafting memoranda, reviewing case files. Those routine activities did little to dampen his quiet elation.

Jeff spent the evening deliberating over the best way to approach the county board about the food stamps and the best way to talk to Andrea about merging their lives.

It was eight o'clock. Jeff paused to reflect on the call he was about to make. Was he taking too much for granted? What if she was still so bitter about her first marriage that she would not dare risk another? But he remembered her many letters, her proposing to him, her working out budgets based on his income, her expressing the difficulties of living with her parents. Vinton was confident. She would accept his offer to share his life. "I'm sure!" he said aloud. "This is no mistake. I'll make sure it works."

The telephone rang but once.

"Hello." Andrea's soft, earthy voice gave Vinton a warm sensation as it always did.

"Hi, is this Betty Lou?" Jeff asked.

"Shur 'nuff," Andrea's affected Southern accent told him. "Is this Billy Joe?"

He hadn't joked like this before, and she hadn't missed a beat. Pretty good, he thought. "How are you?"

"Lonely for you."

"Me too, for you."

"Well, what are you gonna do about it?" she seductively asked.

"Head south."

"What for?"

"Well, for one thing, to see you."

"Anything else in mind?"

"Yes, Andrea," Jeff said, softly but seriously.

She caught the change in his tone. Her heartbeat quickened. "Do you mean that after all of my ploys, all my seductions, all my entrapments, you're ready to give in?"

"I do love you."

"I was beginning to have some doubts."

"Don't."

"Okay. No more doubts."

"Okay. Ready for the big question?"

"Yeah, I'm ready. Been ready for years." She laughed nervously.

Jeff paused for a long moment. He wasn't sure how to handle this. Then he simply said it. "Let's get married." Then, realizing that wasn't very romantic, he began again. "Andrea, what I mean is, I think it would..."

She stopped him in midsentence. "Jeff, I love you, and thank you, and yes!"

"That's great! And thank you!"

"When? When can we get married?"

"I can get some time off in July," Jeff said.

"That's such a long time."

"Would that be okay?"

"How about sooner? Like April or May?"

"How about July?"

"What's wrong, Jeff?"

"July will be better for me."

"Tell me."

"What if I write you?"

"Okay. Love you. I hope I can talk you into next month."

"I'll let you decide after you've read my letter. Okay?"

"Okay."

"Remember, you're spoken for now. Tell all your suitors to stay away."

"There aren't any, Jeff. I'll be waiting for your letter."

16 Jun 67

It was still early morning, the temperature in the low nineties. Lt. Vinton assumed a crouching position. The wetness of his entire front caused him to shiver as drops of sweat from his forehead momentarily blurred his vision. The intense activity of a few minutes ago was now reduced to a systematic exchange of rounds, neither the PAVN nor the American paratroopers being target effective. Vinton looked at Pruitt but turned away on seeing the radioman grimace with pain, then fired a short burst at the greenness of the rain forest, then scanned the skies. Just as he was about to curse again, he saw three specks of gray far on the horizon behind his position. He yelled to his men, "Here comes the air strike. Hang in there!"

"Little Wedge, this is Red Striker. Do you read? Over." The field radio had come alive.

Vinton moved to Pruitt, taking the receiver from the radio still strapped to his back. Pruitt moaned and grimaced again as he twisted to make the receiver more accessible. He recovered and weakly smiled, then turned his head away as another spasm of pain cut through him.

"Red Striker, this is Little Wedge. I can see them now."

"This is Red Striker. Ah ... shall I patch you in? Over."

"Negative. The aircraft are approaching from my rear. I'll throw out more red smoke. Have them strike north. I say again - north of the smoke."

"Roger. Read you Little Wedge. Over."

Moments later, red smoke again filled the air. As it began to obscure Vinton's view of the rain forest, he heard the jet aircraft coming in fast and low. Seconds later, the rain forest erupted in fireballs and smoke and the ground trembled from the exploding ordnance. The deafening shockwaves swept over Vinton and his men. Large clouds of black smoke and orange fireballs continued to rise from the rain forest. Then silver-white phosphorus filled the air. The aircraft made another sweep of the area, this time concentrating on the edge of the forest, approaching on an east-west line of attack. The ground again trembled, the shockwaves expanding outwardly from the point of contact. Vinton heard his men shouting obscenities of joy after the aircraft made their second pass. One grunt stood briefly only to dive back into the few inches of water when he drew fire. The aircraft made several more sweeps before returning to their carrier in the South China Sea.

The departure of the quick-responding jets signaled the arrival of an eerie silence. This was replaced by the sounds of small-arms fire from the rain forest. No mortars, Vinton thought. His men were returning fire when four A-1E Skyraiders arrived at the scene of battle. Those aircraft moved slowly and awkwardly compared to the jets. They seemed out of place in this war, an atavism of a more clearly defined, less troubled war. But, notwithstanding their ungraceful and lethargic flight, they had staying power. For over twenty minutes the propeller-driven Skyraiders raked and bombed the area where the hostile fire had originated. Then they lumbered off, slowly and clumsily in contrast to the sleek departure of the jets.

Vinton and his men got up slowly, warily at first, rifles ready. The more experienced soldiers raced to where the dead and seriously wounded lay. After gathering their ammo, they erratically ran back to their positions. Soon they were more relaxed, checking their weapons, lighting cigarettes. The wounded were attended to, the dead placed at gathering points. The medevac helicopters soon had the wounded airborne. They would be at the field hospital within fifteen minutes.

The lieutenant and a noncommissioned officer from the platoon on Jeff's left flank returned to the LZ. Jeff's counterpart walked over to him. He spoke excitedly. "From the body count, there were at least two companies of PAVN back there. I don't understand why they didn't rush us."

"Don't know," Vinton replied, feeling nauseous.

"We stung their asses. My men counted over a hundred bodies when I left. Funny, you know, they usually haul their dead off. How many KIAs do you have?"

"I know I got some."

"I'd better count mine."

"Yeah." Jeff walked slowly to where the dead were gathered. He felt sick, breathing heavily, hoping not to vomit, thinking the massive intake of air would calm his stomach. The dead soldiers were laid out beside each other, their empty expressions facing the blueness of the sky. The open stomach and chest cavities of two of the KIAs were attracting flies. Jeff took a few steps closer, intending to keep the flies off his men. Then he realized that would be foolish. He stopped but continued looking at the bodies. Minutes ago they were alive. Now they were dead. Jeff could intellectually grasp their deaths, but emotionally he rejected it. Three of these men had been under his command. They were his responsibility, and he was a part of their obscene and terrible failure. They had looked to him for leadership and now existed no more.

Karl Shapiro's words "more than an accident and less than

willed…" taunted him. Yeah, he thought, the guy was right! Those dink sonsabitches were just doing their job. Nothing personal. Just terribly absolute - and final. Requiem on a tailgate. Requiem in a rice paddy. Requiem in a marshland. Requiem and death where there should be life.

For an instant Vinton earnestly believed that he could undo this terrible wrong, that he could breathe life back into the dead. By repudiating death, he should be able to overcome its finality; to use reason and logic to deny the presence of death thereby allowing the young to mature to men, to grow old among their loved ones.

The sun was intense. Vinton removed his helmet, wiped the sweat from his forehead. He was about to vomit. His stomach muscles began churning. Vinton breathed heavily again. He couldn't allow his men to see him become sick because of his too human limitations. One of his sergeants walked toward him. Vinton had to control his retching stomach muscles. He had to appear strong, like a man in charge. Instead he felt weak and powerless. He placed the butt of his M16 on the ground and tried to brace himself, tried to crouch. Then he was falling. Before he lost consciousness, he stretched out to touch and thereby to revive one of the dead soldiers. His arm fell short. He could not reach him.

***

Jeff considered several ways to present the food stamp program to the county board. He'd cite better nutrition, more economic activity, and no cost to the county. It all made sense, perhaps, but the program was not politically acceptable to Harney County.

He walked into the boardroom and sat facing Commissioner Scott. He spoke of the new cases, the patients relocated from hospitals and placed in nursing homes under Medicaid. Even Oldfield complimented Jeff on saving the county money, not mentioning the higher costs when total public dollars were considered.

Vinton mentioned the crippled children's clinic scheduled for the weekend. He cited the caseload and types of corrective surgeries required. Many of the children simply needed adjustments to their prostheses, he explained.

Jeff sensed a feeling of good will from the board members; no arguments, no sarcasm, no obscenities. This was obviously because of his impacting the mental health costs. It's going well so far, he thought.

"And gentlemen, you're aware that I've been looking over options regarding the food stamp program. I've been in contact with counties administering the program and state and USDA officials. It's more work, but it'll help a lot of people. And it's federally underwritten, so no county money's involved. And it's really needed. It'll relieve financial pressures, stabilize marriages, keep families together..."

Commissioner Oldfield was listening but seemed detached.

"...and for the families broken by divorce, at least we can ensure that their kids have fuller bellies. ADC families really have a tough time with what we give them. And the old folks ..."

Before Vinton could continue, Commissioner Oldfield spoke, and Jeff sat astounded. "Scotty, we got a lot more on the agenda, and Ryan and I know the votes are here. So rather than hear Vinton explain why the poor shouldn't work and should get more relief, and how goddamned deserving they truly are, I'll just accept the reality of things and move that Harney County pass any needed resolutions to bring in the food stamp program."

"Is that in the form of a motion?" Scott quietly asked Oldfield.

"Yes."

Scott broke into a modest grin. "Does that include the goddamned Indians?"

"Even the goddamned Indians." Oldfield flashed a silly and artificial smile, then regained his normally dour expression.

"Any further discussion?"

There was none. Reisner called the question. The Harney County Board of Commissioners unanimously voted to bring food stamps to the county.

Vinton looked at Scott in amazement. Now he had to get Lisa on ADC without her father-in-law's knowledge. Jeff decided not to ask about an additional staff member. He'd work that out with Scott.

Vinton gathered up his files, thanked the board, and left the meeting. He realized the board couldn't fire him. Too much was happening: the caseload was increasing, patients were being relocated, and now the food stamp program had to be administered. I'm good for at least another year, he thought. Then he thought of Andrea, knowing he could support his new family.

CHAPTER TWELVE

Andrea wasn't expected for another hour. Her children were splashing in the shallow end of the swimming pool, Joyce watching them from the kitchen.

Joyce had practiced running from the kitchen through the living room, past the patio to the pool. She was never more than a minute from them should they stray into deeper water. Still, she was always uneasy when they were in or near the pool. Joyce stacked the cups in the sink following her coffee hour with a few neighbors, careful not to splash anything on her dress. She saw the neighbor's daughter come through the fence gate to babysit the children. Joyce quietly resented her youth, her fine figure.

"I see they're using more material on bathing suits this season," she said with a hint of a smile.

The teenager became embarrassed. Instinctively, she looked away from Joyce and down to the floor, seeing how little of her breasts her bikini top covered. She reddened and stammered, Joyce enjoying her discomfort. "Andrea will be back in about an hour. Here's the number where I can be reached. Enjoy the sun."

Joyce took a final look in the mirror. Satisfied, she went to her car. After driving for twenty minutes, she entered the main gate of the Coast Guard station. The guard saluted smartly after spotting the blue decal on her windshield. Joyce smiled and waved at the young man, driving directly to the Officers Club.

Entering, she saw Ned sitting in a booth at the far side of the bar. She walked to him while he caught the waitress's eye, signaling for two martinis.

Ned looked at her. "The babysitter was late," he said with a smile, anticipating her comment.

"But let me tell you, that little girl is growing up."

"I've been intently observing that," Ned responded, still smiling. "The little ones getting along with each other?"

"Just like always," she said.

"Well, my delightful wife, thanks for coming all the way over here."

"Five years you've been retired, and you're still hanging out in military clubs," she interrupted, smiling.

"Yeah," he said. "I want to talk to you about our little girl."

"The one who's twenty-seven and the mother of two children?"

"Yeah, that's the one. How is she?"

"Wildly ecstatic. She finally got her man."

"How long has it been since she met him?"

"We were at Fort Bragg. So it's been about five years."

"Quite a courtship. You think she's really sure this time?"

"No question."

"Good. I'd hate to see another disaster."

"Let's not think about it. At least Jeff isn't prone to violence."

"Sometimes a woman can make a man do anything."

"You're worried."

"I'm concerned."

"You know there's nothing that can be done," Joyce said, lifting her glass. She only allowed the gin and vermouth to wet her lips, then set the drink down. "She isn't an easy person to live with," Joyce continued. "God knows she and I get into some terrible battles. But it's difficult for her, having to move back with two kids. Maybe when she gets her own home, and not an apartment like before, she'll be easier to get along with. And she deeply loves Jeff. I do know that."

"He's never been married. Will he resent the products from her previous marriage?"

"Really, Ned, referring to your grandchildren as 'products'."

"Wrong word obviously," he smiled, then resumed his sober expression.

"There's nothing we can do," she replied, sipping her martini.

He nodded. "She's an adult, soon to be on her own again. I often wonder. Did we help her too much? Financially, I mean. Did we contribute to the first marriage not working out? Or didn't we help enough?"

"For God's sake, Ned, we weren't to blame. You act as if we were the ones who broke up her marriage. We didn't."

"I know. I just want her to be happy this time."

"She will be, Ned. She will be."

"Has she heard from Jeff, since the proposal?"

"No. But she's expecting a letter. I guess he was a bit cryptic. She's a little apprehensive, but it hasn't detracted from the bounce in her step, the joy in her eyes."

"Then let's drink to Andrea and Jeff." Ned raised his glass. "May their joy and love be unbridled."

Joyce raised her martini glass to lightly touch his. "They love each other deeply. That's all it takes."

***

Andrea parked her car in the driveway and ran to the mailbox. It was empty. Disappointed, she went to her children.

They were sitting with the babysitter at the edge of the pool, their legs dangling into the water. On seeing Andrea, they ran to her, hugging her, their wetness dampening her hosiery and dress. "Let's get you two dressed. It's dinner time."

"Oh, it's too hot," Bobby immediately objected. "I don't want to get dressed."

"Your grandparents went out for dinner, and so are we. How about a pizza?"

Bobby quickly agreed.

Andrea made sure they were perfectly dressed: Laura in a freshly ironed jumper and blouse, patent leather shoes, and white socks; Bobby in sharply creased dark blue trousers, a short-sleeved white shirt. It wasn't until they stepped out of the air-conditioned house that the heat of the early spring engulfed the children. Bobby again complained. Andrea patted his head. "Wait 'til summer, when it really gets hot. And this winter, you know what we're gonna do?" Andrea opened the door to her car, pushing the seat forward to let them in.

"What?" they asked.

"You and I and Jeff are gonna build a snowman. And it's gonna be very cold, sometimes below zero, and there will be snow everywhere. What do you think of that?"

The children affected a chill, wrapping their arms around each other, saying "BRRR!" laughing at themselves.

She opened the door for them at the restaurant where the air conditioning was operating at its peak. The children entered, again affecting coldness, loudly saying "BRRR!" Andrea smiled at them and those in the restaurant whose attention they had attracted. She took obvious pride in her children, how they looked, even their childish pranks. She led them to a booth without chastising them.

Ordering red wine for herself, she got the children noncarbonated orange drinks and a medium pizza. The pizza and drinks were consumed forty minutes later; Bobby waiting until Laura put down the last thick piece of crust before he grabbed and devoured it.

Andrea drove to the coastline and followed it for about twenty miles, the children sitting quietly in the backseat. She drove home as darkness began to capture the day.

She checked the mailbox again. Her heartbeat quickened as she took out the letter. She rushed into the house, placing the children in front of the television. "Now stay put. No fighting! I want to read a letter from your daddy." Andrea was thrilled. This was the first time she had referred to Jeff as their father, and she had said it so naturally. Warning them again, she went to her room and opened the letter. Her hands trembled from excitement or apprehension; she didn't know which. She set the letter down, going to where Ned kept his liquors. She selected a merlot, pouring a glass. She took several sips, refilled the glass, and returned to her room. She set the glass down, lit a cigarette, and began to read.

Dear Andrea, I don't know where to begin. First, I love you and am eager for us to be together. I feel awkward about what comes next. I wish I didn't have to bring it up, but I really have to deal with it. You may have wondered about the length of our courtship and even detected some hesitancy on my part. That's now behind me and I await our marriage. Although loving you nearly from the start, I was apprehensive. During my college days, I had a good friend who married a girl who was bearing his child. Two years later she divorced him. He took it hard. The pain he bore was more than I could stand. During that time I was with him every night. We almost flunked out of school. It was difficult for him and even for me. It was his experience that made me decide to wait until I'm thirty to get married. On the second of July I'll be thirty. I know it's silly but I'm so scared of divorce; I don't want to be a part of that terrible failure. I know we have the maturity to choose wisely, to decide wisely, and to make that lifetime commitment. So why the hell wait?

I guess I want you to reflect and be sure you're sure. Because when we marry, I'm gonna cling to you forever. So humor me if you will, let's wait until July so there won't be any angry stars looking down on us. And with no faults in the stars, and none within us, we'll make this a lifetime affair. I love you, want this to work, am superstitious, and want to marry you in July.   Love, Jeff.

She placed the letter down. She reached for the wine glass and drank what remained. Her hand was steady as she set the glass on the nightstand. She stood slowly, then, out of futility, again sat down on her bed. Stunned, but feeling intense emotional pain, she reread the letter. It did no good. Her bewilderment was changing to anger. Good God! He was thinking about divorce while proposing marriage; and after she had willingly and joyfully accepted his proposal, thinking only of their life together forever. Good God, what kind of man is this? And all those many months, she with her children, and he with so many women! She had waited so long for this man, a man who made the promise of marriage while fearful of divorce. Goddamn him, she thought. Damn him! Damn him to hell! Andrea was losing control. She wanted to yell out, to scream her fury away, to dispel her anger by purging herself of him. To end this absurdity, to do so this moment! She reached for the telephone.

It rang three times. She was about to hang up when Jeff answered. She heard the familiar voice of her fiancé. She waited a few moments before she slammed down the receiver with all the strength her anger had manifested. She felt better but began to cry. She was still sobbing when her parents returned.

Ned was standing beside her, his hand gently wiping the tears from her face. "What happened, honey? What the hell's wrong?"

Andrea looked up, her eyes red. She handed him the crumpled letter, wet from her tears. Ned sat beside her, trying to console her. He read Jeff's letter. Finishing it, he again wiped away her tears, leaving Andrea in her room. He returned with a glass of water and a sleeping pill a few moments later. "Take this. We'll talk in the morning." Andrea took the pill from Ned, grimacing until she washed it down.

"You call in sick tomorrow. I'll stay home. We'll work this out, analyze it, make some judgments. Perhaps when we look at it in the morning it won't be so bad. I'll tend to the kids. You lay back and rest." He gently laid her on the bed and took off her shoes. He returned to his daughter after putting Laura and Bobby to bed. Andrea had stopped crying, seemed to be falling asleep. He placed a blanket over her and went to tell Joyce what was wrong.

There had been friction between the two women since that day Andrea had asserted her control. Joyce had initially resisted before yielding to the ways of nature, acquiescing to her younger and stronger and more resolute daughter. Joyce would reassert herself from time to time only to cower again at Andrea's outbursts. Joyce had waited patiently during this past year for Andrea's departure and had prayed nightly for Jeff's deliverance. Now she feared that something was wrong, that she would have to continue accepting her inferior role within her own household for months, for years longer. She awaited Ned's arrival with trepidation.

"Is the engagement off?" she whispered to her husband.

Ned shook his head. He closed the door to their bedroom and sat beside his wife. "Jeff wrote that he has a fear, an abnormal fear I think, about divorce. That's why he waited so long, until his thirtieth birthday, until this July. Something about their being mature enough. That's why our dear daughter has been with us these last few years. Anyway, it's nothing serious, but Andrea's upset. We'll talk to her in the morning after she's cooled off."

"Ned, I hope nothing happens. I'm not sure I can take much more of Andrea. She and the kids need their own home. Andrea needs her own man, her kids their own father." Then fear struck her again. "Ned, does Jeff want out?"

"No. He loves her very much."

Joyce sighed deeply and lay back in their bed.

CHAPTER THIRTEEN

Jeff checked his mail, hoping to find a letter from Andrea. There was none. Slightly concerned, he drove to the crippled children's clinic. Only a few parents and their children were there, mainly those who had driven a long distance from adjoining counties. He checked the coffee pot, the soft drink container, the rows of chairs, and medical stations. Satisfied, he watched more parents and their children enter. As the gymnasium filled, Jeff kept looking for the Iron Rope family. Once he walked to his car intent on driving to northwest Union, but he reconsidered. Now the medical teams entered, each specialist going to an assigned station. Jeff walked up to the plastic surgeon before the patients began lining up. "Hi, Doctor, I'm Jeff Vinton, the director here."

"Hi. You got a big group for us I see."

"Yeah, but I'm hoping for one more family. I need to talk to you about them."

"Sure."

"We got a sizable American Indian community here, but they've been left out of things. I'm trying to break into that community to provide some services, but I guess experience has taught them to stay away from guys like me. I think I convinced one family whose son has a cleft palate to get some help." Jeff paused, looking for them. "I think the father is a sort of leadership figure to some of the Indian families. If you're not too busy, spend some time with him. Make him feel comfortable. I'd appreciate it."

The surgeon looked around the room. "I get the feeling I'll recognize him."

Jeff grinned. "Shouldn't be that hard." He scanned the room again, looking for George and Mary. Instead, he saw Jerry Milner. "How long you been here?"

"A few minutes."

"You looking for the same folks I am?" Jeff asked.

"Yeah."

"Hey, here they come," Jeff said, looking toward the entrance.

Junior and his brother wore patched jeans and T-shirts. Mary was in a plain black dress, George in Levis and a sweatshirt.

The Iron Ropes were obviously uncomfortable in this gymnasium of whiteness. Jeff and Milner walked over to them, "Hi, George, Mary," Jeff said. "I want you to meet a guy who works with me. This is Jerry Milner"

Jerry, despite his large frame, crouched down to Junior's level. "Hello, Junior. You gonna see the doctor today?"

Junior grabbed his father's leg and hid behind it.

"Let's get a seat and I'll get some coffee." Jeff led them to some chairs, ignoring a family that rose and moved to another row. Jeff left, then returned carrying cool drinks and coffee. After handing out the drinks, Jeff motioned Evelyn over to complete the application for George. Age: thirty-one. Place of birth: Union. Education level: eighth grade. Occupation: spot labor. Last year's income: $3,400.00. The questions continued.

Jeff was gaining some insights into the plight of the Iron Rope family. He would use this to take advantage of George's leadership role in the American Indian community. The information now in the proper bureaucratic slots, Jeff used Evelyn's pen to approve the Iron Ropes' eligibility.

As they walked to the plastic surgery station, the doctor was examining the results of his earlier handiwork on the youngster before him. "Well," he asked, "which do you like better? Your old mouth or this new one you got?"

The girl spoke slowly, articulating each word. "My new mouth."

"I'm really glad you like the way things are." He looked to the girl's father. "There's no need for me to see this young lady anymore. She's all set. But I'm gonna miss her. You know she stole my heart away." Sensing the father's appreciation, the surgeon shook his hand and turned his attention to his new patient, George Iron Rope Jr. He placed his hands on his knees and leaned toward Junior. "I'm Dr. Helliman. Who are these fine people with you?"

Junior, his speech affected by the deformity, replied, "My mom and dad."

The surgeon stood upright, took the file from Jeff, and opened it long enough to catch George's name. He held out his hand. "Mr. and

Mrs. Iron Rope, I'm Dr. Helliman. I'm glad you brought this lad in. We can fix him up pretty good. Another couple years it would have been more difficult."

He placed Junior on the table and examined his palate, mumbling as he proceeded. "No problem here ... hmm ... take care of that ..." some indistinguishable mutterings. Then he said, "Mr. and Mrs. Iron Rope, I want to attend to this as soon as possible, like next week. Can you get this young man to the capital city next Wednesday? I'll operate Thursday morning."

George, stunned by the real possibility of his son's face becoming normal, buoyed by the physician's kind attention, was so elated he didn't hear the question.

Helliman again asked. George heard this time, but his hope quickly faded. "I don't know," he responded faintly. "We don't have money for the bus, and our car won't make it. And there's no money to eat with. I don't know..."

Jeff grabbed George's shoulder and whispered to him. George's euphoria returned. "We'll be there, doctor. Thank you."

"Good. I'll see you then, Mr. Iron Rope." He reached to help Junior off the table. George and Mary each grabbed one of his hands and then walked backwards in deference to the surgeon, awkwardly bumping into a family. They apologized and walked to the exit. Jeff thanked the doctor, then caught up with the Iron Ropes. "Come to my office Tuesday. We'll have the bus tickets, hotel reservation, and a check for expenses."

Tears were flowing down George's and Mary's cheeks. They couldn't answer. Jeff smiled, his eyes also moistening. "I'll see you Tuesday."

***

Driving to work on Monday, Jeff realized how empty his weekends had been. There was little to keep him occupied except going to his office to catch up on paperwork. But soon his family would be with him. Soon his weekends and holidays would be bustling with activity. He grew impatient and had to restrain himself from calling to tell Andrea they needn't wait to get married. He missed her, more now than just a week ago.

Then, she had represented a fond thought, a loving memory, a pleasant and endearing individual for whom he possessed deep emotion. The telephone conversation had changed her into a most integral and essential part of his being. No longer would Andrea represent fond memories. She was now his future.

He arrived at the office a few minutes late and was pleased to see his staff busily working. After getting his coffee, he sat behind his desk. He had pressing matters before him, but he could only think of his family.

Taking a yellow pad, he jotted down those things he had to do. Scott had fulfilled his part of the bargain by getting the food stamp program approved. Jeff's part, getting Lisa on ADC, would be simple. But the food stamps, with all of the details involved in bringing that program to the county, would be a lot tougher.

Who could he trust with that program? Should he change Milner's assignment or hire a new person? And he needed to meet with the grocers to ensure they applied for food stamp designation. And he wouldn't allow his clients to be treated differently from the regular customers. He would work on that. And he would need to get with the media to get some coverage for the program.

And Dee and her kids. When should he approach her? And how would Andrea and the kids like Union, the High Plains, its weather, and people? And where the hell would they live? Need to find a home! And furniture! Christ! He had no money for that! Lisa Oldfield. He would meet with her. First things first.

He phoned Lisa and made an appointment for ten o'clock. It was a half-hour drive to her home. He could leave in about ten minutes and be there on time. He closed the door to his office. He leaned back and placed his feet on his desk, holding his coffee cup with both hands, sipping.

When he left the office, he didn't mentioned where he was going. His staff would discover the Oldfield file, or see the warrant, or notice the computer printout soon enough. He would counsel his staff again on the need for confidentiality about the work, the files, and the clients.

Soon he was rapping at her door. Lisa invited him in. Awkward moments passed as they stood in the kitchen. Jeff noted the tidy appearance of the house. The youngest child was watching television, the older ones in school.

"Commissioner Scott asked me to drop by and visit with you," Vinton explained. She was tall, he noted, several inches taller than Oldfield, slender, attractive.

She spoke in a low voice. "I appreciate your coming."

"How are you doing?"

Lisa smiled faintly. "Oh, pretty good, I guess."

Jeff noted her pained expression, sensed the depth of her embarrassment. He looked away. "Well, that's good to hear." He looked back at her. She forced a thin-lipped smile. "Yeah, that's good to hear. It's none of my business, of course, but how's your money holding up?"

Lisa said nothing, painfully aware why this welfare worker was in her home. The moments of silence grew longer, both feeling uncomfortable.

Jeff sensed the impasse between them. He broke into a smile. "Lisa, I tell you what. I'm gonna step outside, knock on your door, and you let me in. Okay?"

This absurdity relaxed, even amused Lisa. She smiled. "That's not necessary, Mr. Vinton. You want to know how I'm doing? I'll tell you. Terrible." She maintained her eye contact. "I haven't a cent. I suppose that's because I haven't gotten any money since he left. I can't find a job. I'm in terrible shape."

"How are you and the kids eating?"

"There's still some food around."

"How much are you behind on the rent?"

"The home is owned by my in-laws, rather my ex-in-laws. Anyway, they're not charging me anything. And we go there often to eat."

"Does your father-in-law know you're not getting any money from his son?"

"No. I don't want him to know."

"I think he should."

"Absolutely not."

"Why not?"

She didn't immediately respond, then, "I'm fearful of my husband."

"Of physical harm?"

Lisa couldn't respond verbally. She shook her head.

"Christ." Jeff took out a cigarette and offered her one.

"I haven't had one for three days. Maybe I've broken the habit. But, God, I need one." She smiled. "What the hell! Thanks."

He lit the cigarettes. Neither one said anything. Finally he spoke. "There are programs to help people in, ah, your situation."

"I know. ADC. But I thought you had to be black and live in Chicago to be on that program."

"Some folks think that. It can happen to anyone, even to some of our black friends in Chicago."

Lisa smiled, then let herself laugh. "Anything else?"

"Just general relief. County money. And Commissioner Oldfield scrutinizes those items. I understand that's a consideration."

"Yes," she said, "a consideration."

"In another month we'll have food stamps."

"Mr. Vinton, I can't wait until next month. I've got to do something right now."

"Are your kids getting free lunches at school?"

"No."

"May I arrange it?"

"How?"

"I'll ask the school administrator to send you an application. Just complete it and return it. The kids are obviously eligible. It'll make you feel better, knowing they're eating at lunchtime."

Lisa did not reply. She stared at the tabletop. She finally said, "I can't believe it's my family we're talking about. ADC. Free school lunches. Food stamps. But it is, dammit, it is."

"May I call the school? I'll do it discreetly."

"Let's talk a bit more first. Let me get used to the idea I'm a welfare recipient."

"You know our files are confidential. No one needs to know you're getting help."

"Can you guarantee that?"

"You mean Commissioner Oldfield?"

"Yes."

"Commissioner Scott asked me to do everything I can to prevent his knowing. But yes. He could find out, especially if you're still getting help when he assumes the chair next year."

"What should I do, Mr. Vinton?"

"Have you talked to your husband about your predicament?"

"Yes."

"Do any good?"

"No."

"Is there a motion by your attorney for temporary support?"

"I don't have one yet."

"An attorney?"

"Yeah."

"Get one."

"Okay."

"Pursue all your legal options. But if I were you, I'd apply for ADC. You need help now. I'll expedite the paperwork myself, but it'll still be a month before you get your first check."

"Okay," she said.

Jeff handed her the application form. The daughter-in-law of Commissioner Hank Oldfield was becoming an ADC mother, the grandchildren of Commissioner Oldfield dependent children. Jeff placed the signed application in his briefcase. He lingered a few more minutes, encouraging Lisa to contact an attorney and the school administrator.

Driving to his office, he took perverse satisfaction in having the signed application of Oldfield's daughter-in-law. The irony was overwhelming. The man on the county board who most frequently derided Vinton for using the state's resources to help the poor would now have that same state provide sustenance to his family, to those who would perpetuate his name and image throughout time. Then Vinton reflected more deeply. A sense of sadness overcame him. If this sort of thing could happen to someone as sanctimonious as Oldfield, it could happen to anyone.

Whose philosophy was correct? Vinton's, based on the government's concern, compassion, and involvement in the lives of its citizens? Or Oldfield's, that the government should restrict its activities to collecting taxes and waging war? With Vietnam now a part of his totality, Vinton even questioned the government's effectiveness in waging war. He had witnessed the vast bureaucracy the military had brought to Southeast Asia. Fifteen to twenty support personnel for each rifleman, each drawing combat pay. Many members of the officer corps housed in Saigon's finest hotels, dining in air-conditioned restaurants, enjoying French cuisine, chauffeured in air-conditioned staff cars. One naval captain even insisted on white-walled tires for his staff car. All were busily engaged in their contributions to the effort: purchasing Sony stereo equipment to be sold or stolen from the PXs, overseeing slot machines at clubs, renting chalets, procuring go-go dancers. There were other activities: housing vast amounts of materiel, recording favorable kill ratios, returning KIAs to the correct hometowns.

Jeff wondered how many tons of bombs, shells, and bullets it took to achieve one enemy KIA. It would have been cheaper to bribe the bastards. If a VC captain would surrender his company and its weapons, give him a quarter of a million dollars. A PAVN colonel and his brigade should be worth an even million. We could have bribed a general or corps commander with ten million. We could have made capitalists out of the communist sonsabitches. Instead, we were purists. Bribery was not cricket; somehow immoral. We waged war the correct and proper way, the traditional and moral way. We wounded, maimed, killed, and blew our adversaries into tiny pieces. Fiscal outlays would have been more effective. Nonetheless, we're winning over there. Maybe Oldfield's right: collect taxes, wage wars.

But who would provide for the Lisa Oldfields of the county, the grandchildren of the Hank Oldfields of the nation?

Vinton deliberated these conflicting philosophies: good battling evil, compassion against indifference, Jeffersonian idealism verses Hamiltonian doctrine. But where does the common sense, the truth, the logic come in? Jeff was weary from weighing these absolutes, finding them all too abstract and insoluble. Worse, the polarities were without limits to their spectrum. The sciamachy was frustrating and disquieting.

Driving to the courthouse, he wanted to deal with concrete commodities, items that had metrics, were determinable. He knew he would instead deal with the imprecision of imperfect people experiencing social, economic, and mental duress. And, for all his doubts about how much sense it made, he was part of the support system upon which those people had to rely. Vinton walked into his office, frustrated and depressed.

Evelyn looked up and sensed his mood. She asked what was wrong.

"I'm not sure. Join me. Bring your cup. Maybe you can help me work it out."

"Sure."

She was seated when Vinton returned with his coffee. "Anything happen this morning?"

"Things are fine here. What happened to you?"

"Nothing. I guess I'm just tense, a bit uneasy."

"You sure nothing's wrong?"

"I'm sure."

"Okay." She leaned back in her chair and relaxed for a moment.

After the initial onslaught of clients, the office had settled into its daily routine. This new routine was more accelerated than before but manageable. There was now some time to sit and relax. The two sat for several minutes, saying nothing, doing nothing. She finally stood and smiled. "I'd better get back to typing my DPW 144s."

"What the hell's a DPW 144?"

"That, sir, is just one of the many reports I routinely do, have you sign, and send to the state without your knowing what the hell's on them."

Jeff was surprised by her mild profanity. He smiled. "And I appreciate it."

"I made an appointment for you at one thirty with a John Rediger."

"Who is he?"

"He said he was the director of a CAP."

"What's a CAP?"

"I thought you'd know."

"Okay. I'll see him. Thanks."

A bit later, Jeff told Evelyn he was leaving for an early lunch. He checked the mailbox at his apartment. A couple of bills; a letter from Andrea. He entered his apartment. He felt a strong pang as he looked at the handwriting on the envelope. She was so far away, both in distance and time. He opened the letter.

Dear Jeff, July the 12th will be a beautiful day. I love you. Long, long letter follows. Love, Andrea.

Elated, Jeff stretched out in his chair. The depression that had deepened as he had anxiously waited for her response to his letter was gone. The euphoria had returned. Now things were okay. She loved him. They were going to be married. Jeff lay down on his bed.

The phone woke him. Jeff looked at his watch. He had been asleep for nearly two hours. Picking it up, he was informed that John Rediger was waiting to see him. He went to the bathroom and splashed water on his face. Alert, feeling confident about his future, he adjusted his tie, and went to his car.

Vinton felt a bit sheepish as he entered his office. He apologized to Rediger, invited him to sit, and asked Evelyn to bring coffee. He looked at Rediger, expecting him to speak. Rediger returned his stare. The coffee was brought and the men sipped from their cups. Rediger was short, about five feet four, and had short, neatly-trimmed black hair. He wore an expensive navy-blue suit, red tie, and white shirt. His patent leather shoes shone. His frame was not large, but his belly was.

Jeff put his cup on the desk. "I understand you're with a CAP."

Rediger nodded. "I'm its executive director."

The pomposity of the job title got Vinton's goat. *Director's not good enough. He's got to be the executive director.*

"What does the title 'executive director' mean?" Jeff asked.

Rediger hadn't thought very much about it other than it sounded good. "I'm the chief administrative officer of the CAP."

"Oh, you're the director then."

"Yeah."

"Why then preface the title 'director' with 'executive'? It's a bit redundant, ain't it? Directors execute policy, don't they?" Jeff knew he was being unfair, but he was enjoying himself.

Rediger looked bemused. "That was the job I applied for and got. I kept the title."

Jeff realized Rediger had no idea why he was an executive director. He felt he had sufficiently deflated Rediger's sense of self-importance, and he was a bit perplexed about his hostile bearing. He decided to lighten up, to make the conversation more pleasant. "Do you work for a board of directors?"

"Yes, Mr. Vinton."

"Well, they're the directors. You're the executive director." Jeff smiled. "Does that make sense?"

Rediger's face brightened. "By God, it does. I never thought of that before." He paused, then said with a grin, "Next time somebody asks me what I am, dammit, I'll know." Then, almost philosophically, he said: "It's good to know who you are."

Jeff nodded in agreement. "Well, how may I help you, Mr. Rediger?"

"First, I'm going to ask you to call me John."

"Sure, John. What else can I do?"

"Well, Mr. Vinton, Chairman Scott has appointed you to my governing board. In other words, you're now one of my bosses."

"Well, if my boss appointed me to be your boss, I suppose I should accept the responsibility." Vinton smiled. "I guess I've no choice." He sipped more coffee. "I don't want to sound like a dumb bunny, John, but what the hell's a CAP?"

"How much time can you give me?"

"Probably enough."

"Good. CAP is an acronym for Community Action Program. We're a social service and advocacy agency, a nonprofit corporation authorized by federal legislation and state law. Our funding's mostly federal, but we're governed by a local board. We're a part of LBJ's Great Society. Our federal counterpart is OEO. You've heard of the Office of Economic Opportunity?"

Jeff's attitude changed from indifference to enthusiasm. His mind darted to the allure of the national effort to eliminate poverty. This was an effort he wanted to be part of, if only as a board member. "OEO. Yeah, I've heard of you guys. How long have you been in operation?"

"About three years. The first year we just got organized."

"Funny I haven't heard of you, John. Of course I've only been here a few months. Tell me, what are you doing in Harney County?"

"Not that much right now. I'm gonna lean on you to help get stuff started. We've found some local resistance. Scott thinks you can help."

"He's pretty gracious, but I don't have any clout around here."

"Scott thinks you do, in the low-income community, and that you act as a bridge between the poor and everyone else."

Jeff wasn't persuaded. "I'll do what I can. What programs do you have?"

"We got a Head Start center here. Some Manpower training slots. We have some few vacancies to fill. Maybe you could help by referring someone. We do outreach and referral, community organization, senior citizen activities, and we have some VISTAs."

"What the hell's community organization? What's that program do?"

"Not much so far."

"What should it do?"

Rediger was not sure how to continue. "Have you ever heard of 'power to the people'?"

Alinsky politics, Jeff thought. He grinned. "Is that anything like storming the courthouse?"

Goddamn, Rediger thought. He smiled. "No. Not at all. It's kind of a hazy concept that no one quite understands. It was thought up by some brain trust back East. Its premise is that maintenance programs like the ones you administer keep people housed and their bellies filled but don't really deal with or solve the dilemma of poverty."

"That makes sense."

"Yeah. The concept is to empower people, to try to get some power to the powerless."

"Then community action is the political arm of OEO, organizing the poor into political activists," Jeff observed.

Rediger was astounded. "Most folks, even most CAP directors, haven't picked up on that yet. Perhaps I should watch what I say around you."

"No problem with me. I'm not averse to a little activism."

"Well, regardless, I don't know of any CAP, at least any rural CAP, that's had any success in that arena yet."

"If it ain't working, why keep doing it?"

Rediger was becoming annoyed. "Just one reason. The feds tell us what programs they'll fund."

"So much for local control, huh?"

Rediger decided it was time to go. "You'll be a good board member, Mr. Vinton. I'm pleased you're joining us."

"When's the next meeting?"

"In about two weeks. I'll send you a notice."

"Good. Do me a favor. No. Two favors. Send me all the background information you can. Organizational structures, personnel policies, work programs, audit reports, and evaluations. The whole works. Okay?"

Rediger nodded.

"I want to make sure I know what I'm doing while I'm on your board."

"Sure thing." Rediger was wondering what he was getting into. No other board member asked for all that crap. Rising to leave, he held out his hand.

Jeff grasped it and didn't let go. "The second thing. Have your staff contact George Iron Rope in northwest Union. Put him in one of those job training slots you mentioned."

"I don't know, Mr. Vinton. There are pretty strict eligibility criteria."

"Don't worry. He's eligible."

"Well, we'll have to find a work station. And it must be in a government or nonprofit organization. Frankly, Mr. Vinton, I haven't seen many Indians in county or municipal jobs around here, or even in your office."

Jeff ignored the comment. "Do what you can, and give me a report before our board meeting. Just call me. Okay?"

"I'll do what I can about Iron Rope."

"Good. I'm sure you and our organization can help Mr. Iron Rope. And, Rediger, I'll try to do a good job for you."

"Thanks, Mr. Vinton."

Rediger got in his car, an uneasiness overcoming him. He started the engine, pulling out into the street, thinking aloud. "That is one crazy sonofabitch." He headed for the nearest bar on the outskirts of Union.

He ordered a bourbon on the rocks as his eyes became accustomed to the darkness. Looking around, he saw there were only a few people in the place. Rediger picked up his drink and went to the pay telephone. It rang but once. Pleased at the receptionist's promptness, he listened as she responded.

"Good afternoon. This is your Community Action Program."

A professional sounding voice, Rediger thought. He disguised his voice. "May I speak to the director?"

"Yes, sir. One moment please."

129

A few seconds later, another feminine voice answered, this one lower, earthier. "Mr. Rediger's office."

"Hi, love. How you doing?"

"Johnny," she responded, "she told me the call was for you."

"I know. I was just checking out the dumb broad. She did okay."

"You sure you weren't checking on me," she asked, humor in her voice.

"Yeah. I was just thinking I oughta check you out some more. Can you get away for a few days? Big meeting in Dallas, you know."

"Hey, I'd like that. When can we go?"

"If you can, get us a flight out this evening."

"For sure I will! What should I say the meeting is?"

"Oh Christ, think of something. I don't care."

"You know it's getting kinda hard, coming up with the names of meetings."

"That's one of the reasons I pay you so goddamn much: your productive imagination."

"What're the others?"

"You're kinda cute, and an easy lay."

Jan laughed. "It's a good thing you're into poverty and not diplomacy. How many days?"

"Schedule us back Friday afternoon."

"Sounds great."

"I'm at a bar outside Union. My suitcase is in the trunk. I'll call you in an hour from down the road. Get us on the earliest flight after five. I'll meet you at the airport. And, love, make goddamn sure you get our travel advances. I'm broke."

"I'm already looking forward to Big D. I'll give you our itinerary when you call."

"Okay, love."

"I can't wait, Johnny. Christ, I hope my old man don't get suspicious. This is our third trip in two months."

"That's your problem." Rediger hung up the telephone.

Gulping his drink, he returned to the bar and ordered another. He began anticipating this evening with Jan. He was becoming aroused by the memories of their last trip - to Atlanta - three weeks ago. He finished his drink and purchased a pint of Old Crow. Putting it in his suit pocket, he walked to the car. Patiently, he began driving the hundred miles to the regional airport. He assumed they would be on the six-thirty flight. He opened the bottle, swishing the warm bourbon in his mouth, enjoying the numbness it afforded his gums. He had plenty of time. There was no need to hurry.

***

Milner, his tie loosened and suit coat slung over his shoulder, asked, "What the hell you doing here? It's an hour after quitting time."

"Just catching up on things, and thinking."

"Andrea?"

"Yep."

"I'm looking forward to meeting her and the kids."

"You'll like her, like them."

"Well, I got three more out of Keokuk. That makes a total of nine this month. And my car hasn't broken down yet."

Jeff set aside the file he was working on. "Jerry, have a seat for a minute, can you?"

"We're on my time you know," Milner said, affecting a frown.

"We've got to start thinking food stamps. The board's resolution was forwarded to USDA last week. It'll probably take the feds a couple of months to process it, but we should make plans."

"Who do you want to handle it?"

"You."

Milner remained silent.

"It's a difficult program to administer, so damn many rules and regs, variables, exceptions," Jeff continued. "Because of the BIA checks some of the Indians get, this will be a tougher county than most."

"How long before you need a decision?"

"Pretty quickly."

"Let me think about it. In the meantime, we're on my time. And the county is gonna owe me one helluva mileage check. Let's get out of here. I'll buy you a beer."

"Great."

"That's obviously dependent on your processing my travel claim."

Jeff rose and placed his arm around Milner's shoulder. Both men were tired, but the prospect of some drinking rejuvenated them. They walked to the hotel restaurant and embarked on another fun night.

***

Jeff was marking off the days before he would travel to Galveston. He had crossed out ten since getting Andrea's letter. The wedding date seemed so elusive, so distant, yet each day brought it a little closer. All the forces of the universe seemed to be on his side, causing the time to pass quickly. The days evolved into weeks, and soon the weeks would be months. Thankful that his job was keeping him busy, Jeff marked off one more day from his personal loneliness and emptiness of the present, making these elements a part of his past.

Junior would have some stitches on his upper lip removed next week. The surgeon had done a good job.

George was still hustling spot labor jobs, and his car had made one more trip to the commodity distribution point. He bought a used tire that set him back seven dollars, plus a dollar and a half to have it mounted. John Rediger had been unable to place George in a job-training slot. Jeff's call to him had been unproductive.

Lisa would get her first ADC check next week. Jeff and Evelyn were the only ones in the office who knew.

After negotiating a raise, Milner agreed to head up the food stamp program.

Scott authorized an additional staff member. She was now driving between Union and the state hospitals, saving the county tax dollars, forcing other levels of government to pay more.

Jeff attended his first board meeting of the Community Action Program. He was impressed with the number of programs, the funding levels, the industry and dedication of the staff. Rediger ran a tight ship.

Andrea's long letter was disjointed, contradictory, and confusing. But the last page was filled with love and joy and promise. The photograph she had sent the newspaper was the one that had caused Jeff so much anguish and pleasure. This time, it afforded only joy. The newspaper gave the engagement announcement more space on the society page than Jeff expected.

Oldfield, still wracked with the torture of Lisa's and Jack's failed marriage, joined the other commissioners in congratulating Jeff, then sadly turned away.

CHAPTER FOURTEEN

From the day he announced his candidacy for governor, Bob Elam led in the polls. The last poll Herb Chandler had commissioned was taken four weeks before the primary. The lead had been six points. A UPI poll had given Elam a four percent lead. The pundits judged that to be important because it had been taken three days after the legislature had overridden Norman's veto of LB192. An anti-Norman groundswell was building. But Chandler had been disappointed at the size of the lead. He believed that if the veto had been sustained, Elam would have trailed Norman. In any campaign, it's hard to overcome an initial lead. Chandler now operated on the theory that although there was still much to be done, Robert Temple Elam was one serendipitous sonofabitch.

He was concerned about Elam's initial statewide campaign swing. Bob still wasn't comfortable before reporters. That would kill him. The television journalists would only show the footage revealing his discomfort. It wasn't that the media was in Norman's camp or against Elam; it was just their nature.

To overcome that, Chandler rented a small twin-engine aircraft and scheduled a series of press conferences across the state, starting in the sparsely populated western section. Bob fumbled through the press conference at Union. However, as Chandler expected, except for a single radio station, there was no electronic media. One television cameraman was in Yorkton, the next stop. Bob did better. By the time he arrived in the central part of the state, he was in control. At the press conference in the capital city, with five television stations and numerous reporters and photographers present, Bob was well within his comfort zone; forceful, confident, persuasive. And Pam looked very much like a first lady,

The filing deadline was approaching. Neither candidate faced any opposition from within their parties. Because of Elam's rising popularity within the Democratic Party, Chandler didn't think he would. He did expect someone on the right to challenge Norman in the Republican primary, and he was disappointed that had not happened. There would be no bloodletting in the ranks of the GOP. But Elam was quietly attracting significant numbers of Republicans.

Despite the minor adjustments required during any campaign, the matrix Chandler had produced last summer was still operative. Things were still in accordance with the initial battle plan. Chandler knew what he had to do. Let the momentum gather, maintain the flow of money, and make sure that Bob made no major mistakes.

It was late in the afternoon. Chandler sipped the last of his warm bourbon, snuffed out his cigar, and leaned back in his chair. He had ordered Elam to get away for a few days. Just go somewhere and relax. For the first time in weeks he had his evening free. Not a damn thing for him or Sergent to do. He had already planned the night's activity: retire early, sleep until noon.

With the exception of a two-hour layover at Lambert Field, Bob and Pam were enjoying their flight. The Boeing 707 was on its final approach. Pam looked out the window but only saw wooded and slightly rolling hills. She had expected this area to be suburban with homogenous streets and cul-de-sacs. She was pleased that these woodlands had been protected from developers. Probably federal land, she surmised. The large aircraft tilted slightly. Still, there was no indication of the millions of people who lived in this Northern Virginia corridor. Pam looked out at the other aircraft approaching the airport, each appropriately separated, all converging as if on the spokes of a giant wheel. She thought of the bumpy flight of the campaign's aircraft, her stepping from the small plane, nauseous from each thirty-minute flight, but needing to smile, wave, and be gracious. She nudged Bob. "I'm glad this is Dulles International, not Yorkton Regional."

Bob smiled. "It's gonna be good to be where no one knows us. We can get ourselves lost in this town and not worry about what the hell other folks are thinking."

"It'll be nice."

"We got four full days. I told Herb not to expect us until Monday." He leaned back in his seat and tried to stretch his legs. It was useless; there wasn't room.

Again looking out the airplane's window and spotting the terminal, Pam felt cheated. She wanted her first view of Washington to be from the air. But Dulles was not close to the capital. Disappointed, she leaned back in her seat.

Departing the aircraft, she was pleased with herself. She felt great; no nausea, no queasiness. Flying's not that bad, she told herself, grabbing and holding Bob's hand as they walked through the terminal.

They boarded the shuttle bus after getting their luggage. The ride lasted forty minutes. They were well within the Beltway before she saw some of the anticipated landmarks.

At their hotel, the doorman loaded their luggage on a cart before Bob suggested he could carry them. After checking in and arriving at the room on the tenth floor, Bob begrudgingly tipped the bellhop.

Pam went to the window and pulled the drapes. The seat of the national government was before her, brilliantly pearl white. While Bob unpacked, Pam sat before the window and stared at the magnificence of the U.S. Capitol.

Bob glanced at her from time to time. She continued to be mesmerized. Only when Bob was out of the shower and dressed did Pam move from the window. As the flight had been tiring, they decided to eat in the hotel restaurant. Pam carefully chose the dress she would wear and took an inordinate amount of time applying her makeup.

As they entered the dining room, Pam surveyed the patrons, hoping to spot a face she had seen on television. Even as they were led to a table, she refused to give up. Surely in this large restaurant there must be at least one congressman.

Bob wasn't sure if he should tell her that the restaurant was only filled with businessmen, tourists, and bureaucrats; that the faces she might recognize would not be here. He let her continue her search. After dinner and drinks, they realized how tired they were and returned to their room.

Pam again marveled at the view, Bob once going to her and gently massaging her shoulders. When Pam finally closed the drapes, Bob was in bed, going over memos from Chandler, then making changes to a speech, and checking the latest poll. Six percentage points seemed to be a safe lead, but the eighteen percent of undecided respondents bothered him.

Pam returned from the bathroom and slipped into bed, nuzzling beside him as he placed the memoranda in his briefcase. He then reviewed correspondence from his CPA. Pam, disappointed at his concentration first on the campaign, now on profit-and-loss statements, shifted in the bed, more closely compressing against him. Bob put his arm around her shoulder, continuing to read spreadsheets.

She shifted her head, intently looked at Bob but failing to catch his eye. It became a challenge. She traced her long fingers across his chest, sometimes entwining them within his chest hair. His expression remained unchanged; his concentration intent. Pam continued lightly touching his chest, from time to time reaching up to kiss his nose and cheek then his chest and nipples. He shifted his large frame slightly, but that gave Pam an indication she was succeeding. She again kissed his chest. Bob sat up straighter and placed his hand on her head, compressing her hair, enabling him to continue reading. She rested her head against him, became more bold, more decisive. She moved her hand downward, touching his special parts for long enough to ensure he was fully aroused. She relaxed and laid close to him, looking impishly into his eyes.

Bob looked away from his papers and at her, seriously at first, almost sternly. Then he smiled. "I love you dearly, Pam, but tell me, what's got into you?"

"I don't know. Kind of a rebirth."

"Don't get me wrong. I'm not knocking it. Hell, I'm damned appreciative."

"Good." She again kissed his chest. Several moments of silence followed. Then, in a serious voice she said, "I've thought about this, about me, about us. I think I've traced my libido's renaissance to that night you first told me we were going to run for governor. And since then, as you might have noticed, it's only intensified."

"I've noticed," Bob said, taking her into his arms. "I should have run for office years ago."

"Poor Bob," Pam purred, her eyes sparkling. "Tonight I'm going to make up for all those years of deprivation."

***

It was after nine when Bob awoke. He reached for Pam but only touched the sheets where she had lain. He thought of Pam's innovations from the previous night and yearned for her again. He looked toward the window, expecting to see her there. She wasn't in the room. He leisurely shaved and then got dressed. Fully rested, he enjoyed his acute awareness that he had no meetings, no speeches scheduled. Nothing. He called room service for coffee and a newspaper. He walked to the window where Pam had spent so much time. It was a magnificent view. He looked down to the sidewalk, thinking he might see her, but saw only a few people walking about. Answering the rap on his door, he signed for the coffee and paper, poured a cup and sat down to read. He was a bit intrigued by a news item about ITT lobbyist Dita Beard being spirited off to Denver, but another knock on the door interrupted him. He rose and opened it for Pam.

"I forgot my key," she said, kissing him. "And I really enjoyed our activities last night," her tongue tracing her upper lip.

"It was a fun night, worthy of redoing. Where you been?"

She smiled. "Walking the Capitol grounds. It's only a couple of blocks away. And then halfway down the Mall toward the Washington Monument. God, these blocks are long, and God, my feet are sore."

They seldom used a taxi for the next two days, walking, it seemed, the width and breadth of the city. They stood before the Lincoln Memorial, toured the White House, shopped at the Watergate, spent hours at the Smithsonian, looked at Lafayette's and Kosciusko's statues on the Square, visited Kennedy's grave at Arlington. But before returning to the hotel they would sit on a marble bench, resting and enjoying the grandeur of the Capitol. Pam suspected that Bob was captivated by this magnificent structure and the activities it housed. She wondered if he was looking beyond his years as governor. A congressman? Damn! Pam thought as she became sexually alive again. She smiled, pleased with her recharged libido.

Later, remembering that Pam wished to see Washington from the air, Bob changed airlines, getting a flight out of National. They waited until the last minute at the airport, reluctant to board. They had been able to devote themselves totally to each other. Bob realized this was the first time they had been alone since Pam had been pregnant with their son. He regretted he hadn't done this sooner, sharing time with her and no one else.

Once aboard, Pam took the window seat. Minutes later the aircraft raced down the runway, then climbed steeply. They were on the starboard side and thus afforded a view of the city. Pam stared out the window until the aircraft began banking, assuming a westerly direction. Bob tried to stretch his legs, finally situating himself diagonally, his legs intruding into Pam's space. He dozed for several hours until the aircraft began descending. Awake, he realized how badly his leg muscles had tightened. He smiled, thinking of Pam, her excitement, her insistence on walking from each interest point to the next. He suspected she was suffering from the same discomfort but would never mention it. He looked forward to getting home.

They had needed the respite from the campaign, and they were rejuvenated when they arrived home. But they hadn't been there for long when Chandler called. Pam answered and spoke briefly with Herb before handing the phone to Bob.

"Hello, Herb."

"Hi, Bob, welcome home. I hope you're rested."

"Feeling great."

"Good. What time can I see you?"

"What's best for you?"

"Nine o'clock breakfast at the Enterprize."

"Fine."

"Bob, I got our schedule for the last few weeks before the primary. When you see it, you'll know why I sent you away for a few days."

"But, Herb, I can't lose. I'm the only Democrat running."

"I know. But we want to win big. To do that, we have to energize the Democrats. That means we work every night. Plus, we want to make inroads into the GOP and the independents. Anyway, don't get discouraged. I'll explain tomorrow."

"Okay."

Bob turned to Pam, "Welcome back to the campaign. Herb wants to discuss our schedule for the next few weeks. He says it's pretty tight. I'm to meet him in the morning."

"I'll be so damned glad when this is over," said Pam. Then she thought for a moment. "The election isn't 'til November. Hell! We've got over five more months of this."

Bob looked at her, troubled by what she was saying and thinking.

"Have you ever wished you hadn't got us into this, Bob?"

"No. It'll be worthwhile. I've no regrets."

"It appears we're going to win. What changes will you make?"

"Well, after I get my cabinet officers on board - Did I mention Chandler's heading up an executive search committee? - I'll make sure they know what they're doing, then work on restructuring. A professor at the college is doing a study on that. His initial judgment indicates we can provide more services at less cost. That is if we can stop our departments from competing with each other. This state desperately needs a command and control system. That'll be my first priority. But that's a tough one. To get it done, the legislators will have to cooperate, and if Jake Hammond's typical, they're one crazy bunch."

"Jake Hammond. Have you heard from him since I, since we were up at the ranch?"

"No, my dear, but we will. We will."

The legislators were on break. So were the lobbyists. Thus, the Enterprize Club was nearly empty when Bob entered. Nonetheless, Herb had reserved a room for them to meet. Bob was escorted to the room. Herb and Sergent were enjoying their coffee when Bob entered.

Herb stood to greet him. "Hey, Bob, you look real good. Where'd you get that tan?"

Elam rubbed his hand from his cheekbones to chin, holding it there. "We went to Washington. The weather was beautiful, and Pam insisted we walk everywhere. My leg muscles are still sore, but you're right, I got some sun."

"You look great."

Bob sat, Sergent serving him coffee, Chandler handing him an itinerary. The first item was "Primary-1" and its activities. The last entry was "Primary-20".

"Okay, an overview," Chandler said. "You'll note we're going to concentrate on the Democratic strongholds, the liberal farm groups, factories, union picnics, the Faculty Club. We got a full day scheduled for ethnic neighborhoods, the Irish, Italians, Hispanics. Note P-13. You speak before the Public Employees Union. That's gonna be a tough one 'cause the media are sure to be there, taking notes. We advised the union leadership you won't have time for questions - a quick shoot-in-shoot-out. Chandler stretched his arm toward Sergent. Bill, where's the speech for that?"

Sergent produced a manila envelope from his briefcase. He took out copies of the speech and handed them to Elam and Chandler, keeping one for himself.

"Professor Vogt's doing the white paper on reorganization. He drafted this for you," Chandler explained. "He attended a couple of your speaking engagements and patterned the speech to your style. It's damned good. What you pledge here is no reduction in the work force, but more work, more job satisfaction. No mention of a pay increase. Don't ad-lib it. We've thus far kept your liberalism a secret. Let's keep it that way."

Bob smiled. "Hell, don't worry about me. I halfway believe the stuff I'm saying."

They all laughed. Chandler, though, had an odd look on his face. It didn't change as he motioned Sergent to respond to the rapping on the door. Sergent let the waiter in. They were served fruit salad, mushroom omelets, sausages, and English muffins. Their coffee cups and water glasses were filled every few minutes. The discussion throughout the meal was light, nonpolitical. Bob was surprised they didn't continue plotting out his campaign. Several times he looked at the waiter, thinking he might be the reason. He looked innocent enough. Surely it wasn't him. Regardless, Bob dutifully followed Chandler's lead, talking about the trip to Washington. The moment the meal was finished, the waiter cleared the table, replenished the coffee and water pitchers, and left.

Chandler went back to the schedule. "Now, Bob, we're gonna skip the smaller communities for now. We'll hit the urban areas and the suburbs hard. Once the primary is over, and before we get to the general, I'll want to see you in every backwater town this state has. But now we go with the big groups and population centers. Okay, on P-3 you're gonna address the State Education Association. Now, realize this union has got tentacles in every goddamned town that's got a schoolhouse and schoolmarm. In the smaller towns the teachers are the community's leaders. Hell, in some towns they're the only ones with a degree. Politically, they're the mother lode. We know the association's president. He's our boy, so you'll get a good reception."

Chandler stopped, sipped his coffee. "And Pam will love this," he continued. "We're going to rent the airplane again, starting in Union, crossing the state, ending up in the capital. Now every area we hit, the county chairman is going to have a large crowd for us. This will be a dry run for the general. We'll see which of these guys can produce. For those who can't, we'll send out our people for the general. We can't draft a speech for each stop, so you'll have only an outline to go by. Mix it up at each stop, ad-lib, but speak only in generalities. Okay?"

Bob nodded.

"Good. Let's go over the Farmers Union speech. I'm not sure how familiar you are with what's happening in the hinterlands, but a lot of eastern money has been coming in and buying farmland. They ain't doing it as individuals, and they sure as hell ain't moving their families out here. And they're using some pretty exotic financing mechanisms, things like limited partnerships. Now normally that's used for highly speculative ventures, like a Broadway play, or buying a goddamn baseball team. Only now they're buying farmland. In this speech you say we need a Family Farm Act to ensure local ownership of the land. Read the final sentence of the speech."

Bob went to the last page. "When we win, I assure you that you, the steward, the producer of food, fuel, and fiber, will be the one casting your shadow on the land you work, and love, and own." Bob looked at Chandler. "That's good, Herb."

"You're damned right it is. That's why you're paying me so damned much." He handed Bob a report. "This will be your homework tonight. There's about sixty pages of stuff. After you've gone through it, you'll know what a center pivot is, what the price supports on dairy products are, and what parity is. Bob, it's dry stuff, but know it and understand it. Okay?"

Bob noted that the state university seal was printed on the cover. He thumbed through its pages and placed it in his briefcase. He nodded at Herb, promising he would get through it that night.

"Good. Okay, Sergent, it's your turn."

"Right. Bob, we got a TV appearance for you on P-10, Saturday morning. You can relax 'cause not many people watch television at that hour. Usually the kids watch cartoons. But they're gonna ask some tough questions. It'll be good practice. We left four hours on P-11 for you. We'll do a mock news conference to see just how good you are. Now look at the agenda on P-13... That's gonna be a watershed..."

Sergent's staccato delivery became overpowering. Bob felt weary, as if he and Pam had not gotten away, as if there had been no break to this madness. He recalled Pam asking if he really wanted this. He told himself again that he did. He tried to listen intently as Sergent spoke of critical dates, critical meetings, critical people. Everything, it seemed, was critical.

Bob left the Enterprize in a daze. The breakfast meeting that had extended into the afternoon had returned him too abruptly to this life he had chosen. He thought of his homework as he drove home; the memorizing of terms, numbers, state Democratic central committee members, county chairs, vice chairs, treasurers, Democratic mayors, county commissioners, village chairmen, influential Republicans who had come over. Christ! He arrived home and looked at Pam. Damn her! She was still refreshed from their trip. She could tell he was not. She went to him, hugged him, asked if he wanted a drink.

"Just iced tea, Pam. I'm gonna take a shower. Put it on the vanity, would you? Thanks - and I love you."

Pam felt sad as she watched her husband walk to the bathroom. Their vacation was surely over. "Is there anything wrong, Bob?" she asked softly.

He turned, smiled, and said, "No. Everything's going real well."

CHAPTER FIFTEEN

Their faces revealed an unresolved frustration and betrayed an advanced level of intoxication. Each had served his country by militating against the war and shouting Ho-Ho, Ho-Chi-Minh, becoming nauseous in Chicago, bleeding at Kent State. They were true rebels, unshaken in their knowledge about how things were and how things should be. They had dreamt George Bernard Shaw's dream and were daily asking, "Why not?" They believed their dream must soon become reality. They developed loyalties to losing causes, were the products of JFK's climate of idealism, and existed in the despair of Nixon's miasma of cynicism.

Sitting on the apartment floor, their brashness of a few minutes ago yielded to silence. This was one of their get-togethers. They gathered twice a month to vent their frustrations, each driving over a hundred miles in their gray GSA sedans.

Now the purging was over. They would soon curl up in their sleeping bags, let the early morning hours dissipate the alcohol, then return to the communities the CAP had assigned them.

Dave Goldman, from Delaware, graduate of the University of Pennsylvania, broke the silence. He asked Ron Millard why he hadn't joined the Peace Corps.

Millard, an engineer from Ohio with credentials from Berkeley, looked hazily at Goldman. "This nation isn't being threatened by the natives in Ethiopia or Peru. There's no sense trying to export economic justice 'til we achieve some semblance of it here. VISTA's where the action is, not the Peace Corps."

"But really," Goldman countered, "doesn't Kuala Lumpur or Rangoon or Bangkok sound a bit more exotic, even a bit more erotic, than Union or Yorkton?"

"Yeah. But the hypocrisy would be too great. We'd better get our act together here before we try to fix the rest of the world."

"Yeah, but I'd much rather deal with a satrap over there than the bum we've got here."

"You mean Rediger?"

144

"Rediger."

Bill Jefferson, an agri-economics graduate from Michigan State, the newest, the quietest, the most conservative member of the group, pondered for a moment, then joined the discussion, "Did I tell you what he said to me when I first got here?"

Goldman shook his head. "No," Millard said.

"Well, I guess it's because of my name. Anyway, I get off the plane not knowing anyone and this short guy rushes over to me - I was the only young guy getting off. He grabs my hand, introduces himself, asks if I'm a VISTA, and says - these were his exact words, so help me God - he said, 'Jesus Christ it's good to see you. I was afraid you'd be a goddamn nigger'." Jefferson sat back, expecting laughter. There was none. Goldman continued staring at his boots. Millard kept his eye contact with Jefferson. More silence engulfed the domestic Peace Corps men.

"Of course the whole area's hopeless," Millard finally ventured, "and in the agency it's obvious that Rediger's the problem. Is there anything we can do about him?"

"He's got the board of directors in his pocket because they don't know what's going on," Jefferson offered. "I tried to get to one board member. As I spoke with her, she told me the governing board was only an advisory board. I just walked away."

"Christ," Goldman muttered.

"Who's the new guy from Harney County?" Jefferson asked.

"I checked him out. His name's Vinton. He's a goddamn welfare director," Goldman answered.

"So what? That doesn't automatically make him a bad guy."

Dave Goldman sharply responded to Jefferson. "Yeah it does. I've seen the way Indians live there, in dirt-floor shacks, no plumbing, about zero square feet per person."

"On that footage - is that give or take ten percent?" Jefferson asked.

Goldman ignored him. Not even a smile. "No welfare director with any humanity would allow people to live like that."

"There must be someone on the board. Rediger's got to go," Jefferson offered.

"Why don't the three of us speak to the board at the next meeting?" Millard suggested.

"No. If we said anything meaningful, Rediger would fire us, and they'd never get any more VISTAs," Jefferson countered.

"Yeah, we have to rule that out," Goldman agreed.

"So where does that leave us?" Jefferson asked.

"Well, we could declare Rediger anathema and excommunicate," Millard said.

"What else?" Goldman wondered.

"We could transfer to the Peace Corps," Millard suggested.

"With our luck, we'd be assigned to Saigon," Goldman said.

"I said the Peace Corps, not the War Corps," Millard parried.

"Come on!" Jefferson shot back. "I've watched this guy Vinton. He's a little stodgy, but I'm not willing to write him off. What've we got to lose?"

"Our training was pretty clear on that. Welfare workers are part of the problem." Goldman was adamant.

"What the hell," Jefferson persisted. "You live in that little town on the county line."

Goldman looked up, then relented. "Okay. But while I'm seeing the sonofabitch, you'd better come up with Plan B."

"Let's face it. We're wasting a year of our lives out here," Millard said. "But it's an education. We're learning how the system works. It gives the appearance of movement, but it's designed not to work, only to provide employment to a few poverty barons."

"Is that your better plan?" Goldman asked.

"You see Vinton. If nothing comes of that, we'll start our summer offensive," Jefferson concluded.

"I'll see the sonofabitch tomorrow," Goldman said.

***

This time George and Mary came to meet Vinton as he drove up to Annie's and Horace's home. Vinton saw them walking across the open field followed by their sons. It was late afternoon, and they were perspiring when they got to him.

"Hi. How's it going? And how's Junior?" Jeff knelt down to Junior's eye level. "Gosh darn, the doc did a good job." He went over and shook the hand of their other son, then turned to George and Mary.

"We are grateful," George began. "And Junior, who won't remember how he was when he's grown up, is grateful." Mary looked at her husband with unabashed pride. He had said those words just as he had practiced them.

"Well, good! Junior sure is a handsome lad. But I'm concerned about Dee and her kids, and Grandma and Grandpa Red Shirt." Vinton wondered how George would react to his referring to the Red Shirts as grandparents. George didn't seem to notice.

"Yeah," George said.

"It must be hot and crowded. I want to get Dee out of there."

"How? Where would she go?"

"Get her some money through ADC so she can get an apartment."

"Okay," George responded. He reached to shake Vinton's hand. His grip was strong, signaling a bond between them.

"George, I brought the application with me. Let's get it signed so she can get her first check next month."

George nodded. He went to the door, opened it, allowing numerous houseflies to escape. "Dee, Mr. Vinton wants to see you."

Dee appeared moments later. Jeff went to her, extended his hand. Dee became flustered. Seeing this, he withdrew his hand. She looked at him with a meek smile.

"Dee, we're gonna get you some money so you can get your own place. Okay?"

She looked to George. He nodded. She looked back at Vinton, saying nothing.

Jeff leaned inside his car and pulled a yellow pad from his briefcase. "Where were you born, Dee?"

"On the reservation."

"When?"

"June third, nineteen forty-nine."

"How many children?"

"Four." She listed their names, birthdates, and places of birth – all in Union.

"Here at the hospital?"

"No." Dee looked confused, guilty.

"Where?"

"Right here." She pointed to the Red Shirt home.

147

"Was a nurse with you?"

"Just grandma and her friend who does that."

Jeff wondered if there was a goddamned form for this. "Was grandma the, ah, the …" He searched for the word.

"Midwife," Mary interjected.

"Yeah, midwife." His last question was unnecessary. "There are no birth certificates?"

Dee looked away again with more shame.

"Do you have a birth certificate?"

"No."

"Okay. Sign here." He gave her the multicolored form. "This may be a bit tricky. I'm not sure what we're gonna use for birth certificates. Was there a baptism or anything…?" He sensed her discomfort. "That's okay. We'll work it out."

Dee returned to the house, relieved she had completed her meeting with the welfare worker. George would explain to her what she had signed. She took pride in how neatly she had written her name. It was, after all, a government paper.

George walked hesitantly to Vinton. He started to address Jeff as "Mister," then decided not to. "Uh, Jeff, a few families asked how I got Junior fixed. I told them. They want to meet you to get their kids fixed."

He was anxious. If George could help these families, it would elevate his standing in the Indian community. Two families were of the Deer clan, historically superior to George's. He wanted to use Vinton to strengthen his leadership position, to lessen the rivalry among the clans. A lot depended on Jeff's response. "Could I set up a meeting, let them meet you, and see if you could help the kids?" George's voice was apprehensive.

Preoccupied by the problems that Dee's application entailed, Jeff didn't notice the anxiety in George's voice. Accepting the question at face value, he told George to set up the meetings. Then he thought of Rediger.

"George, did anyone from the CAP contact you?"

"From where?"

"From an action agency. About a job?"

George shook his head. But what was Jeff was talking about? A

148

job? George was afraid of saying the wrong thing, jeopardizing whatever Jeff was talking about. "No. What job?"

"Let me check it out. We'll talk later." That son of a bitch! Jeff thought. He drove to his office, becoming angrier with every mile. He called the CAP the moment he arrived and asked for the executive director.

An earthy voice responded. "Mr. Rediger's office." Jeff identified himself and asked for Rediger.

"I'm sorry, Mr. Vinton, Mr. Rediger is escorting officials from the U.S. Department of Labor. They're inspecting some job training sites in the target areas. May I ask that he call you?"

"Yeah. Do that." Jeff hung up the phone.

He sat back, frustrated with a feeling of betrayal. Well, he thought, I'm one of eighteen board members, one of Rediger's bosses. I'll give him another week before bringing it up at a board meeting. He then turned to the notes he had taken while talking to Dee. He wondered how he could bureaucratically prove the existence of Dee's children.

***

Millard left Jefferson's apartment before Goldman and Jefferson awoke. Goldman, not eager to see Vinton, spent the morning and early afternoon with Jefferson, then got into his GSA vehicle and drove to Union. Turning his attention to the countryside, he was overwhelmed by its emptiness. Back home, one town easily merged with another, separated only by a small sign delineating one from another. Out here, towns took on the appearance of major communities; communities whose existence were difficult to understand.

Heading down the highway, Goldman allowed his mind to wander. In the time he had been assigned to Harney County he had developed a friendship with several American Indians. And during his idle time he had driven across the broad expanse of the land, mesmerized by its stark and monotonous beauty. He had developed a deep appreciation for why the Oglala had tenaciously fought to repel the intruders a hundred years ago. He recalled their stories about Brevet Gen. Lawrence T. Harney, U.S. Cavalry, Harney County's eponym. Harney had been credited with a minor victory in the war with the Plains

Indians. In the late 1880s, troops under his command had killed some three hundred Indians in a dusty and remote little valley. The Oglala descendants of the victims agreed with historians about the number. The slain, however, were women and children, the helpless and infirm.

Goldman had learned to respect the American Indians. No one loves a drunken Indian, but he discovered that those who became alcoholics had done so unknowingly, innocently, and from a richly deserved sense of hopelessness.

A quarter-pint of whiskey consumed by a twelve-year-old at night would numb him from the winter cold and the '54 Ford that was his bedroom. It would allow him to mercifully fall asleep. Liquor would then insulate the teenager against the racism, the poverty, the lack of opportunities. Then the young parent, seeing his plight perpetuated in his children, would come to rely on the effects of liquor to cover himself, as a blanket, from his world of hopelessness.

Dave didn't love drunken Indians, but he shared an empathy with them that no one in this area had felt before.

Goldman observed the proud Indians with a sense of wonder: living in jerrybuilt shacks, sweeping their dirt floors, working menial jobs. Surviving and procreating, guaranteeing the continuance of the race. He also observed the cultural pride and the silent hatred for the imposed white society.

Goldman slowed as he reached the outskirts of Union. He noted the skyline: water towers and granaries. Christ, he thought, thinking of the skylines back East. He looked at his watch. It was after four. He drove straight to the courthouse.

He sat impatiently as Evelyn told Vinton a VISTA wished to see him. Moments later, his tie loosened and shirtsleeves rolled up, Vinton came out to meet Goldman. Shaking his hand, Vinton led Goldman to his office, offering a chair. Goldman lifted the chair and moved it to a corner of the office, sat, and stared at Vinton.

Moments passed. Neither spoke. To evidence further disrespect, Goldman slouched in the chair. He looked at the welfare director more closely. The guy looked decent, almost caring. But he knew that couldn't be. No decent person would be affiliated with this office in this county and allow the inhuman indecencies to continue. The guy's a phony, a con man, a politician who will survive the bureaucratic wars, uncompromising regulations, and cries of the poor. He's here to support the needs, prejudices, and economic security of the crummy middle class. These thoughts gave Goldman a sense of moral superiority.

Vinton was angered by Rediger's indifference to George's situation. It had been a month, and Rediger hadn't even sent anyone to see George. Now this VISTA comes and sits in a corner sulking.

"There's obviously a reason you're here. Perhaps you could tell me just what the hell it is," Vinton said.

Goldman disdainfully continued staring, then lightened the mood. "I'd like to talk about the CAP."

"What's your affiliation with the agency?"

"Pretty minimal. They sponsor me. I report to them."

"Sounds more than minimal to me." Jeff paused. "VISTA's like the Peace Corps, ain't it?"

"Yeah. Our service is stateside."

"I don't know if you know, but I've just been appointed to the CAP's governing board."

Goldman nodded acknowledgment. He did say "governing board." That was encouraging.

"What do you think of the agency's effectiveness?" Jeff asked.

"It's got its problems."

"What are they?"

"That's why I'm here, to tell you."

"Tell me."

"A long story."

Jeff looked at his desk, the stacked papers, the case histories, the completed applications, the thirty-two cases he would present to the commissioners. What the hell, he thought, it's nearly quitting time. "Let's go get a beer."

"I'd like that. But I also want to talk about Harney County."

"Okay," Vinton said, leading Goldman from the office. "How long you been here?"

"About six months. You?"

"A few months longer."

Goldman walked beside Jeff. He was surprised. He had assumed the welfare director had been here a lot longer. That unsettled him; injected a new element. It upset his uncluttered perception. His stereotype might not hold. Goldman entertained the notion that maybe Vinton wasn't a bad guy. If this guy is for real, he thought, what was it like before?

Entering the cocktail lounge, the welfare director of Harney County and the VISTA volunteer from OEO sat and ordered two beers. It wasn't until after they had gotten the drinks that Vinton broke the silence. "Dave, I read your signals. I admit it. Things are pretty bad around here."

Dave looked at Vinton, said nothing.

Jeff rejoined Dave's cold stare. "Now just when the hell are you glory boys from OEO gonna get off your asses and do something?"

Goldman's eyes flashed with anger. "Me? When am I gonna get off my ass?"

Vinton's stare warmed. He smiled, then quietly laughed. Goldman, still taken aback, was unsure what his reaction should be. Then, sensing the irony, joined Vinton in the laughter.

"Tell me about the agency," Vinton said. "You say it's got problems?"

"The agency is screwed up from top to bottom. There are some good people there, but there's no direction. They don't know what to do, so they do very little. They sit around drinking coffee, chatting with each other. There's a terrible inertia. The problem is that Rediger has no vision, no idea what the agency should be doing. In fact, he's usually traveling somewhere, to the regional office, the state capital, Washington, various meetings. I'll bet he's gone half the time." Dave stopped and sipped his beer, looked at Vinton.

Jeff thought of the sensual voice he had heard that afternoon. He was going to ask if Rediger traveled alone but thought that would be tacky. "The agency must be doing something. I was at a board meeting. The reports seemed to be okay."

"It runs the canned programs; manpower training, outreach and referral, planning, several multipurpose centers. But it's motion without movement."

"What should the CAP be doing?" Jeff asked.

"That's a tough question. It damn near has carte blanche. It could do damn near anything."

Jeff looked at Dave, encouraging him to say more.

Instead, Dave sipped more of his beer. Christ, he thought, I got this guy listening to me, and I don't know what to say.

Finally Jeff spoke. "Look, Dave, you say the CAP's screwed up but you offer nothing, not even a suggestion of where to look. You know, maybe you got a thing with this guy Rediger, and maybe he has to go to those meetings or maybe not, but it appears that neither of us know. You give me something verifiable and I might go to bat. But you've got to give me something."

Dave looked at Jeff. "You're right. I'll get something."

"Who's the federal contact? Maybe he could tell me something."

"Yeah. That would be Larry Ashton. I've met him a couple of times. Don't know much about him."

"I'll call him to get acquainted. How about another beer?"

Goldman was embarrassed that he hadn't been better prepared. "No, I have to be going."

"Okay, but one thing you can do for me is get some paper, some information, on the agency. I asked Rediger, but he hasn't sent anything."

"Yeah, I can do that. I suppose you mean program proposals, internal policies, that sort of thing."

"Yeah, I'd appreciate it. Anything else about the CAP?"

"I wasn't very prepared, was I?" Goldman said.

"Nope."

"You seem to be an okay sort of guy."

"Looks are deceiving."

"Yeah. I tell you what. There're two other VISTAs. We'll get together, get our act together, then meet with you. Okay?"

"Sure. Anytime."

Disappointed with himself, Goldman finished his beer, shook Jeff's hand and left. Vinton left a few minutes later, wondering if Andrea might like this place.

***

George knew that Regis Rides Horse Well's son Joseph had a harelip. With Junior's face improving, he, George Iron Rope, was to become the unofficial liaison between the plastic surgeon, Jeff Vinton, and the Rides Horse Well family.

George had spent hours pondering how to best use the healing and helping powers of Vinton's office. He considered the hard-nosed, no-nonsense approach. "I can do these things for you and your family. In return I want these things..."

This would allow him to quickly build a power base; allow him to assert himself as the critical link between state and federal programs and the American Indians of Harney County. As long as he could make the appointments and be present at the meetings, he could parlay his brokerage services into a long list of IOUs. He knew that Vinton was too busy to keep track of all those events. Furthermore, the Indians were too fearful of the wasicu's redoubtable government to initiate their own contacts or ask too many questions.

George knew he had the moxie to pull it off. And as each family had its children attended to, obtained medical services, and received ADC payments, George would be viewed as the one responsible for their good fortunes. Word would get back to the reservation of the good things he was doing for his people. "His people." It had a nice ring.

"Hello, Joseph. Is your daddy home?"

The tribal chairman would contact George to see how he was getting these things done for his people. George would tell him how many he had helped, and the tribal chairman might get him a job with the BIA or at least the tribal government. He could move his family into publicly-financed housing on the reservation: a real floor, running water, a toilet.

Regis Rides Horse Well came out of his hut. "Hi, George," he said in Lakota.

"Hello, Reggie." As George spoke, the exploitation of friendships, the machinations, the fantasizing, the illusions of power all melted away. He could only be himself. He told Regis of how Jeff Vinton had helped his son, how he was willing to help others, how this wasicu was different, how he could get help for little Joseph.

Regis had heard that Junior's face had been fixed, but the tribal culture had kept him from going to George, who was a member of the Wolf clan, for help. The Wolf clan had always camped toward the end of the J-shaped encampment. His clan bivouacked closer to the chief's clan. History and degrees of nobility and rank and prestige, die hard.

Regis couldn't bring himself to seek help from a member of an inferior clan. But now George was here, offering assistance, asking nothing for himself. Regis called for his wife to join them. Upon hearing what George had to say, she openly wept.

***

Jeff marked more days off his calendar. July was fast approaching. Jeff and Jerry Milner spent much of the week with state and USDA officials going over food stamp procedures. Although Jeff appeared to be attentive, he spent much of the time thinking of Andrea. She had written about the furniture her parents were giving them, that the moving company wanted to schedule a delivery date. She had pointedly told Jeff that she needed an address. He had to rent a home.

Vinton had complete faith in Milner's adept bureaucratic mind. He was not concerned, after the officials left, that he knew very little about the food stamp program's administration. Directors delegate. He would delegate. Milner would be responsible for the program.

During that week, the new caseworker had made another trip to Keokuk. In all, the welfare office had relocated more than fifty patients. The savings to the county was over $200,000.

Jeff left his office Friday afternoon and drove to his apartment. Rather than eat out, he heated a frozen dinner in the oven and watched the evening news. McGovern had won two more primaries that week. The Democrats, it seemed to him, were behaving like lemmings – heading for a political debacle. Jeff decided to spend the weekend looking for a home for his family. He went to bed early but didn't sleep well.

George Iron Rope was waiting when Vinton arrived at his office early Monday morning. Before Jeff could pour coffee, George told him of three families whose children had cleft palates. Jeff appreciatively listened as George explained how he had approached the families, what he had told them, the families' heartrending responses.

This guy is doing my job, Jeff thought. He's lining up clients for me. Christ, I should pay him for what he's doing. As George spoke, Jeff thought of what Goldman had told him about the CAP: canned programs, multipurpose centers, planning, outreach and referral. Hell,

George was his outreach worker. Jeff could call Rediger, get a manpower training slot, hire George, and put him to work. Why the hell not? His expression changed abruptly. George sensed it. He stopped in midsentence, looking apprehensive.

Ignoring him, Jeff called Evelyn, asked her to get Rediger. George obviously met the eligibility requirements. But maybe all the slots were filled. He didn't want George to think he had a job for him only to have that expectation dashed. He had to get George out of his office. His telephone rang. He picked it up and spoke to Evelyn. "Is he there?"

"No, but his secretary is still on the line. She says he'll be in about ten."

"Let me speak with her."

"Sure, she's on line three."

"This is Mr. Vinton. How may I reach Rediger?"

The sensual voice, smooth as silk, responded, "Mr. Rediger cannot be reached by phone. He's monitoring the agency's multipurpose centers. May I have him call you?"

"Please do, and within the half hour." Jeff paused, then to underscore his anger, asked, "Do you understand?"

"Yes, sir."

Jeff hung up the phone and looked at George. "Sorry about the interruption. I'm gonna get a call soon. You need to leave when it comes. Okay?"

George, still apprehensive, nodded.

"Good. Now go on. It sounds interesting."

"Well, that's about it. Three kids with harelips. I told them you would meet with the families and try to help their kids."

"Good."

"Can I set up the meetings?"

Jeff looked at his calendar. His telephone rang. Evelyn's voice betrayed a touch of humor. "That didn't take long."

"Tell him I'll be with him in a moment." Jeff turned to George. "I'm gonna have to throw you out now. What's your schedule this morning?" George was surprised. No one ever assumed he had a schedule. He shrugged his shoulders.

"Come back in a half hour." After George left, Jeff spoke coldly into his receiver. "This is Mr. Vinton."

156

"Mr. Vinton, this is John Rediger. I checked with my office and my executive secretary said you called. What can I do for you?"

Hell, he probably was working, Jeff thought. "Yeah, John, thanks for getting back to me so soon. I want to ask how we're doing with George Iron Rope?"

"That's a tough one. I've had my people looking all over Union for a job site for him."

"And no luck, huh?"

"Not a damn thing, Mr. Vinton."

"As I understand it, you got the slot, just not the site."

"That's right. To level with you, I'm afraid it's because George's an Indian. Nobody wants to supervise an Indian. You know, drinking, they come to work late - Indian time, they call it. I'm sure some of it's racism, but as you know, Mr. Vinton, a lot of it is their own damn fault."

"I suppose so. But what if I could locate a work site? Could you put him on?"

Rediger paused. "Well, I told you there's eligibility criteria."

"But certainly your staff checked him out by now. The guy's obviously eligible. They've seen him, haven't they?" Jeff detected the discomfort he was causing.

"I'm sure they have."

"And if George wasn't eligible, they would have told you, knowing your personal interest."

Rediger knew what was happening. He just couldn't think of a way to stop it. "Of course."

"Good. I want to hire him in my office." Jeff paused, waiting for a response. There was none. He continued. "I'll send you a job description. What else do you need?"

"How soon do you want him?"

"Eight o'clock this morning."

"I can't move that fast. There's regulations, paperwork and..."

"You've had a goddamned month. I want him today, eight o'clock."

Rediger didn't respond. Jeff allowed the moments of silence to gather. Finally Rediger spoke. "Okay, I'll have someone visit your office today. You got your boy. And, Mr. Vinton, you owe me one."

Jeff wanted to challenge Rediger's comment, but he backed off a bit instead. "Yeah, I owe you one, and thanks. I look forward to your staffer coming over."

As they replaced the receivers, they both muttered, "That sonofabitch!"

Jeff sat back pleased, waiting for George to return. He was soon at Jeff's door and was welcomed back into the office.

"You don't have a job, do you?"

Diffidently, George shook his head.

"If you like, I could offer you a temporary one, for a year. Forty hours a week, minimum wage, a dollar sixty-five, working here in the office."

George was stunned. He tried to figure what a dollar sixty-five times forty was. He thought of the pride he'd have telling Mary that he had a job, regular hours, in the courthouse.

Jeff waited for George to speak, then asked, "What do you think?"

"When can I start?"

"You've been working since eight this morning. Now it's just for a year, but if things work out there's a chance it could become permanent. But knowing the county board, I doubt it."

"That's okay. Can I go tell Mary? I mean, can I leave for a few minutes? I'll be right back."

"Of course, George. Take an hour off."

George walked to his car, eager to tell Mary he had a real job with a steady income that she could rely on for a whole year. No more day labor, shocking oats or hoeing beets, cleaning grain bins or hauling garbage. A real job, working for Mr. Vinton, an employee of Harney County. As he drove down the paved streets past the nice houses, the well-attended lawns, he thought his family might have such a home someday. He left that area of town where homes had inside toilets, carpeted floors, and children who laughed and played, confident of their future. He drove past the small industries of northwest Union, then over the railroad tracks. He looked at the cattle in the pens, quietly awaiting shipment to the slaughterhouses. Even at this point they were segregated; the reddish-brown Herefords serving as a buffer between the white Charolaise and the Black Angus. George drove past the loading docks, on to the dirt roads, to his home. Entering, he saw Mary sitting, darning his socks.

"Throw those socks away, Mary. I got a job. I'll be working every day. Jeff Vinton hired me. I'm on the payroll right now."

Mary looked at her sewing. "What will you do for Mr. Vinton?"

Her question sobered George. "I don't know. He didn't say. I didn't give him a chance to tell me."

"Will you work in the office?"

"I guess so."

"Then we'd better get you some better clothes." She walked to their bedroom. George was amazed at how calmly she was reacting. She was already taking down a cardboard box from a shelf as he followed her into the room. She removed a newer pair of denims, a plaid shirt, and socks. George sat on a chair and began untying his shoes. Mary replaced the box and, approaching him, gave him the clothing. She looked into his eyes. "I'm very proud of you. You know, you're the first of our kind to ever work in the courthouse." Then she thought for a moment as George removed his trousers. "Except for prisoners mopping the floors."

George looked up at her. "My God! You're right."

She walked behind George and began massaging his shoulders. When George unbuttoned his shirt, she stopped kneading the muscles of his back. He removed his shirt and again felt her familiar hands. He also felt the unrestrained weight of her breasts lightly touching his shoulders. He stood and turned to his wife. He looked at the childlike face, the high cheekbones, the ebony hair falling on each side of her face. Her seductive smile encouraged him to look at her body. The innocence of her face contrasted with the sensuality of her body: the full breasts, the slim waist, the slender tapered legs.

She advanced to him and kissed him. Then, taking his hand, tugged him to her. Falling upon the bed, she felt his weight upon her. George was alive with energy, and they were both exhausted when he too quickly released that power within him.

Later, as George dressed, he looked to his wife lying on the bed. He enjoyed her beauty but said nothing.

She rose, kissed him. "Congratulations on your job." She had begun to say "new job" but caught herself. This was his first real job.

George smiled. "And I've been on the payroll the last hour!"

George wondered how he'd explain being gone for so long as he drove to the office. No one mentioned the time when he walked in. Evelyn smiled, introduced herself, and asked him to call her by her first name. And she said 'welcome aboard' as if she meant it. She said Jeff was waiting for him. Still anxious, George entered Jeff's office.

Vinton looked up, offered George a chair, and leaned forward, his elbows on his desk, his hands joined together. He smiled. George felt relieved. "I suppose you'd like to know, now that you're on board, just what the hell we want you to do."

George was surprised how confidently he replied. "That's right, Mr. Vinton."

"Now it's Mr. Vinton, huh?"

"I thought I should."

"No one else does."

"Okay."

"You're gonna need to hang around until someone comes to see you. They'll have you sign some forms enrolling you in a training program. They'll pay you. I'll supervise you. Okay?"

George nodded.

"After that you go to work. Your job will be to do what you're already doing - finding applicants in the American Indian community for me."

George couldn't believe his luck. This all fit so nicely into his fantasies about helping his people. And for Christ's sake, he realized, they're gonna pay me.

"George, concentrate on services to crippled children. You know, harelips, that sort of thing. The reason is simple. It doesn't cost the county any money. Now if you run across a really bad situation, like Dee for example, let me know and we'll put her on ADC. But we're in a pretty intense political arena, so go slow. Understand?"

George nodded again.

"Good. Too much too quick will get us both fired."

George instinctively understood the reality. "You set the pace."

"Good. And keep track of your mileage so we can reimburse you. Now let me show you your work area." Jeff led George to a desk and chair in the main office area. "This is your home. Evelyn will get any supplies you need; pencils, tablets. Okay?"

"Sure." George sat uneasily, put his elbows on his desk; his desk, his chair, his space in the Harney County courthouse.

Jeff watched him for a few seconds. "Just take it easy. I'll be with you when the CAP people get here." Jeff then left George Iron Rope, case aide of the Harney County welfare office, and George could not erase his silly grin.

For a moment, Jeff doubted that Rediger would send someone to sign George up. Who would pay for his hours if the CAP wouldn't? Jeff knew the county wouldn't. But I got his word, Jeff assured himself, and I'm one of his bosses. He then thought of Goldman's visit, of his judgment of Rediger and the CAP. Picking up the phone, he dialed information to get the number of the federal regional Office of Economic Opportunity. He then dialed that number and asked for Larry Ashton. He spoke with three offices interspersed by long blocks of silence before Ashton picked up the phone.

"Mr. Ashton, I've probably spent ten bucks getting you. I work for Harney County, and I'm on John Rediger's governing board. Would you call me back on your WATS line?"

"Sure. Where are you?"

Jeff gave his phone number. Ashton called back moments later. Jeff told him he had been appointed to the board, had been to one meeting, had heard some good, some bad about the agency, and wanted to hear the fed's version. He waited for Ashton's reply.

"Well, it's a corporation chartered in your state, governed by a board of directors. We contract with it to do certain things. It fulfills its contract. Does that answer your question?"

"Nope."

"I figured it wouldn't. What precisely do you want to know?"

"I'm not looking for anything specific. I just want some general information, such as how good is it? What's your general impression."

"I told you. It fulfills its contract with us."

"You obviously ain't gonna tell me anything else," Jeff retorted, becoming angry.

"Ask me something specific, I'll respond. I don't like fishing expeditions."

"Okay, Mr. Ashton, next time I call I'll have something specific." Jeff was annoyed at Ashton and mad at himself. He realized he had appeared as foolish to Ashton as Goldman had to him.

***

Anxious to hear Goldman's report, Millard and Jefferson were annoyed by his delay. Two hours later, Goldman pulled his car in front of Jefferson's apartment. Entering, he smiled, waved, went to the refrigerator for a beer.

"You're late," Millard observed.

"Yeah," Goldman acknowledged.

"What about Vinton?" Jefferson asked.

"I think he's an okay guy, even a bit quixotic. If we can develop something, he said he'll move on it. But it's got to be something hard, something he can grab on to."

"Is he gay?" Jefferson deadpanned.

Goldman smiled at Jefferson. "And we got nothing hard, nothing grabbable."

"Speak for yourself," Millard countered. Then, "There's rumors about abuse of travel, lack of direction, lack of leadership. But nothing really damning."

"We've got one thing going for us. Rediger's arrogance," Goldman said.

"What the hell's that supposed to mean?" Millard asked.

"I really think this guy's a bum, capable of dishonesty, and I think he's too arrogant to worry about covering his tracks. Somewhere there's a paper trail. We just got to find it."

"Find what?"

"I don't know."

"Well, money leaves a trail," Jefferson ventured.

"Do we know anyone in the fiscal office?" Goldman wondered.

Millard looked to the floor. Jefferson said, "Nope."

"We oughta. There's some young gals there. One's bound to be single," Goldman continued. "Who wants the assignment of having some assignations?"

"What kinda ass?" asked Jefferson.

"Assignations. Secret, romantic rendezvous," Goldman answered. "Indulge in a bit of spawning. You know, make love, not war. And do so in the best interests of the nation's poor."

"I'll check it out," offered Millard, the most attractive of the three.

"Might have known you'd handle that chore," Jefferson said.

"Kings go forth," Millard philosophized.

Jefferson extended the appropriate finger and expanded upon it. "Up yours."

"That's not the way it works," Millard reminisced.

"Well, at least you got half the victory sign," Goldman said, looking to Jefferson. "In an organization as big as the CAP, there's got to be some disgruntled staff members. Folks denied a promotion, got a chewing out they didn't deserve, feel they aren't being properly used. Jefferson, you and I got to get close to the staff. We gotta find these people and get the scoop on what's happening, man!"

"Of course, it's all mighty iffy" Millard said.

"No. No, dammit. Not when you consider we got Rediger's temerity going for us." Goldman spoke confidently.

"I don't know, but I guess that's all we got," Millard conceded.

"Let's see what develops," Goldman said. "By the way, I'm moving to Union. All my stuff is in the car. I gotta go find an apartment. See you next time."

Dave finished his beer and left before anybody could object. This was the first time they hadn't used their biweekly meeting to get drunk. Millard thought of the bookkeeper he was seeing. He felt the need to be with her tonight. Besides, he thought, Dave's already broken with tradition. He rose from the chair and looked at Jefferson. "You know, it's not the same as fighting for one's country."

"What's that?"

"Making love while engaged in the war on poverty."

"Yeah. All in the cause of a great society."

CHAPTER SIXTEEN

The aircraft descended toward the Union airport. The flight had been pleasant with little turbulence. Bob Elam sat in the back of the cabin so he could stretch his legs. Pam had dozed beside him much of the way and now was awaking. Elam watched Sergent and Chandler who sat in the forward seats. They had been going over itineraries for the next three days, making changes on the outline Bob was to use for his speeches, looking at photographs of the Democratic county chairmen, elected officials, and Republicans who had climbed aboard the Elam bandwagon. Bob also spent much of the trip trying to memorize the photographs and names. He closed the loose-leaf binder, knowing further study would only confuse him. He cursed himself for having drunk so much coffee during his lunch. As he took Pam's hand and squeezed it, he could only think of rushing to the terminal's restroom.

Herb turned around. "We're almost there. Off there on the horizon you can see Union," he said, pointing.

Bob squinted, looking where Herb pointed. But the setting sun blinded him. He simply nodded. Herb sat back and tightened his seat belt.

As the aircraft touched down and sped down the runway, Bob saw several people standing outside the fence separating the terminal from the runway. Because the Union airport had few scheduled flights, Bob assumed they were the local Democratic leaders. As the aircraft taxied to the tarmac, he wondered if he could rush to the restroom before meeting them. He figured not.

The aircraft shuddered to a stop. Herb had his door ajar during the last few minutes of taxing, allowing fresh air to enter the cabin. He now opened it and stepped from the aircraft, followed by Sergent. As they helped Pam, Bob, half-crouching, worked his way to the door.

Once out of the aircraft, Bob saw Herb shaking hands with the local Democratic officials, chatting with them. Bob recognized many of them from the photographs. He went to them, acknowledging the good work they were doing, smiling, joking, chuckling at their responses, then he rushed to the terminal. After several long minutes, he rejoined them and saw Sergent placing their luggage in a car, Herb walking toward him.

"Bob, our good friends in Harney County tell me they stand with you." He turned to Frank Wycoff, the county chairman. "You know, if another Democrat declares his candidacy, you're in a potful of trouble."

"No problem, Herb. We'll chance it."

A tall man in a western-cut suit and cowboy boots looked to Bob. "Don't pay any attention to Herb. The Harney County Democrats are behind you a hundred percent." Then he added, "And so are about half the Harney County Republicans."

Later in his room, after drinks in the hotel lounge, Bob wondered if the guy was serious. Did he have that much Republican support? He fell asleep wondering if it would be that easy?

***

Although Herb and Bill had been working since six, they allowed Bob and Pam to sleep until seven fifteen. Then Herb called their room, telling Bob to meet them in the restaurant. Pam could join them at her leisure. Sipping his coffee, he was surprised to see Pam walking alongside Bob. She looked refreshed, radiant, sparkling. She'll make a helluva first lady, he thought. "Good morning, Bob, Pam."

Bob bellowed back a hearty greeting. Pam smiled pleasantly. After placing their orders, they were given photocopies of their itinerary for Union. Pam immediately looked to the bottom of the sheet. It read "Wheels up, Union: 12:00. Wheels down, Yorkton: 12:35. Good God, she thought, those God-awful thirty-minute flights. Then, resignedly, she softly said, "Here we go again."

Herb heard her and repeated with enthusiasm, "Here we go again!"

He turned to Bob. "On this first leg, here in Union, we're gonna give you a lot of time. Then the pace quickens. Your next chance to catch your breath will be after you cast your ballot Tuesday morning. This morning you got an hour for breakfast, then back to your room to refresh. At nine fifteen you and Pam are to walk into the Lawrence T. Harney Room. Sergent will show you where it is after we leave the restaurant. He's our gopher this trip. Don't worry about your suitcases, your rooms, checking in and out. He'll take care of that. Okay? We've planned a thirty-minute press conference, just radio and newspapers.

Just use your normal introductory remarks, then respond to questions. Okay? Out here, you want to stress your Family Farm and Ranch Act. Call it the Ranch and Farm Act."

Bob nodded as the waiter brought his and Pam's breakfasts.

"At nine forty-five we'll have left the hotel and driven about a mile to the home of the party chairman. There will be about thirty to forty people there to have coffee with you. Some of these folks will be Republicans, so stress the unity stuff. Stay away from the partisan crap. You got less than an hour to thank your supporters, workers, and those who sent in money."

"Okay."

"Good. At ten forty-five you make your first speech at a park a few blocks from where we're having the coffee. Like all the others, we want you to ad-lib it. It'll be good practice. We expect about sixty people. But if there aren't that many, don't get depressed. It's tough enough getting people to vote, let alone go to speeches. Incidentally, the people at the coffee are being told to shake your hand, chat a bit, then go to the park to make the crowd bigger. So you're gonna see some familiar faces. At eleven thirty Sergent will have the car directly behind the rostrum. Don't mess around! Stay on schedule! At eleven thirty, stop whatever you're saying, apologize, wave good-bye, and leave. Bill will get us to the airport by noon. We'll go over the Yorkton itinerary while we're flying down there."

Bob nodded again.

"Good. Now eat your meal."

Bob looked at his plate. He hadn't touched it. He ate quickly so he and Pam could keep to Chandler's schedule. They followed Sergent to the Lawrence T. Harney Room. Bob glanced in the room, observing the rows of chairs, the rostrum, the microphone. His heartbeat quickened.

They returned to their room. While Pam packed, Bob brushed his teeth again, checked his appearance in the mirror, then checked his watch. "It's time," he said. "Walk with me." She grabbed his hand and they walked to the elevator, then down the corridor to the Lawrence T. Harney Room.

Entering, they saw five reporters and a couple of photographers. Elam greeted them with his loud but pleasant voice. He and Pam went to the table where the rostrum and microphones were set up, carefully walking among the electrical cords. He wondered where Chandler was.

"Good morning," Elam said, standing and smiling at the rostrum. "It's good to be with you and to be in Harney County. I selected this community and this area, and the vast agricultural industry it represents, to be the first stop of this, my last visit with the people of the state before the primary. I did this for a very specific reason. I want the people to know where Bob Elam stands when it comes to agriculture. The production of food and fiber is the mainstay of this state's economy. If I'm elected, agriculture will be the primary consideration of my administration. You know, a lot of bureaucrats and, I'm sad to say, elected officials in the capital don't realize how important this sector of our economy is." Bob paused, curling the fingers of his right hand into a fist. "But after four years of Bob Elam as governor, they're gonna know!" His knuckles rapped on the surface of the rostrum.

A short pause. "There's a lot I want to talk to you about, but darn it, I don't have much time. I'd like to tell you about the Family Ranch and Farm Act I'm proposing. I really think it's important that the shadow cast on the land be that of the owner and worker of the land. Not the shadows of corporations whose boardrooms are in New York, Chicago, or Houston. If there's any corporation running cattle out here, the boardroom better be in the kitchen of the stockholder. I'd like to tell you how I'm gonna reorganize those bureaucrats back in the capital so that government will make sense to the people of this state, not just the bureaucrats." Bob paused. "There's more I want to talk with you about, but I can learn more if I listen to what's on your mind. If you have any questions, I'll try to answer them with the good sense I hope the good Lord gave me."

Chandler and Sergent were sipping coffee in Herb's room, listening through a closed-circuit hookup. Sergent was taking notes. Chandler said nothing.

"Now what are the good folks of Union concerned about?"

Elam acknowledged a reporter with cowboy boots and a western-cut shirt. "How are you going to persuade the WTO to enable us to sell more beef to places like Japan?"

Bob tried to remember his briefing on the WTO. He hesitated. Then things fell into place. "Excellent question. We need a strong voice for agriculture. One who'll provide leadership for the agriculture producing states, for the beef industry. Someone who'll shape up those bureaucrats at USDA and State and Commerce, make them persuade those exporting nations that we need to export. And we've got products their people want. I heard a good steak costs twenty dollars a pound in Tokyo. We can produce, process, and ship that product to Japan at half the price and still get a profit back to our ranchers. What American agriculture needs is leadership and a strong voice. I want to be that voice, that leadership."

Chandler nodded approval. Sergent grinned.

"What's your stand on abortion?"

"The Supreme Court made that a federal issue. I don't like it, but that's the way it is." The reporter didn't follow up. Chandler smiled.

"Will you appoint people from the western part of the state to your cabinet?" Then the reporter added, "Most governors kinda forget we're out here."

"I sure will."

"Who you got in mind?"

"I can't mention names right now."

"He's okay," Sergent said softly.

Bob was responding to a question about highway maintenance as Herb got up and poured another cup of coffee. As he sat down again, Bob was adroitly handling the complex issue of water usage regulations. Herb and Bill looked at each other. "He's done his homework," Sergent said. They continued listening to the press conference as if they were not involved in the campaign. They were impressed by Bob's delivery, his eloquence, his perceived sincerity.

Bob recognized another reporter. "A while back we got a new welfare director in Harney County. He used to live in the capital, and now our welfare rolls are growing by leaps and bounds. What's your position on welfare and socialism?"

Chandler looked to Sergent. "Go get the car. It's time we move on. He put on his suit coat and rushed down the hallway. As he entered the room, he heard Bob saying "... to get people off welfare, off food stamps, we've got to offer them an alternative. Jobs. And if they haven't got the skills, we've got to provide training. And we've got to pay them decent wages, raise the minimum wage. And we have to view them as they are, decent people under economic duress, people who would rather..."

"Bob," Chandler interrupted, "we're getting behind schedule." Then he looked to the press. "Gentlemen, I'm sorry. Some kind folks have organized a coffee on Bob's behalf, and we don't want to be late. I hope you'll understand." He looked at Elam, feigning deference. "I'm sorry, Bob."

"Gentlemen, this is Herb Chandler. He's running my campaign, and he's always telling me we're behind schedule. Unfortunately, he's always right. I suppose we do have to go." Bob seemed disappointed. "But before I go, I wish to apologize for an unforgivable error. I failed to introduce the gracious and lovely lady beside me. This is Mrs. Elam. She's my wife, and I love her very much." Bob helped Pam, who was blushing, from her chair. They then left with Herb.

Elam sensed Chandler's annoyance as they rode the few blocks to the party chairman's home, but he didn't raise the issue. Herb also remained silent. As they neared the house, they heard the refrain "Happy Days Are Here Again." The host had taped it at a Jefferson Jackson Dinner and was playing it over his teenager's stereo. Chandler turned to Sergent. "Get our luggage, check us out of the hotel, and for Christ's sake get that press conference tape. We'll listen to it on the plane."

Elam was surprised at the mention of the tape recording but said nothing. He got out of the car and walked toward the house, the peppy music buoying his spirits. He surveyed the home. He judged its size and value to be twice as much as his home. He wondered two things about Frank Wycoff, the Harney County Democratic chairman: How'd he get his money? And why the hell was he a Democrat?

Soon he was inside the spacious and well-appointed home, acknowledging the supportive shouts and applause. Christ, he thought, this would never happen back east. They obviously don't see many candidates out here.

Elam shook Wycoff's hand while looking at the large number of people, noticing that Pam too was surprised. Then, as if planned, Pam began greeting people on one side of the foyer while Bob began meeting and greeting people on the other side. Soon they were separated by the legion of Elam supporters. There was no opportunity to speak, only shake each hand as it was thrust before him, utter a meaningless "How ARE you?", then move to the next outstretched hand without waiting for a response. Bob made his way into the large living room, then the dining room. "Hey, it's good to see you!" He moved to the next person. "I'm Bob Elam. So good to be here!" He turned in response to a pat on his shoulder, flashed a toothy grin, simply said "Howdy," and shook the hand before him. He was afraid someone would ask a question requiring an answer. That would take too much time, time he couldn't afford to spend with any single supporter. He was surprised no one did. They seemed satisfied with his platitudes and then stepped back in deference. The minutes passed. Bob kept moving. Once, looking around, he saw the crowd thinning. If only the voters in the capital had the manners of these cowboys, he thought. While shaking hands, he thought again of Frank Wycoff. One helluva guy. One helluva political operative.

He checked his watch. He could stay here ten more minutes. He wondered how Pam was doing, wondered where she was in this large house. As the crowd thinned out, Bob could briefly listen to those whose hands he shook. He heard how a hailstorm destroyed half of a farmer's wheat field. Another grower told him the railroads don't assign enough freight cars to move the grain during harvest time. A banker suggested liberalizing the state's usury laws. As Bob nodded to him, he thought how relative our language is: A banker wanting more liberal laws to conserve and enlarge the resources of the wealthy. It's all how you say things, he thought, moving to the next person. As he shook that hand, he heard the man introduce himself. Elam should have recognized him. But he looked older, more weary than his photograph: Hank Oldfield, county commissioner, Republican. Elam surprised him. "Good to meet you, Commissioner, and I'm real glad to have you with us today."

Flattered, Oldfield responded with a timorous smile. "Haven't been around so damned many Democrats since 'forty-eight."

"Well, I want you to know I've shaken a lot of Republican hands these past months. We both know this isn't really a partisan fight. It's more a difference in philosophy, a different approach to government."

"Well, Mr. Elam, I just came by to let you know I'm in tune with your philosophy, your approach."

Bob looked around. He felt he could spend a few minutes with Oldfield. "How's LB192 going to affect county government?"

"We'll have to live with it, but I don't know how," Oldfield said. "And our welfare costs are going up."

"I hear you have a new director."

"You heard, huh?"

"I hear he's pretty active."

"Too damned active," Oldfield complained.

"I want you to know I'm gonna look real hard at those welfare costs."

"They need looking at."

Elam, wishing to move on, shook Oldfield's hand again. "Well, I appreciate your thoughts. I realize the position that county government is in with this new law. I'm going to work to get more state aid to local governments. I appreciate your support."

"I'd like to help you out locally," Oldfield said. "Have your people contact me. I'll do what I can."

Elam thanked him, made a mental note, then greeted his next supporter. They were fewer now, gathering in small groups. Bob spotted Pam. With immense pride he watched her moving about the remaining people, endearing them to her, capturing their votes for her husband. He walked to her, slipping his arm around her waist. As she turned to him, he whispered, "You're great."

Riding to the park, Elam noticed Chandler's mood had changed. He was buoyant, almost euphoric. Herb turned to Sergent. "How many do you think there were?"

"Just glancing as I drove by to pick you up, I'd say over a hundred."

"Harney County is a damn good jumping off place," Chandler noted, more to himself than anyone else.

As they approached the park, Bob again heard the song from the PA system. *Happy Days Are Here Again*."

Sergent stopped the car as instructed, requiring Bob and Pam to walk through the crowd. He then drove to an area behind the grandstand to allow a quick exit after the speech.

Frank Wycoff walked to the microphone the moment he saw Bob and Pam get out of the car. Grabbing it, he announced the arrival of "the NEXT governor of this GREAT state."

Working his way, Bob responded to those who rushed to him, using his left hand to reach their outstretched hands, to pat them on the shoulder, but not stopping to press the flesh. This facilitated his movement to the rostrum, and it gave some relief to his sore right hand.

The words "the NEXT governor of this GREAT state" kept ringing in his head. He looked around. The crowds were here in Harney County. They were supportive. Some people were even enthusiastic. And this is supposed to be Norman country. Elam remembered past elections in which Democrats led as the automated vote counts quickly came in from the eastern part of the state. Then the returns from the west began coming in, at first eroding, then equaling, then surpassing the Democratic leads. This is Republican country, and Elam was drawing crowds - at least here in Harney County.

Bob and Pam took their seats as Wycoff began his introduction. So far he had taken five minutes and given little evidence of surrendering the podium. Bob glanced to Chandler who was looking at his watch, also concerned. Now they were listening to another joke from Wycoff's inventory. More minutes passed. The county chairman was speaking of Bob Elam and his candidacy. A good sign, Bob thought. He smiled graciously while being described as "a man for all seasons, a man for all reasons." Bob sensed that Wycoff was about to finish. Then Wycoff said there was a season for everything, that this was the time for Bob Elam. Wycoff turned to Bob, his left hand adjusting the microphone to his newly assumed posture. "And it has been written that there is a time for all things..."

Jesus Christ, Bob thought, now he's going to read Ecclesiastes.

"...a time to be born and a time to die..."

Bob noted the cadence of the beautifully structured words, how Wycoff's timing, his pauses, enhanced the rhythm of the phrases. He's a good speaker, Bob thought.

"...a time to scatter stones and a time to gather, a time to embrace and a time to..."

Bob thought of Wycoff's many attempts at humor, some only mildly successful. And now he's going to end with words from the Bible! It didn't fit. It's out of sync. Then he realized what was next. A smile crept across his face. Somewhere JFK did this.

"...time of hatred; a time of war and a time of peace..." The Democratic county chairman lowered his head in quiet reflection. Then, as he raised it, he jabbed his right hand toward the audience. "And may I suggest there's a time to fish and a time to cut bait."

The juxtaposition of this cynical phrase alongside the scripture surprised the audience. But after a few moments laughter swept the crowd.

His timing was perfect.

Then Wyckoff's voice roared, carrying itself across the park. "And may I further suggest it is a time for action, for decision, a time for us to do those things - all those things - necessary to ensure the election of Bob Elam. Ladies and gentlemen, I'm proud to present to you the next governor of our great and sovereign state, Robert Temple Elam!"

The crowd responded well. Wycoff had done a damned good job, but he had cut too much into Bob's time. As Bob acknowledged the applause and walked to the podium, Chandler wondered if Bob could switch the mood of the crowd to his no-nonsense style. Bob wondered who had told Wycoff his middle name.

He stood before the rostrum and shook Wycoff's hand. As he adjusted the microphone, it shrieked in rebellion. The crowd laughed again. Bob stood silently before the podium, looking at the people before him, then looking to Wycoff. "And may I remind the able and honorable gentleman who so eloquently and wisely introduced me as your next governor," Bob paused to allow bits of laughter to abate, "that there is also a time to introduce and a time to sit down."

The crowd responded with more laughter and applause. Bob walked over to Wycoff to ensure the crowd knew his comments were good-natured. He shook Wycoff's hand again and patted him on the back before returning to the rostrum.

Elam checked his watch. His speaking time had been cut substantially. "And there is a time for people who seek public office to meet with those they wish to serve. And that's why I'm here, to meet with you, to talk with you, and to share with you my thoughts. I've already met many of you personally and I've met some of your elected officials. I've heard of the poor maintenance of our farm-to-market roads, and we are going to send help on that."

Bob rattled off subjects that had been brought to his attention, pledging to use the office of the governor to remedy each problem, to favorably resolve each difficulty. As he spoke, he subtly indicated government's expansive role in the lives of its citizens. Searching the faces of the audience, he saw no objection. Bob felt good about this, felt vindicated.

He had been speaking of more and better services. He now rhetorically asked himself something wiser politicians seldom ask, and then only in private. "But, Bob Elam," his voice roared out, "how are you going to improve government services while holding the line on taxes?" His voice carried throughout the park; then his words echoed back to him and his audience. The crowd remained quiet, hearing Bob's words again.

Bob smiled. "I seldom ask myself the same question twice." The crowd again laughed.

"But some questions should be repeated. Once, twice, how many times?" He paused. "Until there's an answer!" He paused again. "Ladies and gentlemen, our schedule's tight, I'm going to leave you good folks and this fine community in a few minutes. But before I go, I'm going to answer that question. The answer is relatively simple yet profoundly difficult for an elected administrator to accomplish. And that's all I will be - just another administrator. You folks are the stockholders. I'll be your hired hand." He paused, deciding how to proceed.

Only then did he realize he was in trouble. It wasn't a smart-ass reporter or a cheap shot from his opponent or a question from a special interest group or the lunatic fringe. It was his question, asked out loud.

He wondered how to describe the waste, duplication, empire building, turf battles, diffused lines of authority, lack of control, lack of accountability, the ingrained and traditional ways and waste of the bureaucracy. Moments were passing. He had to say something. He wondered if these ranchers and shopkeepers and housewives would understand. How can you say you want control and authority without appearing megalomaniacal?

Too many moments passed. Bob slowly began. "The answer to improved government services and restraint in government spending lies in the people's ability to pinpoint accountability. If you're not receiving the level of service you should, there should be one office, one person who should explain what the problem is. And if that person is unresponsive, you should be able to fire him!"

Bob noted the silence. Well, goddammit, I got their attention. "Do you know the governor of this state only governs about forty percent of state government, only about forty percent of the bureaucrats, the employees of state government?" The crowd made no movement. They awaited his next words.

"The rest of state government, sixty percent of your government, is controlled by commissions, boards of directors, boards of regents, authorities, nonprofit corporations. All underwritten by your tax dollars. All housed in state offices. None of which receive the guidance of your governor. None of which are responsive to him. None of which take direction from him. Some of which work against him. Many of them compete for the same tax dollar, for the same client with the same service in the same community. All of them employ executive directors, executive secretaries, administrative assistants, and PR specialists."

His left hand jabbed the air before him. "It is there where the problem is, where the waste is, where the duplication is, where the special interests are. And, if elected, it is where I will be, disrupting this ludicrous and costly playground designed by and for the bureaucrats."

The crowd applauded heartily.

Christ, Bob thought, maybe I'm okay.

Chandler stopped pacing. The applause gave him the courage to look up for the first time since Bob had asked that damning question. He looked to the faces of the crowd: craggy-faced ranchers and cattle buyers in western attire, casually dressed businessmen, informally dressed housewives, blue-collar factory workers. They were all clapping.

Bob raised his hands to stop the applause. He spoke loudly into the microphone to quiet the ones who were still applauding. "I have to go in about three minutes. I raised that question, dammit. Now you gotta let me answer it!"

More applause.

"Don't you?"

Some laughter, then the crowd settled down.

Bob waited, then with a serious expression said, "The problem with government is not the people who pay for it, not the people who work for it. It's a problem of structure. And with a bad structure, many of the noblest goals of government are never realized. If you elect me governor, I will bring managerial practices and principles to your government. We can provide the services you need and hold the line on taxes by making the machinery of government more effective!" After pausing, he said, "This I pledge to you, if you help me with your vote!"

During the applause that ensued, Chandler walked over to Pam in the grandstand. "It's time we go. Go stand by Bob, wave to our friends, and let's get the hell out of here!" As the crowd saw Pam walking to Bob, the applause grew louder. He held out his hand. She grabbed it, closing in beside him.

Perfect, Chandler thought. She's a helluva lady.

Back on the aircraft, Chandler had to shout so that Elam could hear him above the roar of the engines. "Two things," he began. "The tape recording of the news conference sounded okay. But for Christ's sake, don't feel the need to be an apologist for the ADC mothers of the world. If you get another question about welfare, you simply say 'I'm gonna look into it – I'm gonna cut it back!' Regardless of your thoughts, that's the mood of the people. Respect it!"

Bob nodded. But he was dreading what was coming next. Chandler had become more than just a consultant. He was now Bob's mentor, his trusted counselor, a person Bob wanted to please. With uneasiness, he looked to Herb. Chandler's expression conveyed uncertainty, almost bewilderment.

"Now, Bob, about the last part of your speech. I don't know what to say. You violated all the rules and came out looking like a champ. I'm a bit confused." He thought for a moment. "For the time being, don't do it again. But we're gonna want to think about it. You came across refreshingly honest. You pinpointed a problem, identified the dilemma, and did so credibly. Your answer to your own question was damned good. Don't quote me, but we may want to polish it up and do it again, sometime before the general election. But let's wait 'til we hear the tapes, get some feedback, and assess it. Okay?"

Pleased, Bob nodded in agreement.

"And, Bob, never ever say that I'm running your campaign. If you have to identify me, call me an aide or a pal or whatever. Remember. You're the one running this campaign." Chandler paused for effect, then reached into his briefcase and gave everyone photocopies of the Yorkton itinerary. As it generally followed the Union format, he went over it quickly as the aircraft began its descent.

The crowds were in Yorkton too; in greater numbers than Union, reflecting its larger population base. Bob abided by Chandler's instructions. When he was asked about welfare, he said the entire situation would be given close scrutiny. Bob had no compunction in saying this. Human services were where much of the duplication existed. That was where he would first attempt to eliminate the many redundant and quasi-governmental agencies.

He closely followed the talking points on the three-by-fives during his speech at the American Legion hall. Chandler observed that the talk went well, but it lacked spontaneity. Bob didn't exert the energy that he had in Union. By the time they landed in Colfax, Bob looked weary, emotionally drained. But Pam appeared to be generating more energy as the day wore on, seemingly tireless.

Bob got through the events in Colfax okay, although his right hand was swollen. He limped to the hotel room where he welcomed the sight of a bottle of Old Fitzgerald and a full ice bucket. He poured a glass and sipped his drink before showering. The bourbon relaxed him. Apologizing to Pam, he asked her to have dinner with Herb and Bill. Bob could only think of resting. Tomorrow morning he would be in Burke County, standing alongside Jake Hammond.

***

The morning flight was uneventful. Bob was relaxed as he watched the landscape slowly change. The badlands and hill country directly west of Union and the High Plains of Yorkton were part of the fading western horizon. Below him now was a patchwork of small fields, each reflecting its own color in the morning light. The winter wheat and oats had been harvested, their yellow residue contrasting sharply with the greenness of the corn, beans, and alfalfa fields. Occasionally a field had been cleared of its vegetation and lay fallow, its rich blackness adding another dimension of color.

As the aircraft lumbered eastward, Bob noticed the perfectly symmetrical circles of green, some covering an entire section. He had read about center pivot irrigation systems in a background paper. Eastern corporations had purchased large tracts of marginal land; land with soil incapable of holding moisture needed for deep-rooted plants. After installing the center pivots, the corporations planted deep-rooted plants. Two events then occurred. The region's large aquifer began to be depleted, drying up many of the shallow wells as the center pivots pumped thousands of acre-feet of water from the ground. Worse, the heavy application of chemicals on the fields leached back into the ground water. In a number of communities the water had nitrate levels unsafe for children and pregnant women. Bob thought that these green circular products of the center pivots were unwholesome and even menacing. Something a governor should do something about! Then he thought about tilting against windmills and realized how silly his thoughts were. He sat back and relaxed.

Senator Jake Hammond remained at Elam's side during his entire stay in Burke County. Bob gave the appearance of being honored by Hammond's presence; smiling, being gracious, placing his arm around Hammond's shoulder, posing for photographs, and exchanging small talk. Bob shook Jake's hand at the airport while the news cameras clicked away. But Bob was becoming vaguely aware of an undefined ambiguity he felt toward Hammond.

The rest of the stops became routine: Bob shaking hands, meeting key officials, speaking before large audiences, perfecting his techniques for the general election. He was becoming a polished speaker, adroitly equivocal at press conferences, profoundly responsive to complex questions.

These days transformed Bob from a neophyte candidate into a veteran campaigner. He was doing all the right things, building a redoubtable legion of supporters in each area he visited. He had in these few days effectively mobilized his resources, employed to the utmost the techniques Chandler had instilled within him, and successfully improvised when holes appeared in the game plan. Bob had gone through this period of testing and had acquitted himself well. He was now a politician.

As the small aircraft landed at the capital city's airport and Elam saw the large group of supporters awaiting him, he fully realized that he enjoyed what he was doing, liked what he had become.

CHAPTER SEVENTEEN

Goldman called the meeting to order by rapping his beer can on the bare floor.

"Oyez, oyez," chanted Jefferson.

Goldman ignored him. "Okay, what do we have?"

Millard was eager to speak of his sexual prowess. "Well, I got close to one of the bookkeepers, a delightful young thing. And she's receptive to us, more importantly to me. She hates Rediger's guts and is willing to help." Millard paused to gloat a bit. "And she's been mighty cooperative but insists on being properly wined and dined. And that's a problem. You know, I'm damned proficient in this assignment. Damned proficient. But I need an increase in my monthly stipend or at least an expense account. Goldman, would you take care of that?"

"Only if you tell us what you found out."

"We can get anything we need from the fiscal office. And there's stuff we might want to look at," Millard said. "For one thing, Rediger goes to lots of meetings and takes his secretary with him."

"Where are the meetings? In the state capital?"

"Yeah, there, and Washington. Then there's Nashville, New Orleans, Denver, Los Angeles. They really get around."

"Is there a reason other than the obvious why she needs to go?"

"To take minutes of the meetings maybe," Jefferson speculated. "What kind of meetings are they?"

"Professional associations, I guess," Millard replied.

"Normally those are fun things. How often do they go?" Goldman asked.

"At least once a month."

"Lots of bucks," Jefferson observed.

"How can we get this nailed down?" Goldman asked.

"That's easy. I'll get photocopies of their travel claims," Millard said.

"Some stuff may come out of those claims," Goldman said. "Yeah, get them as soon as possible."

"Okay."

"What else?"

A period of silence ensued, broken by Goldman. "Well, the talk about the agency is that one of the outreach workers, an old friend of Rediger's, is a soap salesman."

"What the hell does that mean?" Jefferson wondered.

"Okay. His job is going to the homes of the poor to tell them about the agency's programs."

"Yeah, we know that," Millard said.

"Well, in this agency that means a lot of miles. He uses his personal car and gets mileage reimbursement."

"Okay," Jefferson said impatiently.

"Well, rather than go from town to town to meet with low income people, he goes from town to town to sell soap."

"You're joking," Millard said.

"No," Goldman responded.

"You mean he's paid wages and travel expenses to sell soap? Is that what you're saying?"

"Yeah. And normally his travel reimbursement is more than his paycheck."

"Hmm. Amazing. What else?" Jefferson asked.

"The deputy director," Goldman cryptically threw out.

"What about him?"

"He started out as the economic development director and worked his way up to deputy director, but he kept both job titles."

"Okay, he's wearing two hats," Jefferson said impatiently.

"His job as economic development director is to create jobs for low income folks."

"Right."

"Well, there's a couple of ways to do that. One is to discover local talent, help the poor start an ethnic restaurant or maybe get a lawn service started, that sort of thing."

"Makes sense. But a lot of businesses starting on a shoestring go under pretty quick," Millard said, looking at Goldman.

"Well, that ain't no problem here 'cause the agency decided to do it the other way around, by chasing smokestacks."

"Uh?"

"By inducing firms to relocate factories here," Goldman explained.

Okay. That's tougher, but it still makes sense."

"Yeah. He takes credit for bringing about two hundred jobs to the area."

"What's your point?" Jefferson asked.

"This. While the CAP is paying him for this, he's charging folks for his services as an economic development consultant. Hell, he's even started a for-profit corporation. And get this. The word is that the stockholders are the deputy director, Rediger, and his secretary."

A silence followed. "You guys got a lot more than I did," Jefferson said.

"Did you get anything?" Goldman asked.

"The stuff I got is really minor," Jefferson said. "I learned the CPA who audits the books is also its treasurer. If he's not aware of the stuff you guys found, it's at least a conflict of interest."

"Okay," Goldman said. "Now what do we do?"

They sat back in silence. Goldman got some beer from the refrigerator. "Let's think paper trail," he said, handing each a can. "Let's get the travel claims of Rediger and the outreach worker. That's a helluva start."

"How far back?" Millard asked. "And how about his secretary?"

"Her too. Start with this month. Go back as far as you can. At least a year."

"Okay," Millard said.

"Good. I'm not sure what we can do about the deputy director," Goldman continued. He thought for a moment. "Jefferson, why don't you write the secretary of state?"

"What for?"

"Get copies of his corporate papers, the board of directors, assets, chief stockholders, that sort of thing. The name of the corporation is High Plains Economic Development Inc."

"Okay," Jefferson said, taking notes. "What else?"

"I don't know," Goldman responded. "If we go to a local chamber and start asking questions, Rediger's bound to find out."

"Yeah," Millard said. "Then he'd fire us. That would be okay with me, but we'd get a lousy job reference from VISTA."

"You're right. Even after we get the paper from the state, we shouldn't move on the deputy until we complete the picture." Goldman looked at Millard, "You sure you can get those photocopies?"

"It'll take a while, but no problem."

"Okay, we'll go with that," Goldman said. "But let's keep digging."

***

Jeff asked to speak with the county clerk in her private office. Without enthusiasm, she escorted him to the small office. She sat behind her desk, adjusted her eyeglasses, intertwined her fingers, and lowered her joined hands to the desk. Then she asked how she could help him.

Jeff sat down slowly in front of her desk. "Tell me. If a child is delivered by a midwife and no doctor gets involved, how does the kid get a birth certificate?"

"He can't. It's illegal to deliver a child unless you're a doctor." She paused. "Sometimes, in an emergency, like when an EMT delivers a baby, then the doctor at the hospital signs the certificate."

"But what happens if the child is born and no doctor is involved?"

"It's against the law."

"I see." Jeff wasn't sure how to proceed. "Even though it's against the law, the kid exists. How do we remedy that dilemma?"

"I really don't know."

"Quite a problem, huh?"

"No, not at all. Just tell me who the midwife is, and I'll contact the county attorney. He'll put a stop to it."

"But how will that get the kid a birth certificate?"

"It won't. But we can stop that kind of practice."

"It's not an ongoing situation. It happened several years ago."

"It's one of your Indian friends obviously."

"They're not my friends."

"Whatever."

The conversation was at an impasse.

"I really don't know what to say, Mr. Vinton."

"You haven't been all that helpful," Jeff said.

"I'm sorry."

"Really now, who might know what to do?"

"You could check with vital statistics at the State Commission of

Health."

"Yeah. Good. I guess I'll do that. Thanks." Jeff walked back to his office a bit annoyed.

He called the state office, wondering if by helping Dee he'd get Grandma Red Shirt in trouble. He spoke in general terms. The state employee was as unresponsive as the county clerk. Jeff was confident there was no way to prove the existence of the children.

The problem wasn't overwhelming as far as he was concerned. He had seen the damned kids. He knew they were alive, but the problem of no birth record would plague them throughout their lives. He wondered how the older ones got into school. He wondered if they were in school. Jeff recalled seeing a teenager standing in the dark recesses of the shack. The youngster was about fifteen. What the hell was the story with that kid? Did he live there, too? Was he part of the family? And what the hell constitutes a family to these damned Indians with their various adopted family members? These Indians are an anomalous breed because of their lack of credentials, their bureaucratic nonexistence, Jeff thought, troubled by Dee's children.

He went to refill his coffee cup when he bumped into George. For Christ's sake, he thought, I've got an in-house expert on Indian affairs, my mini-BIA.

George accepted blame for the awkward encounter. "Hey, that's okay," Jeff said. "But I have to see you. Come to my office."

George nodded. As he followed Vinton, he feared he was about to be fired. During the two weeks he had been on the job, George had referred five families to Jeff, all living in situations similar to if not worse than Dee's. Vinton hadn't objected, George remembered, but he had seemed troubled. So rather than be in northwestern Union and accessible to other families, George just hung around the office, doing nothing. No one objected, but George felt guilty. It was a dilemma. Should he do his work, thereby increasing the welfare rolls and Vinton's political problems? Or should he sit, doing nothing, unproductive, but saving the county money? Troubled, he followed Jeff into the office.

"Before you sit, George, please close the door."

He appreciated the way Jeff was going to fire him, in the privacy of his office, behind closed doors. He sat before Jeff's desk.

"George, we got a problem, and it appears there ain't no answer to it."

The collective "we" gave George comfort. "Is it me?" George inquired.

"Christ, no," Jeff said, surprised.

George relaxed. "How can I help?"

"It's Dee. I've got to get the approval to the state if she's gonna get her first ADC check next month. And I promised she would. It's ready to go except for one thing." He paused. "George, this is tough for me to understand, so you're gonna have a tougher time. The problem, simply put, is that Dee's kids don't exist as far as the government's concerned."

"How come?"

"They don't have any birth certificates. Grandma Red Shirt was the midwife. There was no doctor. As far as the state's concerned, only doctors can sign birth certificates."

"That's no problem," George responded.

"The hell you say!"

"No. What I mean is, well, it's common for Indians living off the reservation to use midwives to deliver our little ones." Then, looking seriously at Jeff, he said, "The hospital won't accept us."

"That's another problem, George. We can work on that later. Technically, if a hospital accepts Hill-Burton, and they all do, they have to admit the poor. But ..."

George interrupted. "It's more that we're Indians than that we're poor."

Jeff was saddened by what George had said, but he remained on topic. "There are laws to deal with that. But how the hell do I prove these kids exist? How can we get some paper on the little bastards?" Before George could respond, Jeff went on. "And the five referrals you've given me so far, I'll bet those kids were delivered by midwives, too. The problem is gonna keep coming up the deeper we get into the Indian community."

"I said there's no problem."

"How then ..."

"The tribal courts have a lot of ..." George couldn't find the word.

"Latitude?" Jeff ventured.

184

"I don't know. I guess I mean power."

"Okay. Can they issue a birth certificate?"

"Sure."

Jeff sat back, relieved. "Can they issue four certificates?" he smiled.
George nodded.

"How do we do it?"

"We gotta get Dee, her kids, and Grandma to the reservation.
Grandma must appear before the tribal court, swear she delivered the
little ones, and that they're Dee's. Then the judge orders the certificates
to be issued. We can get the whole thing done in a few hours."

"Could you handle it?"

"What do you mean?"

"Can you get Dee and Grandma and the kids down to the
reservation?"

George looked away from Jeff. He didn't have a spare tire.

"We'll pay you mileage for the trip."

"I'm broke, Jeff."

"How much do you need?"

"Ten dollars for a tire."

"I can't give it to you, but I'll lend it to you."

"We can leave tomorrow morning," George said, thinking he could
get his surplus food commodities while the kids got their birth
certificates.

"Good." Jeff handed him the money. "How about gas money?"

George looked down at the floor. "It's going to take two trips."

"Here's another twenty. Pay me when you get your mileage check."

"I will."

"And tell the judge we'll have to do this again"

"Okay. No problem."

"And not now, but in a few days I want you to tell me about the
other kid living with the Red Shirts."

"Oh, you mean Donny."

Jeff sat back. So there was another kid living with the Red Shirts.
Eight people in that little shack! "Yeah, but before you do, I want Dee
moved out."

George smiled. "I won't be in tomorrow. We'll leave early. I'll go
and tell Grandma and Dee. I'm sure they can go. Is that okay?"

"Sure." Jeff sat back, pleased that George was on his staff.

***

Jeff turned the page on his calendar, prompting a renewed surge of anticipation. Forty more days, he thought. Before the engagement, Andrea and Jeff had communicated only sporadically. Now, the letters and telephone calls were far more frequent. Andrea had sent a list of the furniture her parents were giving them and what he needed to buy. He sent a picture of the house he had rented. He was to move in on the first. The mover would deliver the furniture on the second. Jeff would leave on the sixth. Everything was coming together. He was already thinking of himself as a family man. The world was a delightful place in which to live, to make better, and in which to love.

He looked up from Andrea's picture as Evelyn entered his office. "Good morning," she said as she gave him the stack of welfare checks from the county treasurer. "Today's Mother's Day, you know."

"Huh?"

"Today's the day we mail the ADC checks."

Jeff grinned.

"And each month it's costing more for postage."

"Do I detect a subtle protest?" he asked.

She looked at Jeff, keeping back her smile. "Look, it's my taxes buying all of these stamps."

Jeff looked at the stack. "It does seem a bit thicker than last month."

"The treasurer noticed that, too."

"Is Dee's in here?"

"Yeah, I checked. Here it is. And Lisa gets her second check this month."

"Any problems with Lisa?"

"I hope you don't mind. I spoke with the treasurer last month. She understands and will keep it quiet."

"Hey, I appreciate it. You know, that was a tough spot, and I didn't know what to do, so I ignored it." He thought for a moment, realizing how foolish he had been, how much Evelyn had helped. He looked at her. "You done good."

"I assure you everything's okay."

"Good. Incidentally. Don't mail Dee's. George will take it to her. She's renting a place today."

"I hear her neighbors aren't pleased."

"I suppose not. That's a problem. We're gonna get resistance as Indians move into white neighborhoods. The good people of Union will surely complain to the commissioners. It's a difficult problem." He shook his head. "You know, when I took this job I knew things would get rough. I decided that even if the sky started falling, I'd run the office in accordance with the law. I've no idea what the outcome will be." He stared out the window for a moment, then looked back to Evelyn. "Have George come see me. He's gonna help Dee move."

She turned to leave when Jeff quietly asked, "You still with me? You know we had a pretty rocky start?"

Without speaking, she sat in the chair before him. "You take a little getting used to."

"How do you mean?"

She rose, closed the door, and sat again. "I've really given a lot of thought to what's happening in Harney County. And what was happening before you got here."

"Yeah?"

"It's really hard for me to say it because it explains in a damning way what we were, what we are, what we've done, and what we're doing." She looked down at her hands folded in her lap.

Jeff didn't speak but continued looking at her.

"If you look at us one way, we don't dislike or hate the Indians. And there really hasn't been any prejudice exercised against them. We just never gave any consideration to them ..." She paused, breathed deeply, then said softly, "... as people."

She felt relieved. She had said it. Now she could speak more freely. "They were a subculture. No, worse! A sub-race, not really people. You can't deny human rights to sub-humans. So we weren't prejudiced except in such an absolute way that we were totally prejudiced. But," she paused, "unknowingly, unconsciously, innocently. This is going to surprise you, but George is the first Indian I've ever known. I never gave myself the opportunity to meet the Iron Ropes of the world." She again stopped and looked squarely at Jeff. "Mr. Vinton, this is my way of saying I'm deeply ashamed, and yes, dammit, I'm still with you."

She rose from the chair, looked at Jeff, and forced a smile. "I'll ask George to join you."

George came in moments later. "Wanta see me?"

"Yeah, it's moving day." He decided not to mention Mother's Day.

"What do you mean?"

"Would you help Dee move?"

"No problem. Pat and I are gonna do that tonight."

"Do it on company time. She can't have a lot. You shouldn't need your brother. That way you can be with Mary and the kids tonight."

"Good."

"Here's her first check. Will you give it to her?"

"Sure."

"And, George, tell Dee to get the kids to a dentist."

"Okay."

Jeff finished his coffee, put on his jacket, and tightened his tie. Before leaving, he asked Evelyn about Milner.

"He was kinda nervous. Knowing him as I do, that surprised me."

"Opening day jitters," Jeff dryly commented.

"That, and he took over five thousand dollars in food stamps with him, and five hundred in cash."

"Maybe he felt guilty - absconding with so many bucks."

Evelyn laughed. "You gonna go check him out?"

"Nah, just help him out. He's at the community center, ain't he?"

"Right. We went over there yesterday. Rediger's staff did a good job setting up a place for us."

"Good. Do you have the phone number?"

"Yes."

"Okay. I'll be there a while."

***

Jeff observed the number of people walking to the community center. There were old couples, young women with children, Indians, Mexicans, Anglos; all going to get federal food stamps. Inside, he was astounded to see a long line of Harney County's poor queued up before the office where Jerry Milner was working. Many of the children were crying. The old people looked fatigued. The stench of poverty that had

188

permeated the welfare office during his first months now filled the community center. Jeff asked for chairs to be placed beside the line of people. Soon the older clients and women late in their pregnancies were seated. Then, stepping inside the office, Jeff took Milner aside for a moment. "You look busy. How are the stamps holding out?"

"Can you bring me about two thou more?"

"Sure. Anything else I can help you with?"

"Nope. We set this up as a one-man operation. We better not change now."

"You sure I can't help?"

"Just get out of here, and bring some more stamps."

"You okay?"

"Yep. No mistakes yet, as far as I know."

Jeff lingered for a few minutes, chatting with the people who were waiting, apologizing for the long line, the delay.

No one complained. Some said they were surprised at the number of people. A few personally thanked Jeff for bringing the program to the county. He told them to thank the county board. He was pleased at the large turnout. It gave visible proof that despite the affluent appearance, there were many poor people in Harney County. Furthermore, the fact that most were Caucasian countered the perception that poverty was a peculiarly Indian problem.

After taking the food stamps to Milner, he drove to Grandma and Grandpa Red Shirt's home in northwest Union. George was loading cardboard boxes into his car's trunk. Dave Goldman was there, too, negotiating a mattress through the house's narrow doorway. Jeff went to help, taking one end of the mattress. Its bottom was damp. Remembering that the mattress had been on the dirt floor of this home, he wondered if it was worth taking to Dee's new home. Its odor was obvious even in the outside air. He knew he was transferring the stench of poverty from one place to another. The poverty, although diminished, would linger.

George helped Goldman put the mattress on top of his car. After tying it down, he went to introduce Jeff to Goldman.

"Yeah, we've met. How are you, Dave? And when did you meet George?"

"I moved down here last month. Got to know George through

Donny."

"Oh yeah," Jeff grinned, looking at George. "And tell me, Dave, how is Donny?" Jeff asked, still looking at George.

"We oughta talk about him. And about Rediger."

"Sure." Jeff looked around. "Where are Dee and the kids?"

"Over at the new home," George responded.

"Good. Can she help you unload, George?"

"No problem."

"Okay if Goldman and I take a break?"

"This is the last box. I'm all set." Turning to Dave, George thanked the VISTA.

"Got time for a drive?" Jeff asked Goldman.

"Sure. Why didn't you tell me George was working for you?"

"I didn't know you knew him. He just started a little while ago." Jeff turned his car onto the dusty street.

"What the hell's the courthouse chatter like on that, a damned Injun working in the courthouse? Christ, in the welfare office!"

"Pretty quiet so far. The calm before the storm," Jeff joked.

"Who do you want to talk about first, Donny or Rediger?"

"Donny sounds less controversial."

"Don't bet on it, but okay." Goldman paused for effect. "Donny is sixteen and has spent a total of three days in school."

Jeff looked away from the dusty road to stare at Dave. "What do you mean, three days?"

"Well, he went to kindergarten like all good little Indian boys do. On the third day the teacher told him he was different so he didn't have to come back. And he never did. He's slow, but sure as hell educable."

Vinton remembered the other retarded person in the state hospital. "Jesus Christ," he said.

"Holy Moses," Goldman said.

"What kind of goddamned place is this?" Vinton wondered aloud.

"A typical American community," Dave dryly responded. "Now, shall we resolve the Donny problem, or do you want to go to the Rediger problem?"

The euphoria of getting a home for Dee and her kids, thereby making more room for the Red Shirts, gave way to a sense of uneasiness. Jeff sighed. "What about Rediger?"

"The nonprofit corporation on whose board you sit is corrupt. Corrupt through and through."

"What the hell are you talking about?"

"I mean it."

"You sure?"

"Yep."

"Got proof?"

"Quite a bit. We're getting more."

"Who are 'we'?"

"Two other VISTAs and me."

"That's right. There's three of you guys." Jeff blindly looked ahead. Goldman didn't respond. "I suppose we should meet," Vinton said.

"Yeah. We should get together. But what can you do for Donny?"

"I don't know. Sixteen years. That's a lot of years. What's he been doing all this time?"

"Hanging out."

"There are sheltered workshops where these kids can get some skills plus some classroom stuff," Vinton thought out loud. "They're obviously pretty light on academics. I think the closest one is in Yorkton."

"Could you get Donny in there?"

"I can't really say. I don't know."

"Why?"

"Well, we're getting into bureaucratic red tape. Where does the responsibility lie? Is it a welfare or education problem? I don't know. At first blush, I'd say the school district is responsible. It's a typical dilemma involving bureaucratic jurisdictions."

"What are you gonna do?"

"Look, Dave, I don't know."

"You wanna go on to Rediger?"

"Let's stick with Donny," Vinton persisted. "I'll call the workshop tomorrow. See what it costs. Plus there'll be room and board expenses. There is another consideration. Does he want to go?"

"Probably not."

"A consideration."

"Yeah."

"Let me check it out." Jeff sighed. "As far as Rediger, set up a meeting."

"This weekend okay? Here in Union?"

"Sure. We can use my office," Vinton said.

"Good. Why don't you stop and let me out. I'll walk to my apartment." Goldman got out of Jeff's car. Jeff drove on, disquieted.

***

Jeff received the notice of the CAP's next board meeting. He reflected for a moment and then phoned Commissioner Scott. An hour later he was driving to Scott's ranch.

Scott invited Jeff in and seated him at the kitchen table. Pouring coffee, he asked, "Now, Jeff, what the hell's so important?"

"Remember when you appointed me to the CAP's governing board?"

"Yes. Several months ago wasn't it?"

"Right."

"Yeah, I remember," Scott said impatiently.

"Well, I'm here to report to you." Jeff relayed the information he had gotten from the VISTAs. He did so in detail, even laughing once over the temerity of Rediger and his deputy director. The VISTAs had put together a tight case.

Jeff sat back, sipped his coffee, and waited for Scott to respond. He looked at the commissioner, knowing Scott was morally outraged, wondering what course of action he would dictate. Jeff believed the fair and analytical mind and the sober and honest character of the man were now fully integrated, fully at work. He was eager to get the go-ahead to hang Rediger's ass.

Scott stood and leaned on the chair before him. It was the first time Vinton had seen him objectively. Always before, Jeff was on the defensive, depending on Scott to line up the votes, to soften the impact of Jeff's activities, to advise him when to slow down, when it was safe to forge ahead again. This time Jeff had brought an issue to Scott, and the issue was Rediger's corruption, not Jeff's compassion. He looked at Scott's hands, the prominent veins, the muscular grasp, the scarred knuckles. He looked at Scott's face, noting the loose skin of his neck. He realized that Scott was an old man, a tired man, but still, Jeff knew, an honest man.

"You're getting married next month?" Scott asked.

"Right." A strange question, Jeff thought. "I'm eager for you to meet her."

"So am I, Jeff, but you're gonna miss next month's meeting of the CAP's board. You'll be honeymooning. Do you think it's fair to open up this can of worms at one meeting, then not be at the next? I know it's not the case, but it might be viewed by your fellow board members as a cowardly act."

"When this stuff hits the fan, there'll be calls for Rediger's resignation, or motions for his discharge."

"Not necessarily."

"Why not?"

"It's a lot easier to hire a person then to fire him."

Jeff looked up, perplexed.

"The courts more and more view jobs, what a person does for a living, as property. Just as you can't deprive a man of life or liberty without due process, you can't deprive a man of his job, his property, without due process." He smiled, "Fifth Amendment, U.S. Constitution."

Jeff slowly reciprocated. "Well, what's the U.S. Constitution among friends?"

Scott looked sharply at Vinton. "I can't believe you said that."

"I believe some corrupt congressman from New York said it years ago. But it fits our discussion."

"You're angry at me?" Scott asked.

"I don't know. The possibilities are rising."

"Isn't there some logic to what I'm saying?"

"No."

"Why not?"

"If Rediger doesn't resign when confronted, along with his secretary, deputy, and the soap salesman, then the county attorney should file charges," Vinton reasoned.

"His resignation could be construed as implying guilt," Scott explained. "So it wouldn't be wise for him to resign. And it's damned difficult to prove this kind of corruption. Really now, no money has been transferred except paychecks for hours apparently worked and airline tickets for travel. Rediger could say he simply traveled to the wrong city on the wrong date. A damn dumb mistake, but there ain't nothing illegal about being dumb. Besides, you and the other board members approve his travel. You share some of the blame."

"What is it you suggest?" Jeff asked.

"That you enjoy your honeymoon."

"And?"

"That you love your wife and keep your job to support her."

"I came here thinking Rediger's job was in jeopardy, not mine."

"Of course," Scott replied noncommittally. He paused, then said, "Incidentally, the next governor - you've heard his name, of course, Bob Elam - was talking to Oldfield about you. They both seem to share the same appreciation of you and your work here."

"I can't believe a gubernatorial candidate is concerned with obscure welfare directors in obscure backwater counties."

"Believe it, Jeff."

"Mr. Scott, I've crossed over. Now I'm angry."

"Don't be, Jeff. Look at it another way. The CAP does some good for the poor. Not a lot, but some. And it brings a lot of federal money into the area, into these small towns, money that wouldn't be here without it. So Rediger exerts his energy screwing his secretary. It could be worse."

"Is that the extent of our options? The least worst?"

"Jeff, remember the riots all over the country a few years ago?"

"Yeah."

"At meetings I went to, I heard OEO was behind some of that. Hell, I've heard that CAP directors sometimes threw the first firebombs. I'd really rather have Rediger screwing his secretary," Scott looked intently at Jeff, "and so would the other county commissioners in this area."

Jeff was stunned. Weakly, he said, "I represent Harney County on the CAP governing board. I've brought information to your attention that I believe to be damning. What precisely are my instructions from the county board chairman?"

"Skip the next meeting. Then go get married."

"I don't know," Jeff looked defiantly at Scott.

"Do as I suggest," Scott said firmly.

Jeff rose from the chair and coldly stared at Scott. Scott met Jeff's stare. Jeff slowly shook his head, then lowered his eyes. He turned and walked to the door.

"Oh, Jeff, I signed a hundred dollar raise for you. It's for your work on the mental health mill levy. You'll see it in your June paycheck. It's also a wedding gift from the good people of Harney County."

Jeff walked from the house. He had closed the door without speaking.

Back at his office, he called Goldman.

"Yeah," Dave answered.

"Dave, this is Jeff. I want you to do me a favor."

"Sure, Jeff."

"Keep digging. Get whatever more you can. When I get back from my honeymoon, I'll confront Rediger."

"That'll be three months."

"Yeah, I know."

"What happened?"

"Nothing. I just think it's best this way."

"For Christ's sake!" Jeff could understand Dave's mounting anger. "Why?"

"'Cause he's gonna fight it. And I don't want things to cool down between the time I present it and the time I can push it."

"Sure."

"I mean it! I want to be in a position to pursue this. I don't think Rediger's the type to just quit. He's gonna fight it!"

"So what?"

"If it comes to a vote while I'm gone, he might win."

"Okay, Mr. Vinton," Dave abruptly said. "Thanks so much. See ya."

Jeff held the receiver long after Dave had hung up. Pangs of disloyalty stung his conscience. He had told the VISTAS he would act and he had backed off. He rose from his desk, closed the door to his office.

He spent the next hour mulling over what had happened. He felt cheap, dirty. He had given his word and had failed to keep it.

Then he remembered Scott's mention of the pay raise. A hundred bucks a month. That's about twenty percent, he thought.

CHAPTER EIGHTEEN

It was the night of the primary victory. But it wasn't really a victory. Bob Elam had run against and defeated no one. Yet, typically, there was a victory party.

Following Herb Chandler's orchestration, Bob spent much of the night high atop the city, ensconced in Chandler's dimly-lit, mahogany-walled office behind his massive desk.

Bill Sergent was aware of the scheduling of the guests as he greeted and handed them a drink. He then led them to Herb's office where Elam rose to greet them. Chandler remained in the office reception area, keeping the process on schedule. To Elam, everything appeared unstructured; the visitors entering, chatting, reminding him of commitments they had met and promises he had made, congratulating him, leaving. Bob had no idea that Chandler was telling each guest their allotted time.

Preempting all others was Jack Rutherford of the Farmers' Union. Next was Gene Hartman, Cattleman's Association, followed by Bob Evans of the National Farmers Organization. With agricultural interests assured of their importance to the Elam administration, organized labor was next. Higgins of the AFL-CIO admitted that labor hadn't gotten out the vote but promised a better turnout and additional financial support for the general. Ryan, who headed the Teamsters, was more aggressive yet deferential. Jackson White of the public employees union underscored his members' dependence. He spoke articulately but asked for nothing, only reassuring Elam of his members' support. The teachers union promised to do its part. Then came those representing key sectors, next the thinner line of academe, the leadership of the NAACP, the Urban League, the G.I. Forum, a mixed group representing conservation, chambers of commerce, antinuclear, private education, and so on. These last groups were given less time with Bob. After the homage was paid, Bob was given fifteen minutes to relax and to refresh before riding with Chandler to the victory party.

Charging into the large ballroom with a band playing "Happy Days Are Here Again," Elam pressed the flesh, shook every hand extended to him. There was no opportunity to speak, but Bob caught the eye of the individual whose hand he held and maintained that grip for a few seconds longer than necessary. Bob was making an individual impact on each member of the party faithful.

Chandler let Bob enjoy the night, allowed him to mingle, didn't push him to the raised platform. And although Bob enjoyed each encounter, his hand again became swollen. It hurt each time someone matched the firmness of his grip. Finally, Bob pushed his way to the speaker's platform.

As he and Pam negotiated the last few steps, the band again struck up the familiar chords of the old Democratic war cry. Happy days were indeed here again. Bob grabbed the microphone, smiling broadly. "I hear they're playing Al Smith's song again!"

Jesus Christ, Herb swore to himself. Wrong again. That was "The Sidewalks of New York." Besides, these kids don't know who the hell Al Smith was!

The crowd laughed, applauded, a few began the chant: "Elam's song, Elam's song ..." Soon the entire ballroom picked up the chant. "Holy shit!" murmured Chandler half aloud.

Bob raised his arms to quiet the crowd. "The Democratic Party..." He hesitated. "The people's party has many greats identified with it. Al Smith was among its best." Chandler grimaced. There goes his goddamned liberalism again. "And this song belongs to him, to the Democratic Party, to us." What the hell, thought Chandler, this is the hard core with us tonight. "And I'm proud to be a member of the party of Kennedy, of Johnson, of Humphrey ..." Jesus Christ, swore Chandler as Bob cited the litany of Democratic greats. "... of Jackson, of Jefferson. But above all, I'm proud of you. And Mrs. Elam and I ..." He paused. "... To hell with formality. Pam ... " he emphasized her first name, "... and I love you, all of you."

Bob spoke for a few minutes longer. He and Pam then raised their interlocked hands, repeating the gesture as the crowd roared its approval. Elam escorted Pam from the rostrum, then joined the crowd, shaking hands, embracing old and new friends, engaging in small talk, uttering appropriate and meaningless words, pressing the flesh, being the consummate politician. Pam joined Chandler and Sergent, proudly watching her husband.

The next morning Pam went to a newsstand. She purchased three copies of each the state's major newspapers, returned home, and gave Bob one of each. While Bob read of his primary victory, Pam clipped out stories. As she placed the clippings in a scrapbook, Bob, papers in lap, coffee cup in hand, appreciatively watched his wife.

Herb did not call Elam once during the rest of the week. Bob went to the lumberyard on Friday, conferred with Kreiger who he had promoted to run the business. Bob quickly realized how boring it was. He wondered how he had endured the day-to-day operation of the business. After an hour at the lumberyard, he reassured Kreiger that the business was in good hands and left.

Chandler called the following Tuesday. "I've been waiting for your call," Elam said. "Damn, you know I miss that caustic voice of yours. How's things? Anything wrong?"

"Nope. Nothing big. In general, things are going great. I just thought you needed some time. But now, back to work!"

"Well, I'm ready. What do we do next?"

"You'd better come see me. We can straighten out that little something I didn't mention. It's an error our treasurer made."

Bob felt fear. All kinds of things can go wrong in a campaign besides the personal or political errors of the candidate. Financial errors could be devastating. Bob's mind raced over worst-case scenarios. Did an overly zealous volunteer bribe someone? Did they accept a donation from a crook? Was there a payoff somewhere? Bob's voice betrayed his fear as he asked what had happened.

"Hey, I didn't mean to scare you," Chandler reassured his client. "Actually, the way it turned out, you'll be pleased about our little problem."

"What the hell is it?"

"I'll see you at three, at my office."

"It's nothing serious then?"

"Nah, don't worry."

"Okay, Herb, see you then." As Bob replaced the receiver, he felt a sense of relief that the error wasn't anything big. He felt even better that he was going back to work, returning to the political arena.

Later, after chatting with the secretary, Elam walked into Chandler's office. Herb was awaiting him, a check in his hand. "Sit down, Bob. Want a drink?"

Bob declined, asking Herb about the problem.

"It's a matter of disbursements, Bob."

"What do you mean?"

Herb responded by handing Bob the check. "By your accepting this, we resolve the problem." The check, made out to Robert T. Elam, was for four thousand dollars.

"What the hell's this for?"

"Your wages for working for a chicken-shit outfit called 'Elam for Governor'."

"You're kidding me?"

"I'm kinda embarrassed about the mistake, but no, I'm not kidding. The CPA uncovered it. It's the only error he found while going over the books."

"I'll be damned. To think I'm being paid to work on my own campaign."

"Routine, Bob."

"Where's the money come from?"

"Out of the campaign coffers. Money from unions, corporations, individuals."

Bob envisioned a little old lady, or a struggling family, sending in a check. He felt guilty. Then he remembered seeing some of the contributions from corporations. Smiling, he said, "I'll assume this money came from Mobil, or ITT."

"Nope. They ain't contributing to us," Herb said, then added, "this time."

"Well, for Christ's sake, let's get Sergent on their asses." Then, more seriously, he asked, "How is the fund raising going?"

Chandler responded by handing Bob the ledger sheet. Noting Bob's disappointed expression, he said, "Morry Stans I ain't. But we have a shot at the DNC."

"The national committee?" Bob asked, surprised.

"Sure. You're the Democratic candidate for this state. And the DNC has placed a priority on recapturing statehouses. You just got to let them help us a bit."

"How much are they worth?"

"They've assigned states in our population range twenty-five thousand dollars, but only two-thirds will get the money. They want to meet you, make some judgments about you, decide whether or not you're a winner."

"Good. Where do we meet?"

"At their office in Washington. Here are the airline tickets. The meeting is scheduled for a week from yesterday. You leave Saturday morning. Keep track of your expenses so we can reimburse you."

"Sounds great. What else?"

"Sergent and I want to go over the DNC meeting with you. We can do it now. Okay?"

"Sure."

"Okay." He phoned Sergent to join them. "After this, the rest of the week's yours. Nothing else is planned."

Bob was disappointed the week would be empty of this new life he was so earnestly enjoying. To hide his disappointment, to keep Chandler from seeing how addicted he had become, he forced an empty question. "Where will we stay?"

"We got your reservations. Bill will go over that with you."

"When Pam and I went to Washington, we stayed at a place a couple of blocks from the Capitol on New Jersey Avenue. I'd like to stay there again. Pam really enjoyed the place."

"No problem. Tell Bill which hotel it was."

"Thanks." Bob sat waiting for Sergent. Moments later, Bill walked in carrying several file folders.

Chandler and Elam joined Sergent at a small circular table. Sergent began. "Okay, two DNC guys will spend most of the day with you. They'll pick you up at the hotel and be with you damn near the entire day. During this time, one, then the other will excuse themselves to talk to the guy who actually makes the decision. It will be done so subtly you wouldn't notice if I hadn't told you. Okay?"

Bob nodded.

"Good. Now each man will be looking for different things. Phil Macomber, he's tall, slim, gray-haired. His job is to assess you generally but primarily to test your party loyalty. He'll ask questions about building a wider base for the party. He'll probably suggest something like, ah, 'you should appoint a couple of Republicans to your cabinet. You know, win their loyalty by co-opting them.' What would you say to that?"

"Sounds reasonable," Bob replied.

"Wrong answer." Bill smiled. "The answer is to appoint only Democrats. If you need to appoint a Republican, make him change parties first. But the best answer is an emphatic 'No!' You see, congressional and senatorial races are damned important to the DNC. It obviously wants to control the congress - a lot happens there. But the state races are the bread and butter of politics. That's where the patronage is. The statehouses are where you build your national party. There just ain't much a congressman can do as far as patronage. Even a U.S. senator can't make many appointments. The plum book is only accessible to the executive branches: the mayors, the governors, the president. So it's important that you appoint Democrats, the young, the brash, the politically attractive; people who'll use their offices as springboards for their own political careers. They want you to groom a new generation of Democratic leaders."

Bob nodded. It made sense.

Bill continued. "The DNC wants three things out of the Elam administration." He spoke confidently of the inevitability of Bob's victory. "One, they want a stable of electable candidates coming from your administration. Two, they want Democrats to get jobs in state government. The third is a resurgence of the state's party." Bill paused for effect. "Your job next Tuesday is to convince them you can accomplish these things."

Sergent continued briefing Elam, suggesting persuasive things to say. Bob nodded with confidence. He believed he could.

"Good. Now while Macomber is making these judgments, Corson will assess your winability."

"Winability?" Bob asked, smiling.

"Forgive the coinage. You know what I mean."

"Sure."

"The last hour or so, you'll be with the third guy. He'll have received the assessments of you. Now we don't know a thing about him, but the trick is to look, speak, and feel like a winner. 'Cause we could sure use that extra twenty-five thou."

Bob nodded. Chandler rapped his fingers on the table. "Okay, your little briefing is over." He reflected for a moment. "The hell of it is,

Bob, we can't really prepare you for the visit. We can only tell you the posture you should assume. But it's you the man - the mensch - they'll be looking at."

"I feel good about it," Bob said. Grasping Sergent by the arm as they left Herb's office, he mentioned the name of the hotel. He drove home, eager to tell Pam of the trip they would be taking.

CHAPTER NINETEEN

Hugh Saarson was regarded by both his adversaries and allies as tough, shrewd, and not disinclined to push beyond the parameters of professional and ethical standards to gain his ends. But above all, he was viewed as successful. He had joined the ranks of those with over a million dollars many years ago and had since improved on his position.

Saarson had accepted a position with a large R&D firm in Southern California after earning his MBA from Stanford in '41. When the war broke out, he bided his time, waiting for the machinery of conscription to locate, classify, and order him to present himself for duty. When he was ultimately called, he was declared 4-F because of a back injury.

Hugh continued working for the firm for three more years, then he was released when several costly errors were traced to flaws that were due in some part to his projections. He accepted the discharge in good spirits, viewing his years with the firm as an extension of his college education, a sort of apprenticeship. There was no remorse within Saarson that his errors had cost the firm tens of thousands of dollars. They were honest mistakes, he reasoned, a part of his learning process. He was relieved that the miscalculations had cost him nothing personally and that the firm was large enough to absorb the losses. In the days of fast profits and lucrative contracts, he knew the firm would quickly recover.

Hugh had led a Spartan lifestyle, living in cheap apartments, eating in sleazy diners, foregoing the pleasures of the many lonely women he encountered. The bulk of his wages was invested in companies involved in government contracts, especially those with cost-plus defense contracts. Hugh recognized that these contracts were invariably awarded to the most politically connected firms. That made them good investment opportunities. But as the war effort began to pay its dividends in numbers of enemy captured or killed, tonnage of ships sunk, Pacific islands and French villages retaken, Hugh sold the inflated stocks, placing the windfall profits into savings. He thereupon left the West Coast with his four years of acquired experience and his savings. He moved to the Midwest.

Hugh enjoyed the sparsely populated region. And he observed the price of farmland. He read the obituaries of aging farmers who died while pushing themselves beyond their endurance in the production of food. When the death notices indicated the decedents' sons were assigned to overseas theatres of operation, Hugh met with the widows, offered a fair price, and amassed thousands of acres of land.

Hugh was often asked how he liked this area compared to the more sophisticated lifestyle of the West Coast. To the delight of these Midwesterners, he told them he preferred it here. He liked the simple routine the area afforded him. Although having a disproportionate number of its sons in the military, the people didn't have the martial monomania of the West Coast. Here farmers continued planting and harvesting their crops, small shopkeepers sold their wares, and life went on about the same as it had before the war. Since there were no training bases nearby, young men in uniform were seldom seen except when hitchhiking through the region or when troop transport trains stopped for refueling. The war only deeply affected those whose sons, husbands, or lovers were in the military, but they endured these separations with dignity. The vagaries of the seasons, the prices of grain and livestock, as well as the progress of the war were the primary subjects of conversation.

As the number of acres he owned or controlled increased, so did his appeal to the women in the area. Although his life on the West Coast, with its relaxed morality, had been characterized by a near celibate existence, here in the Bible Belt he learned the pleasures of love and lust. And although he dined and danced with the women who were available - the single, the married, the widowed - it was a widow of a U.S. Marine with whom he fell in love.

Caring for the Marine's daughter was a joy to Hugh. However, tolerating the activities of his adulterous wife became inconsolable anguish. It ended the night a police officer awoke Hugh and told him of his wife's death. Details were conveyed to him by sundry means the next day. His wife and two sailors, all very drunk, were killed when their car simply ran off the road and into a tree. The speedometer remained on eighty-five after the car had come to rest. The policeman, out of a sense of decency, had placed a blanket over her naked corpse.

After the sixteen months of marriage and unrequited love, Hugh resumed a lifestyle of celibacy, devoting himself to the stepdaughter who was now dependent upon him and whom he had grown to love, and to the business in which he could immerse himself.

Now, twenty-five years later, Hugh's total being was again filled with anguish because of the stepdaughter he had adopted. It was, he thought, in her blood, absolving himself of any personal blame.

Five years ago, the marriage of Hugh's daughter was the high point of the capital city's social calendar. As Amy was given away by her father before the altar in a large Episcopalian church, the governor, a U.S. senator, and three congressmen representing all but two of the state's districts were in attendance.

Hugh learned to love the grandchildren his daughter's marriage gave him. But he sadly watched the marriage dissolve into nothingness and end in divorce. Amy had remarried within a year, this time to Greg Allen, an affable young man with a law degree, a gregarious personality, and an inability to support his family. Hugh quietly observed the difficulty of Amy's second marriage, fearing his interference might make the situation worse. He continued giving money to his daughter during periods when Greg had no clients, but he knew he was throwing good money after bad.

So Hugh decided to try to resolve the situation himself. After evaluating the problem and checking with those firms his son-in-law had represented, Hugh knew he didn't want Greg working for him. He gave serious thought to where Greg might be able to succeed or, failing that, do his employer minimal harm. It was one of his associates who produced an answer that was simple, time-tested, and achievable: a government job.

Basing his strategy on the premise that incumbents are usually reelected, Hugh arranged a meeting with Governor Norman.

Unfortunately, and unlike most people, Hugh Saarson wasn't intimidated by the executive office of the governor. Instead of being awed by its grandeur, he only saw its flaws: the chipped paint, the cracked leather, the faded velvet curtains.

Familiar with the way in which deals are struck, he cut right to the chase. He offered Norman a cash contribution of $25,000. The only stipulation was that his son-in-law would get a cabinet-level position that he would hold throughout the governor's second term. To

Saarson's way of thinking, the offer was sound, one that Norman should readily accept. Norman would receive a large sum of money to apply to any venture he desired. In return, he would appoint an individual from a good family, with impeccable credentials, legal training, and an ability to favorably represent the administration.

Saarson would ensure that his son-in-law had a respectable, perhaps prestigious, position for the next few years earning $25,000 a year. Then, after faithfully serving his governor and state, Greg could get a job with a white-shoe law firm or even enter the political arena himself. It was a sound business deal, Hugh thought. No one loses, and he wins.

Norman was stunned by the blatant offer of the bribe. He sat back, buying a few moments before he tried to respond without any hint of culpability. He hoped his expression wouldn't betray his shock. After all, Hugh Saarson was not a man to be taken lightly. Norman then realized he shouldn't be personally insulted, that Saarson simply viewed this as a quid pro quo.

He leaned forward, his elbows on his desk, the tips of his fingers almost touching. "I tell you what. Have your son-in-law present his credentials to my administrative assistant. I'll tell him Greg will be by to see him in the next few days. You know, we always need bright young people in government. Perhaps Greg is just the man we're looking for."

Saarson leaned forward to again explain the financial aspects of the offer, but Governor Norman cut him off. This meeting was clearly over. With some confusion, Saarson rose from his chair. "I'll sure do that, Governor. I think once you meet my son-in-law, you'll discover he's a man you will want in your cabinet." With that, he shook the governor's hand and departed, not knowing he had committed a criminal act but realizing full well that his son-in-law had no chance of being hired by Norman.

He called Herb Chandler the following week. The call was hardly spontaneous. He had used the time to determine which Democrats would run against Norman. After several calls to politically connected friends, he learned that Chandler was grooming a candidate. He was also told that Herb had an eye for a winner, seldom involving himself with a candidate unless the individual could be elected. This time Hugh moved more subtly - for two reasons. Time wasn't important, and he realized that any strings attached to contributions had to be dealt with delicately.

Chandler had invited Saarson to the meeting at the Plainsmen Hotel. And he suggested to Elam that he spend some time chatting with Saarson.

After hearing Elam and seeing the crowd's response to him, Hugh knew he was in the presence of the next governor. After Elam had finished speaking, Hugh wrote a check for two thousand dollars, walked directly to Herb, and handed it to him. He was gaining a degree of sophistication. You don't deal with the candidate in these matters; that's what his aides are for. When he shook Elam's hand, no mention was made of the contribution.

Hugh telephoned Greg immediately after getting home on that snowy night. They met for drinks the following afternoon. Hugh asked how Greg's practice was doing. Greg said business was slow, but he expected it to soon pick up.

"That means you have some free time now?"

"Yeah, some."

"You want to get involved in an exciting venture?"

Greg looked up from his drink. It's about damned time, he thought, wondering what Hugh had in mind; obviously something speculative, oil drilling on some of Hugh's land, he heading up that new component. Or was it the development of a shopping center near the outskirts of the capital? Hugh owned land there, too.

He then realized his current predicament: an attorney with no clients. He felt an appreciation for Hugh. His answer, however, was a bit flippant. "I've always liked the long shots, Hugh. Something with nothing substantial up front but lots of possibilities, something wide open for imaginative thought. Are you going to start a new subsidiary…" He noted Hugh's expression, then lamely finished, "… or something?"

Hugh didn't lose his temper. Evenly he said, "No, it's nothing I'm involved in - or my company. You'll have to make your own entry, your own contacts, prove your own worth."

Clearly disappointed, Greg shifted his weight in the chair. Damn him! He still won't trust his only son-in-law in the family business. "What the hell you talking about?"

"I know who the next governor is going to be."

"Yeah, so what?"

Hugh could not hide his disappointment this time. He's dumb, lazy, and shallow. "Jesus Christ," he swore. "Let me ask you. Who do you think it will be?"

"No idea."

"Neither do most people. Does that suggest anything to you?"

"Not really," Greg answered, disappointed he wasn't going to work in one of Hugh's ventures.

"For God's sake, Greg, think for a moment."

Greg looked back with a blank expression.

"Look, governors govern," Hugh explained. "They run the machinery of government. They need lots of aides to assist them. Now are you getting the goddamn picture?"

"Norman is gonna be reelected. He's already got his aides," Greg countered.

"No, he won't. He's a loser. The next governor of the state is a guy most people haven't heard of, a guy you certainly haven't heard of. His name's Bob Elam. Can you see a role for yourself in his new administration?"

Greg's eyes opened wide. "Could you get me a job with him? Running an agency or a department?"

"No. But I might be able to help."

"How?"

"That's not important now. The important thing is to make some contacts with his campaign staff. Start volunteering, get on board before the train leaves the station."

Greg now fully appreciated what Hugh was saying. "You mean in the campaign?"

Disappointed that the husband of his only child took so long to grasp the obvious, Hugh simply nodded.

"Who's heading it up?"

"Go see Herb Chandler. I'll give you his telephone number."

"Okay, Dad, I sure will." Then he added sincerely, "And thanks."

They finished their drinks and parted. Hugh sent another check to the Elam campaign that evening.

Chandler assigned Greg to the boiler room, doing the unsung tasks required in every campaign. Greg realized the chores were far from the policy level he had envisioned, but he relentlessly undertook them. When Amy returned from work, she would find Greg and the children folding campaign pamphlets or stapling campaign signs onto wooden stakes. Their living room was always in disarray with boxes of campaign literature and bumper stickers, their garage filled with yard signs.

Throughout this process, Greg was changing. He was cheerful, no longer chiding or belittling Amy. His relationship with the children became closer than ever before. Despite Greg's lack of income and the constant untidiness of their home, Amy again enjoyed being with her husband. She watched with appreciation as Greg worked with the children. She would prepare chilled drinks when they came home after placing campaign literature at neighbors' homes. Greg then volunteered to canvass areas of the city where others hadn't gotten the job done. He got a map from the municipal planning department, and he and the children plotted out these neighborhoods, ascertaining the quickest routes to each home. Before the primary, he used voter registration lists to deliver the pamphlets to Democrats. Now every registered voter's house received them. On weekends Greg and the children loaded up the backseat and trunk of the car with signs; pounded them into the yards of those he persuaded to climb aboard the Elam bandwagon.

Those in charge of Greg commended his work to their superiors. Word was getting around the Elam camp. Greg Allen, son-in-law of Hugh Saarson, successful lawyer on leave of absence from his firm, was a fulltime volunteer and one helluva campaigner. Because he was frequently at the campaign headquarters, Greg often met Elam, and while being the consummate sycophant, he was never perceived as an opportunistic toady. Soon he was invited to sit in on a program task force. Eventually he headed up a subcommittee of the Welfare Reform Committee. Greg acquitted himself well; once preventing an embarrassing blunder by advising the committee of the categorical nature of Title XX. Shortly thereafter he was assigned the task of reviewing the state's OEO programs, charged with developing an action paper that would become the new administration's position on the programs.

Greg Allen, respected jurist, political activist, and devoted campaigner, was now Elam's in-house expert on the state's antipoverty programs.

Hugh Saarson, for the first time, took pride in his son-in-law. Amy was again happily married. And Greg Allen - he had arrived!

CHAPTER TWENTY

The rangelands had depleted the moisture provided by the spring rains and surrendered their lush greenness to the brown of autumn. The cattle herds had been thinned out so that fewer head would have to compete for less food come winter. The streams had lost their sparkling clarity and now listlessly carried minute particles of the earth to the muddy rivers into which they flowed. The moist and warm winds from the southeast were now drier, colder, and from the north. As the leaves had fallen and trees stood naked, the High Plains reverted to the lethargy of the season.

It was that time when one retreats to the comfort of home, where steamed windows and the warmth of kitchen are a reassurance of the stability of one's life and basic purpose.

Minor problems are magnified by the intensity of the season, the closeness it mandates, the isolation it enforces. But the pleasures of life can also be magnified and enhanced by the same intensity and closeness. It simply depends on whether one is riding the zenith of joy or mired in the depths of despair.

Today it was loss that was being experienced. Saddened as he stood among and shared the sorrow of the mourners, Jeff Vinton witnessed the remains of Commissioner Brian Scott being lowered into the frozen earth. Seeing that Andrea was shivering from the cold, he placed his arm around her waist and drew her close. They stood awkwardly as did the others after the casket had been lowered to the bottom of the grave. Jeff then saw many of the people walking to where Mrs. Scott and her sons were seated. Realizing that Andrea was unaccustomed to the cold, that she continued to shiver, he motioned her to their car.

After letting her in, Jeff ran around and entered the vehicle, starting the engine. They remained motionless because their car was parked between two unoccupied automobiles on the narrow road that led through the cemetery. Jeff looked at Andrea, admiring her beauty. "You know, I'm proud you're my wife."

She smiled. "You look troubled. I guess he was your friend in addition to being your boss. I'm sorry I never met him."

Jeff wondered if he should mention the problems he foresaw because of Scott's untimely departure. During the six months of their marriage, he had kept from her the vitriolic exchanges between him and Oldfield. He decided not to tell her. There's nothing she can do, and she's better off not knowing, he reasoned. Also, he wanted her to perceive him as being in control of his, of their, destiny. "Yeah, I guess we thought he'd come out of it. He was getting better before that last attack."

The car engine warmed and he turned on the fan, heating the interior. Finally the car ahead of them left, and Jeff drove from the cemetery onto the highway. He was in a pensive mood, attempting to review the recent events and project their impact. Scott's death would cause changes, most of them adverse to Jeff and the direction he had set for the welfare office. It had happened too suddenly. He hadn't had time to sort things out. He looked at Andrea and, catching her eye, smiled and turned on the radio. He didn't want to talk. He wanted to think about his position, his options, the actions he should take.

Andrea knew it was best to leave him alone when he was in one of these moods. She looked at the frozen countryside passing by.

Jeff had relied too much on Commissioner Scott's strength of personality and character. He had done little to create relationships with the other commissioners whom he might have won over. Instead, he had let Scott handle the necessary compromises and tradeoffs. Jeff didn't even know on what issues Scott had yielded to accomplish the concessions. It's too late now, he lamented. He inventoried his political strengths. Initially, and significantly, there was the mental health mill levy. He had removed over a hundred patients from the state hospitals. The county's cost for their care had decreased by $450,000. That was a lot of money. Pretty persuasive stuff! He turned to Andrea, thinking he might explain this bureaucratic coup, but she was engrossed by the monotony of the bleak countryside.

Relieved, he returned to his thoughts. The food stamp program. The merchants would tell the commissioners about their increased business activity. He would check with Milner to see how many dollars had come to the county via the program. And the ADC checks. All new money. And Medicaid. The poor were now advised of medical and dental coverage. Christ, he had no idea how many teeth had been filled, pulled, replaced. It was a lot. He began to feel okay. Maybe he wasn't in trouble after all. The local AMA and ADA members would quietly speak to Oldfield. So would the chamber of commerce members. He would ask the clerk of the court to tell the commissioners about the mental health savings. And she would tell them! Satisfied, he continued driving to Union.

It wasn't until he entered the city that he realized the folly of his thoughts and how far he had removed himself from reality. For Christ's sake, no doctor or merchant would defend the conduct of his office, the socialization of Harney County, regardless how much they benefited. There was a vast chasm separating his practice of public involvement in personal duress and the ingrained conservatism of everyone else. He realized his remaining days as the welfare director were few and would be controversial and painful.

He looked to Andrea who had entrusted herself and her children to him. He felt guilty, unsettled, scared. He grabbed her hand and held it tightly, gaining comfort. She looked at him, perplexed. Minutes later, Jeff drove up their driveway. Andrea watched as the northerly wind blew tumbleweeds across the stubble of the wheat field west of their home. She remained seated in the warmth of the car, unmoving. Then she remembered her children walking into the restaurant last March. She looked at Jeff and parroted them. "BRRR!" Jeff looked surprised. In return, she smiled. "I don't expect you to understand, but this South Texas blood just got warmed up." She looked out at the coldness of the day. "Okay, let's brave the elements and I'll make lunch." Jeff hurried to the house and unlocked the front door. Seeing it was open, Andrea raced through the wind.

After lunch, Jeff went to the courthouse. He sensed that Scott's specter and the ramifications of his death were present, a precursor of another finality. Jeff entered his office and closed the door. Then he realized that action reinforced his staff's fears. Sensing it was futile to alter their perception, he still had to try. He asked Evelyn and Milner to join him. Moments later, faces glum, they entered his office.

Jeff forced a smile. "Christ, what the hell's going on?" Then, with the dark humor he had used in Vietnam, "You'd think someone got knocked off."

"It's not the newly departed we're concerned about," Milner

smiled.

"I'm afraid the word's around the courthouse, Jeff," Evelyn said. "Oldfield's gonna try to fire you."

"I suppose he's got the votes," Jeff said, looking to Milner.

"The chatter is he does."

A silence ensued, interrupted by Evelyn. "I'm concerned, Jeff. Do you have anything lined up, jobwise, in case he does?"

Jeff shook his head. "No. I hadn't expected to be changing jobs so soon."

"Does Andrea know?"

"Not a hint."

"It'll probably take a while," Milner said.

"Yeah," Evelyn agreed.

Jeff looked up. "Well, in the meantime, let's keep going as usual. Okay?"

"Sure," they said, leaving Jeff alone in his office.

Well, it couldn't last forever, he reasoned. But goddammit, why so soon after Andrea and the kids had moved here? Then in a moment of unemotional clarity he realized he was entering a period of grace. He knew that only at the beginning and end of a relationship could one act with impunity. He could now do all of those things he wanted to but was unable to do because of political reasons. It would take a few months for Oldfield to lock up the votes, to contrive a reason to get rid of him. He thought of Rediger. He dialed the regional Office of Economic Opportunity, asking for Ashton.

Ashton answered several minutes later.

"Ashton, this is Vinton, from Harney County. I earlier spoke to you about John Rediger."

"Yeah, I remember. How are you?"

Ashton's personal inquiry caught Jeff off guard. "Okay. Yourself?"

"Enough chitchat. What is it?"

"Remember our last conversation?"

"Vaguely."

"The board meets in three weeks. I ain't fishing no more."

"Whatcha got?"

"Be at the meeting. I'll tell you and the board then." He impulsively hung up the telephone. Moments later he called Goldman, asking if he was free. It was their first conversation since Jeff had told him he was going to hold off taking action.

"Why?" Dave asked tersely.

"I'd like to invite you over to my home."

"What for?"

"Some wine, maybe some cheese."

"What else?"

"To ensure I've got everything current for the board meeting."

A silence followed. Then, "You gonna do it?"

"Yep."

"Damn! Sure. What time?"

"About eight."

"Okay if I bring George? We got a meeting but can leave early."

"Sure." Jeff replaced the phone. He felt good in spite of Oldfield and the forthcoming demise of his job. He walked from his office, advising Evelyn he was leaving early. She was perplexed by his good spirits and smiled sadly.

Andrea was surprised by his early arrival. Jeff told her George Iron Rope and a VISTA were coming over that evening. He then realized that George had surely heard the courthouse rumors, had probably told Goldman. He would intercept them before they mentioned his difficulties in front of Andrea. He took a cup and poured some coffee, sitting at the kitchen table. "How's things?" he asked. Andrea stepped away from the stove. She reached out her hand, holding his for a moment.

"You think we got time?" he asked.

She looked at him for a moment, then laughed, "Heavens no. The kids will be here any moment now."

"Shucks. Well, just checking."

"I'm glad you're over this morning. You looked pretty shaken."

"Yeah, I'm okay now." Changing the subject, he asked, "You remember George, don't you?"

"Yeah." She appeared lost in thought for a moment, then, "I read in the paper that Joe Pipe On The Head was arrested for public drunkenness." She paused. "I think their damned names are part of their problem."

"Hmm. Could be. Never thought of it. Anyway, the other guy's a kid from the East Coast. I think you'll like him. He has the same accent as some of your relatives I met at our wedding."

"God! It'll be good to hear an eastern accent again. I've forgotten what it sounds like."

"Do we have any cheese to go with the wine?"

"Sure. But we haven't any wine."

"How's the money?"

"Low."

"Can we spare a couple bucks?"

"I suppose so." She got out the checkbook. "Ten dollars okay?"

"Sure we can afford it? You know, I haven't been privy to our finances since we got married."

Andrea recognized the complaint cloaked in Jeff's humor but chose to ignore it. "You make it, I'll spend it," she said in an offhand way before giving the checkbook to Jeff. She then leaned forward and kissed him lightly.

The doorbell rang at eight o'clock. Dave and George were right on time. Jeff had positioned himself near the door during the last few minutes. "It's them, Andrea. I'll get it." Jeff stepped out into the cold.

"Have you heard, George?"

"Yeah." George answered, looking away from Jeff.

"Did he tell you, Dave?"

"Yeah."

"Well, for Christ's sake, don't mention it to my wife."

They nodded. Jeff, holding the door, motioned them in. Andrea was walking into the living room as they entered. Jeff observed her beauty once again, proudly introducing her to Dave. Andrea invited them to sit. Laura and Bobby lowered the volume of the television, moving closer to it. Soon Andrea brought in the red table wine and a block of cheese. "Before you guys get started, I got to ask you something, George."

"Sure, Andrea."

"You may not like it."

"That's okay," he smiled. "Take your best shot."

Andrea was unsure how to begin. "Well, in the various places I've lived, there were a few Indians. But their names weren't ..." She hesitated. "Didn't have the ..." She stopped in midsentence. She began again but again floundered.

Dave smiled at her discomfort. "What Andrea is asking, George, is how come you guys got such screwed up names?"

"The hell you say," George rejoined, laughing.

"Seriously," Jeff joined in. "What is the story? Some are damned ludicrous. I ran across a file that had the name Dorothy Bad Milk. Probably a delightful young lady but with an atrocious name."

"I never thought much about it," George reflected. His father's name was Iron Rope. He passed it on to his sons. He never thought to ask where it came from.

Dave leaned forward. "You know, I met a kid named Carl Crooked Eyes. I'll bet the little bastard's gonna need glasses in another six months."

George cut a piece of cheese. "More county money, huh?"

"Christ," Jeff exclaimed. "We gotta get that kid back to the reservation, or at least across the county line."

George looked at Andrea. "I don't know," he said, this time intrigued. "I guess the missionaries couldn't pronounce Lakota words. The language is difficult, but the sounds are beautiful."

"What's your name in Lakota?" Dave asked.

"Wican Muza."

"WHY KHAN MUSE ZAH," Goldman said phonetically. "Like an Oriental poem."

"What's Poor Bear?"

"Yosma Kameko."

"And Standing Soldier?"

"Ahkichi Ta Nagi," George responded.

Dave became angry. "That's great, but why the hell do you call yourself Iron Rope? You're George Wican Muza. Just because some damned missionary couldn't speak Lakota eighty years ago doesn't mean you can't now!"

Jeff interrupted. "I know a guy named Pesek. In Bohemian, Pesek means 'little dog'. If the missionaries ever got hold of him! And how about Schlegelmilch, and Vrbka? If we Anglicized Indian names, why didn't we do the same to Russian, German, and Czech names? How come we just picked on you guys?"

George smiled. "That's okay. We're used to it."

"No!" Andrea protested. "Do something about it!"

"What?" George asked, surprised by the emotion in her voice.

Andrea was taken aback. Then it occurred to her. "You should un-translate them. That way American Indians would have American Indian names!"

"Hell yes," Jeff said. "If a tribal court can issue a birth certificate, it can sure as hell change a name!"

"I suppose," George said after thinking for a moment. "But you know, if it did, they somehow wouldn't be Indian names."

"But it would enhance cultural pride, tribal identification, respect for what you were and what you are," Andrea persisted.

No one spoke. Andrea's expression betrayed her impatience. Everyone was in agreement except George, the American Indian.

George slowly shook his head. "I just don't know, Andrea."

"You better get the Crooked Eyes family out of the county," Dave grinned, looking at Jeff.

Jeff smiled, contributing to the silence.

Exasperated, Andrea walked to Laura and Bobby. "Time for bed." After a few futile protests by the children, Andrea led them down the hallway. Halfway down the hall she stopped and turned. "I still think that in a subconscious but fundamental way those crazy names are a part of the Indians' problem." She turned, following the children to their rooms.

Dave looked at Jeff. "Quite a gal you got there. She coming out to Harney County and spouting the rhetoric of Eldridge Cleaver."

"Huh?" Jeff looked at Dave. "Isn't Cleaver the guy who fled to Algeria or somewhere to avoid prosecution?"

"Yeah. He's also the guy who said, 'If you're not part of the solution, you're part of the problem'."

Jeff was surprised by this bit of trivia. "I'll be damned. You know, I saw a rancher driving his pickup, rifle in the rear window, with a bumper sticker quoting this guy Cleaver."

"If only he knew," Goldman mused. He looked at Jeff and in a low voice asked, "How's the job security?"

"Pretty bad," Jeff said, annoyed by his answer.

"Why haven't you told Andrea?"

"I want to get something lined up first. Besides, it's only a rumor."

Dave's expression revealed his skepticism. "Okay."

Jeff had to change subjects lest Andrea overhear. "How's our friend Rediger?"

Dave placed his wine glass on the coffee table. "We didn't think you'd move on it. We shut down our investigation."

Jeff nodded. "No problem. I understand. I still got the photocopies you gave me. That should be enough. I told Ashton to come. I'll go with what we've got."

Dave nodded. "Should be enough."

"Any suggestions as to how to present this mess?"

"You shouldn't have any problems. Just be low key, unemotional, aloof, persuasive, non-confrontational, and eloquent," Dave said.

Jeff nodded. "Like you said, I shouldn't have any problems."

Dave and George were leaving as Andrea returned to the living room. Disappointed, she invited them to come back again.

"Sure," George said. "How soon?"

Andrea smiled. "We'll finish the wine and cheese tomorrow night. About the same time?"

They returned the next evening, and the next. As the days passed, they became the only ones outside of his family with whom Jeff could relate, share experiences and expectations, and relieve his tensions. And if Jeff's passion reflected an innate sense of justice, Dave gave it a political and philosophical foundation. The discussions provided Jeff with internal support, and they exacerbated his difficult relationship with the commissioners and the people of Harney County.

Dave's discussion of the War on Poverty gave Vinton greater insight than he had gotten by being on the CAP board. Dave supplied him with OEO instructions, guidelines, mission statements, and the public law enabling the effort. Lacking the eloquence of Jefferson, the legislation spoke in arcane terms of government's dependence upon the governed. The law supported the active participation of low-income people in government. One OEO regulation contained a Bill of Rights for indigents.

The discussions occurred nightly. Goldman enjoyed himself, giving substance to his views as he articulated them. "Take the food industry for example ..." He rambled on. "Vertical integration ... limited partnerships ... corporate farms ... land grant colleges marrying agribusinesses ... machines picking tomatoes ... center pivots ... nitrate levels ... water mining ... capital intensity ... energy intensity ... .

The night before the board meeting, Dave and Jeff reviewed their evidence. There was a question of tactics. Should Jeff begin with the less important items, building up to the more damaging ones? Or would the board be more decisive, act more quickly if they were shocked by first hearing the worst? "We're taking this too seriously, Jeff," Dave said. "No matter how you present it, they're gonna fire the sonofabitch and the bums around him. If they don't – then there ain't no God."

This eased Jeff's mind. "You really think so?"

"Sure. Those board members are basically bigoted, dumb, and reactionary. But when it comes to tax dollars, most of them are honest."

"I hope so," Jeff said unenthusiastically.

"So whatcha worried about?"

Jeff smiled. "It shows, huh?"

Dave nodded.

"Well, I haven't spoken with any board members. And I'm committed to go with this thing because I told Ashton I'm gonna do it. And me, an outsider, is gonna attack a local boy who's brought a lot of money to the area and who's caused damn few problems. Really, why should they believe me?"

"Christ, you've got photocopies, and you've photocopies of the photocopies, a goddamned personalized packet for each board member. And in those packets you've got damn good stuff, and the figures don't lie, can't be refuted."

"I hope you're right," Jeff said, not fully persuaded.

***

It was dusk as Jeff left Union to drive to the board meeting. In his briefcase were the documents for his fellow board members. Jeff used the time to again organize his thoughts, structure his presentation.

Arriving at the CAP office, he remained in his car for a few minutes. Scott's death and Oldfield's ascension to the chair were clear signals of his impending job loss. Would his vigorous attack on Rediger, his causing that dismissal, make it easier for Oldfield to have him fired? And what of Andrea and the kids who were the innocents in this ugly war of bureaucrats? What would they be subjected to because of his actions? And Rediger. Did he have a wife and kids? Jeff had no idea. But how about the poor who were being cheated out of programs that could help them? Shouldn't they have some consideration? Troubled, Jeff walked into the meeting room knowing no victor would emerge.

He sat at the directors' table, nodding to those who arrived, waiting as the room filled. Fourteen board members were present. He saw the VISTAs in the back of the room. He looked around, wondering where the hell Rediger was. Then he felt a light tap on his shoulder. He turned and looked up.

"Vinton?"

"Yeah."

"I'm Larry Ashton."

Jeff rose and shook his hand. "Good to meet you."

"Yeah. You got a minute?"

"Sure."

"Let's step outside."

"Sure."

Outside, Ashton asked, "What you got?"

"It's enough to make me wonder what you feds have been doing all this time."

"If your stuff is good, if it's hard and fast, I'll try to help. If it ain't, you'll get what you deserve."

"Fair's fair," Jeff said, smiling weakly. "I'm freezing my butt off. Let's go back inside."

"Okay," Ashton said, Jeff noting concern in his voice.

Reentering, he looked around again. Rediger still wasn't here. Had he heard what was going to happen? Maybe he won't show up because of a guilty conscience, Jeff thought. He leaned back in his chair, finding comfort in that idea. Then the agency's executive director entered the room accompanied by Commissioner Oldfield. Why the hell was Oldfield here? Jeff saw both men's eyes riveted on him. He noted Rediger's smug expression, Oldfield's disdain. What little certitude Jeff had quickly plummeted. He watched as they separated, Oldfield patting Rediger on his shoulder, then sitting, Rediger walking to his seat at the directors table. Once situated, he shuffled some papers, then turned to the chairman but spoke to the entire board. He apologized for being late. The chairman asked an attractive woman in her thirties to call the roll.

That must be Jan, Rediger's traveling companion and bedmate, Jeff concluded. He looked at her from a sexual perspective. For a moment he envied Rediger, then his attention was redirected to his own situation.

The chairman was advised a quorum was present. He looked to Rediger.

"Mr. Chairman, I've a couple of housekeeping items. First, there's a letter from the Harney County Board of Commissioners. It reads: 'Dear Mr. Chairman: Please be advised that in official business conducted during the February 19 meeting of the Harney County Board, Mr. Jeffrey Vinton is relieved of his duties representing Harney County on the governing board of the Community Action Program. Furthermore, effective this date, Chairman Hank Oldfield is hereby appointed to replace Mr. Vinton.'

"This communication is properly signed." Rediger looked up. "Mr. Chairman, Mr. Oldfield's credentials appear to be in order. I recommend the board accept and welcome him. I also think a token of appreciation to Mr. Vinton for his brief but fine service to this agency would be in order."

Jeff sat back in his chair stunned. Goddamn, it was Ashton, he realized. The fed had set him up. He cursed himself for the stupidity of that call to Ashton.

"So ordered," the chairman said. "Mr. Rediger, you are directed to officially extend to Mr. Vinton this board's appreciation." He looked at Jeff. "And on an informal basis, Jeff, this board thanks you. We wish you could have been with us longer."

Still speechless, Jeff realized that at least the chairman had not known this would be happening. Then Jeff felt a pat on his shoulder. It was Oldfield, smiling, wanting to assume his rightful place at the directors table. Jeff gathered the manila envelopes and placed them in his briefcase. He rose, surrendering his seat.

Embarrassed and powerless, he walked to where the VISTAs were sitting. They were as stunned as Jeff, but the cynicism their training afforded them allowed them to more quickly recover. Jeff remained bewildered.

"You've got to go with your stuff during the part of the agenda set aside for new business. And you've got to do it as a private citizen," Millard whispered with a sense of urgency.

Jeff nodded, still disconcerted.

"You think you can do it?" Goldman asked.

"I have to, because Rediger and Ashton know I'm going to."

"Let's step outside and regroup," Goldman said.

Oldfield couldn't prevent his smug smile. With detachment, he listened to the reading of the minutes. He was more interested in watching the duress Vinton was experiencing. After watching Jeff and the VISTAs leave, he turned his attention to the meeting. He became bored while listening to the report on the number of poor people served last month. Next was the fiscal officer's report on cash flow, monthly expenses. Oldfield almost interrupted her to inform the board he had another meeting to attend and that he would have to leave early. God he could use a drink to ease this boredom. Instead, he listened to a report of the agency's job training program. Realizing that George Iron Rope was paid by that program, he listened more intently. He had decided that George would leave the courthouse the same day Jeff did. Hell, he thought, Lisa could use a few extra bucks. She could replace George. But he reconsidered. He didn't want any of his relatives, or ex-relatives, replacing a goddamned Indian or involved with the goddamned welfare office. It wouldn't look right, he being a county commissioner; hell, he being the chairman of the board. His thoughts kept wondering. Then he saw Vinton and the VISTAs return. He hadn't expected that. He looked at his watch. Nearly an hour had passed. Well, he thought, the chairman won't let this drag out much longer.

Pleased that the meeting was proceeding in a timely manner, the chairman asked if there was any new business. Then he saw Vinton standing in the back of the room, his hand raised. A few words from the departing director, he thought, a nice windup. "Yes, Mr. Vinton. Have you any farewell thoughts for the board?"

"Yes I have." Jeff walked to a small table before the directors. Placing his briefcase on it, he took out the manila envelopes. "I've come across some information regarding the conduct of this agency and its staff. As a director, I was compelled to share it with the board. Now, as a private citizen, I still have that responsibility."

The chairman's expectation of getting home early was suddenly dashed. He looked at Rediger, who reciprocated with a deadpan smile, then at Jeff. "What is the nature of your information?"

"The information appears to lead to four charges. These charges involve conflict of interest, unauthorized travel, submission of illegal payroll and travel claims, and, because of the widespread practice and that federal funds are involved, conspiracy to defraud the U.S. government."

The chairman was unprepared for this: "... conspiracy to defraud the U.S. government ..." Jesus Christ! He looked to Rediger whose face was ashen, then to Ashton. "You represent the federal government. Do you know anything about this?"

Ashton stood. "Only that if Mr. Vinton doesn't have the facts to back him up, he'd better get a lawyer. I can see legal actions coming out of this."

"Jeff, Mr. Ashton may be right" the chairman spoke sympathetically. "Have you conferred with an attorney?"

"No, I haven't."

"Don't you think you should? Then come back next month?"

"No. I'm prepared to go now."

Oldfield, now alert, leaned forward. "For the record, Mr. Vinton isn't acting as a representative of Harney County. Anything he says or does is as a private citizen, no connection with the county."

The chairman became flustered. Christ, he was just a goddamned shopkeeper appointed to serve on a board overseeing an agency about which he knew nothing. Then, for Christ's sake, he was elected chairman, even got his picture in the paper. Everything was going okay. How the hell did he get into this mess? More important, how could he get himself out of it? He looked to Ashton. "As the federal representative, can you give the chair some advice as to how to proceed?"

Ashton stood, his hands in his pockets - almost slouching. He looked at the chairman obliquely. "There have been serious charges made. This board will have to deal with these allegations. I'm not an attorney. I can't advise you how, but you must deal with them."

Ashton had infuriated the chairman. "Any other bits of advice?" he sarcastically asked.

"It's an internal problem," Ashton continued. "I'll monitor your response, your reactions. But you're a private corporation. If you have a lawyer on the board or attorney of record, I'd suggest you involve him as soon as possible."

Enraged, but keeping a calm exterior, the chairman thanked Ashton. Then in an effort to postpone the inevitable, he turned to Rediger. "Have you anything to say about this?"

Rediger had regained his composure. He smiled. "I don't know what the hell Mr. Vinton is talking about."

Hearing this, Oldfield let out a loud laugh. Several board members joined him.

Damn, I've lost my initiative, Jeff thought. They're circling the wagons.

The chairman could delay no longer. "Well, Mr. Vinton, I guess it's up to you. If you wish, we could go into executive session. That might relieve you of some legal difficulties."

"Thanks, but I have friends who should hear what I have to say. I'll speak from here."

"Point of order! Point of order!" shouted Oldfield.

"What exactly is your point of order, Mr. Oldfield?" the chairman asked, fearing he was losing control.

"I really don't have one," Oldfield admitted. "But I need to speak."

The chairman saw humor in the situation. He looked at Jeff. "Mr. Vinton, you have the floor. Will you yield to Mr. Oldfield?"

Jeff made the best of the situation by exaggerating its awkwardness. "The Harney County welfare director yields three minutes to the honorable and distinguished chairman of the Harney County Board of Commissioners."

With unexpected eloquence, Oldfield barked back: "The chairman of the Harney County Board of Commissioners thanks the competent and able director of the Harney County welfare office. And within my three minutes, I wish to inform this board that Mr. Vinton may have a self-interest in making these accusations against our executive director. He knows that the mismanagement of his office has caused the county board concern and that his continued employment with the county is questionable. What I'm saying is that Mr. Vinton is looking for a job and may have zeroed in on Mr. Rediger's."

This caused a buzz among the board members. Oldfield looked at Jeff, enjoying the discomfort he had caused the welfare director.

Jeff was becoming intimidated by the events. But he realized no one but the VISTAs knew the information he possessed. "Mr. Chairman, I'm ready to proceed."

"Please do."

Jeff's nervousness had been replaced with cool anger. "Thank you. As I said, there are three primary accusations as well as conspiracy to defraud the government. The first is conflict of interest. I will provide the following documentation to substantiate that charge." He looked at the pile of manila envelopes, then asked Goldman, who had come up beside him, to separate the material relative to the specific charges.

"This conflict involves the deputy director and economic development director. You're aware that one individual holds both positions. Item one consists of the minutes of six city council meetings that have within them authority to pay this agency's economic development director fees for services as an industrial recruitment advisor. Those payments are to a corporation about which I will speak shortly. Item two consists of photocopies of time sheets and expense vouchers of the same individual charging the agency for the same services to the same municipalities during the same time period."

Jeff asked Dave to distribute the photocopies corroborating that accusation. He gave his former colleagues on the board a few minutes to scan them. "These documents suggest the possibility of double payment, fraud, and conflict of interest." He allowed silence to ensue. "I also have enclosed documents from the secretary of state regarding a for-profit corporation named High Plains Economic Development Inc. The nature of its business is providing technical assistance. It is the same corporation I earlier spoke of. Please note that the officers of this corporation are the CAP executive director, deputy director, executive secretary, and her spouse."

"The next items concern an outreach worker. Item three is correspondence from The Great Mobile Soap Company. The letter states that the distributorship for this area is unavailable and names the person currently owning that distributorship. That individual has the same name and address as an employee hired by the CAP to do outreach work. Item four consists of several signed statements by this individual's customers stating the times and dates that he delivered their orders."

"Item five is this individual's travel claims submitted to the agency, indicating visits to the same towns on the same dates his customers say he makes his soap deliveries. Item six consists of photocopies of travel claims and cashed checks reimbursing him for his travel."

Jeff asked Dave to hand out the photocopies, again allowing the board members time to examine them. He glanced at Oldfield who was intently chewing an unlit cigar, then at the smirking Rediger, then at the board members. A few had completed their scrutiny of the documents and were waiting for other shoes to drop. Some of the board members looked shocked. One smirked like Rediger. Ashton was taking it all in stride, another day in the life of a federal bureaucrat.

"The other charge also involves unauthorized travel and the illegal submission of travel claims. Again, taking a total perspective on this, the charge of conspiracy is obvious." Vinton took a deep breath. "Item seven: A list of trips by Mr. Rediger and his secretary during the last twelve months. You will note that twenty-five trips have been taken to sixteen states. The employees were paid wages during this travel in addition to airfares, lodging, and per diem. If one doesn't question the necessity of Jan Roberts traveling with the executive director, there are still significant questions."

"The last item consists of twelve letters from chambers of commerce in cities where official travel was taken to attend conferences and conventions during the indicated dates. These chambers denied their cities had hosted the cited conventions during those dates. One chamber researched past conventions and stated the indicated organization had not met there in the past three years. They further checked with the national chamber which has no record of such an organization existing." Vinton paused. "I would submit the possibility that these trips may have simply been pleasure trips, paid for by the agency and the taxpayers but for no official purposes."

The board members sat in stunned silence. Then they all began talking at once. A steady hum emanated from the directors table. Finally, the chairman tapped his pen against a coffee cup. "The meeting will come to order. Have you anything else, Mr. Vinton?"

Jeff thought that if he mentioned the lesser charges, Rediger could muddy the water by responding only to them. "Yes. But I prefer to present them at a later time."

"Well, I guess what you've given us is quite enough," the chairman said. He looked around, hoping someone would say something. The room remained silent. He looked at Jeff. "What do you suggest we do?" he lamely asked.

"Since I'm no longer affiliated with this agency, it would be inappropriate for me to suggest a course of action," Jeff coolly answered. "But as a taxpayer, I expect something to be done."

The chairman looked to Ashton. "What do you recommend?"

Ashton rose. "It appears you've got some problems. But you must use your local resources to resolve them." Ashton sat back down.

"Well I'll be goddamned," the chairman murmured, but loudly enough for those near him to hear. He turned to Rediger. "What do you have to say?"

Rediger took a moment to answer. "Just that Mr. Vinton will hear from my attorney in the morning."

"Nothing else?"

"Nope."

Exasperated, the chairman again looked around. The other board members looked away. "The chair will entertain any suggestions as to how to proceed."

Finally Oldfield spoke. "I move that we appoint an investigative committee to examine Mr. Vinton's charges."

"What do we do in the meantime?"

No one spoke. Then Oldfield said, "I call the question."

The chairman wasn't angry, just annoyed. He patiently spoke to Oldfield. "You're out of order. There's been no second."

Several board members quickly responded.

Oldfield again called the question.

"The question has been called for," the chairman acknowledged. "The motion has been made and seconded that we establish a committee to investigate the charges. All in favor indicate so by saying 'Aye'."

There was a spontaneous outburst of "Ayes."

"Those opposed, say 'Nay'."

Silence ensued.

"Motion carried. I charge the executive and personnel committees to merge and form a select investigative committee. I charge them to meet as necessary and to submit a full report to this board at its next regular meeting. I remind the committee that provisions do exist for emergency board meetings. Furthermore, I appoint Commissioner Oldfield the committee chairman."

"Sonofabitch!" Jeff said to Dave.

A motion to adjourn came from the end of the table. It was followed by many seconds. The vote was unanimous. The Community Action Program's governing board adjourned for another month.

The other VISTAs walked over to Jeff and Dave. Jefferson spoke first. "Something may still come of it. Who knows? The feds might force the board to act."

"I really thought the board would move tonight, at least suspend Rediger if not dismiss him outright," Jeff said, discouraged.

"Maybe next month. You did good," Millard countered. "Let's get drunk."

Jeff finally arrived home a little after two o'clock. The lonely drive back to Union had helped to sober him and had forced him to face the reality of dealing with his future. He was careful not to awaken Andrea as he got into bed. He would explain everything the next day.

Jeff arrived at the office on time the next morning. He was tired. Worse, he was hung over. He got some coffee, walked to his desk, and slowly sat. His mild headache was annoying, but it was the queasiness of his stomach that caused him the most discomfort. Still, that was manageable. It was the mental pressure, the self-doubts, the lack of personal security, the responsibility of family, and a strange sense of guilt that caused him greater uneasiness.

Dave Goldman walked into his office at ten o'clock and told him the VISTAs had been fired.

Jeff, his mind clouded by the residue of alcohol, thought he hadn't heard Dave correctly.

Dave repeated what he had said.

It took Jeff another minute to comprehend. "It figures. Rediger's retaliation," he surmised. Dave moved his chair to the corner of Jeff's office where he had sat the day they had met. He bore the same cynical expression of that day.

"Can you appeal it? Or do you want to?" Jeff asked.

"Second question, perhaps. First question, I don't think so. The board gave Rediger widespread administrative authority. I'm pretty sure he's got the power to fire us," Dave said.

"When is it effective?"

"I don't know. I have to call our regional office."

Jeff thought of his predicament. "It appears unemployment is on the rise in Harney County. What are you gonna do?"

"I was accepted at Columbia Law School. I'll hang around for a while, then in a couple of months go to New York, get an apartment, get ready for school."

"I didn't know. Congratulations. About law school, I mean."

"Thanks."

"How about Jefferson and Millard?" Jeff asked.

"I don't know. They're pretty burnt out."

"Too bad. I'm glad you're gonna be around for a while.

"How about you?"

"Well, I'm still employed. The board hasn't acted yet."

"Yeah." Dave underscored the obvious impermanence. "Officially you're still employed."

Dave's mention of his precarious situation annoyed Jeff. At this moment he wanted to escape that reality. He stood, signaling that he wished to be alone. Dave ignored him for a few minutes, staring at the tile floor, then stood. Jeff reached out his hand. "Keep in touch," he said, smiling. Dave shook his hand and departed. Jeff walked to the coffee station to refill his cup. The telephone rang as he passed Evelyn's desk. "It's Jan Roberts, Mr. Rediger's secretary," Evelyn told him as she handed him the receiver.

He was surprised she was calling him, especially after last night. "This is Mr. Vinton."

"Mr. Vinton, Mr. Rediger asked me to contact several of our job training sponsors. We just received instructions from the regional office to decrease our number of slots. Mr. Iron Rope has been terminated, effective close of business today." She said, "Thank you," and hung up before Jeff could utter a word of protest.

Jeff sadly shook his head as he handed the receiver back to Evelyn and returned to his office. If not the long knives then certainly the short ones, he thought as he leaned on his desk, his stomach churning. First the VISTAs. Now George Iron Rope. How could he tell George that his own goddamned honesty had cost the Indian his job? No bother, he thought, I've got all day. Then he realized the folly of making George work until five. He picked up the phone, asking George to come in.

"Yeah?" George peeked into his office.

"Come on in."

George entered, sat down, looked to Jeff. "George, there are winners and losers in this world. You teamed up with a loser."

George knew what was next. He was about to lose the only real job he ever had.

Jeff looked at him painfully. "George, we're being chewed up by a meat grinder. Rediger's fired the VISTAs, now you. I can only pay you to the close of business today. I'm sorry."

"I understand," George said.

"Go ahead, take off, and figure out a way to tell Mary. There's no reason to return."

"Sure." George shook Jeff's hand.

"I'm sorry, George."

"See you." George walked to his desk. Then, realizing he had nothing of his own there, he walked from the courthouse to his car. "Jesus Christ," he swore. His left rear tire was flat.

***

Hank Oldfield spent the morning in the conference room. The county treasurer placed another ledger on the long table. Moments later she brought a file drawer and placed it next to the ledger. "These are the invoices and warrants for September, Mr. Oldfield. Should I take any of the others back?"

Oldfield grunted, chewing on his unlit cigar. He didn't even look up.

"If you tell me what you're looking for, I could probably help," the treasurer offered. Oldfield continued leafing through the invoices, then he shifted his attention to the ledger. "Don't really know," he answered.

The treasurer returned to her office.

Oldfield didn't notice her departure. He continued to examine the county's invoices.

***

Milner was grim as he walked into Jeff's office. Jeff looked up, sensing his mood. "You heard about the VISTAs and George, huh?"

"Yeah. But that's not the real problem."

Jeff had been numbed by the morning's events. What the hell's next? Quietly, he asked, "What you got?"

Jerry sat on the edge of the chair. "It's one of the nursing homes we've been placing patients in."

"What about it?"

"I heard on the news the State Health Commission is trying to close it."

"Why?"

"The home is charged with some health violations. Stuff like overcrowding, inadequate staffing during the night hours, inadequate diets, and there's an indication of patient neglect."

"Jesus! Which one is it? And how many we got there?"

"It's the one down in Yorkton. We got twelve clients there."

Jeff's face lost its color. He sat back. "Christ, we take people from a facility that's adequate and place them in one that's not. What should we do? Pull them out now, or wait 'til the license is revoked?"

"The care won't get any worse. It'll probably get better during the investigation."

"Christ, Jerry, I can't think right now. Call the State Health Commission. Get their advice about what we should do."

"Okay." Jerry began to leave, then turned around. "Heck of a morning, huh?"

Jeff only shook his head. "When you get off the phone, let's have lunch."

"Sure."

Twenty minutes later Vinton and Milner walked out into the gray coldness. They walked without speaking, Milner sensing Jeff's need for silence. As they approached the restaurant, Jeff said, "Keep walking." When they reached the Elks Club he said, "Here we are."

They left the club an hour later and returned to the office. Milner had handled his martinis well. Jeff was tipsy and smelled of beer. So much so that Oldfield, who had been waiting, immediately knew where they had gone to lunch.

"Been waiting for you, Mr. Vinton," he said, knowing Jeff was at a disadvantage. Jeff smiled at Oldfield then asked him if he wanted some coffee. With a sense of superiority, Oldfield smiled. "Why don't you?" Again Jeff's grin appeared. "Yeah, I think I will."

"Shall we go into your office?"

"Yeah. Sure. Let me get my coffee."

Oldfield was seated when Jeff walked to his chair. He had closed the door as he entered. He sat, now somewhat sobered.

Oldfield slowly adjusted his eyeglasses and glared at Vinton. "What the hell are these?" he nearly shouted, thrusting several invoices toward Jeff.

Jeff reached for the documents. He recognized them as invoices from the Youth Opportunity Center. Anxiety overcame him. "They're the monthly tuition bills for one of our clients."

"Who authorized the expenditures?" Oldfield snapped.

"I did."

"Who's the client?"

"A retarded youngster. His name's Donny."

"A goddamned Indian, I suppose."

"Yeah, I think so."

"Figures. Did the board approve it?"

Although aware of his predicament, the alcohol made Jeff bold enough to say: "Must have. The invoices were paid."

Oldfield looked coldly at Jeff. "I assure you of one thing. The county's paid its last buck for this goddamned Indian. Goddammit, Jeff, we're the county government, not the goddamned Board of Education."

"I spoke with the school superintendent. He said the board wasn't responsible. I didn't think we should keep the kid out of school any longer."

"It's not our responsibility," Oldfield countered. He sat back in the chair, slowly shook his head with some resignation. A few moments passed. He looked squarely at Vinton. "Jeff, you're not a bad guy. You're just screwed up. Make no mistake, though. I'm committed to your leaving the employ of this county. You know that, don't you?"

Vinton didn't answer. He reacted calmly to Oldfield's stated purpose.

Oldfield continued almost apologetically. "I think in other circumstances we'd be pals. But make no mistake. Politically, we are complete opposites. Dammit, we can't do everything for everybody. And goddammit, you're convinced you're responsible for the welfare of every sonofabitch in the county. You're wrong. Those bastards are responsible for themselves. And you and your goddamned socialistic practices have got to go. We don't want you in Harney County. I'm gonna give you a month to find a job to support your family. Then I'm gonna move against you. You're going! And in the meantime, get that kid out of school. The county ain't gonna pay the bill any longer."

Donny's plight was far removed from Jeff's thoughts. He sat back, then leaned forward to protest, to save his job, to maintain the means to support his family. But he knew it would be hopeless. Then anger rose within him. He wanted to lash out at Oldfield; to tell him how his goddamned grandchildren were adding to the county's welfare rolls because his goddamned son wouldn't support his own children. Then, strangely, Jeff felt sympathy for Oldfield. He didn't want to hurt the old man. He remained silent.

After Oldfield had departed, Jeff sat and plotted the best way to explain his, no, their predicament to Andrea. Although eager to leave the damned office, he delayed his departure. Finally, realizing there wasn't a good way to share bad news, he prepared to go home. Before he could escape the events of this day, Milner called to him: "State Health says the nursing home is really bad news. Recommends we get our people out immediately. They feel so strongly, they're sending a certified letter."

"Okay," said Jeff, trying to bring some order to his confused mind. "Let's wait 'til we get it, but make plans for their removal. We'll talk tomorrow." Jeff departed the office eager for the comfort and warmth of family and home.

His thoughts as he drove were fleeting, almost erratic in nature. Filled with self-doubt, aware of how he had failed those who had entrusted themselves to him, Jeff dreaded his arrival. He envisioned his kids sitting before the television, the warmth, and smells of food from the kitchen, the soft music flowing from the FM station, his lovely wife. During these months of marriage his perception of Andrea's beauty had only been enhanced, those flaws in her appearance relegated to a nonexistence. Furthermore, while his professional difficulties lowered his own self-esteem, her insistence of complete control of their household elevated her level of competence in his eyes. Andrea brought order to the house and family. Jeff's anxiety increased as he neared his home. He was reluctant to disturb the serenity of the home, to explain their uncertain future, to confess his inability to control his circumstances.

As Jeff entered his home, Andrea was screaming loudly. Jeff hung up his coat, expecting things to calm down. They didn't. Laura began crying, holding her hands to her ears to shut out Andrea's piercing, angry words. Andrea reciprocated by raising her voice. Andrea was further angered by either Laura's actions or words. She stormed to her daughter, jabbing and thrusting her finger before her, yelling more intently. Laura was hidden from Jeff's view by Andrea, but she must have said or done something that caused Andrea to sharply grab her, jerk her around, and spank her. Laura shrieked from surprise and fear and pain. Jeff sat down, stunned by what he was witnessing in his home. Laura was now wailing, Andrea having stopped the spanking. Bobby had been cowering in a corner of the room. He stood, began to protest. Andrea walked over and slapped him.

Jeff could not understand what was happening. It was totally beyond him. He stood up quickly. "Goddammit, Andrea, enough's enough!" He shouted above Andrea's yelling, Laura's wailing, and now Bobby's sharp cries.

"Don't tell me how to raise my kids," Andrea snapped back, her face contorted, an intense loathing spilling forth. Jeff moved between Bobby and Andrea, partially separating them with his body. This enraged Andrea. She released Bobby, then she struck Jeff sharply on his face. Her blow barely made an impact. It was the reality of his wife striking him that caused the pain. Andrea stepped closer, angrily intruding into his personal space. She jutted out her face. "I suppose you want to hit me now, don't you? Well go ahead. Hit me!"

Bewildered, Jeff looked at Andrea. He was beginning to feel a dull throbbing on his cheek. Andrea maintained her intense stare, clenching her teeth. Jeff looked at the children. They were bewildered and scared but calming down. "Go to your rooms," Jeff said.

Relieved, they darted to their bedrooms. Jeff walked to the kitchen then back into the living room, trying to compose himself. He looked at his wife, seeing her as he had not seen her before. "What the hell's going on?" he asked almost inaudibly.

Still agitated, but now outwardly in control, Andrea responded, "Oh, nothing. I just got mad at the kids."

"Over what?" Jeff asked as calmly as he could.

"They were fighting over the TV."

"You were really angry," Jeff observed.

"Not really. I didn't expect you home so soon."

Jeff pondered that statement. After a few seconds, and feeling the need to keep the conversation flowing, he added, "Yeah, I needed to come home early."

"Why?" Andrea was completely calm, as if the events of just a few minutes ago hadn't occurred.

"We got to talk."

"Oh?"

"Yeah. How about after dinner, when the kids are asleep?"

"Sounds serious."

"Kinda."

"I'll finish getting dinner."

As he was trying to assess what he had just witnessed, the telephone rang. He picked it up.

"Mr. Vinton?"

"Yes."

"This is the credit department at Montgomery Ward. I'm calling from our district office in Tulsa. You've missed your last two installments. May we expect a check from you soon?"

"You sure you got the right account?"

"Yes, Mr. Vinton. May we expect a check soon? The amount overdue is sixty-four dollars."

"Sure," Jeff said, replacing the receiver.

He looked at Andrea. She was serenely preparing dinner.

CHAPTER TWENTY-ONE

As soon as Governor Charles Norman won the Republican primary, running unopposed, he began losing the general election. Initially it was a slippage of a half percent. The next poll reflected a drop of two points. Fearing this erosion, he contacted his advisers, those hard-nosed politicians intent only on political victory, and told them to develop a plan to redirect his campaign during these last weeks. He told them to meet at his hunting lodge far out in the country. He would receive their recommendations the following week.

Inactivity, however, was not his forte, and he found the day's schedule intolerably empty. He needed to do something, so he drove to his lodge and unexpectedly joined his advisors. He had intended to impart confidence, to empower, to give his charge. But Norman was fatigued, dispirited, his thoughts disjointed. He spoke of the lofty goals of the discredited reorganization bill; how he needed another term to achieve those objectives. He spoke as a man obsessed with efficient, responsive, accountable government. The jaded and cynical party pros looked at each other in disbelief. The moment Norman departed, they continued their task, effectively discounting the heady thoughts of Governor Norman. The report was submitted to Norman that Monday.

It contained three salient steps: Be a caretaker - not an innovator. Continue the status quo. Leave the commission form of government untethered.

Norman reacted to this in-house report with a press release. It pledged an ongoing battle against government inefficiency, an assault on the unresponsive bureaucracy, and an unrelenting attack on the commission form of government.

Those independent units of government responded with a passion, exploiting the activism of their clienteles and their collective power. It was a decisive counterattack. By November, Norman was eleven points behind Bob Elam. Election day proved the pundits and polls correct: Elam won in a landslide.

During his concession speech on that sad night, Norman spoke eloquently and wisely and well. He spoke of those ideals on which he had based and lost his campaign. He said he wanted to end the commission form of government. He said he hoped the governor-elect shared his goals. But no one was listening. The supporters remaining in the ballroom were mostly drunk with cheap booze and depressed with pervasive dysphoria. Governor Charles Norman, now a lame duck, wept as his chauffeur drove him and Mrs. Norman to the governor's mansion.

Across town, in a suite at the Plainsmen Hotel, Bob and Pam Elam, Herb Chandler, and Bill Sergent watched Norman's concession speech. A general sympathy swept through the suite. Tears trickled down Pam's cheeks. Her thoughts were with Mrs. Norman, and with herself on some future night.

No one objected when Sergent switched off the television. The governor-elect and Mrs. Elam, followed by his aides, departed the calm of the suite to join their jubilant supporters. Greg Allen, the man who envisioned himself as the antipoverty czar, positioned himself to be first to congratulate Bob as they entered the boisterous ballroom.

***

A week later, while looking over his schedule, Chandler was only mildly surprised to see Sergent's name. "What's Bill want?" he asked his secretary.

"I don't know. He didn't say."

"I know!" He frowned. "Move things around. I'll see him first."

She nodded. Bill walked into his office ten minutes later.

Chandler looked up. "Whatcha got for me, Bill?" He noted Sergent's sheepish demeanor.

Bill stammered for a moment, unsure of how to begin. He shifted his weight, asked if he could have a seat.

Herb weighed the options of causing Bill some additional discomfort or making this always awkward moment between employer and employee a little easier. He decided to be understanding. He looked at Bill who was still deferentially standing. "Of course, Bill, please grab a chair." Herb let a few moments pass, then he smiled. "And give me the goddamned letter."

Sergent looked up from the floor. "You know?"

"Been in the business a while. It happens, sometimes to the advantage, sometimes the disadvantage of my employee."

"What do you mean?"

"It all depends on the personality, the strength of the individual. My judgment is that you'll get chewed up. You're too decent. You try to inject fairness into an unfair world. You think it's a just world and don't realize it's just a world. I'm afraid you'll be quickly outmaneuvered, then totally frustrated. But," he smiled affectionately, "I may be wrong."

"I can play hardball, too," Sergent said defensively.

"I hope so. What position?"

Sergent didn't know how to answer until he understood the question. "Elam's administrative assistant."

"Not bad. Better than a cabinet officer. A part of the inner circle, a key member."

"Yes."

"Okay. I accept your resignation, if that's what you want."

"It is."

Herb rose and walked over to Sergent. "You know, by their very definition, politicians are an amoral, shallow, and expedient lot. They view themselves as the prince, and the only loyalty a prince has is to himself. Play it cool. Watch your back. Test the firmness of the ground before you walk on it. Learn how to be a bit ambiguous. If you can't tell how the winds are blowing they'll blow you away. Moral courage and strong convictions are fatal flaws for a political aide. So during your time as a political lieutenant, do your damnedest to avoid criticism by speaking eloquently and forcibly but without substance, by making as few decisions as possible."

Bill began to protest, but Chandler persisted. "I know this all sounds a bit cynical, but it's good advice. And one more thing. Don't give all your loyalty to your prince. Keep some in reserve for someone who can help you after the Elam administration is no more. I assure you, there's nothing more pathetic than a man who walked alongside the prince, made decisions affecting the people of an entire state, directed the flow of millions of dollars and the activities of hundreds of staffers, and after it's all over can't find a job. Serve your prince well, but give a damn about yourself. There is nothing more fleeting than appointees and appointive power. The office and power you'll have is not inherent, only derivative."

Chandler walked to his desk surrounded by the trappings that were solely his, attained by his skills, personality, and tenacity. With sorrow, he looked at his young and unsophisticated aide. "All the luck in the world, Bill. I really mean it."

***

Greg Allen walked into the Plainsmen Hotel lounge, the latest edition of the capital city newspaper tucked under his arm. As his eyes adjusted to the dim light, he noticed two women at a table. Sitting at the bar, he ordered a drink, then purposefully swiveled his chair toward the women. After catching their attention, he proclaimed, "We may not be much, but right now we're all this goddamned place has got!" Then, sensing a forthcoming smile on the face of the younger one, Greg laughed loudly.

"Since there aren't many of us, perhaps we should just huddle together," she said with a sparkle in her eyes.

Greg responded with another artificial and boisterous laugh. "Yeah, safety in numbers."

"Now don't you go worrying about safety," she said, her eyes fixed on Greg. "I had my tubes tied."

Her friend feigned embarrassment by holding her hand over her eyes. Hot damn! thought Greg as he picked up his drink and walked to their table, sensing a stirring within him. "I'm Greg Allen."

The younger woman regally held out her hand. "I'm Sharon. She's Denise."

Greg, with grandiose exaggeration, bowed to lightly touch his lips to her hand.

"Well I'll be damned," Sharon laughed.

"It's the only saving grace for folks like us," Greg said.

"What?"

"Being damned."

"Makes sense." Sharon turned to Denise. "Doesn't it?"

More nervous laughter.

"You live here?" Greg asked.

"Nope. Just in for a few days," Sharon replied.

"From where?"

"Yorkton. Out west."

"Oh, I'll be going out there soon."

"What kinda work do you do?"

"I'm a lawyer," Greg modestly admitted. "But right now I'm changing jobs."

"To what?"

"I've just accepted a position with Governor Elam."

"Oh." Sharon was obviously impressed.

"Yeah, it's just official." Grandly placing their drinks to one side, Greg laid out the newspaper. His picture was on the front page. The headline read ELAM'S POVERTY CZAR. Greg had persuaded the reporter to use that sobriquet over drinks the night before.

"I'll be damned!" Sharon again said.

"We already covered that topic," Greg said, laughing, placing his hand on her exposed knee.

Later, in Sharon's room, as he eased himself into her syphilitic vagina, Greg was pleased he had called Amy, advising her he'd be late. Affairs of state, he had told her.

***

Sergent sat before Elam in the governor's ornate office. After the secretary brought coffee, Elam began. "You know, before we get this administration going full swing, I thought it might be well if we set some broad parameters – kinda set the climate."

Bill was ill at ease. This was his first meeting with his new boss. He remembered Herb Chandler's words of caution: Speak eloquently but without substance. Let no decision be solely traceable to you.

"Sure. Good idea," he responded.

"Good," Bob smiled. "Now that we've got this goddamned office, what the hell do we do with it?"

An awkward silence ensued.

"We must be aware," Bill ventured, "that we need to operate on two distinct levels. The first concerns products, the second, perception."

"I think I know what you're saying, but flesh it out."

Bill tried to swallow away his nervousness, recapture some moistness for his dry mouth. "I have the impression that governments usually run themselves regardless of what the executive wants or doesn't want. The bureaucrats are the only survivors of political wars."

"Yeah."

Sergent felt like he was in over his head. He was glad it was only he and the governor sitting in this large office. He had to go on, but he couldn't think quickly enough to change the direction he had set. "So until we know more about the workings of the bureaucracy, maybe we should concentrate on the public's perception of us rather than any new initiatives."

Elam simply stared at Sergent. Sergent's discomfort heightened.

Then Elam recalled JFK's administration: the flurry of activity, the few accomplishments. Yet the image of JFK in the minds of the people, even some of the jaded analysts and historians, was favorable. It was a matter of class and style, not substance and products, he thought. "You may have a point. Go on."

"Well, I suppose the procedural steps would be something like this." Bill had no idea where he was going, but he knew he had to continue advising his governor. "It obviously can't be in memo form, but we should call in all the newly-appointed department heads and instruct them to do nothing. Just maintain the status quo. We would cloak this in language like '... learn the workings of your department, study your legislative mandates, get to know the capabilities of your people ...' We'll say 'exercise prudent administration, not innovation, during these early months'."

Elam interrupted. "Okay, perhaps for the first few months. But dammit, I intend to be an active governor, not a caretaker. Anyway, go on."

"Secondly, we'll dust off the surveys we took last year. Again see where the people stand on the issues. We'll put out press releases courageously aligning this administration with those politically safe but emotional issues." He reflected for a moment. "I did most of your releases during the campaign. I could make that chore a part of my job."

"Good. And that will give us some time."

"Right," Sergent said, relieved.

"We'll go with that thrust for the first three months," Elam projected. "Then in April we'll announce plans to take control of the bureaucracy. You know, reorganization, elimination of the commissions, that sort of stuff. And in the meantime, I want you to get with Greg Allen. You've met him haven't you?"

Bill nodded.

"By March thirty-first I want you guys to have a comprehensive framework underway to reorganize this state's human services. He's a good man. You'll enjoy working with him. Okay?"

"Sure." Sergent realized that Allen was one of Elam's political crony appointments. He went to his office, just a few steps from the governor's, and pulled out the surveys and studied them thoroughly again. He began his first press release for the new governor an hour later.

FOR IMMEDIATE RELEASE

For further information
contact William P. Sergent,
Administrative Assistant to
Governor Robert T. Elam

ELAM TO GET FREELOADERS OFF WELFARE

Governor Robert T. Elam today announced...

***

Sergent was sipping his coffee when the telephone rang. It was the receptionist. "Mr. Greg Allen, for his ten o'clock."

"Good. Have Greg come in."

Sergent looked up as Allen stood before his desk. "Have a seat. The governor has assigned us the task of improving the state welfare programs. We should be able to make some substantial reductions in costs through economies of scale. Did you get my memo?"

"Yeah, I just went over it last night," Greg tentatively responded.

"Good. Now our final product will be a structure under which virtually all human services programs will be included. We intend to eliminate the commissions and make cabinet-level directors report to a kind of a czar." He recalled the news article about Allen's appointment. He looked up for a reaction. There was none. A bit surprised, Sergent continued. "Since you're a lawyer, I'll want you to scrutinize the federal and state legislation affecting the following agencies ..."

Greg barely heard Sergent listing the government units. He was preoccupied by the chancre that had appeared on his genitals last week and by the certainty that he had infected his wife. He wondered how the hell he could get Amy to go to the doctor with him to receive massive injections of penicillin at the same time. He figured that he could fake having the flu, tell her how contagious it was, and insist they get the shots together. He would claim that the influenza was so debilitating that she had to get a shot to prevent her from getting really sick.

"...after we determine how much we can jack these programs around without losing federal funds, we'll recommend appropriate legislation - Hammond will sponsor it - changing commissions to line agencies, line agencies responsive to a single agency..."

...for Christ's sake, I wish she was a dumb broad. I could tell her I got it off a toilet seat or something...

"...we'll call in the department heads to tell them what we got in mind - we'll do that sometime in April - tell them to cooperate or resign..."

...I could plead innocence. Accuse her of playing around. Yeah, maybe she has...

"...by the end of the fiscal year, we should be all set to move. D-Day is one October. Okay?"

...the first thing I've got to do is get myself squared away. I'll see a doctor this afternoon...

"Okay, Greg?" Sergent repeated.

"Sure," Allen replied, returning to reality. "Could you send me a memo encapsulating this?"

"We just went through it, for God's sake," Sergent said. Then he remembered that Allen was close to Elam. "Yes, of course."

"Thanks. I'll see ya."

After Greg left, Sergent strolled into Elam's office. Looking up, the governor said, "You been meeting with Allen, huh?"

"Yeah."

"He's a sharp guy, ain't he? How did it go?"

"I don't know," Bill replied with a troubled voice. He returned to his office and sat before his typewriter.

FOR IMMEDIATE RELEASE

For further information
contact William P. Sergent,
Administrative Assistant to
Governor Robert T. Elam

ELAM CHASTIZES BUREAUCRATIC INFLEXIBILITY

Governor Elam today took some powerful shots at those government employees whom he believes are more intent on job protection than public service...

***

For the next few weeks, Sergent had trouble making any progress at work. Too often the results of many hours of toil were crumpled up and thrown away. One evening, as he threw out his latest drafts of organization charts, flow charts, bureaucratic matrixes, and integrated functions, he realized the task was too complex for his skills. Frustrated, he left his office sensing his inadequacy. Driving home, everything seemed to fall into place, but he knew it was because he was too exhausted to grasp the many complexities of restructuring the disjointed but ingrained infrastructure of government. His fatigue made it all seem simpler than it really was.

Bill called his old mentor the next morning. Forty minutes later, he got out a legal-size tablet. To the extreme left he began. Agencies fully consolidated, integrated, operational ... Ω-300. He continued working through his lunch hour. Things easily began falling into place: Human Service Czar appointed ... $\blacklozenge$-184. Hammond's LB enacted ... Q-280. Statutory research accomplished ... £-130. Gubernatorial approval gained ... Σ-275. Gubernatorial lobbying ongoing (public and legislative) ... Σ-75-300 ...

After long, long hours, after he completed the reverse-logic matrix, Bill enjoyed the same smugness Chandler had known months before. "It can be done!" he said aloud. He looked at the many lines representing movement, coordination, interaction, the achieved benchmarks, the limned action steps, the resultant meshing of the various institutions of government; the executive initiative; the AG inhibiting judicial involvement; the legislative deliberation; the lobbyists' intervention; the bureaucracy's submission ...

It was all plotted out, superbly designed, governmentally achievable. Sergent sat back, exhausted, satisfied. Then he noticed that all of the elements operated on different timetables, parallel to each other - except at Q-80. Here the lines converged. This critical juncture was manned by Allen. "Jesus Christ!" He reached for his telephone. Allen answered after the second ring.

"Yeah, Greg, this is Sergent. I got to see you. Can you come right over?"

Greg entered Sergent's office ten minutes later.

Bill looked up. "Christ, Greg, you don't look so good!" he said, noting Allen's ashen complexion, the shadows under his eyes. "What's wrong with you?"

Greg responded in a subdued manner. "Oh nothing. Had the flu. I saw my doctor yesterday. Got a million cc's of penicillin."

"Good. I hope those cc's knock out the little sonsabitches," Bill smiled.

"Me too," Greg said, knowing he would soon reinfect himself.

"How we doing on the legislative research?"

Allen had to think for a moment. Then he remembered the assignment. "Just cleared my desk of a lot of stuff. I'll get on it this afternoon."

"Yeah. Be sure and do that. We're going to reach a point in time when nothing can move without that being accomplished."

"Consider it done," Greg said, rising.

"Okay," Bill responded, thinking again that Allen might be preoccupied. "You know, we really need that stuff, and it won't hurt you to be the one supplying it."

"I appreciate the assignment," Greg said before walking out of the office.

Sergent's attention returned to the matrix, his eyes falling upon Q-80. He felt troubled. Sipping his coffee, he considered the wisdom of sharing his doubts with Elam. The governor, certainly by inference, gave the impression that Allen was one of the administration's fair-haired boys. Yet, dammit, this entire project could be trashed by Greg's preoccupation or indolence, or both. He wondered if he should get a backup for Allen – maybe someone from the AG's office. But what if Allen is closer to Elam than he is? What if there's a political or personal connection he didn't know about? And he'd better get Elam's approval before involving another constitutional office. Jesus Christ!

The excessive amount of coffee Sergent had drunk last night was producing a mild headache. To hell with it! He rose and, without knocking, walked into Elam's office where the governor was conferring with another man.

"Oops. Sorry, Governor, I didn't know."

"That's okay, Bill. Come help us make a decision."

"Sure."

"I'm afraid that this model might be a bit too ostentatious even for a governor," Elam said to his visitor. "But how about this smaller Continental?"

Bill smiled. "The old Plymouth's giving out, huh?"

"Not really, but I think it's time for a new one ..." Elam's voice trailed off.

Sergent was annoyed that Elam was doing business with a car salesman in the office of the governor. He was also relieved he couldn't discuss his doubts about Allen. "I'd go with the smaller model," Bill advised.

"Good thinking on your part. Thanks." Then, in afterthought, Elam asked if he could help with anything.

"Well, we may have a soft spot on the horizon. Let me monitor it for a while; see if we'll get the proper response. I'll get with you on it later."

"Okay, Bill." Elam returned his attention to the salesman. Sergent departed, somewhat relieved, somewhat disappointed in his governor and himself.

Three weeks later, Sergent's disillusionment had not eased. Elam was obviously becoming more concerned with cosmetics, less concerned with issues. Bill had moved to a smaller office for a few days while the governor's office was redecorated. Now he observed new and modern office furniture being moved in. He lamented the departure of the admittedly old but substantial executive desk and captain's chairs.

Sergent's disappointment in his boss's behavior was unexpectedly offset by Greg Allen's activities.

Allen had begun his scrutiny of the human services programs by examining services for the aging. What he discovered was nothing less than a conspiracy to thwart the intent of Congress.

Now, as Allen stood behind Sergent's chair, he pointed to a part of the federal law governing aging programs. "Now read this and tell me what it says."

Bill looked at the federal law Greg had placed before him. "You mean here? Section 307?"

"Yeah."

Sergent scanned the legal language then looked up at Greg. "Well it says that the local area agencies on aging – the AAAs - can't directly provide services." He paused for a moment, then asked, "Why?"

"That gets to the intent of Congress," Allen said. "It says why. Right here - both in the law and the Code of Federal Regulations."

"Where?"

"Here, in the CFR. Read this part. 45 CFR 903.1"

Bill read from the code. "Okay, 903.1(e) states 'funds made available under this part shall be used primarily to provide maximum incentive for attracting support from public and private agencies which have resources for programs for the elderly'." Bill thought for a moment, then answered his own question. "Okay, the AAAs are designed by Congress to be advocacy and monitoring entities and money funnels."

"Right. Now read (f)(1) and (2)."

"Okay. Paragraph (f) says 'Funds made available under this part may be used to provide social services only when it has been clearly shown that: (1) The social services are needed and not already available, and (2) No other public or private agency can or will provide the social services'." Bill looked up. "So what?"

"Would you be surprised if I told you that, in clear violation of the law, the AAA's are directly providing services while other units are willing and able to do so?"

"Yeah. I'd be surprised."

"Then be surprised."

"You mean they are? In violation of congressional intent?"

"Sure as hell!"

Sergent smiled broadly. "Okay. This is the kinda stuff we want to put a halt to. Document this and we'll use it with the legislature, and ..."

He was interrupted by Greg. "Remember I mentioned a bureaucratic conspiracy?"

"Yeah. What's that all about?"

"Well, it goes from the top of the bureaucracy in Washington all the way to the bureaucrats here." Greg moved around the desk and sat before Sergent. "But it's awfully arcane stuff, cloaked in legalese. Let me give you a backdrop to the whole thing."

"Shoot."

"Okay, here we go. First, the law prohibits AAAs from directly providing services. Second, despite the law, in most of the states, including this one, they're directly providing services. Third, if bureaucrats don't like the law, they change it."

"How do bureaucrats change laws? Laws enacted by Congress?" Bill was bemused, wondering if Allen was pulling his leg.

"Simple. The bureaucrats write the regulations. And once the regs are approved, they have the force of law. So if the bureaucrats don't like what Congress legislates, they undo it. They effectively change laws through the regulations they publish in the CFR." His index finger tapped the voluminous codification on Bill's desk.

Bill incredulously looked at Allen. "I'm having difficulty believing you."

"I've got a good example. But more background first. When the regs are printed, there's a period for comment. Then the bureaucrats review the comments, determine their relevancy, and decide what to put in and what to take out. Then they finalize the regulations and the law is extended to include these regs."

Sergent could only chuckle. "Go on."

"The trick of the bureaucrats is to use all their skills of legerdemain to create such abstruse language patterns that the people don't know what the hell they're saying."

Sergent began to see Allen in a new light. Maybe Elam was right, he thought. This is one sharp sonofabitch.

"Okay, back to specifics," Allen continued. "The bureaucrats have just published new regs to change the law to conform to their wishes."

"What's their gimmick?"

"It's so far out that I think only a lawyer could detect it."

"Try me," Sergent challenged him.

"Sure. The proposed regs state that the local units can disregard the intent of Congress by directly providing services if - and now I'm gonna quote Section 1321.103 (C)(1)(i) of the proposed regs. Now remember, this is proposed as an exception to the intent of Congress."

"Okay."

"This is the bureaucratic proposal: 'If the area agency was providing the service before the agency's initial designation after the effective date of these regulations and requiring it to stop would result in a disruption of the service'."

"Pretty legalese, but it sounds okay to me," Sergent said.

"It sounded okay to me too until I read Section 1321.61 of the proposed regs. That section speaks of a redesignation process for all AAAs." Allen showed Sergent the newly proposed regulations. "In paragraph (d), it sets a time table for redesignation. The critical phrase then becomes 'initial designation after the effective date of these regulations ...'"

"It's a bit too recondite for me. But then, I'm not a lawyer," Sergent confided to Allen, smiling.

"What the bureaucrats are saying, despite Congress's wishes and the law's intent, is that when they re-designate the AAAs, they can deliver services directly. The operative phrase is 'initial designation ... after the effective date of these regulations'."

"Forgive me. I just don't get it," Sergent admitted.

"Don't feel bad. Me and the lad who wrote them - and his boss - are probably the only ones who do."

"I guess I can see the bureaucrats' intent," Sergent said. "But dammit, bureaucrats shouldn't have that much power."

"Once the regulations are finalized, it takes court action to change them. Lawyers and courts cost bucks."

"The old joke," Sergent mused. "'How much justice can you afford?' And more importantly, who gives a damn?'"

A silence engulfed them. Then Sergent spoke forcefully. "I do. And I want this bureaucratic sleight of hand documented. I want the present practices of our state and local units of aging documented. It's bureaucratic crap like this that will get us legislation to correct this goddamned mess. Damned good work, Greg. Get it all on paper."

Greg gathered his files. As he rose to leave, Sergent stopped him. "Greg, I'm confused by all of this. Tell me why - what's the motivation for these bureaucrats?" he asked naively.

"It's a matter of turf - and the trappings that go with it."

"Turf, huh? Give me a specific example."

"Sure, we'll use the AAAs as examples. They have vertically integrated their programs so that no other agency can get a piece of the action. That way, they build a political constituency dependent on only themselves. It becomes a goddamned political machine, subsidized by the taxpayers. That's why Norman got his ass chewed up so badly with his reorganization plan. Their clientele went to war because the bureaucrats told them to. You see, in that case, the bureaucrats work for a commission, removed from the control of the governor or any other elected official."

"So that's why. Self-interest. And the 'how' is real simple," Sergent said. "The bureaucrats increase their power by bribing their constituents with tax-supported services."

"Right," Greg said. "The AAAs, and only the AAAs, feed and care for their constituents at publicly-funded eating places. These bureaucrats provide a critical aspect of the old folks' lives, and they've built one helluva political machine."

"But they've done so illegally."

"No. Nothing is legal or illegal in government," Allen reflected. "It's only bureaucratically effective or ineffective."

Sergent sat and reflected. Allen slouched in his chair, satisfied with himself. "Well, our governor is not going to tolerate that kind of activity," Sergent said. "Get it documented, Greg."

Allen nodded and left Sergent's office. Bill was shocked at what he had just learned, pleased with Greg's research, glad he was on the Elam team.

Allen, however, grew troubled again. He hadn't thought of his personal difficulty during the meeting. Now it was again overbearingly present. He was sure that his wife had given him syphilis. "Goddamn her!" he swore.

Governor Elam walked into Bill's office a bit later. "Wasn't that Allen in here?"

"Yes, sir."

"What you got him working on?"

"Human services reorganization."

"Good. I also want him to concentrate on the community action network."

"What's that?"

"You know, I'm not sure. I think they're 501(C)3s getting federal money. Part of LBJ's War on Poverty."

"Okay. Anything special?" Sergent asked.

"Yes. I got a call from a county commissioner in Harney County."

"Way out there, huh?"

"Yeah. The action agency out there is in some kind of trouble."

"Okay. Shall I have him look into it in general? Or is there something specific?"

"Better make it specific. Commissioner Oldfield said there's a troublemaker out there. Guy named Vinton. He's teamed up with some VISTA volunteers. I don't know the specifics, but we don't want bad press about anything that even looks like government. Have Allen quash this thing before the press picks up on it. Tell him to use Oldfield as the local contact. He's a good man. He helped us with our campaign out there."

Sergent wrote down the instructions. He set the yellow pad down and looked up at the governor. "I'll get Allen right on it. Incidentally, the guy's doing yeoman's work."

"Good." Elam began walking back to his office. He stopped and turned around. "And, Bill, keep those press releases coming. My pollster tells me the people love them, especially the ones about the welfare bums."

CHAPTER TWENTY-TWO

The arctic front raced southward, first mixing with the warmth and moisture, then overpowering those gentler forces. The result of this interplay thus far was four inches of snow.

Weather forecasters were predicting six more inches. By the time the full extent of the storm was known, Commissioner Hank Oldfield was in Yorkton. Knowing he could not travel back to his ranch, he checked into the Airport Ramada then drove to the airport.

The aircraft the Community Action Program's newly-elected chairman was on would be the last to land at or depart from the airport for the next two days. Oldfield rushed to meet him as he deplaned. "Good to see you. I thought my drive down here would be for nothing. I'm surprised they let you land."

"Helluva storm," Chairman Craig Baker noted.

"I checked in at the Ramada, made a reservation for you. You'll need it, won't you?"

"Nah. I live on a little acreage right outside Yorkton. I'll get home somehow. Let's go to your room. I got a lot to tell you."

They stopped to buy a fifth of bourbon on the way. Oldfield uncapped the bottle and took a swig while negotiating his vehicle through the drifting snow. In the motel room, the chairman mixed his drink, lit a cigarette, and relaxed.

"Well, what happened?" Oldfield asked.

"At first the staff at the regional office came off as self-righteous SOBs. They're the middle management bureaucrats - guys like Ashton. I told them to go to hell and insisted on seeing the regional director. He's a Nixon appointee, you know. Well, the moment I got to his office, I asked to use the phone. With him standing next to me, I called Congressman Leighton. I spoke to his chief of staff, told him to get the regional office off our ass."

"Yeah?"

"He talked to the regional director. We got our time," Chairman Baker gloated.

"Good!"

"Yeah, it turned out pretty good. This is what we got to do. First is the restitution of about ten thousand dollars of Rediger's and Jan Roberts's travel expenses and wages while they were out frolicking around."

"You call it frolicking, huh? Where the hell do we get that kinda of money?" Oldfield wondered.

"No problem. I worked it out with the regional director. We can repay it with in-kind bucks."

"What kind?"

"In-kind. That means noncash dollars. Things like the value of volunteer labor, donated items, rent-free space. The agency can always mobilize those kinds of bucks. And since it's not money, the auditor doesn't examine those entries."

"Damn. You got some good work done. I was concerned about the money."

"So was I," Baker admitted.

"What else?"

"The soap salesman has got to either quit the agency or quit selling soap. It's a conflict of interest."

"It's more than a goddamned conflict," Oldfield said. "It's outright theft. But I have to admit, it's a reasonable solution. What else?"

"The regional director told me he didn't want to mess with the economic development director and his chamber of commerce activities. He said some cans of worms just shouldn't be opened. No criminal charges. We just got to make him stop, or quit."

"We're getting off real easy, so far."

"Yeah, I talked my ass off," the chairman modestly confessed, sipping his bourbon.

"Do we have to get rid of Rediger?"

"No. But no one travels anymore without board approval. I view that as mine to give now that I'm chairman."

"I'll back you on that. What's Ashton think of all this?"

"You know, that sonofabitch tried to threaten me these last few months. I mentioned that to the regional director. He relieved Ashton of his assignment to our agency. We'll get another field representative next week."

Oldfield went to pour more bourbon in his glass. He turned and, with his glass, saluted the chairman of the CAP board. "You did one helluva fine job. We should underwrite more of your travel."

"But you know there's one hard spot left," Baker remarked.

"What's that?"

"Your boy Vinton."

"Why? What can he do?"

"The VISTAs have been fired, and they've left. Only Vinton remains in the area. He could still cause problems."

"No problem. I'll fire the sonofabitch."

"Good. That should take care of things."

"Vinton's wife's been in the hospital down in the capital. I don't think he's got any health insurance. He's probably broke and in debt over his head. After I fire him, he'll have to clear out of here quick."

"Then we're all set."

"You really did one helluva fine job," said Oldfield in admiration.

"Yeah. But I had to use damn near all my IOUs with the congressman."

"I'm glad you had them to use," Oldfield said. "You got us off the hook very cleanly, with no one getting hurt."

***

Andrea had again suffered severe abdominal pains a month earlier. The doctor had prescribed antibiotics and painkillers. After several days of persistent pain and negative results, he told Jeff he was baffled. The tissue was healthy, blood count normal, no fever. He suggested a specialist in the capital city.

Andrea was annoyed by the children's petty arguments and bickering during the long drive. Jeff tried to ignore her shouting at the children and her cries of pain as he drove. It was a mentally exhausting drive. Jeff asked Andrea if she was okay after they got into their room."

"Yeah, I feel better now," she said smiling. "God, Jeff, I hope they can find out what my problem is."

"They got more sophisticated equipment down here. We'll get you squared away." Then with a pang of guilt he asked, "Andrea, do you feel well enough to look after the kids for a few minutes?"

"Sure. Like I said, I'm feeling better."

"Okay if I go down to the bar? I need to relax."

"Of course. It's been a long trip. I'm sorry I yelled so much. I hope it didn't bother you."

Jeff merely nodded and kissed her lightly on the lips.

Entering the lounge, he stepped to the bar and ordered a beer. Hearing loud and boisterous laughter behind him, he turned to see two women with a man who was a few years their junior. Jeff judged by their level of intoxication that they'd been here a while. Worried about Andrea, mentally exhausted, he turned away from them. But not before he heard the man shout, "Governor Elam says it's okay if I make love to every woman in this goddamned state." Again the loud and boisterous laughter, then a woman's voice: "Well, you'd damned well better get started!"

Jeff returned the grin of the bartender and continued his interest in the conversation, turning his chair to face the intoxicated threesome.

The man responded, his voice slurred. "Get started? Hell, I've been working on this assignment ever since I was eleven years old!"

"Don't stop now!"

(Giggles).

Jeff turned to the bartender. "Friendly little place you got here."

The bartender smiled. "You won't believe it, but the guy says he's an aide to the new governor."

"I guess there's gonna be a lot more Democrats if this guy can keep it up."

"Yeah," the bartender noted, "and they'll probably all grow up to be lousy politicians or bureaucrats. God save us."

Jeff didn't reply. He finished his beer and rose. He walked past their table as he left the bar. He wanted a closer look at this aide to the new governor.

Andrea was better two days later even though the test results were inconclusive. As they packed to leave, Jeff gave fleeting thought to the expense of the trip. He didn't want to dwell on that. Worry about it later, he decided. The drive back was uneventful, the children sleeping much of the way.

The events of the past weeks had weighed heavily on Jeff. Andrea's illness had been emotionally draining, but she was all right now. He still hadn't told her about his job difficulties, and, worse, he sensed his fuse was shorter. Most troubling, though, were the events he had witnessed that terrible evening he arrived home early. He couldn't forget the screaming, the slapping. Yet it hadn't recurred. The children were happy and carefree. Laura had just turned ten, and Andrea had thrown a birthday party for her. Without telling Jeff, she had purchased numerous gifts. His concern increased when she wheeled the bike in from the garage. But he couldn't blame Andrea because he hadn't told her he was losing his job. In fact, he had made a conscious effort to shield her from that possibility. It's too late to tell her now, he lamented. We can't return Laura's gifts after giving them to her. He made a mental note to ask Andrea to talk to him before buying any more nonessential items.

The generous celebration of their daughter's birthday was a flaw borne of love. Hell, he would have gone overboard too. It was her first birthday with her new family.

When he left for work the next morning, he only vaguely remembered that the county commissioners would hold their monthly meeting that day. He was surprised when he saw Milner and Evelyn sitting in his office, enjoying their morning coffee. "Good morning," he said.

"We just effected a palace coup," Milner laughed. "We've taken over this damned place."

"Why not?" Jeff smiled, walking to his chair. "What's up?"

"We just thought we might review some of this office's accomplishments since your arrival," Milner continued.

"What for?"

"To share with the county board."

"You know something I don't?"

"No, but we should be ready. Besides, this stuff should be shared periodically with the board."

"They should know what's going on," Jeff agreed. "What do you have?"

"The stuff's damned impressive," Milner said. "As far as new federal dollars coming into the county, our best judgment, including food stamps, federal share of the maintenance and medical payments, sets the amount at about two point three million. Of course," Milner smiled, "there's an error margin of plus or minus 2.1 percent. Seriously, we can't be precise without investing a lot more time - time we ain't got. And people being served by this agency have increased significantly. But we don't want to mention that."

"I know," Vinton replied. "But dammit, they're entitled to the benefits if they're eligible. We don't make the laws. Congress does that. Why can't the board realize that poor people have rights? And we're here to protect those rights. And to track down runaway pappies like Oldfield's son, for Christ's sake! Who's gonna take care of his kids? Oldfield isn't!" Realizing he had let Milner in on the in-house secret, he lamely added, "That's for damn sure."

"The county board recognizes their right to remain silent and to move to the next county," Milner said dryly.

"I know they don't agree with me," Jeff said. But dammit, we should be telling people about our programs, not hiding them from those who need ...'"

"Whoa" Milner chided him. "We're preparing you for the county board, not the Welfare Rights Organization."

"Sorry."

"And now for the *piece de resistance*. Your office has saved the county over $750,000 in mental health costs because of the initiative to get people out of the state hospitals. And we got the folks relocated from the Yorkton nursing home – the one they closed down – without the newspaper doing a story on it."

"That was good work you did regarding the Yorkton facility. But, Jerry, is it really three-quarters of a million?"

"Yep."

"I hadn't been keeping track." Jeff reflected a moment. "Lots of bucks," he finally said.

"Lots of bucks," Evelyn echoed.

Jeff had a sense of well-being as he entered the commissioners meeting room. He noted that all the commissioners were present. Their faces reflected the dourness peculiar to this board. As Vinton seated himself, Oldfield spoke. "Morning, Jeff. We won't take too much of your time today."

"That's okay," Jeff responded, feeling at ease.

"The time I spoke of earlier has arrived, Jeff." Oldfield said.

Jeff was oblivious. "Sir?"

Oldfield looked intently but not unkindly at Jeff while he made the motion to discharge the Harney County welfare director.

Jeff heard the second to the motion, the motion to call the question, the vote. It was unanimous. He rose and walked back to his office. He thought of Andrea, of Laura, of Bobby. He felt a deep sense of shame - empty and powerless.

16 Jun 67

The brief but intense windstorm caused by the helicopter lifting into the sky, and the spray of the marshland water which was a part of its wake, were the first sensations Lt. Jeff Vinton felt since passing out.

The effect of the filthy water coupled with the swirling wind caused him to shiver again, his body quickly reviving itself. He was still nauseous, his eyes trying to focus on the tall individual standing over him.

"You're one cool sonofabitch," said the lieutenant whose platoon had been set down on Vinton's right flank. "You're in a firefight one minute, then the moment it's over you take a goddamn nap."

Vinton was still disoriented. His mental processes hadn't revived in sync with his body. He slowly stood, looking at the scene of the now terminated engagement. The sky was still blue with a few thunderheads massing to the southeast. The heat was still oppressive. He grinned at the lieutenant, but his mind was still groggy.

"You okay now?"

"Yeah."

"This your first firefight?"

"Yeah."

"Don't let it bother you. It happens."

"Sure," Vinton said, embarrassed by his conduct.

"The trick is to stay awake while the sonofabitchin' slopes are shooting at you. Ain't nothing wrong with takin' a break afterwards."

Vinton leaned down to pick up his M16.

"We'll be on the last boat out of here," the lieutenant continued. "The 'copter'll be here in about fifteen minutes. We'll be hitching a ride with our KIAs."

Vinton surveyed the valueless landscape where three of his men had lived their final moments. The kunai grass was now flattened and windswept. The black patches at the tree line contrasted starkly with the eternally verdant forest that had escaped the bombing and strafing. But this ugliness would only intensify the impact of the sun, causing new growth. The blackened holes would be replaced by greenness in a few weeks. The skirmish, insignificant to all but those involved, had already been reported to the G-3 staff that had duly logged the action and was now looking for new targets of opportunity. They were viewing aerial photos of an area sixty-five kilometers to the north. PAVN activity had been observed there. The tactics would not change. Inject U.S. paratroopers, expect them to draw hostile fire, call in air support, achieve a favorable body count.

Jeff looked again at the battered rain forest. Housed within the dead vegetation were the remnants of a PAVN infantry unit. The enemy KIAs were the products of this insane machinery of which Vinton was an integral but minor part; this extension of American foreign policy.

But Vinton's compassion did not extend to the enemy KIAs, the kids who had worn the uniform of the People's Army of Vietnam. In fact, he had no feelings at all for those who had been killed while trying to kill him and his men.

The pain and anguish and feelings of absolute powerlessness returned to him when he thought of his own KIAs; an Anglo, a black, a Chicano. Dead Americans. Dead paratroopers. Dead kids. He looked to where they had been placed. They were now encased in black plastic body bags. Vinton found comfort in knowing that flies could no longer walk upon their open eyes, could not explore the gaping holes in their chests and stomachs. In the distance, he observed another pile of body bags. This time he controlled the retching of his stomach.

He looked again to his counterpart. The lieutenant had been observing him closely. "You sure you're okay, Vinton?"

"I suppose I'll get used to it," Jeff said with resigned remorse.

"Hey man – remember. It don't mean nothin'! Stay loose. When we get back to Bien Hoa, I commandeer a jeep. We'll go to Saigon and tie one on."

Jeff looked at the blue sky and simultaneously saw and heard the lone helicopter approaching from the east. He watched it drop down to receive the first part of its cargo. He observed three paratroopers carelessly throw the bodies onto the floor of the aircraft, then climb aboard themselves. The Huey slowly and awkwardly lifted above the horizon, then approached the second pickup point. By the time the helicopter reached Jeff's position, the bodies had been neatly stacked on the floor of the aircraft. They nearly occupied all of the helicopter's floor space. While the other lieutenant stood by, Jeff helped place more dead soldiers onto the aircraft.

He handled the bodies with care. The enlisted men, noting Jeff's rank, did as he did, gently lifting and stacking the bodies. As Jeff helped lift another, he wondered if it was one of his men. He noted that the frame of the dead soldier was slight – a short man. Jeff assumed it was Morales.

Vinton was the last to climb on. As the helicopter rose, then banked, its sharp list caused the neatly stacked bodies to tumble toward starboard. Vinton, standing next to the open door, felt the weight of one of the corpses as it fell against his leg. In the middle of the aircraft, one of the grunts let out a macabre laugh. The soldier then lifted his feet from the bodies that had engulfed them. He first just stood upon one of them, then walked over several more to get to an area devoid of the body bags. Soon the other living passengers in the helicopter extricated themselves from the layer of the dead, they too walking on the black bags and the nonliving they housed. Jeff remained where he was, allowing the body to rest against his leg. He refused to walk upon the lifeless mass. It was only his massive intake of the cool, fresh that kept him from vomiting.

CHAPTER TWENTY-THREE

Bill Sergent was nervous. He was at that point in his career when he had to commit to a precise course of action. Worse, it wasn't an issue to be dealt with in the inner chambers. This item, the government reorganization plan, would be hotly contested on the legislative floor in full exposure of the media. And the special interest groups, the appointed officials, and the bureaucrats would be clamoring to speak and would be effective in their testimony, expert in their knowledge.

Sergent had to rely heavily on Greg Allen. And Allen was a queer duck, almost a split personality; sometimes lucid and penetrating, more often strangely preoccupied with a suggestion of indolence. Yet, he was Elam's boy, and Sergent had to work with him and sometimes around him.

Sergent recalled Herb Chandler's counsel: Never be solely identified with any one issue. Stay fluid. Always offer alternatives. Talk much but say little. But he was stuck. Even the lower levels of the bureaucracy knew about and resented him. Every state worker felt personally and professionally threatened. It was, Sergent thought while gathering his papers, one helluva note.

Unusually diffident this morning, he walked to the door to Elam's office. He shifted the papers to open the door when he heard Hammond's voice. He listened for a moment. It wasn't Hammond's conversational voice. It was his Legislative Voice: deep, resonant, orotund. Sonofabitch! He paused for a moment before the door.

"So this gal, whose most outstanding feature was her sheer bulky corpulence, she sits down to offer testimony before the committee. Before she can say a word, I say, 'I see you're getting your food stamps okay. How about your ADC checks?' Then she says, 'But sir, it just ain't enuff.' So I says, 'Anymore and we'd have to buy you a bigger car and build you a bigger house.' She says 'It's my glands, sir.' and I say 'I believe that our state veterinarian college could benefit from a complete and total examination of your glands'."

Sergent heard the Legislative Voice change to a boisterous Legislative Laugh.

"To this day, I don't think she knew what I was saying!" More Legislative Laugh.

As Sergent opened the door, his eyes fell on Elam and he sensed Bob's disdain. On the other hand, Hammond was rocking with laughter, repeatedly slapping his thigh with his open hand. Sergent was encouraged by Elam's distaste for Hammond's humor and his presence. He recalled how Bob had almost recoiled from Hammond in Burke County during the campaign. But now Elam needed Hammond. And so did he. Now his work would be presented to Senator Hammond who would judge if the framework had merit. If it didn't, in Hammond's judgment, Bill had to go back to square one, to begin anew. The goddamned legislature, he thought, a bunch of tipsy, womanizing, prima donnas. He thought of the efficiency of governments ruled by philosopher kings. Government by fiat. Realizing there are no philosopher kings, he was prepared to afford deference to the senator, to speak persuasively and well, to effectively respond to questions.

Hammond turned in his chair as Sergent entered. "Billy-boy, how are you?" Hammond asked as if he was on the campaign trail.

"Just fine, Senator, and yourself?"

"Couldn't be better, Billy-boy. Bob tells me you've been working your ass off on this reorganization plan. I suggested you run it by me before you go further. Hope you don't mind." His last sentence was meant to humor Sergent.

"I'm pleased to have the opportunity, Senator, and appreciate your time and your concern. We all know the legislature and this governor wish to effectively deal with the bureaucracy."

"Ah, them! You know they're aware of what you're trying to do."

"I suppose they've heard some scuttlebutt ..." Bill hesitated, "... but we don't intend to decimate their ranks. And when this gets through the legislature, they'll be able to take more pride in their work, their departments, themselves."

"Billy-boy, you don't understand the mentality of bureaucrats. They're in it for the long haul. You know we got a damned good retirement plan for them."

Bill smiled. "I would hope so."

"Yeah, it's a fine plan," Hammond continued. "But what you've got to understand is that people in general resist change, and bureaucrats in particular resist change. They believe change in government should only occur slowly, if at all; that the most potent force of government is its own inertia. And if you get the bureaucrats' dander up, they can be an ugly lot. They've the power to delay, impede, subvert, and sabotage damn near anything they want to."

"I don't believe it necessarily must be that way. Their having so much power," Sergent countered.

"Well it is, because it was designed that way."

Sergent began to ask "By whom?" But he was tiring of this preliminary discussion. He wanted to make his presentation, return to his office, and get away from Hammond. "Then, Senator, this plan will unplan that."

Sergent wondered why the hell the governor wanted Hammond to guide this bill through the senate, especially after he had zapped Governor Norman's bill. Or maybe, because of that, he's the perfect one to get this bill passed. But that didn't make sense either. The whole thing seemed out of whack. He looked directly at the senator and smiled. "Here then is our Unplan."

Three hours later, with organizational charts, program integration diagrams, and joint funding plans displayed on stands or strewn on the floor throughout the large office, Bill Sergent abruptly sat down. He had presented a workable framework for governmental reorganization as well as anyone could have. After he sat, he realized his shirt was wet with perspiration. He looked to Elam and sensed the pride the governor had for the well-developed plan and for his administrative assistant. He looked to the senator. He could not read his thoughts.

Long moments of silence ensued. Sergent was mentally and emotionally exhausted. The governor was waiting for Hammond to speak. The Legislative Voice and Presence were clearly in the room as Hammond began. "Your plan, although well-conceived, strikes at one of the basic safeguards of government. Your plan makes no provision for the checks and balances of government. All told, it is a very unwholesome, unworkable, and very unutterable thing you've done."

Bill was stunned. He looked at the senator, then to the governor. Elam was serenely puffing on his pipe. "What the hell are you talking about?" Sergent shouted at Hammond.

Before Jake could respond, Elam spoke to his aide. "It's a matter of

Senator Hammond's long government service, Bill, and his undying respect for our system of government."

Sergent wondered just what the hell that meant. Furthermore, he was angry. He had spent days and nights working on this plan and its presentation. And now he was getting this gibberish. He barked at his governor. "Notwithstanding his long government service, tell him to speak plainly."

Hammond had gained a respect for Sergent during these past three hours that was similar to the respect he had gained for Elam when they had met at the Enterprize. He spoke before the governor could respond to Sergent. "The feds won't allow your plan to become operational, Bill."

"Why not?"

"Because each federal categorical program has a piece of legislation attached to it. The legislation forbids the mass and wholesale integration you're recommending. The Congress and federal departments don't want their programs to be consolidated or lumped together. They want them separate and distinct and identifiable. Programs that congressmen and bureaucrats can take credit for. Not mixed together in this hodgepodge you suggest."

"Under my plan, every program will be identifiable," Sergent retorted. "And their administration will be streamlined, duplication will be eliminated, and more money will be available for more services." Bill looked with total frustration and some desperation to Elam who remained strangely silent.

"Federal law forbids what you propose," Hammond said.

"What law prohibits what I propose?"

Elam quietly observed how Sergent had personally identified with the reorganization plan.

"Each law has a section prohibiting precisely what you propose," Hammond pointed out. "Damn, Billy-boy, you've just suggested that every damn program the federal system's presented to the states, to this particular state, be substantially affected. For example, look what you propose for a simple little program, the Elderly Nutrition Program. Now this was just to be a little thing Congress did to get food to old folks, to keep them healthy and out of nursing homes. You know, save on Medicare and Medicaid. Nothing fancy, just a soup line operation.

However, as the politicians astutely noted, a helluva popular program. But Jesus Christ, Bill, you take this simple little operation and make it as complex as a goddamn ICBM. Hell, you got Department of Labor training the cooks, Department of Transportation hauling around the doddering clients, USDA providing the food, Extension Service writing the menus, OEO recruiting more people to feed. FHA and HUD building the senior centers, HEW checking their goddamn urine and blood pressure. Christ, you even got SBA monies starting cottage industries for them." He paused. "Did I leave anybody out?"

"Yeah, a couple. AoA, CFN, some Social Security titles, and FNS," Sergent answered. "Also, we should be able to use some VISTAs and Senior Aides. And there's a program that serves free lunches to kids during the summer. We'll just throw another potato in the pot, haul the food over, and serve it at a youth center or park or somewhere; exert more economies of scale. But that's just one of the programs the plan addresses."

Sergent paused, looking at Hammond. "Hey, I know it sounds crazy, but it can be done, and it can be super cost-effective. It's just a matter of planning a totally integrated operation. With central control, we can do that." He noted the dour look on Hammond's face. It didn't deter him. "I'm damned excited about the prospects. What do you think specifically is wrong with it?"

Hammond didn't know how seriously he should regard this aide to the governor or how seriously the governor perceived him. Sergent's terribly complex proposal was amazingly workable. It therefore challenged the sole precept of Hammond's concept of government: Never give any department or individual too much power. Keep programs disjointed; bureaucrats dispirited and demoralized.

"It can't be done because it's wrong," Hammond fired back. "That's what the hell's wrong with it! But then," his voice lowered, "you're just too young and headstrong and brash to realize that. The other reason is it's illegal."

"Who says it's illegal?" Sergent snapped.

"Federal law says it's illegal," Hammond said with the confidence of an experienced legislator. "The feds won't let you mix up all those monies."

"No. No, you're wrong," Sergent said coolly. "Wrong as hell!"

266

"The hell you say," Hammond smugly and sarcastically responded.

"Whatever you say," Bill spoke softly. "But what about Section 204 of the Intergovernmental Cooperation Act of '64."

"Never heard of it."

"Here it is." Bill handed copies of the four-page law to Hammond and Elam.

Elam was the first to speak. "I'll be damned. Listen to this." He began reading aloud.

" 'Notwithstanding any other Federal law which provides that a single State agency or multimember board or commission must be established or designated to administer or supervise the administration of any grant-in-aid program, the head of any Federal department or agency administrating such program may, upon request of the Governor or other appropriate executive or legislative authority of the State responsible for determining or revising the organizational structure of State government, waive the single State agency or multimember board or commission provision upon adequate showing that such provision prevents the establishment of the most effective and efficient organizational arrangements with State government and approve other State administrative structure or arrangements; Provided that the head of the Federal department or agency determines that the objectives of the Federal statute authorizing the grant-in-aid program will not be endangered by the use of such other State structure or arrangements.'

"I'm not sure, Jake, but I think this says Sergent's right – and you're wrong."

Hammond was caught totally unaware. He had never heard of this obscure law. How the hell had this novice Sergent, this nobody, discovered it? Weakly, he said, "There's that damned word 'notwithstanding' again, Bob. I swear it's used at least once in every law."

"Well, notwithstanding your previous objections regarding this plan," Sergent said, "I want you to help me get it through."

Almost paternalistically, Elam took pride in his aide. Hammond, however, was enraged by this young upstart's presumptive attitude. He had simply had enough. His anger was apparent, and only he and Elam knew its source and its depth.

Jake waited until he had regained control of his emotions. Then,

267

staring at Sergent and in an even voice, he said, "Look, you presupposing sonofabitch, I haven't the time nor propensity to attempt to edify you as to why it's not only wrong but it's goddamned dangerous. I don't care about your legal obscurities. Suffice it to say it's goddamned wrong." Then, looking at Elam, he added, "Let's you and I go over this after I've had my aides scrutinize it. But, Governor, I simply can't live with it the way it is now! After we tone it down, I'll introduce the damn thing. And, since I gave my word, I'll shepherd it through the senate. But goddammit, Bob, I'm gonna change the hell out of it." He had risen from his chair while speaking. He reached the door as he spoke his last word. He left the governor's office without uttering another.

The next day, still licking his wounds, Sergent saw Greg Allen's memo. Allen had returned a few days earlier after reviewing the antipoverty and welfare programs in Harney County. The memo's length surprised Bill because Greg normally did things in a hurried, cursory manner. Bill then recalled the many press clippings that had crossed his desk. Some of the headlines came back to him: CAP AND WELFARE DIRECTORS EXCHANGE ACCUSATIONS; CAP DIRECTOR SURVIVES ANOTHER BOARD MEETING; WELFARE DIRECTOR VINTON FIRED; CAP EXECUTIVE SECRETARY SUED FOR DIVORCE; OEO GIVES CAP CLEAN BILL OF HEALTH. Bill refilled his coffee cup and immersed himself in the memo.

TO: GOVERNOR BOB ELAM
THRU: BILL SERGENT, ADMIN ASS'T
FROM: GREG ALLEN, POVERTY CZAR
RE: RANGE WAR ON THE WEST FORTY

Bill smiled at Allen's self-proclaimed job title and his description of the controversy. He began reading.

"BACKGROUND: To recap (no pun intended) the situation, several months ago the Harney County welfare director, Jeff Vinton, allied himself with several VISTAs, a band of hostile Indians, and an OEO middle management employee. This motley group attempted a palace coup, i.e., to force the discharge of the executive director of the local community action agency, and to replace him with Vinton.

"For purposes of explanation, a community action agency (CAA), often called a Community Action Program (CAP), is a nonprofit corporation primarily financed by public (federal and state) monies. Its purpose is to serve and be the advocate of the low income. Its primary funding is from the U.S. Office of Economic Opportunity (OEO), the federal flagship of the War on Poverty (WOP). (OEO is reportedly riddled with malcontents, radicals, and, it is suggested, socialists and communists.) OEO and other funding sources contract with these locally based, locally controlled corporations (CAAs) to perform specific tasks: e.g., X number of houses weatherized, X number of school days to Head Start students, etc. Since funding sources are limited, the agencies are susceptible to the whims of federal field representatives, virtually the local agency's only contact with the federal system and dollars. Needless to say, a bad field representative can jeopardize even a well-run agency.

"Specifically, throughout my investigative inquiry I visited numerous individuals involved in or affected by the controversy surrounding the CAP. Chief among them, and upon whose comments the bulk of this report is based, are: Hank Oldfield, Chairman of the Harney County Board of Commissioners and member of the CAP's Board of Directors (and an early Elam supporter); John Rediger, the CAP's Executive Director; several members of the CAP's governing board; Jeff Vinton, former director of the Harney County Division of Public Welfare (DPW) and former member of the CAP Board of Directors; sundry Injuns, an ex-VISTA volunteer and other militants.

"OVERVIEW: After making a series of libelous accusations against the CAP and its Executive Director at a board meeting, Jeff Vinton was withdrawn as Harney County's representative to the board. He was subsequently discharged as the DPW director. The DPW has since recalled its retired director (Agnes Moore - a real sweetheart!). That office has now stabilized after the hectic and erratic administration of its former director.

"At its next meeting, the CAP board summarily dismissed Vinton's specious accusations and the agency continues to discharge its responsibilities in an exemplary manner.

"The local media no longer views the matter as newsworthy and now confine themselves to such items as the rise and fall of pork belly futures.

"DETAIL: I arrived at Yorkton on 16 April and within the hour met with the recently elected CAP board's chairman. He is pleased that since his ascension to the chair the controversy has leveled out. He places much of the blame for the unfortunate matter on the agency's former field representative, Larry Ashton. The board chairman believes that radical elements have infiltrated OEO and that these federal employees have encouraged local individuals to militant activity. He undoubtedly views Ashton as one of these militants, and had demanded that Ashton's relationship with the agency be severed. This was accomplished by the interest of and good offices of Congressman Leighton.

"I headquartered in Yorkton, driving long and hard hours to numerous communities during my two-week investigation. This was done to facilitate frequent and ongoing communication with the CAP board chairman, who resides near Yorkton.

"I spent some time speaking with Jeff Vinton who still resides in Union. He's an interesting sort of a guy with screwed up ideas and ideals. He's been ostracized by the community, relating only to a radical Jewish ex-VISTA from the East Coast and some drunken local Injuns.

"Vinton seems out of place with these disruptive elements, having earned his BA from State University and served in Vietnam. (It should be mentioned, however, that most GIs in 'Nam became heavily involved in the drug scene and otherwise got screwed up.) Vinton has a nice wife, two children, and they are expecting a third. In conversations with him, he comes across as a radical leftist, covering the spectrum of lamenting corporate involvement in agri-economics to being involved in welfare rights organizations. He tempers his radicalism with idealism resulting in a disabling naïveté. He is currently unemployed, doing spot labor with his Injun friends. The whole matter is a pathetic situation for his family - his wife has lots of class.

"Because of the nature of Vinton's accusations, Rediger rightfully has taken legal action against Vinton, charging defamation of character, libel, and slander (See enclosure).

"Rediger has been the CAP director since the agency's inception and has done a lot for the area's economy, bringing in many federal dollars over the years. He runs a tight ship and is well perceived by the governing board and local, state, and federal sources. I several times had dinner with Rediger, his executive secretary, and an acquaintance of mine who lives out there. Suffice it to say I'm impressed with Rediger's administrative competence, the loyalty he commands from his staff, his acceptance by local governmental and business leaders, and the concern he has for the poor he so well serves.

"RECOMMENDATION: This situation has vastly improved since Vinton's departure from official position. The current disinterest of the media in the controversy has helped defuse the situation. I will, of course, make periodic trips to the area to monitor the CAA's progress.

"Also, at this end I will encourage state and federal agencies to invest in this CAA more than others and will use my office to facilitate Rediger's grant applications. It is my judgment that John Rediger runs a helluva good agency!"

Bill finished his coffee. Pleased with what he had read, he initialed the report and forwarded it to the governor.

***

Greg passed the Plainsmen Hotel on his way home. For a moment, he considered stopping for a drink, then reconsidered, driving straight home. But in that moment's hesitation, his thoughts returned to when he first met Sharon; to her delightful freedom from sexual inhibitions; the feel and smell of her body; her total submission to him. Coupled with these romantic thoughts were his concerns about the venereal disease – the syphilis – that he was sure he had gotten from Sharon. But within this ambivalence, as always with Greg, the libido prevailed. He had not yet resolved that tricky situation and its ramifications. Yet he thought of Sharon often, already planning another trip to Yorkton. His job was secure. He didn't need Saarson anymore, or, for that matter, Amy. And anyone could get a dose of something these days, and now Amy was obviously infecting him.

Sharon had denied his heated accusations when he had confronted her. After the accusations had been made and denied, and they had again given themselves to each other, things seemed right. Sharon honestly did not know she had transferred those indicting bacteria to Greg, nor did she know she had since contracted gonorrhea and would also transfer that infection to him. And because of their intoxication and physical attraction to one another and the abandon with which they pursued their sexual pleasures, knowledge of that transferal would not have subdued them.

Greg arrived home knowing without any doubt that he cared deeply for Sharon. Amy was sitting at the kitchen table. He noted the haze in the kitchen from her cigarettes. He wished she wouldn't smoke so much. At night he would draw her to him, then, smelling the smoke in her hair, would release her, turning his back to her. He looked objectively at his wife. She wasn't the beauty he once thought her to be. She was shorter than he liked. And lately she'd been aloof, almost cold to him. And she carried within her those goddamned spirochete. He viewed her as tainted, damaged goods. And she hadn't bore him a son, or even a daughter. She's sterile, Greg summarily judged.

Not warmly, he said "Hello," poured himself a drink, and sat before the television to watch the evening news. After dinner, Greg played a game of Monopoly with the kids, decisively beating them. He noted Amy walking from the kitchen. He had hardly spoken to her during dinner, and he didn't speak as she walked past him and the kids.

She reminded the children it was bedtime then retreated from her husband's silence down the hall toward their bedroom. She entered the adjacent bathroom, closing the door behind her. She was half-undressed when she caught her image in the full-length mirror. She stopped and looked at her reflection. She leaned closely toward the mirror, perhaps too closely. She noted the flaws in her complexion. But her makeup covered those small pockmarks and other minor imperfections. She committed herself to wearing makeup those evenings when Greg was home, not when he was on his many business trips.

Continuing her scrutiny, Amy felt reassured, satisfied that she was still an attractive woman. She ran her fingers through her hair, then began brushing it with harsh, determined strokes, a cigarette dangling profanely from her lips. She noted the slight movement, a jiggling of her right breast a split second after her right arm had completed its downward sweep. This delayed movement of her breast amused her. She felt randy. She switched the brush to her other hand and almost scratched her scalp while tugging downward. Her left breast responded with its own little motion. The movement of her breasts, those utilitarian but erotic parts of the female anatomy with which men, with which Greg, were so obsessed caused her to feel sexy, desirable. She would, she thought, brush her hair some evening in front of her husband. Some evening soon. She removed the cigarette from her mouth, turned to observe her profile in the mirror. She was assured of her femininity, pleased that the inexplicable programming of her father's sperm and her mother's ovum had produced the embryo of a female. She wondered about that moment of ecstasy long forgotten. Had they known all the elements were right that night? Where Alph the sacred river ran ...

Amy enjoyed wearing skirts that ended just above her knees, scoop-necked blouses, silky clothing. She liked herself, her femininity; that which she was. Then she painfully remembered the cause of her self-examination, this self-imposed scrutiny. What in the hell is the problem with Greg?

She finished undressing and again viewed herself in the mirror, slightly separating her legs. She was okay! Then the terrible thought came to her. Had Greg become gay? She pondered the question for but a moment, remembering the last time Greg stood before her, fully aroused. No! Of course not, she humorously judged. It must be another woman. And I can deal with that! I can compete with any woman!

Completing her bath, Amy walked to the bedroom without putting on her nightie. She picked up a book she had begun. Slowly, feeling sensuous, she walked to their bed, hoping Greg would soon come. She heard the television from the living room. The ten o'clock news must be on. That surprised her. She must have luxuriated in the bathwater for over an hour. She propped up the pillow and slipped between the coolness of the sheets. The bath had completely relaxed her. She lethargically stretched out, neatly tucked the blanket around her waist. Raising and separating her knees, she rested the book in her lap. The sports update was on. Greg would be coming to bed soon. She began reading even though she clearly wasn't interested in the book. She patiently waited for the news to end.

It was one thirty when she finally placed the book on the nightstand. She only had two chapters left to read, but it was a dull book. Greg, she surmised, had probably turned off the TV and fallen asleep in his chair. She turned off the light and tried to sleep.

CHAPTER TWENTY-FOUR

George Iron Rope leveled the rifle barrel, aligning the front and rear sights. Jeff Vinton, standing behind George, turned away. He didn't want to observe the act. George waited until the animal had turned its head in profile, then squeezed the trigger. George felt a slight recoil in the pit of his shoulder as the rifle discharged. It was a clean shot, the round penetrating the brain of the steer. The fattened animal stood motionless for a second or two, then its legs buckled and the animal slowly toppled over on its side, its legs pointlessly extending beyond its frame. The other cattle whose own demise had been deferred were uninterested in the event. They responded to the rifle's report by raising their heads for a few seconds, then returned to their grazing. The death of one of their kind went unnoticed.

Jeff backed up the tractor to the fallen steer. That encroachment caused the cattle to move slowly away. Jeff tied the rear legs of the steer together and tethered them to the tractor. Minutes later, the carcass was towed to the barn, the skinning of the animal began. In spite of the relative warmth of the spring afternoon, steam rose from the point where the hide was separated from the flesh. Later, the more difficult task of removing the belly was accomplished. It was done without the large sac being penetrated by the cutting knife. Now it was a simple matter of further gutting the animal, halving it, hanging it up to cure.

It was nothing like the mechanized slaughterhouses, yet there was a certain efficiency to the operation. The light was fading by the time they finished, so a naked light bulb hanging from a rafter had been turned on. Jeff and George lifted the large stomach and entrails into a wheel barrel and dumped them behind the barn. Their clothing and bodies captured the distinct and offensive odor of the animal's innards. The rancher gave each man twelve dollars and a can of cold beer. They opened the windows of George's car as they drove off, allowing the smell to escape. George let Jeff out at his home forty-five minutes later and drove to northwest Union.

Since being fired, Jeff had frequently returned to his home filthy with the residue of whatever spot labor he could find. But it had never been this bad. He walked into the garage and asked Andrea to bring his tennis shorts. As he placed the foul clothing in a pile, he thought how drained Andrea's face appeared. Finances, he thought. He remembered how angry he had been with Andrea for not telling him about their financial situation when he was still employed. Now he was glad he didn't know, glad she kept that pressure from him. But he knew the bills must be piling up. How was she doing it? The kids were well-dressed, the food tasty and plentiful. She's quite a gal, he concluded.

Jeff's muscles weren't accustomed to the physical labor he was subjecting them to. Although he came home physically exhausted, the mental pressures precluded him from sleeping well. The unfairness of the situation disturbed him the most. Agnes Moore, who had disregarded the law and done nothing to help the needy for twenty years, had returned to the Harney County welfare office as the interim director. John Rediger remained the CAP's executive director although his travel budget had been substantially reduced. Still, Jeff and George had seen Rediger and Jan heading down the highway. Probably to the goddamned airport, Jeff thought. He had slouched down in his seat so they wouldn't see him because he was embarrassed about his station in life. Later, he wondered why he felt shame. Christ, he had done nothing wrong! Yet he sure as hell was being penalized. Sonofabitch!

Jeff ate dinner without speaking. He showered again, went to bed, sleeping soundly only for the first few hours.

George and Jeff had been working for about three hours when Andrea drove up the following morning. In spite of the cool midmorning air, Jeff's shirt was wet with sweat. His face and arms were covered with fine dust from the grain he was shoveling.

Andrea surveyed her husband as she walked toward him. Maybe our luck's changing, she prayed. She ran the last few feet to Jeff.

He looked up at her. "Take it easy, Andrea. Is there anything wrong? The kids? The baby?"

"No. Nothing's wrong." Andrea smiled, breathing heavily. "As you can see, he's tucked safely inside me."

"A 'he', huh?"

"Of course."

"Well so be it. What's up?"

"Larry Ashton from OEO called. He wants to talk to you."

"What about?"

"I don't know. He didn't say. I told him you'd be home at noon. Can you come?"

Jeff looked to George who nodded back. "Sure, just fix me some lunch."

As Andrea drove away, Jeff wondered why Ashton would call him. Having no answer, he went back to shoveling grain.

It was shortly after twelve when Jeff answered the telephone.

"Jeff, this is Larry Ashton. Remember me?"

"Sure. Sorry about the way things turned out. I read some nasty stuff about you in the local press. Stuff like militant, communist ..."

Larry interrupted him. "Yeah, yeah. I got copies sent to me through interoffice distribution. They came down from the national director's office to the regional director's office to my boss's boss's boss. You know."

"Too bad. I'm sorry. You surviving the bloodbath?"

"Oh yeah. I'm still with OEO. Got transferred from that CAP to another one. Incidentally, I read some stuff about you. I think we were in a couple of the same articles. How are you doing?"

"Not so well."

"I figured. You looking for a job?"

"Sure am. Looking hard."

"An agency in the eastern part of your state is looking for a director. The job's been open a couple months. The agency's really screwed up. It pays twelve thou."

"Christ! That's a lot!"

"Shall I tell their field rep you're interested?"

Jeff looked at Andrea's anxious face. He smiled at her. He redirected his attention to Ashton, his voice filled with gratitude. "God yes. Please do."

"How soon can you be available?"

"I'm ready right now."

"Good. I'll ask their field rep to suggest they contact you. They could make you the acting director and get you right on. No guarantees, but you might get a call."

"Larry, you don't know how much I appreciate this ..."

"You got a rotten deal. This is to make it up to you."

"Thank you, Larry." Jeff was becoming emotional. He hung up the phone before his voice betrayed him. He turned to Andrea, smiled. "I think it's gonna be okay."

The telephone rang at eight o'clock the next morning. Andrea answered it then ran to Jeff. "It's the call, Jeff," she said, handing him the phone. "His name's Anderson."

Jeff stretched the telephone cord so he could sit at the kitchen table near his coffee. "Good morning, Mr. Anderson."

Anderson didn't return the greeting. His voice was gruff, his manner of speaking terse, businesslike. "Sorry to bother you so early, Vinton. I wanted to get you before you left for work."

"I was told you might call, so I hung around this morning."

"I understand you're willing to take on a tough assignment."

"Well, I'm not averse to it," Jeff answered as confidently as he could.

"Good. 'Cause we got a mess out here. I really don't know why I waste my time staying on the board, but I'm gonna see us out of this before I quit. Anyway, the man from OEO says you can shape this place up. Are you willing?"

Jeff didn't want to appear too eager. "Yeah, I'd be willing."

"Good. How soon can you get up here?"

"How soon do you need me?"

"About a year ago. That would have been three directors ago."

"I could be there at noon tomorrow." Jeff realized the error the moment he finished his sentence.

"Tomorrow!" Anderson was surprised at the immediacy of Jeff's response. Jeff moved to preempt him. "Yeah, I arranged to take some time off." Then to change the subject, lest Anderson ask about his job, he asked, "What's the situation?"

"We need you for a month. We'll call you our acting director. If you like us, we like you, we'll make it permanent. I was told you're looking for a job change."

"Yeah, I am. It sounds okay."

"Fine. We'll pay mileage, per diem and fifty a day consultant fee. Okay?"

"Okay."

"Can you find the place?"

Jeff felt flushed. He had no idea about the name of the agency or where it was. "What's the address?"

"We're in an itty bitty little town. When you get to Flatwater, that's in Otoe County, just ask anyone where the agency is. Or just follow the drunks. I'll be in your office, our director's office, at noon tomorrow. Look forward to meeting you." Anderson severed the call before Vinton could respond.

Jeff handed the receiver to Andrea. Relief overcame him; his whole body and mind relaxed. Christ, he thought, a job that might result in a job. Twelve thou, twice what I was making. No more spot labor, begging ranchers and storekeepers for work. A job so I can support my family, my children - my new child.

He had ignored Andrea while savoring the possibility of a real job. She was eager to learn what had happened, but she didn't want to intrude on his thoughts. She knew the call had dramatically improved things. She saw that in his face. Finally she asked, "Well?"

"Andrea, I swear to you, this last couple of months will never happen again. I've learned my lesson. I'll no longer be the conscience of the bureaucracy. From now on those ugly sonsabitches can do anything they want. I ain't gonna blow no more whistles. I'm a man with a wonderful wife and children. I'm going to take care of you."

Later in bed he told her what he knew about the job. It was temporary. It might become permanent. He'd be away for at least a month, perhaps longer. They might have to move across the state. She had quickened him to orgasm to hear these things. They were now relaxed, the pressure removed, the future less uncertain. They slept soundly. The children awoke them when they returned from school.

Jeff stayed in bed as Andrea rose to greet them, to prepare dinner. He dozed off several times, once falling into a deep sleep. At ten thirty, Andrea nudged Jeff as she lay beside him. His entire essence had been consumed by his employment situation and its accompanying concerns for these past few months. Her closeness and his renewed arousal made him realize that this afternoon was the first time in weeks they had enjoyed each other. He hungered to share that joy again. Jeff reached for and caressed her left breast, toying with its nipple. Andrea sensed his need and smiled. "Before we start, let me tell you some things. First, your suitcase is packed for a two-week stay. I don't know if you plan to come home next weekend. It's an eight-hour drive. The alarm's set for three o'clock. The oil was checked - it needed a quart - and the gas tank's filled. I put it on the Sunoco card. We're up to the limit on that one so don't use it. Use the others, but not the Mobil card either. And I packed a lunch. It's in the refrigerator. And let's see, what else? She looked into his eyes, hers sparkling like they hadn't in months. "Oh yeah. We're broke but I put twenty dollars in your wallet."

"Good. I'll apply for my travel reimbursement right away and get it to you."

With urgency she said, "We really need it, Jeff."

Even while hearing this, his recharged libido and her presence aroused him. He drew her to him.

The next morning, Jeff drove through the northern tier of counties then traveled southerly through the buttes and canyons and hill country before the sun rose. Driving in the darkness, he fell into spells of melancholy. This would be the first time away from his family, his wife. That made him sad. But his mood changed when the sun was sitting on the horizon before him. He had a job, albeit a temporary one. He could look at Andrea and the children with pride, not in the downcast manner he had recently assumed. He tried to plan what he would say to Anderson, how to assure him he could effectively run the agency, make it work. After searching for the proper buzzwords, the necessary ingratiating phrases, he realized he didn't know what to say or do. Crossing a bridge, he saw that the river was wider, straighter, browner. He reached for the lunch Andrea had prepared.

***

Andrea snapped shut the latches to the lunch boxes, sipped her coffee, and called to Laura and Bobby. Then, making sure the children looked presentable for school, she shooed them out of the house. She sat at the table with her coffee. A sharp pain struck her pelvis. She cringed with discomfort. She had been having these recurring symptoms ever since moving to Union. But symptoms of what? She had seen the doctor routinely during her pregnancy. And even earlier she had been assured she was okay. But the assurances didn't deter the sometimes-excruciating pain. She tried to ignore the current discomfort, commanding her mind to concentrate on something else. She thought of Jeff, of last night, the pleasure she had brought him. It occurred to her that she too experienced enjoyment, but not that much. The ecstasy hadn't been there. The honeymoon's over, she lamented. And where might they be moving to? Flatbush? Flatrock? No, for Christ's sake, Flatwater!

She recalled driving the kids along the coastal waters of Galveston. And now they were moving to Flatwater.

It wasn't really what she had expected. And what about Jeff? He had traveled to Singapore, to Bangkok while in Southeast Asia. Could he be satisfied with a place called Flatwater? This was a temporary setback. Of course he couldn't be satisfied with Flatrock, or water, or whatever. She got out a map. Looking on the eastern border, she located the village. It was, for Christ's sake, right in the middle of an Indian reservation: dusty streets, substandard housing, drunken Indians. She felt crummy. She looked to the bottom of the map. Population: 380. Jesus Christ! She thought of the pool at her parents' house, just steps from the kitchen. And she had left that to live on a goddamned Indian reservation. The pain in her groin intensified. She should call Joyce to tell her Jeff has a job. Her parents had been worried. Andrea thought of the many calls to them, several lasting over an hour while Jeff was working. She thought of the telephone charges and dreaded the arrival of the bill. It was good that he was away, but she always got the mail anyway. And she would have hidden the bill.

She tried getting up, but the pain was too great. Stooping, she went to the coffee pot. Returning to her chair, she picked up the phone and began dialing. Joyce answered moments later. Andrea started crying, alarming her mother.

"No, Mom, the baby's okay, and the kids, they're alright. They're in school now. I'm just real sad. I really miss you and Dad. And I keep having these terrible pains."

Joyce was weary of these calls. With some exasperation she replied, "I know, but you told me the doctors say there's no medical problem."

Andrea didn't reply. Several moments elapsed. Joyce then said, "Ned's downtown. He should be back soon if you need to talk with him. How's Jeff doing," she paused, "job-wise?"

"Oh, we think he's got a job. He left this morning to go to it. It's in the eastern part of the state."

"I hope it works out," Joyce sincerely said. "How's your money? These phone calls can't help."

"I know. But we're so far apart. I get so lonely for you."

"How are things otherwise?"

"I've got a lot of pain. The pregnancy, I guess. But worse than before."

"I'll send some more money," Joyce said. "That'll help."

"I hate to ask. I wish Jeff was more successful."

"He's doing his best." Joyce's voice was firmer this time.

"But I couldn't make the money stretch before, when he was the welfare director. It's impossible now. No one could do it with this size family."

Joyce reflected for a moment. "You should have let what's his name see his kids. That child support would be real useful now. But there's no sense thinking back. The judge relieved him of that responsibility." She then reiterated, "I always thought you should have let him see Bobby and Laura."

Andrea experienced another sharp pain in her groin. "Mom, we've been through that. He was so violent with them, with me."

"Okay, Andrea," Joyce said, skeptical of her daughter's repeated accusations. "But remember, dear, a year ago Jeff was single. Now he's got a family of four, soon to be five. He's got a lot of adjustments to make. And he seems to be doing everything he can. What kind of job did he get?"

Andrea tried to describe what an action agency was, the tentative nature of the job. Joyce mentioned she'd fly up when the baby came. Then Ned arrived home, got on the phone. Andrea described her health problems again and mentioned how well Bobby was doing in school. Bobby was Ned's favorite. An hour passed before Andrea said good-bye to her parents.

Immediately Andrea felt guilty. Jeff had earned twelve dollars the last day he had worked. The call had probably cost twenty. She should have called during the evening hours when it would have been cheaper. She hobbled to the kitchen drawer where she kept the bills. She had placed them between the dishtowels. Most were dated before Jeff had been fired. And things had gotten worse. It wouldn't do any good to go through them now. It would depress her more. She walked painfully to the bathroom, took a mild sedative, then went to the bedroom to rest. Because of the baby growing within her, it took several minutes to comfortably position herself. She willed herself to sleep, telling herself she was happily married. Her last thought before sleep was her love for Jeff.

***

Checking the map, Jeff left the state highway and turned onto a gravel road. He reached the crest of a rise twenty minutes later. The village of Flatwater sat in an oval-shaped valley below. The town was positioned on the west bank of a muddy creek. To its northeast were rolling hills, pastureland where cattle grazed. Rows of cultivated corn and soybeans were planted on the hills' gentler slopes and were several weeks ahead of the wheat and sugar beets of the western part of the state. But the scene appeared different to Jeff. The large reservation south of Union had only barren, unattended flatland. The land on this reservation looked lush by comparison.

Vinton drove into Flatwater a couple of minutes after noon. The streets were paved, but mud from the spring rains, now dried and crusty, gave the town an unkempt appearance. He counted four bars in the town. He drove down the two blocks of the business district, made a U-turn, parked, and stepped onto the sidewalk. He was the only individual wearing a business suit.

He walked until he saw the Community Action Program office. Its name and the OEO logo were on the door. He entered, attentive to the layout. The desks were situated in an orderly manner. They were the institutional gray that Jeff remembered from the military. Government surplus. He approached the receptionist. Late forties, neat appearing, Caucasian. Another anomaly. "I have an appointment with Mr. Anderson," Jeff said without mentioning that he was a few minutes late.

A broad smile brightened her face. "You're Mr. Vinton." She rose. "Mr. Anderson is in the director's office. Let me escort you. I'm Gwen Antonine, your executive secretary," she added.

Jeff nodded. Everyone who works for a CAP is an executive

something, he thought. They walked the narrow hallway, Gwen rapping on the door at its end.

"Come in."

"Hi there," Jeff extended his hand to Anderson.

Anderson was seated behind the substantial desk of the director, slowly rocking and turning in the large executive chair. He ignored Jeff's extended hand, leaned his head against the chair's high back, spoke without amenities.

"As I understand the concept behind OEO, its purpose is to place decision making in the hands of the poor, the unemployed, the uneducated. 'Power to the people' and all that crap." Anderson turned his chair and faced Jeff. "Well, Mr. Vinton, this agency has excelled beyond anyone's expectations in achieving that goal. To press the point, I don't believe anyone working here has a high school diploma or even has held a job for more than a few months. We've put the poor on the payroll, provided them with a damned good board, turned over hundreds of thousands of dollars to them. One result of our purist obedience to the OEO philosophy is that this agency is on probation, to be closed in six months. It's riddled with corruption, incompetence, indifference, absenteeism, a lack of direction, and a lack of production. We've gone through four directors in the last two years. Charges have been filed in U.S. district court against our last director. The FBI has been in and out of here the last few weeks going over the books. Two weeks ago a newspaper did a story on us. We were identified as the personification of everything that's wrong with LBJ's Great Society.

"During this period the governing board's become disillusioned. We haven't had a quorum in six months." He paused as if to confide a family secret. "The board's split along racial lines. They call us rednecks. We call them dirty Injuns. Neither side means those things. The damn agency is dividing the community it was designed to bring together. There's been threats of physical harm made to board members by other board members. So far it's just property damage - slashed tires, nothing big yet. One member confided to me that he carries a handgun to the meetings." Anderson's voice trailed off.

After moments of silence, he continued with more resolve. "One board member moved that we dissolve the corporation - the agency. It's one of the more intelligent motions the board's entertained." He paused again, this time looking blankly at the wall behind Vinton. "We've advertised for a director for a couple of months now. Damn near every staff member we got applied for the job, plus a few more from around these parts, mostly relatives of the staff." A long pause. "The real problem is that this area desperately needs the agency and the hundred or so jobs it offers. And make no mistake, the actual survival of this agency is very questionable."

With his eyes lowered, Anderson continued. "I have a packet for you to go through that will shock you but nonetheless give you an accurate profile of the agency." He looked directly at Jeff. "Anyway, I don't know a damn thing about you, but our options are limited." A longer pause, then with some desperation, he asked, "What do you think?"

"Are you the board chairman?" Jeff asked.

"No. He's out of town today. The chairman's a radical priest. A Jesuit."

"He'll be my contact with the board, or will you?"

"He voted for Humphrey. I voted for Nixon. Take your pick. We're not fussy out here."

"I drove all the way over here. I'll commit to a month."

"Good. Damn good to hear. You must have a helluva good employer, letting you go for a month at a moment's notice," Anderson observed. "Where do you work?"

Jeff didn't flinch as he responded. "Oh, I've been doing some consultant work." It was the best answer he could muster, but he couldn't help notice the cynical expression on Anderson's face.

"Well, regardless, I've prepared a contract for you," Anderson said. "The terms are as we spoke. From this point it's your agency. But you can't fire anyone without permission of the personnel committee. I want you to know that's not my idea. It comes directly from the Society of Jesus."

Jeff grinned. "Okay, I'll review the contract and sign it later. And protocol dictates I interact with the chairman."

"That's fine. Just give the contract to Gwen. She'll file a copy, give you one, and mail me one. Any other questions?"

"Yeah. I'm gonna have to work closely with somebody. Who can I rely upon? Who in this agency can I trust?"

"Ain't nobody."

"I see."

"Good luck."

Anderson departed, leaving him alone. Jeff felt like that first day in Harney County, ill-equipped, unknowledgeable, unprepared. He felt very much alone here in Flatwater.

He had sat on a CAP board for a few months, but he knew nothing about an agency's inner workings. He thought of those who were employed by this agency, now dependent on him, his leadership. He was faceless, unknown to them. They were relying on him, someone they didn't know. He then thought of his own predicament; a family, a kid on the way. To hell with this agency and its staff. Fifty bucks a day plus per diem. A thousand plus twenty-five a day, including weekends. Over seventeen hundred a month. He figured he could live on ten a day. That would mean over fourteen hundred to Andrea this month. What the hell, it beats slaughtering cattle. He walked out of his office to where Gwen was. "Come join me."

It took Gwen a few minutes to locate someone to replace her. Jeff sat in the high-backed chair. He liked it.

Gwen entered. "Glad you've joined us."

"Quite a place, this agency I mean, from what I've heard," Jeff said as casually as he could.

"Yep. Quite a place."

"How long you been with the agency?"

"About eight months."

"Where did you work before?"

"I was a farm wife. I guess I still am."

"So you're new to bureaucracies. What do you think of them?"

"It confirms everything I've heard about bureaucracies, about government."

"How so?"

"What did Mr. Anderson tell you?"

"That we got problems."

"Yeah. Problems we got."

"Well, we're not the government," Jeff observed. "We're the private sector using public money, kinda like General Dynamics or Dow Chemical. We contract with the government to do specific things as well as we can."

"Whatever," she said, not warmly, not unkindly, certainly not convinced.

"What are this agency's strengths?"

"Most of us mean well."

"And?"

"The folks around here are really poor. We're needed."

"How many are on the payroll?"

"Little over a hundred."

"This place is empty. Where is everybody?"

"In the field, the community centers.

He nodded. He asked where he could stay this evening.

"There's an old hotel down the street," Gwen informed him. "Years ago this was a railroad town. The hotel was built then. It's mostly empty now. And it's not very nice. Or, about forty miles north, there's some nice motels in Jackson City. That's a town of about sixty thousand."

"Get me a room here in town. And send the fiscal officer over. I'll start going through this paperwork Anderson gave me."

"Okay. Pay attention to last year's audit."

"Oh?"

"Our CPA recommended that some of our expenditures be excepted. The regional office accepted that recommendation."

"So what do we do? The money's obviously gone," Jeff said.

"We're going to have to make it up somehow."

"Christ. I'd better start reading this stuff."

"You know all the staff's coming in tomorrow morning."

"What for?"

"For you to meet them, talk to them."

"I've nothing to say to them. How far do they have to travel?"

"Some over eighty miles."

"Cancel it."

"Yes, sir. Is that all?"

"Yeah, for now."

"Okay," Gwen agreed. "Incidentally, I took a call from the OEO this morning. They've assigned a new field representative. He's due in tomorrow morning."

Jeff looked surprised but said nothing.

"Shall I cancel that too?" she asked, a smile overcoming her.

Jeff returned her smile. "I suppose we should let that stand."

Jeff left the office at five o'clock. He walked to the only cafe in town. Gwen had told him it closed at six.

It was a lonely meal. He read the county paper to occupy himself. It promised to be a lonely town. He was the last to leave, then he walked to the hotel. It was a two-story frame building that had fallen into disrepair. It appeared to lean to one side. The porch supports were giving way on its north side.

He checked in and carried his suitcase to his room, its single window overlooking Main Street. It was a small room, but clean. The furniture was old, unattractive. He opened his suitcase and removed only his toilet kit to underscore the temporary nature of his stay. He would live out of his suitcase. After changing clothes, he went back to the office to read the program evaluations, audits, and correspondence. One letter from the State Department of Integrated Human Services gave notice it would initiate an investigation. The final paragraph of the letter from Mr. Greg Allen stood out.

"Please be advised that my office will not forgive or tolerate the antics of your agency; nor will this Administration allow your agency to expend its resources in a reckless and injudicious manner and with the apparent impunity the agency enjoyed under this state's previous governor."

The letter was dated three months ago. Jeff could not find any subsequent correspondence from Allen. Allen - Greg Allen. The same sonofabitch he had seen in the hotel lounge. The same sonofabitch he had spoken with in Union. Jesus Christ! Jeff pondered the lack of follow-up after such a threatening letter. He made a note for Gwen to locate further correspondence from Allen. He looked over the audit reports, the agency's evaluation reports, the personnel policies, the staff's personnel files.

Although tired from his long day and long drive, he had difficulty falling asleep after he returned to the hotel. Finally, he fell into a restless sleep.

***

It was a little after eleven when Gwen told him the new field rep from OEO had arrived. Jeff put on his suit coat and walked out to greet him. Surprised, Jeff smiled as he made eye contact with Larry Ashton. It was only after his office door was closed that Jeff spoke. "God, it's good to see you. Are you this agency's rep?"

Ashton nodded. "Just been reassigned. My boss thought we could work together."

"Great. I don't know how long I'll be around, but I'm glad you're here. And I appreciate being on a payroll again, even if it's just for thirty days." Jeff looked to the floor, then renewed eye contact. "But, Jesus Christ, if Anderson's analysis is right, there's nothing I can do in a month to bring this place around."

"Just bringing some stability to the place would be something," Ashton countered. "If you can, persuade your employees to show up for work even if they don't do anything."

"How'd this place get so bad? Christ, I thought Rediger's CAP was bad. And dammit, I still think so. But this place - from what I read ..."

"Yeah?"

"I just don't understand what's going on. I've only seen two CAPs, and they're both screwed up. That's two for two."

Ashton smiled. "What's your point?"

"Why's all this tolerated?"

"The regional director is a presidential appointee. We take orders from him. Does that help?"

"No, it really doesn't," Jeff said after a few moments of thought.

"Well, with this president, OEO has become politicized."

Jeff thought that over for a moment. "What contributions can inept and corrupt agencies make to a political plan?"

"There's a lot of speculation about that within OEO and within Congress," Ashton said.

"And?"

"Well, it's an over-simplification, but the consensus is that the president wants the agencies run this way. He wants them screwed up! But that's probably presumptuous."

Jeff was perplexed. "One thing at a time. First, why is that presumptuous?"

" 'Cause I'm not sure Dick Nixon is all that concerned about one of the smallest agencies with one of the smallest budgets in government. In other words, I'm pretty sure Nixon doesn't think about OEO the minute he hops out of bed each morning."

"I suppose not," Jeff agreed. Then, taking up Ashton's premise, asked, "But how about the staff who speak for him? He's got some crazies around him."

"Could be."

"Second question. Why does he want the CAPs so screwed up?"

"Well, he's really got this thing about OEO," Ashton reflected. "Christ, maybe he does think of us the first thing each morning."

"Okay. So he hates us. So he's obsessed with us. But you bureaucrats control the purse strings, the money going to the CAPs. You can say, 'Shape up or I'll jerk your funding'."

"Now we've gone full cycle, back to the regional director," Ashton said.

"What do you mean?"

"The career employees recommend that the worst agencies, and this is one of them, have their funding cut or be closed. But the regional director ignores the career employees' recommendations."

"You're one of the good guys, huh?"

"Of course," Ashton acknowledged self-effacingly.

Becoming serious again, Jeff continued, "Nothing positive happens because the president of the United States wants the agencies to fail. Is that what you're saying?"

"Yep. Not only a few agencies, but the entire structure, i.e. OEO."

"Damn."

"If we continue getting bad press like this agency routinely gets, local folks'll write their congressmen, congressional support will erode, dry up. Then Nixon will have Congress do his dirty work."

"Astute," observed Vinton. "Do the congressional advocates for OEO know what's going on?"

"Probably."

"Can't the oversight committees call hearings or something?"

"It's a tough nut to crack. To your first point, Nixon would only use the oversight committee's reports to his political advantage. And remember, the executive executes. He appoints cabinet-level officers to administer. Nixon appoints incompetents to administer agencies he doesn't like."

"And appointing incompetents ensures the failure of those programs," Jeff finished Ashton's thoughts.

"More or less. One OEO director made his secretary call him fifteen minutes prior to any appointment he had."

"Sounds reasonable."

"It was to wake him up."

"Oh."

"And the same thing at the state level. Some governors don't like OEO."

"So where does the buck stop? The responsibility begin?"

"Good question. But as usual in government, nowhere."

"Oh come on!"

"Okay. Let's take this agency," Ashton explained. "OEO funds it, the governor lets the money in, the governing board accepts the money, the staff spends the money. Now you tell me, where's the accountability?"

"Either with OEO or the local board, I guess."

"Well, if OEO funds it, the local board ain't gonna refuse the money."

"I hope not for the next month."

"Forget your self-interest for a moment and consider that the governor oughta know what's going on. Hell, OEO even gives him money to hire someone to monitor the CAPs. In this state it's a guy named Allen. Maybe the buck stops with him."

Jeff ignored Ashton's reference to Allen. "I see what you're saying. Power is too diffused. Everybody takes credit when things are okay or blames everyone else if they're going bad. There's no accountability unless someone volunteers."

"And nobody, no bureaucrat, no politician, is gonna volunteer."

"Christ!"

Ashton was becoming weary of this chatter. "Now let's step away from these cosmic considerations and talk about this goddamned agency."

"From the ridiculous to the sublime, huh?"

"Yeah. But before we start, there's no reason why this agency can't work. I want you to remember that as we go through its problems. As you learn more about the agency, your inclination will be to pack up and go back to Union. But, remember, there's nothing wrong with this place except its leadership." He looked at Jeff. "Okay, I've conferred with the former field rep, and we made a list of priorities. Get out a yellow pad."

Ashton settled into his chair. "The first thing to deal with is the money the former director allegedly stole. There's a general suspicion that the former board chairman was in on it, too. He's since resigned from the board. Your action steps are: One: Ask the FBI for an update on their investigation. Two: Contact your bonding company and seek reimbursement. Three: Review the agency's fiscal safeguards. Four: Immediately cancel all agency credit cards. Five: Involve a board member as a signatory on all agency checks. Six: Take a good look at your fiscal officer and make a judgment if she can be trusted. But never rely on people. Rely on systems, safeguards, processes.

"Your second problem: Your staff's not working. They come to work late or not at all. They're either drunk or hung over. They routinely falsify their time sheets." Aston waited until Vinton stopped taking notes and looked up at him. "I'll leave the action steps on this for you to develop. This and the rest of the problems.

"Your third problem: Your agency's work programs. Review them and adhere to them. Get some production out of this agency.

"Fourth: This agency is officially on probation. For the record, be advised that OEO will stand behind you for another five months before we pull the plug. I don't know about the other funding sources. Contact them. Tell them you're in charge, that you're gonna shape the place up. Your fiscal officer can tell you which agencies are funding you and who the contacts are.

"Fifth problem: Your PR is lousy, and it's killing this agency. Meet with the local media. Try to impress upon them that what's done is done, that this is a new day. But don't try to deceive them. If you do and get caught, they'll kill you. Just remember, this agency can't take any more bad press.

"Sixth problem: Virtually all of your programs are operating in one county. Now that's where most of the poor are, here on the reservation. But you've got to do something in the other eight counties. Either that or have them withdraw from the agency. We can't give you any more money 'cause you've mismanaged the money we've already given you.

"Seven: There's vibes that one of your program directors is about to yank his program out of the CAP and set up his own not-for-profit. He's supposed to have selected his board members. Ironically, some are from your board. And it's not that these members are disloyal. They're just ignorant. Anyway, stop him. This corporation can't afford to lose any programs.

"Eight: Technically, by state and OEO regulations, this isn't a corporation anymore. Your governing board hasn't had an official meeting, with a quorum, in over eight months. You damn well better have a quorum this month.

"Nine: Your cash flow of OEO money is thirty percent accelerated. In other words, slow it down or you won't last the program year. You're way overspent.

"Ten: While your federal spending is too high, you're way behind on your nonfederal spending. That's in-kind money, stuff like volunteered services, labor, rent. If you don't improve your local contributions by the next reporting date, I'll cut back your federal share in direct proportion.

"Eleven: The last three annual audits haven't been closed by the OEO fiscal people. Find out why and get them closed. You'll have to negotiate on these, and, off the record, appeal every adverse decision the regional director makes, even if he's a hundred percent right. We need movement on these audits, but it's not the most urgent thing. The appeals will buy you time.

"Twelve: There's a program audit of your Head Start program starting next Tuesday. It'll last four days. The evaluation team comes from the regional HEW office. I spoke with the team leader. He'll try to be nice to you, but put something together for him. You've got to give him something he can hang his hat on or he'll burn your ass."

Jeff's hand was tired from writing.

"Thirteen: I'm told the board won't let you fire anyone during your interim directorship. That's probably best. But be a sonofabitch. Take names, kick asses. If they hire you, have a list of your incompetents. Get rid of them in one sweep.

"Fourteen: When you fire someone and they successfully appeal, you're screwed. If they hire you, I'll have our EEO fly down to teach you how to fire people.

"Fifteen: In everything you do, lay a paper trail. Always cover your ass with paper. Especially with the bucks, the audits, the adverse personnel actions, the ..."

They worked through the lunch hour, Gwen bringing them coffee and sandwiches. By five o'clock Vinton could write no more. His mind and hand were too weary.

Ashton stood up. "I made an appointment with Father Dunn for nine o'clock tomorrow morning. He's your board chairman. See you there. Good night."

Ashton left, driving his rented car to Jackson City. Jeff walked slowly back to the hotel, his mind swimming with everything that Ashton expected him to do.

***

Vinton was parked outside the rectory when Ashton arrived the following morning. Together they walked to the priest's residence. Minutes later they were sitting in the living room, sipping coffee. The priest maintained a coldness, especially toward Jeff. He was tall, gaunt. Jeff judged he was in his late thirties. After the initial amenities, Fr. Dunn looked at Jeff.

"Scuttlebutt has it you're a welfare director."

"Yeah, until recently."

"As I would hear confessions, I sometimes would need to absolve those who had turned to an amateurish form of prostitution."

Jeff had no idea what prostitution had to do with the agency's problems. As the priest was looking directly at him, he weakly responded, "Oh?"

"Yes. They couldn't find work, their husbands had left, their kids needed to eat."

"That's sad," Jeff could only say.

"In the confessional, I would ask them why they didn't go to welfare to get help."

This time Jeff maintained the silence that followed the priest's statement. Finally Ashton spoke up. "What's your point, Father?"

293

Jeff knew where he was heading.

"They told me welfare refused to help them." Fr. Dunn had not relinquished his intense eye contact with Jeff.

Ashton sat back, realizing this was Jeff's battle.

"You should have told them to appeal. Every administrative decision can be appealed."

"I did. They did. They lost the appeal. Then they lost their kids. The court took them away. I did not serve these women, or their children, very well. The kids are now scattered all over hell, different foster homes, different counties. A couple of the mothers couldn't handle it. They're in the psychiatric wards of area hospitals. Welfare's paying for that."

Jeff looked away from the priest. "What can I say?"

"I know what I can say. You, Mr. Vinton, and your kind are a part of the problem. The fact that you're here indicates our pickings are slim. But as long as you're on my payroll, you damn well better help, not hurt, the poor."

Jeff became angry. "From what I can see of this place, Father, you haven't done a helluva lot for the poor yourself. And regardless of the philosophical perspective I'm coming from, it ain't gonna make any difference. The month I'll be here will be spent on administrative matters; trying to inject some order into this agency. I doubt if I'll ever see a poor person."

"Probably just as well," the priest said.

Two hours later, when they finally left, Fr. Dunn's only assurance was that he would muster a quorum for the next meeting.

Walking to their cars, Ashton asked why Jeff hadn't countered the priest's accusations.

Jeff didn't immediately respond. Finally he said, "It's like trying to deny you're a communist. It doesn't do any good."

The following week, Jeff welcomed Bob Buren in his office. He ran the agency's work training programs. Jeff judged him to be about fifty-five. He was tall, lean, ruggedly handsome, an American Indian. He had been identified to Jeff as a political and religious leader of the tribe. His eyeglasses were tinted, impeding Jeff's ability to look directly into his eyes. That annoyed Jeff.

"Please sit down," said Jeff, nodding toward a chair.

"I'd rather stand."

"Okay," Jeff said, sitting down. "How's things going?"

"Other than the goddamn rampant racism, I guess okay," Buren replied.

"Oh?"

"That's the problem with this area."

"I see."

Next, the director of the nutrition program knocked before she entered. She was a large-framed woman with bulky legs.

"Sit down please."

"Thank you." She seated herself with great care.

"You're one of the few Caucasians on the staff," Jeff observed.

"And are we ever happy to see you," she replied.

"Oh?"

"Yes. It's been very difficult working under the direction we've had."

"I see."

"When the people over you and the people under you are all Indians, and they won't work, what can you do?"

"Makes it tough, huh?"

"Well," she spoke crisply, "now we will have our opportunity."

"How's that?"

"Just that things like breeding and education and middle class values will be recognized and rewarded."

"I see."

Jeff saw four other component directors that day. He detected a similar pattern.

Gwen entered Jeff's office just before quitting time. "Well, you haven't been here that long and already I've noticed some changes," she said.

"Oh? For the better?"

"Oh, yeah. Some of the staff are actually coming to work. Not only here in the central office, but even in the field offices."

"That's something," Jeff smiled.

"You know, the staff don't know what to think of you."

Jeff didn't respond.

"You haven't said much to anyone so far. We're all kinda scared of you," she confessed.

"It's not intentional."

"You have a family?"

"Yeah. Two kids, and Andrea's pregnant." Jeff smiled. He started to tell Gwen that he had needed his travel check as soon as possible to send to his wife, but he checked himself. "How about you?"

"Oh yeah, but the kids are grown, and Walt's disabled now. That's why this job, this agency, is so important to me."

"What happened to him?"

"Car accident. He was broadsided on a county road by a drunken Indian."

"Too bad," Jeff sympathized.

"The guy had no insurance. Really a bum deal. You know, he turned out to be a cousin of Walt's. Small world, at least in these hills."

Jeff returned to the hotel room, tired and discouraged.

16 Jun 67

The gunner, a specialist fourth class, ignored Jeff's rank. "MOVE, DAMMIT!" He was firing the M60 at the jungle below an instant later. Lt. Vinton saw the three small holes in the skin of the aircraft from the rounds they had taken. He realized he had to move away from the open door to afford the M60 its full field of fire.

The helicopter was attempting no evasive action. It continued its relatively slow flight in a southeasterly direction.

As Jeff obeyed the orders of the gunner, his first step was on firm matter, but only the middle of his boot seemed to make contact. He felt no contact under his toe or heel while standing on the black plastic bag. Jeff had to assume that he had stepped on the head of a KIA. He quickly pivoted and took another step, coming down on something less firm but with greater bulk and width. He knew it was the chest of a corpse. This matter upon which his foot temporarily rested would afford him greater leverage. He allowed his foot to sink in, to firmly implant itself, his knee to bend more acutely. He placed his weight on his rear leg to continue his momentum and then pivoted from that point to the other side of the Huey. His forward foot lit in an area where there were no black bags. He drew up his rear leg and also placed it on the naked, metallic floor of the aircraft.

He had successfully negotiated the width of the aircraft by stepping on but two dead Americans. He was pleased with his agility.

He looked to the gunner. The soldier had taken a round in his left shoulder, just beside his flak jacket. His field jacket began to darken from the blood. Also, his left wrist and hand were bloodied as he continued squeezing the automatic weapon's trigger. But the darkened patch was not getting any bigger; the round had probably not hit a vital area. The old cliché, "just a flesh wound," worked its way into Jeff's consciousness. The gunner continued to spray the area below them. They had probably flown five clicks from the point where they had taken fire. Probably just a VC patrol. Jeff looked around. No one else was hit. And they should be at the base camp in another ten minutes.

Jeff looked out the door of the 'copter. Sometimes the gunner or the M60 obstructed his view, but more often Jeff could see the greenness below him, the haze before him, the blueness above him.

They were effectively safe now, out of the free-fire zone. The gunner had stopped firing moments ago and was now examining his wound. They were close enough to the base camp that paratroopers would periodically patrol this area, giving martial evidence that this part of the jungle was within the U.S. sphere of influence.

Jeff sighed with relief. He had survived his first firefight. Then he remembered his nausea, his unconsciousness, his walking upon the lifeless members of his command.

Having lost three men, Jeff judged he had not acquitted himself well this day. It wasn't completely his fault. The LZ had been hot; the PAVN had been target-effective. But he would learn to do better. He would toughen up. And he would allow the moments of this firefight to occupy only the deep recesses of his memory.

But walking upon the dead! He knew he would always remember stepping on the head of one and the chest of another dead paratrooper encased in blackness.

***

Vinton was in a reflective mood the following morning. He began making comparisons between his first days at Union and here at Flatwater. At Union he had five staff members. Here he had over a hundred. Therefore he reasoned he had twenty times the options, twenty times the opportunities to implement changes. And where virtually all of his budget in Union had gone for payments to the recipients, here the funds went primarily to personnel whose efforts he could channel: maintenance versus local initiative monies. Managing these bucks would be more fun. Furthermore, the nondescript bureaucrat who had gotten him the job in Union had never contacted him afterwards. Here, Ashton had already visited him and promised to stay in contact. And he remembered that his last job in Union had been slaughtering a steer. There were greater opportunities in Flatwater.

He reviewed his notes about the twenty-three priorities Ashton had identified. If the regional office staff knew about these problems, how many didn't they know about? The board meeting was the following Wednesday. He needed to convey to the board the severity of its problems in such a way that the members wouldn't simply throw up their arms and resign. He had to strike a delicate balance. He must be factual yet let them know the problems could be solved. He decided to list the priorities as Ashton had, and then develop action steps to resolve each one. Those that were too asymmetric, he would simply not bring up.

1) On a yellow pad he boldly printed the words:
1. FISCAL INTEGRITY
 A. RESOLUTION OF ALLEGED FISCAL
IRREGULARITIES.
He listed the allegations, then Ashton's action steps,
paraphrasing them; then
B. CASH FLOW OF FEDERAL (HARD) MONIES
1. MORATORIUM ON ALL HIRING AND DEFERRING
ALL MERIT AND INCREMENTAL SALARY INCREASES.
2. CANCELLATION OF PENDING AND PROJECTED
CAPITAL PURCHASES
3. CESSATION OF EXTERIOR (OUTSIDE NINE-COUNTY
AREA) TRAVEL
4. REDUCTION OF INTERIOR STAFF TRAVEL
5. SCRUTINY OF PROCUREMENT PRACTICES
6. STAFF SUBMISSION TO BOARD OF DRAFT POLICY
REGARDING POSSIBILITIES OF PAYMENT DEFERRAL,

OPTIMIZATION OF INTER-ACCOUNT FUNGIBLE
TRANSFERRALS, ACHIEVEMENT OF PERSONNEL AND
PROGRAMMATIC INTEGRATIONS
7. BOARD DEVELOPMENT OF REDUCTION IN FORCE
PROCEDURES CONSISTENT WITH EEO/AAP
He made a note to have the fiscal officer set up bar graphs
indicating the money expended and time elapsed.
C. CASH FLOW OF NONFEDERAL (SOFT) MONIES
He would use the same graphs, percentages, and amounts. He
began listing the action steps.

He continued with the same format, identifying issues and offering
steps for resolution. At one thirty, without being asked, Gwen brought
in a sandwich and a quart of milk. In exchange he handed her the paper
he had produced during the last five hours. "Just rough draft it, Gwen,
and thanks."

He called Andrea once. She was fine, the baby within her growing,
the kids okay. He told her he had sent his first week's check of two
hundred and fifty dollars and a hundred of his per diem. Then he spent
the weekend working on his presentation to the board, reviewing the
Head Start work program and staff reports, preparing for the evaluation
team.

Christ, he wearily thought, a HEW regional evaluation and board
meeting in the same week. And Larry Ashton was to be at the board
meeting.

***

Gwen set another pitcher of water before Jeff. He looked at her,
expressing gratitude. "The eleventh priority involves a clear
pronouncement of the governing board regarding the possible spinoff
of agency programs." He stopped speaking long enough to fill his water
glass and sip from it. His throat was dry from speaking for almost two
hours. "Anytime an agency is as crippled as we are, we're bound to see
a few wolves on the horizon. The question the board must respond to is
obvious. Is it your wish that the agency transfer some of its programs to
other agencies should the opportunity present itself, or should it
maintain its present configuration?"

Accustomed to the normally dismal staff reporting, Anderson was impressed by Vinton's presentation. But he was perplexed by this item. "What is the basis of this discussion? It seems like a kinda moot sort of issue."

"We want to maintain its moot status, not allow it to become a practical consideration," Vinton answered.

"You know something we don't."

"Nope. Just a precaution during awkward times."

"What is the staff recommendation?" the Jesuit asked.

"Staff recommends board approval of the following policy statement." Jeff signaled Gwen to hand photocopies to the board members. "You will note that upon acceptance of this policy, the board forbids any staff member from conferring with any other entity, be it governmental, quasi-governmental, corporate, or religious, with the intent or appearance of intent of transferring any agency program without prior written board authority. And that the policy statement be distributed to all staff, and noncompliance be grounds for summary termination."

"You sure you ain't telling us something?" asked a member from down the table.

"Yep."

"Move that we adopt the staff recommendation," a director said.

"Second."

"Call the question."

The vote was unanimous.

"Next," Jeff stated, "is Item Twelve..."

Vinton had the meeting well organized and moving quickly. Anderson suggested they take a recess just before eleven o'clock. Jeff sat back, relaxed for the first time. He was satisfied with the board's response to his leadership. They had accepted each staff recommendation and charged Jeff with the implementation. Jeff looked to Ashton, noting he too was pleased. Jeff stretched out his legs, staring at the ceiling, exhausted, ignoring the hum of voices. Fr. Dunn nudged him.

Jeff looked to the chairman. "I'm sorry. What?"

"Before we can take a break, we have to act on the question before the board. For that, we need your answer."

Jeff tried to quickly reengage his mental processes. A few board members laughed at Jeff for being so oblivious the last few minutes. "Please restate the motion," the chair asked.

"I move that Mr. Vinton be relieved of his duties as acting director and be employed as the agency's executive director," a board member stated. He then added: "The real question is whether he's dumb enough to take the job."

More laughter.

Jeff looked at those before him, then caught Ashton's eye. He saw Ashton shaking his head. Jeff wondered why.

"You'd better take it now, Mr. Vinton," someone said. "We might not have a quorum for another year!"

More laughter.

Jeff looked again to Ashton. He again shook his head.

"What do you say, Jeff?" the Jesuit asked.

Jeff was at an impasse. God knows he needed the security of a job to support his family, to move them here, to be with them. But Ashton kept shaking his head. What's going on? He had to respond to the board. But what to say? Slowly he began. "Mr. Chairman, I'm complimented by the gentleman's motion, and it would be a real challenge. But at this point I think it would be prudent for the board to be a bit more cautious in selecting its new director."

Jeff heard muted discussions around him. They think I don't want the job, he thought. To neutralize those thoughts, he said, "Let's give ourselves a month to get to know each other better. At the next meeting, the board can set up procedures for selecting its new director." He then looked at the man who had made the motion. "But I hope you keep that thought."

"I'm sure I will," he replied."

Jeff went to Ashton after the meeting. "Why?" he asked.

Ashton waited until most of the directors had left the meeting room. He led Jeff to an area of the room free of those still remaining. He leaned toward Jeff's ear. "You'd be giving up your tax-free per diem." He grinned at Jeff. "Let's go get a drink. On me. You done damned good."

The HEW evaluation team's exit interview lasted for two hours on Friday. The team confirmed the chaotic condition of the agency. Most critical was the alcoholism of the staff. Some teachers were either drunk or hung over while with the kids. The agency did get high marks for relating to the children's cultural background. The last words of the team leader were that the program would continue with the agency. However, within thirty days a list of special conditions would be placed on the contract. Failure of the agency to accept and comply with the conditions would be cause for grant termination.

Jeff thanked the team members and walked them from his office. Returning, he called Gwen, asking if his check was ready. She brought it to him moments later. "What are you going to do this weekend?"

"My suitcase is in the car. I'm heading home."

"That'll be good for you. Say 'Hi' to your family for me."

"Sure. But before I do that, I'm gonna hire a babysitter for about three minutes."

Gwen was nearing her desk before she realized what Jeff meant. She smiled as Jeff was backing his car from its parking spot.

CHAPTER TWENTY-FIVE

"Fortunately, it's not a political problem yet. But things aren't getting any better. In fact, they're getting worse. I want this thing resolved." Governor Bob Elam looked at the door impatiently. "And where the hell's Allen?"

"We could begin without him," Bill Sergent suggested. "I'm sure he'll be here any minute. Meantime, I'll give you a rundown on what I've picked up."

Displeased, Elam nodded agreement. Senator Jake Hammond sat in silence.

"Most of the constituent calls for the governor come to me," Sergent began. "I take notes, refer the matter to the appropriate department. My point is, I've taken some complaints about these CAPs. Most lament the waste of tax dollars on social programs, thinking they could be better used for defense – as if we could do anything about that. But a few have come from folks who are not your typical rednecks. They were concerned about corruption and incompetence. And they've been pretty specific. One went so far as to accuse this office of a whitewash out west - with Rediger's CAP. He said this guy Vinton was right; that Rediger's a bum."

"Isn't Allen on top of that? I remember a memo ..."

"Yes, Governor, he's been out there several times."

"Well, okay. What about the others?"

Taking his cue, Sergent began discussing other agencies. "The FBI is still in and out of Flatwater."

"Yeah. Problems there, that's for sure," Elam said.

"Incidentally," Sergent continued, "Vinton, the guy from Harney County, is up there as a consultant."

"I'll be damned," Elam interjected. "I'll be goddamned!"

"Another CAP has got a board of directors that's more like a chamber of commerce than advocates for the low-income. The community's poor folks are picketing its office - alleging racism. Sounds like that one's really screwed up. And there's another one that's just running canned programs, but not running them well."

Hammond interrupted. "The problem is that nobody's in charge of those critters."

Sergent looked at Hammond then quickly took the advantage. "Are you saying the goddamned power is too diffused, Senator?

Hammond took the sarcasm well. He smiled and nodded. "Yes, in this case there's a lack of structural accountability."

"No one's in control, huh?" Elam said to Hammond.

"It certainly appears not," Hammond agreed, more seriously.

"Can our reorganization bill address this problem?"

"In this specific case, I'm not sure. They're private corporations," Sergent reminded the governor. "But we could certainly impact their funding."

"Dammit, I want a handle on these CAPs," Elam said. "They're 501(C)3s, but they're doing governmental work, and the public thinks I'm responsible. And I'm taking the heat. I want this cleaned up." He continued looking directly at Sergent.

"I'll put Allen on it."

"I thought you already had," the governor pointedly said.

"You're right. I'll follow up more closely."

"Incidentally," Hammond asked, "where is your fair-haired boy?"

Elam looked to Sergent.

Sergent wasn't sure what to say. Should he mention Greg's erratic behavior, his lack of contribution to the reorganization plan? No, not with Hammond here. Besides, he was merely a liaison who facilitated communication between the governor and his department heads, whereas Greg reported directly to the governor and was closely connected to him. Sergent never had determined how. Surely it ran deeper than pounding yard signs in the ground. "He wasn't looking well yesterday," Bill said. "I'll bet he's come down with something."

Elam had been closely watching his administrative aide. A few moments passed. "Well, I don't want to spend any more time on these goddamned CAPs. You just handle them, Sergent."

Bill nodded.

"Now our real purpose today is to discuss the reorganization bill," Elam continued. "Senator, you want to recommend some changes. Let's hear them."

The senator now felt as if he was finally, and rightfully, the focal point of this meeting. He began, using the legislative voice, by looking only to Elam. Sergent was to be ignored. "Thank you, Governor. The overall plan for this so-called Integrated Human Services Department does possess some economies of scale. It would streamline control between service provision and funding sources, effectively merging four large and five smaller agencies into this new super-department. That would, of course, result in a reduction of administrative costs. Now the savings could either be plowed back into programs, increasing the level of service provision, or we could return the non-earmarked funds to the state's coffers."

Hammond was enjoying his governor's attention. "I would personally recommend the latter. You never know when bucks become important. You could develop a rainy-day fund or perhaps even recommend a tax cut." He paused, still not looking at Sergent or even acknowledging his presence, "You and your staff have done a damn good job. There's some innovative thinking in this plan. I'm impressed with the theory of it: a nice academic piece of work. And finding that obscure law, the Intergovernmental Cooperation Act, must have taken some long hours in the law library. All the things you suggest here can be done. I hate to admit it, Bob, but the concept is plausible."

Elam was puffing on his pipe, his head softly nodding.

"On paper, it looks good. Personally, I don't like it, but it's achievable." Although he was being ignored by Hammond, Sergent was pleased with what the senator was begrudgingly saying.

"Okay, Senator, if the theory looks good, what about its practicality?" Elam asked.

Sergent sat upright in his chair, roused from his short-lived smugness. Elam's question perplexed him. In his proposal, he had touched on damn near every contingency. Theory and practicality were not diverse poles, not in his plan! The polarities had been carefully tempered. The reverse-logic process had taken this whole matter from the hypothetical to the practical. He had plotted out each step. ∫-45 dealt with consolidation. ‖-115 established press liaison. Theory? What the hell was Elam talking about? He began to formulate a rebuttal, an incisive statement that would explain away this doubt the governor seemed to have. The Legislative Voice interrupted his thoughts.

"The plan doesn't address the human factor. It's the people who ultimately screw you every time. And it's not because they're evil or they want to or they've sold you out. Power goes to their heads. They gain a sense of unwarranted self-importance. They use their offices to get back at real or perceived enemies. They undermine their supervisors. They have kids who get arrested on drug charges, have unfaithful spouses, go through nasty divorces. They drink too much, have designs on every damn woman in their agency. They try to build their own political base at your expense. They become liabilities. Now I'm not saying this always happens. With the current structure, you're not dependent upon one person. Under this proposed plan, one man would have too much power. One person can hurt you badly. I suppose this whole structure is dependent upon the director of the Integrated Human Services Department?"

Sergent looked to Elam. The governor nodded.

"And is that individual Greg Allen?"

Elam again nodded.

The senator turned away from Elam, shaking his head. "As I just said, it's your own people who will do you in. This structure makes you vulnerable." Then, again facing the governor, Hammond continued. "As your friend, I have to say I don't like it. But you have my word. I'll push the sonofabitch through if you want it. But Bobby-boy, the key word in government is diffusion. So I'm gonna use my considerable skills to dissuade you."

Sergent looked surprised. He had never heard anyone call the governor Bobby-boy.

***

Greg Allen's absence that morning was based on events that had occurred the previous evening.

Amy had been waiting for him, sitting on the sofa in their living room, sipping coffee. She had sent the children to a friend, indicating that she might not pick them up until morning. Her friend, sensing problems, didn't ask why. Amy sat patiently.

Greg had gone to work at about ten, stayed late, then stopped for a few drinks. He saw Amy waiting for him as he entered the house. That was odd. She usually was cleaning after dinner. And the kids were gone. That was very odd. But then, with Amy's statement simply spoken, everything made sense.

"I went in for my Pap test last week. The doctor called me this morning, asked me to come in."

Greg knew this day would eventually arrive. He had always been quick on his feet, able to easily sidestep an issue, to defuse a situation with a clever line, a quick joke. And he had had several months to work out a solution to this situation. The whole thing had tormented him to the detriment of his job, his relationships with his friends, his sense of well-being. Greg feared how the governor would react to the messy divorce of one of his key aides.

Amy, therefore, had to be somehow effectively dealt with. But how? He had been unable to come up with a plan.

He had finally decided the problem would just have to work itself out, no matter how painful. There was no quick fix. The moment was here.

"Hope everything's okay down there, hon." Greg seldom used endearments. "As much as I love your mind, I admit a certain bias for your body." He walked to the kitchen to appear nonchalant. He was pouring himself a drink when he heard Amy speak. She didn't yell or even raise her voice. She spoke matter-of-factly.

"Things aren't okay, you son of a bitch."

Greg stepped back into the living room, his drink in his hand. "Is something wrong?" he asked with all the sympathy he could muster.

Amy had expected this sort of response. It didn't surprise her. "The doctor told me I have syphilis and gonorrhea. He needs to know who my contacts were."

Greg sat in the chair beside the sofa. His face became ashen. His hand trembled as he placed the drink on the coffee table. Then from somewhere within he summoned enough chutzpah to take the initiative, to respond aggressively. "I damn well think you'd better tell me too, Amy, just who the hell are these paramours of yours. Have you been cheating on me?"

"You rotten son of a bitch!" she replied. Her voice was still flat but very firm. He had expected her to scream, to throw things, to strike him. Instead, she sat quietly and simply called him a son of a bitch.

Goddamn it! Greg thought. This was the worst possible scenario.

Her lack of histrionics convinced him she had nothing to hide. His goddamn wife has been faithful to him. There was, he determined, no reason to continue to lie. But now what should he do? Tell Amy there were many, none of whom meant anything? Or should he tell her that there was just one for whom he felt true affection? Which scenario would she consider the lesser of the two evils? He didn't know. "I'm sorry, Amy," was all he could say.

"I've got VD, and you're sorry. Does that somehow make everything all right?"

Greg wanted to go to her, to embrace her, to comfort her. But he decided that would not be appropriate. He continued sitting. "I'm truly sorry."

" 'Sorry' doesn't fix it," she countered. "How many women in this damned town should I start avoiding? Which of our friends should I walk away from?"

"It's not like that," he said.

"Well, whatever it's like, I'm seeing an attorney tomorrow. I can't live with you any longer. The whole thing has just been a lie to you." Her voice began to crack, tears appearing in her eyes.

This show of emotion encouraged Greg. "Is there anything I can do - or say?" Greg felt he was gaining control of the situation.

"No. Nothing." She was weeping now.

"You know I love you. I love you very much."

"Me and who else? And how many others?"

"I got drunk one night. At a meeting. That one in San Antonio. Really drunk. Remember that business trip? Remember I asked if you could come with me?"

"No," Amy replied flatly. "You never asked me to go on any of your trips," she added after a few moments.

"Anyway, I was really drunk." Greg continued. "I don't remember anything about it, or her. I was with a bunch of guys from other states. Each of them had picked up a gal. I was drunk. We were at this bar. I needed to do what they were doing, to prove I could, I guess. I was really drunk. I'm so sorry, Ame." He had previously used that nickname while making love. He used it now for effect, knowing he would have to come up with another endearment in the future - if he could get out of this nasty mess.

"Just one time?"

"So help me god. I don't even remember it. I was really drunk. Not myself."

Amy sat silently, tears reappearing.

Greg was encouraged. He began to feel good. He had taken the best from both scenarios. Eclectic, he thought smugly. "I can't blame you if you see an attorney. But you have another choice. You could forgive me. Forgive me for this one terrible mistake. It hadn't happened before. It hasn't happened since. It won't happen again."

Greg had been eloquent. Amy was crying unabashedly.

"I do love you, Ame. So very much. I'm so sorry."

Minutes passed. Neither spoke. He had done good, damned good, he thought.

A half hour passed.

Greg intently watched Amy as she rose. Then he relaxed. She couldn't do anything tonight, he reasoned. She'd have to wait until morning. He sat back. I can still work something out, he told himself. Then he realized he truly loved his wife, and he began to feel real fear.

She walked to the telephone. She continued looking away from Greg as she dialed. "Alice? Would you drive the kids home?"

She turned toward Greg after hanging up, still not looking at him directly. "You will sleep on the couch," she announced, her voice without feeling. "And you'd better see our doctor tomorrow."

Greg slept soundly that night. He had saved his marriage. And he realized again how much he loved his wife. He resolved that his days of priapism were over. He slept until noon the next day. Amy had called her office, reporting in sick. Then she went about getting the kids off to school, working quietly in the home, and doing her wifely chores.

Three weeks later, when the public health official stopped by, Greg simply handed him a typewritten list of the contacts Greg could remember. The cities on the list looked like his travel itinerary for the past few months. No words passed between them, except the low-level bureaucrat complimented Greg on his spacious office.

And Greg kept his word to his wife. He remained faithful for well over four months.

CHAPTER TWENTY-SIX

As in all blocks of time, these months of Jeff's life produced a mixed lot. Most joyous was the birth of his son. Andrea had a difficult pregnancy, days filled with nausea and nagging pelvic pain. Now she held in her arms the tiny product of her nine months of pain and discomfort. And she was obsessed with this infant whom she would breastfeed at odd hours, would bathe and cuddle, would watch intently as he slept. Jeff, Laura, and Bobby were secondary. The infant named Jeffery Theodore seemed to be Andrea's only love. Andrea would surrender the baby when she needed to rest or bathe but then would quickly reclaim him. She affectionately called him Ned and would hold him close to her breast. "Isn't he just beautiful?" she would ask everyone.

Joyce flew up to help with the chores in the modest house in Flatwater where Jeff had moved the family well before the baby was born. One evening, as the quiet and melodious music flowed and Jeff was drying dishes, Joyce looked to her daughter nursing little Ned. "That little guy has certainly stolen her heart."

Jeff looked to his wife and first-born. "What more can a man ask for than a wife who loves his kids?"

"You got it all then," Joyce said, looking out the window. The dehydrating plant down the street was drying the year's final harvest of alfalfa. The nauseously sweet smell overpowered even the richly spiced foods Joyce prepared nightly. A truck had just unloaded its cargo at the plant and passed loudly by their home. The dust from the previous truck had not yet settled.

Joyce stayed for two weeks. As Jeff drove her to the airport in Jackson City, she quietly but firmly said, "I don't think Andrea likes the town you've chosen to live in."

"San Francisco it ain't," Jeff replied.

"Even Fayetteville it ain't," she added.

Jeff had been stationed at Fort Bragg, North Carolina, while going through jump school. After he earned his paratrooper's wings, he had several weeks before being reassigned. At night he would go into

Fayetteville. He remembered the town's center had an open-air structure where, it was said, slaves had been sold.

And there were the pawnshops, the bars, the bordellos. ("Take your goddamned platoon to a whorehouse," his friend told him. "Now that they got their wings, make paratroopers out of them.") All the parasitic merchants who preyed on the military seemingly were well represented in Fayetteville. It was, he remembered, a lousy town.

"Come on now. It ain't that bad," Jeff responded to Joyce. "Is it?"

She smiled. "Just don't get too settled into your job. Keep your eyes open for something else."

"I know what you're saying. As soon as we get some bills paid, we'll go somewhere else, or at least find a better home."

"That's good, Jeff."

After her departure, Jeff realized how much Joyce had helped. But as soon as everyone adjusted to the routine without Andrea's mother, things took on a new normality. That didn't affect little Ned; he continued to monopolize Andrea.

At the agency, things were taking on a sense of order. Compared to the county board meetings, the CAP meetings were enjoyable events. Jeff was putting distance between himself and Harney County. Then one day Andrea handed him an envelope postmarked Union. Inside were two clippings from the Union newspaper. No message, not even a name. Jeff read one of them aloud:

OLDFIELD PROJECTS COUNTY TAX REDUCTION

County Commission Chairman Hank Oldfield today projected a seven percent reduction in next year's county taxes. The mill levy had been rising each of the last four years. It stabilized this fiscal year at 15.1 mills.

Oldfield was elevated to board chairman, replacing Commissioner Brian Scott who died last year. Scott had served as chairman for four years prior to his death.

"This reduction will get county government in line with the spirit and intent of LB192," Oldfield said. LB192 was passed by the legislature a year ago and vetoed by then Governor Norman. The bill later became law upon the legislature's override.

Oldfield cited economies he brought to county government since ascending to the chairmanship as cause for the projected tax decrease.

Oldfield specifically mentioned the new direction of county welfare. "We tightened up a lot in that office," he said.

He also gave credit to the sheriff's department for curtailing overtime costs. Further, he stated, "the clerk of the district court reduced her budgetary needs substantially." He attributed this to his closely monitoring the county's mental health costs.

"It really pays to approach government as a business," he said. "I'm running county government the way I'm running my ranch. Damn frugally," he said, as an afterthought.

Jeff barely looked at the article announcing Lisa Oldfield's wedding plans. He crumpled the clippings and threw them into the wastepaper basket. "That bastard!" he said.

***

An attrition began after Jeff began asserting himself as the agency's director. Some people didn't return to work after being reprimanded. Others quit after their pay was docked for days they hadn't come to work. One employee handed the board chairman his resignation during the board meeting. The Jesuit read it aloud to the full board. The staffer complained of Jeff's racism, the chaos he brought to the agency, his dictatorial manner. The board held firm, not even questioning Jeff. And the agency's production increased while staffing levels were reduced.

Soon Jeff had sufficient funds to hire a deputy. He wrote to Jerry Milner, offering him the job. Milner thanked Jeff but said no. Jeff called Goldman. After a few minutes, Dave admitted he wasn't ready to go to law school. He said he'd take the job; that he and Mary and George and their kids would arrive next Monday, ready for work.

"I suppose I'd better find a slot for George, huh?"

"Yep," Dave laughed.

Jeff hesitated for a moment. "Okay, tell him he's my new outreach director. He'll have twenty or so staff reporting to him."

"I'm not sure he's ready for that," Dave cautioned.

"The guy who had the job wasn't all that sharp, and he quit a couple days ago. I think George can handle it."

"I don't know ..."

"I'll ask my secretary to help him with the paperwork. He'll do fine."

"If you think so," Dave said slowly.

"I'll have to hire you guys as acting. After you're in for a few months, I'll hire you officially."

"You know what you're doing," Dave said.

"See you Monday."

Driving home, he was eager to tell Andrea that Dave and George would be moving here. She'd like that, especially because of Dave with his eastern accent. Dave reminded Andrea of her scattered family members living on the East Coast. She once asked Dave how he could afford a Pentax camera on his VISTA stipend. Affecting a New York accent, he told her it fell off the truck. She told him stories of her Uncle Louie in Hoboken. Dave once mentioned going to the Preakness in Meerland. Andrea had no idea what the Preakness was but knew exactly where Meerland was. To Andrea, Dave seemed like a kid brother from home while they were displaced on the great American desert.

But Andrea had been acting strangely lately. The move from Union had been hard on her, being six months pregnant. And though the CAP had paid the moving expenses, Andrea had to handle most of the details.

But when Joyce arrived, Andrea became happy again. She and her mother grew closer than they had ever been before. They talked endlessly about her father, about friends who had retired with Ned, the parties at the Officers Club, how Ned missed the kids, how much they had grown. Jeff's only opportunity to speak with Joyce was while Andrea napped. He learned not to try while she was awake.

Her depression set in following Joyce's departure. Andrea withdrew into herself and little Ned. But Jeff hoped that with Dave coming, Andrea's spirits would improve.

Arriving home, he noticed the familiar aroma of Andrea's cooking. Relieved he didn't have to fix dinner, he walked to her, kissing the back of her neck. For a moment he thought she resented that, her body stiffening, but she turned and smiled. "I guess it's time I get back to work."

"Ain't no question the kids prefer your cooking to mine," he said, "and that I love you."

During dinner he told her about Dave and George moving to Flatwater. She tried to sound pleased but really wasn't interested. He was disappointed that evening when she again got ready to sleep in little Ned's room. Seeing his expression, she explained, "I want to be near him in case he needs me."

Andrea had wine and cheese for George and Dave the evening they arrived. George explained he was keeping his family in Union until his first payday. As Jeff poured the wine, he saw it was a burgundy. From that clue, he assumed their indebtedness was lessening. Before, they only offered table wine. Jeff took delight in seeing his old comrades. He inquired about the whereabouts of Millard and Jefferson. Dave said they were having a rough time. Both were looking for work. And that Millard felt bad about his friend in the fiscal office being fired.

"It's a shame I haven't the bucks to hire them, and her," Jeff lamented.

"No problem," Dave replied. "George and I'll write a proposal for that, a Hire-the-War-on-Poverty-Vet Program." Then, more seriously, he cautioned Jeff: "You'd better hire some locals next time."

They chatted about Harney County. Dave mentioned that several letters to the editor had been published after Jeff had left. Each mentioned the fortunate departure of "socialistic elements."

"I hear Lisa's getting married," Jeff said. "Has she been on ADC all this time?"

"No idea," Dave said. "Milner might know."

"I heard from him last week," Jeff said. "He's teaching again. Really likes it."

Andrea had been in and out of the living room, never staying for more than for a few minutes. Dave noticed her apparent preoccupation. He and George left about eight thirty, returning to the hotel.

The next day Jeff asked Gwen to have Dave come to his office. Replacing the phone, Gwen realized she resented Dave and George. They were outsiders brought in from the western part of the state. God knows there are enough people around here who need jobs. And why was Jeff getting rid of so many of the staff? Surely he was forcing them to leave. And Dave, barely out of school, had such a youthful face. Just a kid with that damned eastern accent. And he was the deputy director, he with his jeans and T-shirt. And George! Hell, he isn't even of the same tribe as her husband and the other Indians around here. A dog-eating Sioux. I'll bet he doesn't even have a high school diploma, and he'll be making more than me! She went to Dave, tersely telling him to report to the director's office.

"Yeah, Dave, sit down," Jeff said. "I want to talk to you before I call George in. I want to do everything we can to make sure he gets started on the right foot; that there's no resentment toward him that would make his job even tougher. I want him to look like he knows what the hell's going on."

"Well, remember he was a damn good outreach worker in Union." Dave grinned. "And don't dismiss the good work he did in the barns."

"What can we do to make him a star?"

"Knowledge is power," Dave trifled.

"We ain't got time to train him. His staff comes in on Monday."

"Well then, let's make him an expert."

"Expert in what?"

"Entitlement programs."

"Specifically?" Jeff asked.

"Let's list damn near every program there is, then share it with him."

"Good thinking."

"Then we'll come up with a family with as many problems as possible," Dave continued. "Then we'll match the problems with the programs. He'll look like a goddamned genius."

"Sounds good."

Vinton spoke seriously when George joined them. "Listen good. We're gonna go through an exercise."

"Okay," Dave led off. "A woman with three kids."

"How old are the kids?" Jeff inquired.

"Two, seven, and ten, and one's retarded."

"Husband?" Jeff inquired.

"Two of them. She divorced one. The other's a runaway pappy."

"Was one of them a veteran?"

"Sure thing. Decorated," Dave affirmed.

"Good. Does she drink?"

"An alcoholic," George joined in.

"Does she work?"

"She did, but she got hurt on the job. Lost two fingers in an industrial accident," Dave continued.

"Tough. Where do she and the kids live?" George joined in again.

"Ah ... with her parents," Jeff ventured.

"Well, how old are they?" Dave asked Jeff.

"Oh, they're ... let's see, sixty-two and sixty-five."

"Does she have a kid with a cleft palate?" George asked.

"Of course," Dave said. "What else?"

"We'll keep building as we go along," Jeff said.

On a large flip chart, Jeff wrote at the top of the sheet: RECOMMENDED PROGRAMS.

They began the list.

"Well, obviously food stamps," Dave started.

"And the old folks can go to an elderly nutrition site," George offered.

Jeff began writing: FOOD STAMPS.

ELDERLY NUTRITION.

"WIC," Dave said.

"What's WIC?" George asked.

"Women, Infants, Children supplemental nutrition program," Dave answered.

WIC, Jeff wrote on the flip chart.

The list kept growing: AFDC – AABD.

WORKMAN'S COMPENSATION.

"Right! Big bucks there, plus job retraining," Dave said.

VOCATIONAL REHAB.

VETERAN'S BENEFITS (FOR THE CHILDREN).

SCHOOL LUNCHES (FREE).

SUMMER NUTRITION.

"They can get free lunches when school's out," Jeff contributed.

HEAD START.

"Of course."

SSI.

CHORE SERVICES.

DAY CARE.

"Is she sexually active?" Jeff wondered.

"Don't ask me," George answered.

"Like a minx," Dave affirmed.

FAMILY PLANNING.

UNEMPLOYMENT INSURANCE.

CETA.

TITLE XX, SSA.

URECSA.

"What's that," Dave asked.

"The Uniform Reciprocal Enforcement of Child Support Act. It runs down runaway pappies," Jeff said.

"Good. What else?"

STATE HUMAN RIGHTS COMMISSION.

CRIPPLED CHILDREN'S SERVICES.

"Yeah," George smiled.

DEVELOPMENTAL DISABILITY SERVICES.

STATUS OF WOMEN COMMISSION.

SOCIAL SECURITY.

GENERAL ASSISTANCE.

LOW-COST HOUSING.

LEGAL AIDE ASSISTANCE.

ALCOHOLIC TREATMENT PROGRAMS.

DRUG TREATMENT PROGRAMS.

A few minutes of silence followed.

"SURPLUS COMMODITY PROGRAM," George ventured. "And let's not forget community action and AAAs."

COMMUNITY ACTION

AREA AGENCIES ON AGING

Thinking of Rediger and his deputy, Dave smiled. "And don't forget ECONOMIC DEVELOPMENT PROGRAMS."

Jeff rolled his eyes. And another. WEATHERIZATION SERVICES. "To insulate the low incomes' homes," Jeff volunteered. Then he said, "And of course LIEAP."

"What's that," George asked.

"Low Income Energy Assistance Program, to help pay utility bills." Jeff added LIEAP to the list.

"Good start." Jeff looked at George. "Familiarize yourself with these programs. Their eligibility criteria, extent of benefits, local offices administering them. You've got the rest of the week. Then on Monday you dazzle your staff. It would probably be well to develop training for your staff the same way we did it here. Suggest a family with a lot of problems and ask your staff what they would do. That way you'll get to know how much they know and impress them with how much you know. And, George, learn the legislative authority for two or three of the programs. So you can say 'the so and so program authorized by the Economic Opportunity Act of 1964, as amended, will do so and so', or 'Title IV of the Social Security Act provides this and that'." He smiled to George. "It'll make you look a bit erudite."

"A bit what?" George asked

"Like you gots lots of smarts," Dave defined.

"Okay," Jeff said with a tone of dismissal. "I'll leave the flip chart here. As we think of more programs, we can add them."

"Not a shabby start," George said, writing down the programs on a yellow pad.

Jeff also copied the list and put it in his briefcase. The rest of the week he kept it on his nightstand, adding programs as he thought of them at night.

The following Monday George Iron Rope dazzled his staff with his knowledge of federal domestic assistance programs and erased any doubts about his leadership abilities. By the time the meeting ended, his staff regarded him as a walking encyclopedia on ways to help the poor.

Gwen rushed into Jeff's office four days later. "Some guy named Ned is on the line. He says it's important."

Jeff picked up the phone as Gwen departed and gently closed the door. "Is that you, Ned?"

"Jeff, Joyce died last night."

Jeff was speechless.

"She died peacefully in her sleep. The doctor says her heart just gave out."

"Damn. Have you told Andrea yet? And Ned, I'm so sorry - so very sorry."

"You better break the news to Andrea. She's gonna take it real hard."

"How are you, Ned?"

"I'm okay. Probably still in shock. But I got a lot to do. The arrangements, notifying relatives, change my will ..." His voice trailed off into tears.

Jeff sensed his duress. "I'm so sorry, Ned. Christ, she was just up here. I'm glad she got to see Andrea and the kids and little Ned. God, how God-awful unfair!"

"I don't know the best way to tell Andrea. Even though they fought all the time, they were close."

"I'll handle that, Ned," Jeff assured him. "You look after yourself. When's the service?"

"Not sure yet. Probably the ninth. I'll call Andrea this evening after you've had a chance to tell her, after she's settled down."

"That'll be good. I'll ensure she gets down there. I won't be able to make it, Ned." His work schedule wouldn't allow it, and he'd have to look after the kids. He wondered if they could afford Andrea's airfare. "After I tell Andrea, she'll call you about her travel plans. Ned, look after yourself. I'm so sorry."

Jeff explained to Gwen what had happened. He told her he'd have to take some vacation time, that she could call him at home if anything came up. He left the office to be with his wife, to share her grief.

Driving home, he tried to think how to tell Andrea. He couldn't believe it himself. Joyce had looked so good when she had been with them. Tears fell from Jeff's eyes. Joyce had been his friend during the long courtship. Ned had been aloof. Joyce. Dead. Damn.

His eyes were wet with tears when he got home. Andrea asked what was wrong.

He told her as gently as he could.

CHAPTER TWENTY-SEVEN

Bob Elam heartily shook Sergent's hand. "Bill, it's good to see you."

"Thanks, Governor. How was your meeting in Newport Beach?"

"Great, Bill, really great."

"I'll bet Mrs. Elam enjoyed Orange County and its salt air."

"She sure did, and so did I. Come on in, I'll get some coffee." Bill walked to a chair, his curiosity aroused. This wasn't Governor Bob Elam. This was Politician Bob Elam. What's up? he wondered.

After he had had taken a sip of coffee and lit his pipe, Elam smiled broadly. "Well, what did you and the lieutenant governor do with my state in my absence?"

"We annexed Texas," Sergent deadpanned.

"Damn," Elam said. "Now I'll need to learn Spanish just to get reelected."

"No, I'm sorry," Sergent stated, "just east Texas."

"Good thinking on you and the lieutenant governor's part. I can handle those goddamned east Texans. Seriously, how's things?"

"Not much happened in your absence. People kept buying liquor and cigarettes. The state of the state's treasury is sound."

"Bless them all," Bob said. Then with a more serious expression he asked, "How's the reorganization going?"

"On schedule. The legislature begins its new term in a couple of months. Hammond will introduce the senate bill, and our friend, what's his name, will introduce the house bill."

"Good. Let's talk about that."

"Sure."

"Remember our meeting with Hammond? The one several weeks ago?"

"I sure do."

"You know, the guy's been around a long time. I think he raised some legitimate issues. What'd you think about his qualms?"

"Nothing we can't handle."

"I suppose not. How's Allen doing?"

Moment of truth, Sergent thought. Now just how the hell do I respond to that? "Okay," he finally said.

Bob leaned back in his chair, slowly sucking on his pipe. "Ah, let me ask that again. How's Allen doing?"

Absolute moment of truth, Bill thought. He sipped his coffee. "In all candor, Governor, I can't figure Allen out."

"How so?"

"He's sometimes erratic, terribly erratic."

"Oh?"

"Yeah. He's been better lately, but he runs hot and cold."

"Why haven't you told me?"

Sergent thought on that one for a moment. Finally he said, "Many reasons, and no reasons. A big gray area. I personally like him, but I can't always rely on him. He seems preoccupied much of the time."

"With what?"

"Hell, I don't know."

"I pay you to know." Elam was becoming angry.

"You know, Governor, we never did work out the organizational chart because I supposed we were gonna change it with this bill. Hell, right now I haven't anyone under me. I have difficulty getting a memo typed. Does Greg report to me, or to you, or to both of us? And do you have a special interest in him?"

"You're my goddamned administrative assistant. Of course he reports to you."

"Oh."

"My only interest in Greg Allen is that he capably serves this administration."

"Oh."

"Do you think he can handle the job? Organizing a new unit of government, managing hundreds of millions of dollars?"

Sergent hadn't fully comprehended that the super-department he conceptualized would be funded with that much money. But of course it would. "He does report to me then?" he responded without answering the governor's question.

"Pretty much," Bob replied.

"Just what does that mean?"

"It means you can't fire him. I don't want to be dismissing any of my cabinet during our first year. Politically, I don't think that would play well."

"Peoria's way back east, in Illinois," Bill said. Then he asked, seriously, "Will you back me up on orders I give to Greg?"

"Sure."

"Okay, that better defines my parameters."

A minute or so passed. Elam ended the silence. "Do you think you could get a resignation from him?"

Sergent was stunned. The governor was moving too quickly, changing basic allegiances almost on a whim. Then Bill remembered Chandler's words. "Nothing is more ephemeral than appointive power." This could just as easily be me we're talking about, he reflected. And just what the hell did the governor mean by "get a resignation?" He was getting confused. "I doubt it," Bill replied. "He would raise hell, lots of it. He's got a drinking buddy who's a reporter with the paper."

Bob looked annoyed, thinking of Allen as a potential liability. "I don't want any bad press. So drop the other things you're doing, Bill, and concentrate on Greg Allen."

"You've given me a tough assignment, you know."

"I know. But I know you can handle it, Bill."

Back in his office, Sergent called his old mentor. An appointment was set for five at the Enterprize. Bill got there around four fifteen and sat drinking, waiting for Herb, putting his drinks on his former boss's tab.

Chandler's greeting was hearty, sincere, almost paternal when he joined Sergent. After ordering a drink, he asked how things were going.

"Okay," Bill responded, knowing Herb would sense his anxiety. "The state of the state is sound. At least that's what we'll tell the joint session of the legislature. And how's your business?"

"Same old prosaic stuff. None of the excitement abounding in the governor's suite. But, we're doing some PR work, a little sampling of opinion for AP. Oh, and shepherding a client onto the supreme court."

Bill remembered that he once had such an assignment while working for Chandler. Only that was for the Third Judicial District.

"Ticklish stuff," he recalled. "How's it going?"

"Already I call him Mr. Justice Ferguson."

"Funny, that name hasn't come across my desk. As a matter of fact, there are no openings on that bench," Bill said, surprised.

Chandler raised his eyebrows. They were dancing, his eyes twinkling, his mouth quietly smiling. He didn't have to say anything. Sergent realized a justice was about to retire. Herb had learned of the upcoming retirement, but the justice hadn't told the governor.

"This is all off the record of course," Chandler said.

"Only if the rest of our conversation is too."

"Sure," Chandler sat back in his chair.

"It'll take a while."

"Good. I've got nothing else planned."

"Okay, here we go." Sergent explained his predicament in great detail. He went over the reorganization plan, again thanking Herb for the reverse-logic system. He discussed Hammond's initial dislike, even anger, for his plan and then how, at the last meeting, the senator quietly accepted it. He commented on the oddly shifting relationship between the governor and Hammond. Sergent also spoke of Allen, his conduct, his erratic personality, his irregular work. He mentioned that morning's conversation with the governor. When he was finished Sergent simply sat there, patiently waiting for several minutes for Chandler to respond.

Chandler spoke slowly. "It's no surprise about Allen. He's been an embarrassment from day one. You know, the bar association was astounded at his appointment. He was worthless as a lawyer, and he's bad news as an appointee. The governor should never have hired him and ought to get rid of him. If you want to know about your antipoverty czar, go to the Plainsmen Hotel bar, ask the bartender, or wait until Greg comes in. That man has badly served his governor."

"Why the hell haven't you told me?" Sergent asked.

"It's not my style to get into that sort of stuff. Besides, you never asked me. But take my word for it. Allen's bad news. But you realize Allen's not your real problem. Just fire him. Or if that's not politically palatable, move him where he can't hurt you. No, he's not your problem. But Senator Jake Hammond, now there's one interesting sonofabitch."

Sergent chuckled. "Well said."

"From what you've told me, you've got a problem with the senator."

"No, I don't think so. I told you he promised Elam that he would introduce the bill, and he repeated that at our last meeting."

"No meetings since?"

"No, none that I know of."

"Hmm. How are you and the governor getting along?"

"Okay, I guess."

"You must assume there's been other meetings. You just weren't invited."

Bill felt his face redden. He wasn't sure if it was from anger or embarrassment.

Herb noted Bill's discomfort. "Don't feel bad. There's always intrigue in the palace." After a pause, he set aside other considerations and focused on Hammond. "You know, governmental consolidation isn't Hammond's cup of tea. In fact, he's vehemently against that sort of thing." Then another delay, this one longer. Sergent stared at his drink as Chandler thought this matter through then looked up when Chandler spoke again. "Bill, what's happened is simply that your reorganization plan is only that, a plan. Hammond has zapped it."

"You mean in the senate?"

"No. In the governor's suite."

Bill again felt his face redden - this time from anger. "No," he protested, "the governor isn't deceitful. And that's what you're suggesting. Dammit, he would have told me."

"Deceitful to whom?" Chandler observed. "But you're right. Elam's an okay sort of guy. But don't you realize that he's already begun to tell you? And he'll continue telling you. And before the legislature convenes he'll finish telling you. But he'll do it so you won't be hurt. He'll probably even talk you into recommending the plan be scuttled."

Sergent's sense of betrayal overcame him. He was speechless. He sat back in his chair as a defeated man. Totally absorbed, he didn't notice Senator Sloane approach them.

"Bill, you've met Senator Sloane haven't you?" Chandler asked.

Sergent snapped out of it. "Of course. How are you, Senator?"

"Fine. And yourself, Mr. Sergent?"

"Okay, I guess," Bill responded.

"That's good," Sloane said. "I just came by to say hello. I ..."

"Why the hell are you still in town?" Herb asked with a laugh. "All your colleagues are back home. Didn't they tell you they adjourned a couple of weeks ago?"

Herb's attempt at humor fell flat. In fact, it was damned unfortunate.

"I've been in to see my doctor," Sloane explained. He looked concerned. "Besides, part of my district extends into the capital city. A lot of folks forget that. They think I'm just a country bumpkin. I only live twenty miles outside of town."

"Of course," Chandler replied in a more concerned tone. "About the doctor. Nothing serious, I trust."

"Nah. Just a little problem I got. But I better be going."

"Let us walk you to your car," Herb offered. "We're heading out of here, too."

***

It was a more cynical Bill Sergent who reported to work the following morning. He leisurely reviewed the reorganization plan. Today he saw it differently, abstractly. It was an academic thing, an intellectual exercise, something that could have become landmark legislation – except for the human element; except for Jake Hammond. Perhaps years from now political scientists would discover this revolutionary concept of providing services to the people. Surely it would be placed somewhere in the state's archives. It would endure. Perhaps it would even become law in some form or other. But, for now, it was an illusory thing. And that was a damn shame.

Sergent responded slowly when the governor summoned him. Unlike before, he lit a cigarette and finished his coffee. Only then did he walk into the governor's office. "Yes, sir?"

"Bill, I'm really concerned about what you said about Allen yesterday. Have you given it any more thought?"

"Yes, Governor, I have."

"And?"

"I think we can deal with the personalities. I believe we should go ahead."

"Maybe. But perhaps more gradually, huh? Maybe sort of evolve into it?"

"No," Sergent stated. "I think we should move decisively. Would you have a problem with that?"

"No."

"Good."

"But who's to head it up?" Elam asked.

"That's a personnel matter."

"But a critical one, nonetheless."

"Right," Sergent admitted. "I just don't know, Governor. You've got a guy who expertly jockeyed himself into the position of heir apparent." Sergent thought for a moment. "You know, you could appoint a really sharp deputy director and order Greg to let him run the new department. Let Greg just do the PR stuff. He'd probably prefer it that way."

"I suppose you're right," Elam acknowledged. "Are you still working on that riparian rights bill?"

"Yeah. I sent it over to the AG's office with a couple of questions. Mr. Attorney Madersen should get back to me soon," Sergent explained, noting how quickly the governor had apparently dismissed the reorganization proposal.

"Good," Bob said. "Well, you'd better excuse me. I'm gonna meet with the state's 4-H leadership."

"Pretty heavy stuff," Sergent smiled.

"Gosh darn heavy stuff," the governor affirmed.

CHAPTER TWENTY-EIGHT

After Jeff had left for work and the two older children had gone to school, there was just Andrea and little Ned. Andrea checked his diaper. She changed it even though it was barely damp. She looked into her infant son's eyes after she buttoned up his blue outfit and before laying him on his back in his crib for his morning nap. Her pain was back, along with a sense of guilt. Was she really sick, or was it all in her head? She summarily rejected that idea again, but she could not shake the hopeless feeling that was also caused by the pain.

She took her coffee cup into the kitchen and stared out the window for several minutes, observing nothing. Then her eyes began to focus: on the house across the street, the dehydrating plant up the street, the silhouetted trees, the utility poles and their web of wires. And she saw the gray cloudbank descending from the southwest.

Sipping coffee, she observed the progress of the storm front, the effects of the wind. Leaves that had lain dormant on the lawns and in the gutters were now being vigorously blown about. She felt a draft in the house. She should place a blanket over little Ned. But she was mesmerized by the flurry of activity around her - the leaves and other debris being forced northward by the strong wind. One moment everything was orderly and still, complacent with its lot in life, its station. The next moment was filled with erratic, unthinking movement. But movement nonetheless.

A large trashcan hurtled down the street, spilling its contents as it bumped along, adding to the confused and disorderly activity. Newspapers, empty cans and bottles, paid and unpaid bills, abandoned toys, all items discarded from a home were relentlessly being driven down the street, out of the community, perhaps out of the county.

It is, she surmised, the natural order of things. The thought comforted her. But soon, she realized, the wind would change and all these items would travel in the opposite direction to where they had been before, to that place they had fled. She thought of how senseless it all was, and her depression deepened.

When would she ever be at peace with herself? When had she last experienced sustained happiness? When she was first married? She had married twice. Which marriage had produced any happiness? Both? Neither? When she was with her parents between marriages? No. Certainly not then. Not when she had to live with her children in someone else's home.

But the pool was there. And the neighbors: friendly, always in and out of her parents' home. But here in Flatwater these folks were a queer lot. Once she got into an argument with the grocer. What was it over? She tried to remember. It was over produce. Was it the quality or the selection? Maybe the price. She couldn't remember. She did remember yelling, the other customers staring at her. They were mostly old, big boned with weather-beaten skin. Farm wives. A hardy breed, but completely uninteresting, certainly not physically attractive. A queer lot.

She suddenly realized that the argument was the only sustained dialogue she had had with anyone in the community since moving here.

She again looked to the sky. The grayness was all that was left of the brief storm. The wind had subsided. The leaves were still. New debris replaced the old. But it looked the same. Everything was unchanged. No real movement had occurred. The sustained presence, the static ever-present prevailed.

Little Ned's cry snapped Andrea from her thoughts. She realized how chilled the house had become. And it was time for the little man to be fed. She turned up the thermostat as she walked to his bedroom. She took him from his crib and checked his diaper. It was still dry. Holding him closely, she walked to the rocking chair in the living room. She unbuttoned her blouse and held him to her breast.

A serenity engulfed them both. While he was being nourished by her milk, she was being nourished by his dependency.

Andrea worked about the house, attentive to little Ned's faintest cry. Her pelvic discomfort kept recurring, and when the pain came again she stoically ignored it, pretending it did not exist.

Her thoughts drifted to when Joyce had been with them. She had been so busy during those days, and the time that her mother had been here seemed so brief. She would rise and attend to little Ned, then prepare breakfast. She made breakfast every morning. Eggs, sausage or bacon, pancakes or French toast, always a big breakfast. Then, after breakfast and after getting Jeff and the kids off, she and Joyce would make another pot of coffee. And they would talk. Nothing serious, nothing heavy, just comfortable talk. The antagonisms she had routinely experienced in Joyce's home never surfaced. She had known it would be that way. Andrea wouldn't allow those petty arguments to occur in her home. Instead, they talked, they laughed, they joked. But they talked less when Jeff was home. The spontaneity wasn't there. Did Jeff inhibit her? Goodness no! No one could inhibit her. But the spontaneity wasn't there. Why not, Andrea mused. Why not?

Joyce. Dead. How unfair. No tears came. Only pain.

The kids came home. Soon they were arguing over TV programs.

Andrea yelled at them. That subdued them for a few minutes. That gave her time to attend to the ribs. She spooned barbeque sauce over them and then placed them back in the oven. The oven heat caused steam to gather on the window. The aroma filled the kitchen, then the entire house. Jeff would be home soon. The smells and warmth of their home pleasantly awaited him.

Andrea yelled at the kids again. Why did they fight so much? Then little Ned awoke. Andrea asked Laura to entertain him for a few minutes. Laura defiantly told her she would not; that she hated her little brother. Andrea spanked her. While Laura was crying, Bobby took little Ned from his crib and played with him.

Andrea prepared the table as Bobby shouted, "He's wet, Mom."

***

Little Ned's faint cries awoke Andrea. She rose and put on her slippers and robe. She looked at Jeff who was snoring lightly. It must be only a maternal quality, hearing those cries in the night. While envying Jeff's undisturbed sleep, she shuffled to little Ned's room. Still half asleep, she attended to his diaper, then flicked up the thermostat on the way to the rocking chair.

A half hour later he was no longer tugging at her breast. She looked at his small face. He is truly beautiful, she thought, rising, taking him to his room. She kissed him lightly on his forehead, laid him in his crib, and covered him. Then, tired beyond belief, she climbed back into bed.

The house was quiet when she awoke again. She reached for Jeff and realized he was gone. She looked at the clock. It was after nine. Jeff and the kids had left, and she had slept through the noise and confusion of their departure.

She went to the bathroom, then to the baby's room to check on him. He was sleeping soundly. She went back to bed and stretched out within the warm sheets. Another day. There was little light coming through the curtains. It must be another cloudy, cold day, probably windy too. Winter days up here were all the same; gray, cold, lifeless. She remembered when she would pack up the car and take the kids to the beach. She would do that in November. Now she just wanted to stay within the warmth of the bed. To go nowhere, just to languish, to wait for spring.

I've got to snap out of this, she thought. Maybe see a doctor. No, that hasn't done any good. And, Christ, the bills still haven't been paid for my illnesses in Union. Besides, the doctor would just do another D&C. And the pain would come back. "No fever, healthy tissue, good blood count," he would say. She was sick of hearing how goddamned healthy she was. If her tissue was so goddamned good, why did she hurt so badly, and why the depression?

She remembered that the doctor in Union and the one in the capital city had suggested she see a psychiatrist. She had cursed them both and forbidden them to tell that to Jeff. But maybe they were right. Maybe she should see a shrink. She'd do anything to end this depression. And now they had health insurance.

But she reconsidered. I'm not crazy; just depressed. Postpartum blues. Still, she had entertained the idea: psychiatric therapy.

She did it a week later. She called a doctor and made an appointment. She would need the car next Tuesday. She would tell Jeff she was going shopping. The neighbor would babysit the kids. She would drop Jeff off at work, see the doctor, actually do some shopping, then maybe she and Jeff could have a quiet dinner somewhere. She felt better.

***

The reception area was typically sterile, but when Andrea entered the doctor's office, she noted the subdued décor of autumn colors:

browns, orange, dark reds. "Good morning, Doctor, I'm Andrea Vinton."

Dr. Lowenthal rose from behind his desk. He motioned her to a large overstuffed chair as he sat on the davenport. "How are you, Ms. Vinton?"

Andrea smiled softly. "I'm here."

"That's probably good. Why are you here?" His voice was gentle.

"Depression."

"I see."

Silence.

"Sometimes being depressed is a natural response to life," Lowenthal said.

Silence.

"How long have you experienced this depression?"

"Quite awhile."

"How long is that?"

"I don't know."

"A week? Three weeks?"

"Longer."

"I see. Tell me about yourself."

"I have three children. I'm a housewife."

"Sounds wholesome."

She nodded.

"How can I help you?"

"What do you mean?" Andrea asked.

"I don't know."

Silence.

Continued silence.

Overwhelming silence.

"Let's try to determine the cause of your depression," the doctor suggested.

"Good."

"You haven't told me if you're married."

"Oh, yes."

"Does your husband love you?"

"I suppose."

"You don't know?"

"I know. He does."

"That's good. That's important."

Silence.

"How about if I prescribe a happy pill?"

"Will it work?

"It doesn't exist."

"I see."

He shifted his weight in his chair.

So did Andrea.

Silence.

"What's your diagnosis?" he asked.

"I'm not qualified to make one."

"You're better qualified than I am."

"Because I'm me, huh?"

"Right."

"I've never been happy."

"Never?"

"Never," she affirmed.

"What is happiness to you?"

"I have no idea. I've never experienced it."

"Sad. But not terminal."

"Good."

"Tell me about yourself."

"I thought I had."

"You haven't begun."

Forty-three minutes later he asked, "When may I see you again?"

"Tomorrow."

"So soon?"

"Yes."

"Amazingly, I do have a cancellation, at two thirty."

"That's good. Thanks," Andrea said, somewhat relieved.

"Good. See you then."

When she said she needed the car again, she asked Jeff not to ask why. She was surprised at how readily he agreed. Initially, she was offended by his lack of interest. Then she perceived it as evidence of their trusting relationship. She later realized it was neither. He was preoccupied with his work. After she cleared the dinner dishes, she went to him, rubbing his shoulders, asking what he was doing.

He looked up from the paperwork he had brought from work. He began to answer but then said it was too complex to explain.

He didn't notice that she had stopped rubbing his shoulders. He didn't realize she had been hurt, had been insulted by what he had said.

"It's good to see you, Andrea," Dr. Lowenthal greeted her the next afternoon. "How'd things go after you left here yesterday?"

"About the same."

"No worse, huh?" he said, chiding her a bit.

"About the same."

"Good. You know, I've been thinking about your frequent illnesses, your hospitalizations."

"Oh?"

"Yes. I think it's all related."

"To what?"

"To your depression."

"How?"

"Chemistry."

"Chemistry," she repeated flatly.

"Yes. You might be suffering from a chemical imbalance."

"Can you prescribe something?"

"No. It's not that easy. It also involves electrical impulses, the circuitry within your body. We don't know much about those things yet," Lowenthal admitted.

"So where are we?"

"Let's talk some more."

"Here I thought we were close to solving the problem. Now you tell me again there are no happy pills."

"But you see, the pain you experience is real," Lowenthal explained. "It's the signals being transmitted to your brain that are false. It's like a person whose leg has been amputated. There can't be any pain in that leg because there's no leg. But the person feels pain, and the pain is real. What we're going to do is work on the false signals, the phantom pain."

She nodded.

"The important thing to realize is that you can beat this thing. You control the entire environment."

"What do you mean?"

"It is only you who's hurting yourself. There are no external factors outstandingly present. They're all internal things, things within you."

"I see."

"If you were grief-stricken, for example, over a death, then the difficulty would be outside of your control. Or if one of your children were ill, then that would be external. Or if your husband was unfaithful, the problem would be based on someone else's actions and your reaction to that situation, to those external threats to your well-being. So you see, in your case we've got the handle on the problem."

"I see what you mean. That's encouraging."

Andrea answered the psychiatrist's questions as honestly as she could. But, as she feared, no pattern emerged. When her session was over she didn't ask for another appointment because she didn't think she needed to meet with the doctor again. On the way home, however, a sharp pain struck her pelvic area.

Then she remembered what she had told Dr. Lowenthal. Did she really mean those things?

CHAPTER TWENTY-NINE

Bill Sergent's subsequent meetings with the governor, sometimes including Senator Hammond, confirmed Chandler's analysis. Bob Elam had lost interest in the reorganization effort. Sergent knew Hammond was as responsible for Elam's change of heart as was, in all likelihood, the employees union. Anyway, it was clinically dead. Now it only remained to be seen how much dignity its death would be afforded.

Each time Sergent analyzed the outcome, he found there was no plausible reason other than politics. That increased his level of frustration and feelings of powerlessness. Other times, he fondly reviewed the matrix of action steps, the cleanly drawn tables of organization, the detailed narrative that meticulously addressed every eventuality. The plan was logically developed, systematically compatible, and, above all, it made sense. He hadn't attempted to project the cost savings. An error? Maybe if he had, the governor would not have scuttled the plan. But such a financial projection would have been too conjectural and intellectually dishonest.

If only he had. But the plan was too revolutionary to try to estimate the potential savings. And it was not within Sergent's character to be imprecise. If he could not with exactitude specify an amount, he wouldn't estimate.

I was too goddamned honest, he told himself as he placed the plan back in a drawer and out of sight. It was just politics, and politics trumps all else, he lamented.

Sergent painfully remembered his last meeting with Elam. He had learned that several Department of Labor programs would not be included in the proposed Department of Integrated Human Services. Much of Title XX of the Social Security Act had been removed during the meeting before that. The WIC program would remain with the Commission of Health, and the state was to return the administration of the summer nutrition program to the federal regional FNS, USDA. Christ, the agency was being stripped bare. What would be next?

Sergent became increasingly bitter, and this resentment was obvious to the governor. Their relationship was being strained, and neither tried to conceal the impending schism.

Elam's position was obvious. He was the elected administrator of the machinery of state government. It was his judgment in which the people had placed their trust, not that of his aides'. It was he who would face the voters during the next election. And the only way to measure the success of a politician is to see if he wins the next election. Beyond that, it was his ass on the line in the history books. Anyway, the goddamned plan was too fraught with pratfalls, too damned complex.

Sergent understood these things. But the reorganization plan could have made Elam a statesman, not just a goddamned caretaker. National leaders would draw upon his expertise, his gutsy, decisive way of organizing things, of making government work. Hell, Elam could be the HEW secretary if a Democrat won the next presidential election.

And Sergent could have been an undersecretary.

"Yes, Governor, I'll be right in." Sergent had been startled from his fantasizing by the telephone. He rose and walked into Elam's office.

He was relieved to see that no one else was there. It was bad enough to swallow the bitter medicine he was being meted out on a daily basis. To do so in Hammond's presence made it all the more unpleasant. He sat and took out his pen. "Yes, sir?"

"No need to take notes. I just wanted to chat a bit."

"Sure."

"Have you seen Greg Allen lately?"

"I speak to him nearly every day he's in town, and he hasn't been traveling lately."

"How's he taking things?"

Sergent wanted to force the governor to directly speak to the point. "Which things?" he asked.

"The Department of Integrated Human Services."

"That name is quickly becoming a misnomer."

"Dammit, Sergent, I know how the hell you're taking it. What I don't know is how the hell Allen's taking it."

"Luckily for him, he's still preoccupied."

"But?"

"His ego, his total self is pretty much wrapped up in his self-designated job title."

"Antipoverty czar," Elam sarcastically said.

"Yeah."

"I know you and he don't like what's happening, how it's taking three years to accomplish what you propose be done in one, but that's the reality of things."

That surprised Bill. "Then the plan is still alive? You're just gonna stretch it out?"

"Of course," Elam lied. "But I don't think Allen has the patience. What the hell are we going to do with him?"

Sergent was dubious, but he played along. "What do you suggest?"

"Can you explain to him what's going on? Could you tell him we've decided to take more time with this? You could say 'to allow you more time to get to know your staff, your federal contacts, and all that stuff.' You could tell him we just prudently thought we'd stretch it out. Could you do that?"

"Yeah. But not persuasively."

"And just why the hell not?" Elam asked angrily.

Bill recalled that Elam didn't want to discharge any key staff members this early into his administration. He judged this would apply to the governor's administrative assistant. He spoke boldly. "Because, Governor, I'm not sure I believe you."

"I see."

The meeting lapsed into an uncomfortable silence – a sort of standoff. Elam lit his pipe. Bill lit a cigarette. It was Governor Elam who spoke first. "Bill, you and I are in a sorta symbiotic relationship. We need one another, but I have the upper hand. So I'm gonna give you an order. Until we can find another home for Mr. Allen, I want you to keep him in check." Bob smiled slightly. "And I want you to do so persuasively."

Bill rose to return to his office. He took several steps before he turned to face Governor Elam. "Yes, sir."

Back at his desk, Bill felt uneasy. He was the governor's administrative assistant. He had been given his instructions, and the order was legal. He had but two options: resign or carry out the governor's wishes. He reached for the telephone. "Yes, Mr. Allen please. This is Bill Sergent calling."

The secretary quickly responded. "Yes, sir, Mr. Sergent. One moment please."

Greg was on the phone seconds later. "Yeah, Bill, what's up?"

"Not much. I was just wondering if we might get together for a drink."

"You sure there's nothing's up?" Greg's voice was apprehensive.

"Sure I'm sure. I just don't think we've ever gotten together informally. Thought it'd be a good idea."

"Yeah. Sounds good."

"Where do you do your serious drinking?" Sergent asked.

"How about the Enterprize Club?"

"I'm not a member."

"Neither am I. We'll crash it."

"Sounds good. Drop over about five and we'll walk over." He wondered how he'd tell the poor sonofabitch that his tent was collapsing around him. He was still considering that when Greg dropped by.

They walked the four blocks through the coldness. The sun was low in the sky, and they had no chance to catch the sun's fading rays as they walked in the shadows of the tall buildings.

"A guy's got to be some kind of a masochist to spend winter in this damned town," Greg grumbled.

"You mean folks like us?" Bill's teeth were chattering.

The express elevator transported them to the thirtieth floor and the Enterprize Club. As they stepped out and walked to the bar, Allen was scanning the place, looking for a member he knew. He then turned to Sergent, "You wanna drink off the insurance lobbyist or NAM?"

"NAM sounds good."

"National Association of Manufacturers. Good choice! They got lots of bucks." Greg walked to their lobbyist. He motioned Sergent over a few minutes later. "Bill, you know Tom Kohler don't you?"

"Bill Sergent," he said, offering his hand.

"Sure. I've heard your name often enough while chatting with the legislators," Kohler said as he firmly gripped Bill's hand. I hear you're gonna shape up those damn bureaucrats. Maybe even get some work out of them. And, off the record, Greg's got my vote to be the man to head up the new department. But let's sit. Whatcha drinking?"

A half hour later, Kohler saw the minority whip enter. He interrupted one of Greg's boring stories. "I'm sorry. I've enjoyed chatting with you guys, but I've got to get to work. Stay as long as you wish. Please," he emphasized. "You're on my tab so enjoy yourselves." Kohler walked over to the minority whip. They were huddled in a quiet corner moments later. Sergent stretched his legs. A smile crept across his face while looking at Allen. "Do you do this often?"

"What's that?"

"Drink free at the Enterprize."

"Two, three times a week," Greg smiled.

Bill remembered his talk with Chandler. He spoke softly. "The word's out that the Plainsmen is one of your haunts."

Allen's face registered concern for just for a second. Then, recovering, he said, "Not so much anymore."

"Oh?"

"Yeah."

"You know your department's in serious trouble?"

"Huh?" Greg looked distressed. Then he asked, "You mean DIHS?" He pronounced it DICKS.

He's already got his acronym worked out, Sergent thought. "Yeah," he replied. "DICKS."

"How serious?"

"Well since I view it as my creation, I'm probably too close to be objective, but I'd say damn serious," Sergent continued.

"What's been happening?"

"You haven't heard anything?"

"No." Greg thought he'd better explain. "I was having some problems at home." He paused. Then he tried to reassure Sergent. "Everything's okay now. But for a while I was kinda flaky."

"You were preoccupied at times," Bill said kindly.

"Yeah. But that's all behind me. Now what's going on?"

"DICKS is being cut back, right to the bone." Sergent paused, wondering if he was telling Allen too much. "This, of course, is all off the record."

"Why? Why, for Christ's sake, are they destroying my department?"

"I really don't know."

"Jesus Christ!"

Sergent ordered another round while Greg stared out the window. It was dark now, and the capitol building was bathed in its amber floodlights. Greg spoke again. "Can it be salvaged?"

"Not if Elam has anything to say about it."

"Are you suggesting we go right to the legislature?"

Sergent spoke carefully. "I thought about it. But that would be disloyal to the governor. My job is to support the governor."

"But just where the hell does that leave me?"

"I don't know," Sergent answered candidly.

Greg gulped at his drink. "Sonofabitch!"

"How about going back to the private sector, to your law firm?" Sergent instantly knew he had misspoken.

"No! Hell no! No way!" Greg angrily retorted. Then he asked more soberly, "Did the governor tell you to ask me that?"

"No. Not at all," Bill lied. "It's just that I know how disappointed you are. And dammit, so am I."

"Then let's develop a strategy to save it. The bastard's your brainchild after all. We could get it through the legislature. Elam would have to sign it. In the public's eye he's still behind it. It's still his bill. We could box him in."

Sergent saw that Greg was grasping at every straw he could think of. He just shook his head. "No."

They were so engrossed in their conversation, their mutual plight, that they hadn't noticed the stillness around them. Then Sergent overheard a woman at the table behind them. "Well, I suppose that makes Jake Hammond about the happiest guy around these parts. He hated the senator."

Bill interrupted Greg's jeremiad, turning his attention away from him. He leaned slightly toward the woman, listening to her every word.

"How old was he?" the woman's male companion asked.

"Early fifties, I think. But he had been having heart problems for over a year now."

"A heart attack, huh?"

"I suppose."

"How is Mrs. Sloane taking it?"

"Hell, I don't know. He just died an hour ago."

Then the conversation shifted, for the Enterprize Club was above all a place of politics. And the woman, a lobbyist for the Teachers'

Association, began to project. "Who do you think the governor will appoint to replace him?"

Bill couldn't hear the man's response. He saw that Greg had joined the eavesdropping.

"That's right! His district does extend into the capital city. Christ, I hope he doesn't appoint another goddamned farmer. Now we got this civics teacher - a moxie sorta guy, politically, I mean. Christ, if I could ..."

Bill looked to Greg. He remembered seeing the senator a few weeks ago right here in the Enterprize. Sloane had mentioned something about seeing a doctor, but he had said that it wasn't serious. Obviously, it was. Sergent was annoyed by the efficiency of the lobbyist. Damn, she could have waited before she started talking about his replacement. Sergent looked at Greg. "Well, so much for the senator's requiem," he said. "Let's get the hell out of here."

CHAPTER THIRTY

Driving down the highway, Jeff experienced a pervasive but undefined uneasiness. Unable to pinpoint its cause, he dismissed it after reaching the office. A fiscal clerk gave him the month's checks. After he signed them, she drove forty miles to the board's treasurer. After he signed them, she drove back to the office. It was admittedly cumbersome, but it helped assure the corporation's fiscal integrity. Jeff believed the safeguard was well worth the cost.

After a few telephone calls, he had forgotten his dysphoria. He was drafting a memorandum when Dave Goldman rushed into his office.

"Did you hear about last night's meeting?"

"No. What happened?"

"Have I stuff to tell you!"

"Tell me stuff."

"It's something really far out."

"How far?"

"Far and long. Really long-range stuff."

"Has it anything to do with poor folks?" Jeff smiled.

"Of course, but only in the long haul." Dave paused. "But I should warn you. Politically, it's dangerous as hell."

"Sounds like our kind of thing," Jeff said, his quixotic leanings coming back to life. "What is it?"

"George has been getting some strange folks to our meetings. Last night he had a bunch of farmers."

"That's unusual," Jeff said.

"The meetings, of course, share with the poor how much money the agency gets and then ask them which programs they need to get out of poverty."

"Yeah, I know. But I can't believe George is getting farmers to go to the meetings. Usually it's just old folks and ADC mothers."

"Yeah," Goldman agreed. "Anyway, some guy in bib overalls says 'You ain't gonna solve any poverty problems around here until you raise the price of corn'."

"That makes sense," Jeff replied. "But so what? Farm supports are such a complex thing. I'll bet the secretary of agriculture doesn't understand what parity is."

"Funny you should mention parity. 'Cause all of a sudden there's this priest who starts talking about parity. He complained about USDA, Congress, the whole damn system. But he always came back to parity. By the time the meeting was over everybody was calling him the 'parity priest'."

Jeff laughed.

"It gets better. They started talking about insurance companies buying a lot of farmland around here."

"Interesting."

"Then we got to corporations. Remember when we first met? We talked about corporate involvement in agriculture, vertical integration, and all that stuff?"

"Yeah," Jeff said, "a long time ago."

"Well, these damn farmers were talking about the same stuff. The priest mentioned the Goldschmidt study, corporate tax codes. Jeff, it was amazing. These farmers are an enlightened bunch of sonsabitches. They actually know why they're going broke. They've actually figured out that the USDA is their adversary. Amazing!"

"But what can we do about the price of corn?"

"Oh, I've no idea. But let me go on."

Jeff nodded.

"The folks at the meeting need some research done."

"What do they propose we research?"

"The extent of corporate involvement in the state's agricultural economy."

"Specifically?"

"How much farmland are the corporations buying? How much do they already own?" Dave explained.

"How do we do that?"

"Oh, that's simple. Just check the records in the county court houses. See who owns the land, how many are corporations."

"Okay. Then what?"

"Compile it. Then publish a report. Get the media involved."

"We're gonna need money for staff and travel," Jeff cautioned.

"Right."

"We ain't got any for that."

"Right."

"So?"

"So listen to this. The CAP board chairman, the Jesuit, has a kid brother who's an aide to the bishop."

"I didn't know that. But so what?"

"The county we're talking about is mostly Catholic," Dave continued. "There's damn few Protestants anywhere in the whole damn county."

"Go on."

"It all fits together. Don't you see?"

"No, I don't."

"The parity priest, Catholic farmers losing their farms, their way of life, their asses, the parish priest, Fr. Dunn, the bishop connection."

"We got a bunch of poor farmers who are Catholic. That's all."

"That's all we need."

Jeff just looked at Goldman.

"The Campaign for Human Development," Goldman continued.

"What's that?"

"It's the antipoverty arm of the U.S. Catholic Conference; the OEO of the mother church."

"You're saying we can wire it - for bucks?"

"It'll take about two months to do the legwork."

"And?"

"Three months for church politics."

"And?"

"We got a shot at a grant."

"Hmm," Jeff pondered, "to document and disseminate the extent of corporate involvement in the state's agriculture."

"And to name the corporations doing the buying. Then try to boycott them, or get proxy votes - or something."

"We'll take a lot of flak," Jeff warned.

"From who?" Goldman said, smiling.

"From the corporations and their politicians. That's who."

"Of course."

"Okay," Jeff said. "Form an advisory board. Fill it with farmers, farmers' wives, priests, any heavies you can pick up. Have them present their proposal to the board. You, of course, help them with their proposal."

"Right."

"I'll try to wire the board. Have some priests call the Jesuit."

"Right," Goldman said. "One more thing. We need Jefferson."

"Who?"

"How quickly we forget. Jefferson, the VISTA."

"Oh, of course, Jefferson. But we ain't got any bucks to pay him," Jeff said.

"I checked last month's cash flow. I project fifteen hundred uncommitted dollars over the next three months."

Jeff smiled at Goldman.

"He works cheap. I've already contacted him," Goldman added.

"How cheap?"

"Five hundred a month."

"A convenient amount. Is he working now?"

"Nope. I don't know if you remember, but his degree is in agri-economics. That'll come in damned handy."

"Hire him as a temp. If we get the grant, we'll have him head it up. But be sure he knows, his job is reliant on us getting the grant," Jeff instructed.

"You mean it?"

"Yeah. Start moving. It sounds exciting."

"Damn," said Goldman, excited.

"Damn," said Jeff, more subdued. "The Jewish-Catholic Land Reform Movement."

"Damn," said Goldman.

After Dave left, Jeff quietly sat. There was, he reflected, a certain excitement to it. Organizing small family farmers, Caucasian farmers. Ain't no community action agency ever done that! Amazing, he thought. He recalled that some of the money Nixon was impounding was USDA bucks. Maybe his politics were forcing the poor bastards to come to us. Ironic, he thought.

After lunch, Jeff took a call from Larry Ashton. He was told he had to travel to Washington next month for training for new CAP directors. Also, the regional office was accepting applications for a special purpose grant. The guidelines were like most RFPs: broad. One criterion was that any program started by OEO money must be ongoing after the grant period. Ashton told Jeff the money was competitive. "I've been telling folks how good you're doing. Don't let me down. Come up with good concepts and good paper. The proposals have to be in within twelve working days."

He told Jeff he needed to advise his other agencies. Jeff hung up and called for George.

George was apprehensive whenever Jeff called. He just didn't know how long his luck would last. He had rented a house and moved his family here several months ago. The home had rugs, a bathroom, running water, and a lawn.

The kids were in school, and Mary was happier than ever. George was making $550 a month, which was incredible. That allowed him to send eighty dollars a month to Patton. And Christmas was coming up. The kids would have their first real Christmas. However, his last job under Jeff had been taken away from him. So he wondered if this dream had also died as he knocked on Jeff Vinton's door.

"Come on in."

"Yeah?"

"George, we need a bunch of meetings in addition to or as a part of the meetings you're now having."

George breathed a sigh of relief. Now relaxed, he asked, "What for?"

"We got a chance for some more bucks."

"I'll chat with my guys. Get things lined up."

"Good. Dave tells me you're doing great."

"You know he's helping a lot."

"That's why he's here. But like I said, you're doing good. I appreciate it."

George wanted to shed the stereotypical image of the American Indian. He wanted to thank Jeff for changing his life. He really wanted to. Instead, he nodded.

Jeff, Dave, and George sat down a week later to sort things out. Jeff looked to Goldman who responded: "Poverty continues to be a pervasive way of life around here. In our western counties we've got small farms and small communities. The land is marginal and the farmers are Catholic. In other words, thin soil and big families."

"Lot of kids, huh?" Jeff asked.

Dave nodded. "Lots of kids. But that's their lifestyle. There's nothing inherently wrong with that. Except commodity prices keep falling, seed and fertilizer prices keep rising, and there's been a couple of dry years. But they're a hardy group. Closely knit families. Church oriented. You know it's amazing. You drive past the homes in the small towns, and each one has a garden. And not just a small plot. It usually takes up the whole yard. These folks have pretty basic values."

"And another thing," George said. "In every town there's two schools. One church, one public. The church one is always bigger."

"And they can't afford one, let alone two," Dave added.

You know," George said, "the kids are picked up by the school buses about six a.m. By the time the bus makes its rounds through those hills and drops the kids off at school, they've eaten their lunches."

"So they have nothing during their lunch hour, huh?" Jeff asked.

"I suppose not."

"It gets back to the price of corn," Dave said resignedly.

Jeff sat back. Things fell into place. "We got two things to work with."

"We got nothing," Dave said flatly.

"The hell you say," Jeff said, now more excited. "We got gardens, and we got empty bellies during lunchtime. The best of both worlds."

"You're right. Those things we got," George said.

"Then let's go with them," Jeff said.

"Go with what? How?" Dave asked impatiently.

"Dave, contact the Ball Corporation in Muncie. Let's use part of the money to set up a food preservation center so they can preserve the produce from the gardens. You know, Mason jars and stuff. Find out how much it costs. Then find one of our community centers that's got the plumbing and electrical capabilities, then prepare a proposal for a canning center."

Dave thought for a second. "Sounds good. Once we buy the equipment, it'll operate at a minimal cost. Just an employee we already got and increased utilities. Most of the costs are already there."

"Okay. But how about the empty bellies?" George asked.

"Yeah. That'll be a bit tougher. George, call regional USDA. It's got a program to help set up school kitchens to prepare hot lunches. But it's only for impoverished communities, and it's on a match basis. The schools put up part, USDA puts up the rest. We'll grant the schools the match money. Dave, find out what the match is and what the guidelines are. You got until tomorrow to get that stuff. Wednesday we start writing."

"Super," Dave replied.

"Good. George, talk with the schools. Tell them everything's tentative, that maybe we've got a shot. We'll try to help fund these school kitchens in three towns. But we'll only do one school per town. Then that school will transport the hot lunches to the other. The issue will be politically hot in these small towns, so let the local folks work out who does what."

"But you're suggesting we match federal money from USDA with federal money from OEO," Dave pointed out. "Is that legal?"

Jeff thought for a moment, then frowned. "Damn, you found a hitch. You can't match fed with fed." Jeff looked discouraged.

"So much for empty bellies," George said.

"Dave, really research the CFR. Find us a loophole," Jeff directed after mulling over the dilemma. "You know, any damn fool can read the regs. It takes a bright lad to figure out how to get around them. Try and figure out a way to wash that money, and ..."

"No problem," Dave interrupted. "We'll rent a Mexican laundry truck."

Jeff nodded and smiled. "Well, George, I guess we'll soon find out just how bright our fair-haired Jewish boy is. Then we'll meet with the info you've gathered and put pencil to paper. Now, if you will excuse me, I'm gonna take off early. I'm heading home."

Driving down the highway, Jeff found satisfaction with the day's events in particular and with the conduct of the agency in general. George was the most pleasant surprise. Jeff hadn't been sure that George could get a bunch of paraprofessionals working toward such an amorphous, ill-defined goal as "community organization." But George was getting results.

George once told him how many single-parent households there were in the nine counties. Divorce, it seemed, was reaching epidemic proportions. George had used the list of programs to identify ways to help the families. More fundamentally, Jeff simply couldn't imagine all of those men abandoning their wives and their children. He was incensed at every one of the runaway fathers. But that was a reality. Some guys are just like that, he figured.

George had his staff transport the abandoned mothers to the county attorney offices to file complaints against their former husbands before referring those women to specific programs. While these runaway pappies are still enjoying the good life, Jeff reasoned, we can at least make sure their kids are getting some help. George's staff had responded well. In fact, Jeff had received several calls from county attorneys complaining about those referrals. But only after the mothers had signed papers against their ex-spouses would George's staff open up access to the cornucopia of aid programs. The abandoned families were receiving local, state, and federal assistance like never before.

There was one difficulty. Some of his staff resented working for an Indian. But George was slowly winning them over.

And there was Dave. Dave did not surprise Jeff. He was fully living up to Jeff's expectations because of his intellect, enthusiasm, and industry.

Even Gwen was begrudgingly recognizing the two men's commitments, capabilities, and contributions.

Three diverse individuals: an Indian who had resigned himself to a life of spot labor; a Jew who wanted to be an assistant U.S. attorney; and Jeff, whatever he was. These three had completely turned the agency around. And they were helping poor people – especially children. Furthermore, he and Fr. Dunn were beginning to develop a mutual respect for each other. Damn! Jeff felt good. He sped down the highway toward home.

Light snow began to fall as Jeff arrived. There was little wind, so the snow fell gracefully, quietly. It was the first snow shower of the season, thus making the warmth of home even more inviting. Inside, the children were again mesmerized by the afternoon's TV cartoons. But the volume was unusually loud. And there was a cacophony coming from the kitchen. Jeff waved to his children, pausing to watch little Ned crawl between his siblings. He went to the kitchen to greet Andrea. Then Jeff identified the strange noise. Andrea had a hard rock station on the radio.

The volume was deafening. Jeff raised his voice so he could be heard. "I didn't know you like this music." But she didn't hear him. Jeff moved closer. "Your taste in music has changed."

Andrea turned to him. "Just recapturing my lost youth." She had to shout.

"Okay if I turn it down a bit?"

"Sure. I'll get it." She turned the dial back a bit, but the music still remained loud.

"Thanks. Now I won't have to raise my voice to you."

"You had better not." She simply looked at him. No emotion. She turned back toward the stove.

"You know, in three weeks I'll be in Washington. I'm already beginning to miss you and the kids."

"Oh, I think I'm gonna need the car again," she said.

"Okay. When?"

"I'm not sure."

"No problem. If you can wait until I head east, you'll have it all to yourself for the two weeks I'm away. How's your day going?"

"Okay."

"Good." Jeff stood awkwardly for a moment, then reached for a coffee cup. He sensed her need to be alone.

Later, after some opposition, Andrea persuaded the children to go to bed early. She spent a few minutes with each of them before coming to the living room. She asked Jeff if he wanted a drink. He had just put down the office paperwork and was settled in to watch a television special.

"Yeah," he replied. "Bring me a beer."

Andrea poured herself a glass of wine then joined Jeff in the living room. "You got time to talk?" she asked.

"Don't you want to watch the show?"

"Not tonight."

"You mind if I do?" he said.

"We got to talk."

"Sure," he said. "You look tired."

"I'm still having problems." She paused. "I've been spotting a lot lately, even hemorrhaged once. All this loss of blood is making me weak. I've lost three pounds in the last two weeks."

Jeff could not hide his exasperation. He no longer knew how to deal with her continuing medical difficulties. Finally he asked her, "You think you should see a doctor again?"

"No," she said stoically. "I'll just put up with it."

Jeff changed the channel to a classical music station. The only sound that came from the set was soft, quiet music.

"I've been thinking back," Andrea suddenly said. "How long were we together before we were married?"

Jeff was pleased she had changed topics. Her recurring medical problems were baffling him. "Well, eleven months at Bragg, then I went overseas. Then, let's see, you visited me several times, and I went to Galveston twice."

"It was really a long-distance romance," she observed.

"Well, no problem. Everything's turning out good."

"I'm not sure it is," she said.

"What do you mean?"

"Maybe it was a mistake."

"Oh, no. No mistake!" He looked at her and set down his beer. She suddenly seemed different.

"I'm not sure I like being with you," Andrea continued.

"What?" His tone and face revealed his alarm.

"I don't like the way you look at me."

"I'm sorry." He forced a quick smile.

"No. Not just then. You stare at me a lot."

"I didn't know." He paused. "What's going on?"

She began to reply when the telephone rang. She stopped speaking. The phone rang four times. "Aren't you going to answer it?" she asked.

"No. Tell me what's going on."

"Please answer it."

"Okay." Jeff lifted the receiver. "Hi."

"Mr. Vinton?" a man asked tersely.

"Yeah. This is he."

This is the credit department at Sears. We've called numerous times before and spoken with Mrs. Vinton. You're going to have to do something about your bill."

"What bill?"

"You've only made partial payments during the last five months."

Jeff remembered the earlier call he had taken from a creditor. This time he didn't challenge the company representative. "I see. How much do we owe?"

"Well, in all, thirteen hundred and four dollars. But your delinquent payments amount to three hundred and forty dollars."

"Oh...ah...let me find out what's going on. We'll send you something soon."

"We will require payment in the next five days or I'll transfer your account to a collection agency. You've been warned before."

Jeff looked at Andrea. He knew she was aware that he was speaking to a creditor. But she looked strangely uninterested. "I'll speak with Mrs. Vinton. Call me tomorrow at my business number. I'll have some information then."

"We'd rather have a check, sir."

"Please do call me," Jeff repeated, giving the man his office number

"All right, Mr. Vinton. I'll call tomorrow. Thank you."

After replacing the telephone, he looked to Andrea. "That was Sears."

"Oh yeah," Andrea said. "There's a mix-up in our account."

"They don't think so." His voice was rising.

She looked away.

"Andrea, what the hell have you been charging at Sears? Let's get out the bills and go over them. Let me help you with this."

"No. That's my job, running the household." She stared defiantly at him.

"Do we have any money to send them?" he asked.

"No."

"How much do we completely owe everyone?"

"I really don't know." Seconds later she shrieked with pain.

"What's wrong?"

"Pain! Call the doctor. The pain's terrible."

Jeff looked at her. She grimaced with each spasm.

The doctor administered a hypodermic shot twenty minutes later. Andrea soon looked relaxed, the pain gone. Jeff turned to the doctor, thanking him. As he prepared to leave, the doctor asked Jeff to carry his medical bag to his car. He'd hurt his wrist from a nasty fall on the ice, he explained.

"I didn't know you folks made house calls," Jeff joked as he opened the door."

"Just us country bumpkin GPs." Outside, he looked at Jeff. "You know there's nothing wrong with your wife, don't you?"

"Then what the hell's wrong? Christ, her pain seems real."

"Oh yeah. The pain's real. And she needs medical help. But I can't give it to her. The pain's coming from her mind. Her tissue is all healthy."

"I suspected as much," Jeff said. "What can I do?"

"I've tried to talk her into seeing a psychiatrist in the capital city. You know, I've made many a house call to your home. At fifty dollars a visit, it must add up. You must have a good job, Mr. Vinton."

"Who's the doctor in the capital city?"

"I've got his business card. Here, here it is."

"I'm to be away on a business trip for two weeks. I'll talk with my wife about seeing this guy when I get back. Good night, doctor, and thanks. Thanks so much."

Jeff stood in the cold air, watching him drive off. Then, minutes later, he realized how cold he was. He walked inside. Andrea was now relaxed. He sat by her on the sofa.

She sensed his presence although her eyes remained closed. She then opened them, but for just a few moments. Just long enough to say one sentence. "I don't love you anymore." The narcotic then took hold. She fell fast asleep.

Jeff brought a pillow and blanket from their bed. After ensuring she was comfortable, he checked on their children. He returned to his wife, kissing her lightly on her forehead.

By then, however, she was sleeping soundly, comfortably. She was dreaming of being in Galveston with Ned and Joyce. Her kids were in the pool. The temperature was in the eighties. Joyce looked so good, so healthy. Andrea was laughing. It was in response to something Ned had said. She smiled softly.

CHAPTER THIRTY-ONE

"Gosh damn, from the sound of your voice it must be serious. Let me see." Sergent looked to his calendar, "Yeah, I'll move things around. Come right over." He called the AG, postponing his meeting.

Waiting for Greg Allen, Bill picked up a draft of a speech Governor Elam would be giving at the state Farm Bureau meeting. A sentence caught his eye. He reread it. "Blaming the food producer for the high prices at the grocery store is tantamount to blaming the cornstalk." Christ, who wrote this? It's got no flair, no panache! Bill began to toy with rhetorical absurdities. Let's see, young couples can't afford to start farming anymore, so most farmers are in their fifties. That means they were born in the twenties, probably were in the service during World War II. How to relate the price of corn to the war? His mind ranged the full gamut. Pearl Harbor changed their lives. How could farm income relate to Pearl Harbor? To the bombs that fell? Fell like hailstones? Falling. Damn! He began editing. "Blaming the farmer for the prices at Safeway is ..." He crossed out the cornstalk. Right! Sonofabitch! He rewrote the sentence. "... the family farmer for food prices is like ..." The telephone rang. He finished the sentence before answering. Damn! That's good! "Yeah, have Mr. Allen come in." Then he injected the phrase "... the attack on ..."

Bill was still writing when he noticed Greg standing before him. "Sit down, Greg, and listen to this." He picked up the drafted speech, that section replete with the markings of his pencil. "I'm just doing some editing."

Greg was preoccupied, but he nodded.

Sergent read the changes he had made to the governor's speech, parroting Elam's inflection and style. He then looked up at Greg who only forced a smile. "I'm sorry," Bill said. "You've obviously got something more important on your mind. Whatcha worried about?"

"My job," Greg simply said.

"Oh. I see." Sergent was sympathetic to Greg's awkward status. "You know there's no plans to dismiss you. It's just that your department is being dismantled before it's been put together."

"I really wanted to see your plan become a reality, Bill. Isn't there anything we can do?" Allen was clearly hoping for a miracle.

"No. Not really. Hammond's principle of diffused control has become this administration's policy."

"Dammit, Bill. I really studied your proposal. The savings in tax dollars, the increased services. It can be done just by eliminating the departmental redundancies."

Sergent smiled sadly. "I know."

"Christ, I don't know when the next shoe will drop, but right now all I've got to oversee is LIEAP, forty percent of Title XX, some home economists, and those damned CAPs."

"Come on, Greg. It's not that bad. But it's not what we envisioned."

Greg shook his head. "What should I do?" His face betrayed desperation.

"Well, if you want to stay in government, you might look around, see what's available. Check with your contacts at the federal level. The pay is certainly better. Or look at municipal government or even here in state government. There's bound to be someone who quits, gets fired, or dies." Sergent looked at Allen. His sympathy obviously wasn't easing Allen's troubled mind. He lowered his head, staring at the desktop. "Just take it easy, Greg, and bide your time. Something's bound to come up."

"Okay, Bill, and thanks. I know you're as disappointed as I am."

"Let's keep loose. You know how things have a strange way of going flip-flop. Why not plan some vacation? You and Amy get away. Let the dust settle."

"Yeah, maybe we will. But you know, your earlier advice wasn't all that bad either. Do you know any department heads I can undermine?"

"Sure," Sergent laughed. "And I'll shoot you a memo with their names as soon as you put your request in writing."

Sergent went back to the speech after Allen departed, correcting syntax here, making a phrase snappier there, deleting awkward sentences, and adding witty one-liners. When he was satisfied, he sent the draft to the governor's secretary for its final typing.

Greg returned to the DIHS. His secretary flashed a smile, but the smile faded when she noted his expression. She resumed reading her novel after he entered his office. Allen called her moments later. He didn't want to be disturbed. Big deal, she thought. This office hasn't been disturbed by anything or anybody since he took over. She was amazed how a once busy office could become so inactive so quickly. But there were no other jobs that paid as much as this one, and she had become comfortable in her position. She had hoped that Sergent's reorganization would liven things up. But now that too was obviously dead. Oh well, she thought, things will turn around eventually. She returned to her novel.

Meanwhile, Greg was compiling a list of departments and their directors, where he might land another job. He ruled out some of them. Environmental Control: too technical. Water Resources: too geoponic. Health was headed by an MD; not a chance. State Procurement: again no chance, the director's an old buddy of Elam's – but, he reasoned, a lot of kickbacks there. Insurance Commission: a possibility. He drew a line under that department. Still, he was dissatisfied with his efforts. He began thinking of his acquaintances in the federal structure. The pay would be better, and the feds had a great retirement plan.

He had gotten drunk one night with the regional DOL deputy director while at a meeting in New York. They had employed two prostitutes for the evening. It had been the deputy director's idea, and Greg had gone along with it. He wasn't averse to prostitution per se, only the proprietary aspect of it. He had fond memories of the four of them in the hotel suite. It had been great fun.

His mind returned to his predicament. Damn, he thought. I'm riding this dead horse, and everyone knows it's dead, and I'm being made a fool of. In a bureaucracy this big, there's got to be something I can shoot for. Who else does the governor appoint? Members of the State Parole Board. Yeah! They make thirty grand a year. Let's see, what else is there? As soon as I figure out what I want, I'll see Elam. To hell with Sergent! He hasn't done anything to help me! He's probably the guy who's zapping me! Right! From now on, I deal with the governor.

***

Elam summoned Sergent to his office the following week. Bill continued to dutifully respond to the governor, but without the enthusiasm he had originally brought to his role as administrative assistant. The collapse of the human services reorganization effort had eroded much of his respect for Elam. The illusions were gone. Elam was just another boss. Bill's job was to do his best to follow his boss's instructions. But the excitement, the fervor, the crusade had ended. Bill walked into the governor's office carrying his coffee cup, his shirtsleeves rolled up.

"Yes, sir."

"Bill, it's good to see you. I'm in a bind, and I need your help."

"Sure."

"There's a special, not quite an emergency, but a pretty important meeting of the Regional Governors Association."

"Yeah?"

"I've got to leave tonight. The meeting's tomorrow. It'll last three days."

"Oh, I see. You can't give your Farm Bureau speech. How about Evans, the head of Agriculture?"

"He's going with me."

"Who then? The lieutenant governor?"

"I was thinking of you."

"Governor, the bureau wants a celebrity, or at least an office holder. Not a bureaucrat."

"You're the one who polished the speech," Elam pointed out. "And you did a damn good job. You deserve to be the one to give it. And you are the governor's chief aide. Besides, I already spoke to the bureau's president. It's you."

"Alright, Governor, I'll leave tonight, too." He smiled. "But rather than depart from the Intercontinental Airport, I'll get a Ford from the motor pool."

"Thanks, Bill. I appreciate it. Good luck with your speech."

"Thanks, Governor. Enjoy your meeting."

Sitting at the table on the stage, beneath the large Farm Bureau banner, Bill lowered his head as the chairman of the state bureau's governing board introduced him. "... and although Governor Elam is not with us ... he and his agricultural director are at this moment carrying our water for us at the Regional Governors' Association ... as a matter of fact, I've just received this telegram from Governor Elam ... but the young man the governor asked to represent him ... one of agriculture's strongest advocates in the Elam administration ... it is my privilege to present to you ..."

The speech had gone well. Sergent had been interrupted numerous times by either laughter or applause. The farmers and agri-businessmen applauded for several minutes when he was finished. Bill was satisfied he had done a helluva job; both in polishing the speech and, today, in its delivery.

Heading toward the exit, Bill stopped to chat with the bureau's leaders and several members of the press. Then, on the way to his car, he saw it was only three thirty. He should be home by seven.

He turned on the radio, selecting a capital city station, as he eased onto the Interstate. The news came on a few minutes later. The weather conditions were deteriorating, a man's voice told him. A cold front had pushed its way through, and the temperature was falling. The light rain was turning to sleet as Sergent drove. He tested his brakes. The car slowed evenly. He resumed his driving speed. He turned up the volume as the newscaster spoke of the governor's trip. "Governor Elam again emphasized on his arrival in Evansville the need for agricultural exports ..." Bill accelerated the car slightly. It was biting the road well.

"In a related story, Governor Elam announced the temporary appointment of Greg Allen to the state senate. Allen, who is currently serving as the state's antipoverty czar, will fill the seat of Senator Patrick Sloane, who died last month. As state senator, Allen will be paid $32,000 a year, a five-thousand-dollar increase over his current pay. Allen has been a key member of the governor's inner circle since the earliest days of the administration. Allen, who is thirty-four and a lawyer, played a prominent role in Elam's successful gubernatorial campaign. As state senator, he is expected to closely follow Elam's policies ..."

Bill was stunned, inadvertently accelerating the car on the wet highway. He let it to return to the speed limit. But his state of shock was absolute. Greg Allen! Sonofabitch!

"... taking over Allen's position as antipoverty chief, the governor announced, will be William P. Sergent, currently the governor's administrative assistant. Sergent, a close aide to Elam during the campaign, worked with a public relations firm prior to joining state government. His pay remains unchanged. Governor Elam stated he was fortunate to have an individual of such high caliber whom he could appoint to this important office ..."

Sergent remained in a state of shock for the next twenty miles. The sonofabitch could have told me, he thought. Then he remembered that Elam usually made his appointments public while he was out of town. He remembered Elam's rationale. "Every time I appoint someone, I make enemies. You know, people who think I've done them wrong. The trick is to get the hell out of town after every appointment. Let everyone cool off for a few days."

Professionally, Bill realized the wisdom of this practice. Personally, he was pissed off that Elam hadn't told him about these changes in private. I could kill the sonofabitch, he thought. I am his goddamned administrative assistant! Well, to hell with him and his inaccessibility. I'll catch a plane to Evansville tonight. I'll confront the sonofabitch! And tell the sonofabitch off! Bill's anger continued to mount. Then he suddenly relaxed, became almost philosophical. What the hell, he said to himself. This is the governor's style: cheap, cowardly. No class! He resigned himself to his fate. So he was to head the Department of Integrated Human Services. The same do-nothing job whose importance he had recently tried to impress upon its former director. Now the Honorable Mr. Allen was a state senator, and he is what Greg was.

Politics, he thought, is strange.

CHAPTER THIRTY-TWO

Jeff Vinton noted how easily Andrea glided the car down the highway. The scent of her perfume filled the vehicle. Unusual but pleasant, Jeff thought. He looked to her lap, then followed the contour of her hip. Her high-heeled foot evenly depressed the gas pedal, her other foot rested near the brake. The movement of her legs had worked her dress above her knee. Jeff observed his wife erotically. He was, it seemed, addicted to her.

"So you're leaving for D.C. Thursday, huh?" Andrea asked.

"Yeah. They sent the tickets to the office. I'll be leaving from Jackson City. You can drive me there, can't you?"

"That won't be a problem."

"Good." He smiled. "More window shopping today?"

"I just need to get out of the house."

"That'll be good for you."

They were silent until Andrea let him out at the office.

"Have fun, but don't spend any money," Jeff said. "See you tonight. Love you!" He watched the car depart. Andrea drove with a certain authority, like everything she did.

Jeff still hadn't learned their level of indebtedness. He hadn't asserted himself. The timing wasn't good.

Nodding to Gwen, he stuck his head into Dave's office, waving good morning. He filled his coffee cup and went to his office. Reading memoranda, drafting letters, and taking telephone calls occupied Jeff for two hours until he was told that Larry Ashton was on the phone.

"Yeah, Ashton, this is Jeff."

"Jeff, you sonofabitch, you've done it," Larry said excitedly.

"Is that good?"

"You pushed the string beautifully."

"How so?"

"That phrase you found in the CFR, '... to attract public and private monies ... ' "

"Yeah?"

"And the error we feds made by not restricting the match of federal resources for this subsection about matching OEO monies with USDA money.

"Yeah?"

"You know, the school lunch startup."

"Yeah."

"Well, this principle of using OEO money to make local governments pony up has been our basic tenet. But you forced the issue. Damn! Then I insisted the whole question go to the regional counsel. He agrees with you. Do you know what the hell I'm talking about?"

"I think so."

"Right. Well, the regional counsel ruled that monies granted under this subsection don't require match. More importantly, they can match federal money. The regional director bucked the thing to the national counsel. After reading the law, he agreed. So you set a national precedent! From now on, monies under this subsection don't need to be matched. And can be matched with other federal dollars. Just to be sure, our counsel went over to USDA and talked with their counsel. Talked him into it. Jeff, you got your three lunch programs! No problem. But do you realize how important this precedent is? By using our monies from this subsection to match other federal bucks, we can multiply the impact of our dollars several fold. That is, until Congress sees what we've done and amends the law. Or someone takes us to court. But in the meantime, you've got your grant - all hundred thousand of it."

"That's great, Larry. Thanks for your help."

"You know you got everything you asked for – which, incidentally, is more than I told you to ask for."

"Yeah, we were a little greedy. But we didn't think we'd get it," Jeff confided.

"Don't thank me! I've got to advise six of my grantees they'll be getting less. But again, congratulations. Oh, and enjoy your trip to D.C."

***

Andrea walked into the offices of Woods, Buckner & Carr. She told the receptionist she wished to see a lawyer. Ten minutes later, she was told that Mr. Carr would see her. The receptionist escorted her to his office. "Good morning, Ms. Vinton. May I get you some coffee?"

"Yes. Please."

Minutes later he returned with two cups, steam rising from them. "You got a problem?" Carr asked, smiling.

Andrea crossed her long legs, sipping the coffee. She drew out a cigarette. Carr lifted a lighter from his desk, leaned over, and lit it. Andrea inhaled deeply. She spoke deliberatively. "I believe I want a divorce."

A barely discernible smile crept over Carr's face. He looked at Andrea's wedding ring. It was a plain gold band. Can't tell from that, he thought, but she's a class gal. Probably got some bucks.

"Well, do you or don't you?"

"I'm not happy," she confided.

"The Constitution guarantees your pursuit of happiness. Now why can't you pursue it?"

"My husband."

"Then you want a divorce."

"Yes."

The pursuit of happiness bit usually helped the wavering to decide in the affirmative. It'll probably be worth a couple of thousand bucks, Carr thought. Although he was a trial lawyer, he had given up that aspect of the law. Things got too complex. Too much work. Divorce was where the quick money was. You could handle ten or twelve cases at the same time. A quick in, a quick out. Usually no more than three weeks in this state. "You wanna continue living with him?"

"No," Andrea said.

"Well, you're in luck. There's no law that says you have to live with someone."

That gave Andrea the final bit of encouragement she needed. "I want a divorce," she said, firmly this time.

"How about your soon to be ex-husband. What does he want?"

"When I dropped him off to come here, his last words were that he loves me."

"He doesn't suspect."

"No." Andrea was beginning to feel remorse, some guilt. Carr picked up on that. He needed to dispel her compunction. "When they don't suspect anything and they're served with the papers, they can become violent. Is Mr. Vinton violent?"

"No."

"Could he become so, under duress?"

"I suppose so. He was in the infantry, a paratrooper, in Vietnam."

Carr feigned a disturbed look. "We'd better have the court issue a restraining order to protect you."

Andrea had a restraining order placed against her first husband. She agreed.

"Okay, let me get the particulars, and we'll whip this right out," Carr said. "Where were you married?" A few minutes later he flipped back the pages of his yellow tablet. "Why don't you have some more coffee. I'll show you to our conference room. We'll get this typed up, and you can sign it." He looked again at Andrea. "He has no suspicion, huh?"

"No. None," Andrea said as she rose.

The poor sonofabitch, Carr thought.

Carr walked into the conference room ten minutes later. "Sign right here. This is the petition for the divorce. Let's see, here we ask that he pay all the legal fees and child support until the hearing. Yeah, sign it here. And this one is your request for a restraining order. We say that Mr. Vinton is predisposed to violence. That way, the judge will be sure to sign it."

Andrea's hand was steady as she signed the documents.

"Okay, that takes care of the paperwork. The work's done," Carr explained, signaling the meeting was over. As Andrea stood, he said, "You know, you're lucky you live in a state with no-fault divorce. There's nothing he can do to stop it. In three weeks you'll be one helluva attractive divorcee. Oh, and another thing. You'd better get to a motel tonight. Don't let him know where you are. That way he can't hurt you or the kids."

"Right."

"I'll have these taken over to the clerk of the district court. The papers will probably be served this afternoon."

"Good."

"Have a good day, Ms. Vinton."

***

Gwen looked into Jeff's office. "We're the last ones here. And I for one am out of here. Good night," she smiled at him.

"Good night, Gwen. See you tomorrow."

She looked back again. "Do you need a ride?"

"No. I'm waiting for Andrea. Thanks, though." Jeff rose to lock the door behind her. While doing so, he looked up the street, hoping to see Andrea driving down the hill. There was no sign of her, so he returned to his office. He reviewed the grant application for the corporate farm ownership survey and looked over Goldman's presentation to the governing board. They looked good, damned good. He checked his watch. It was a little past six. He decided to get a beer. He wrote a note telling Andrea where he'd be and taped it to the door. The wind was gusting, and flurries were falling. He was chilled by the time he entered the bar. He walked to a table and sat down. Before he ordered a beer, one of his employees came over. She worked in the fiscal office; a divorcee with two children. Kinda cute.

"Hi. Haven't seen you in here since your family moved up."

Jeff smiled. "Yeah, I'm waiting for Andrea. She's running late. Sit down and join me, won't you?"

"Sure."

An hour later two more staffers had joined them. Jeff was becoming increasingly concerned. It occurred to him that Andrea might have been in an accident. "I'd better get going," he said, rising.

"Is Andrea here?" the divorcee asked, looking to the door.

"No. And I'm getting worried."

Jeff put on his coat and returned to the office. He called home but no one answered. Thinking he had misdialed, he tried again. Still no answer. Jeff was no longer worried. He was damned scared. He wondered what to do. If she was in an accident someone would be trying to call, he reasoned. I'd better get home. He went to the fiscal office and took the key to one of the agency's cars. He had difficulty starting it but soon had it going. The flurries turned into a snow shower as he sped down the highway. The snow was falling heavily thirty minutes later as he entered their home.

The house was balefully empty.

He called the highway patrol. There had been several accidents, the officer told him, but no one named Vinton. He thanked the officer, then he called the Jackson City police. Same report. Relieved, he put down the phone. They're okay, he assured himself, but where the hell are they? He made some coffee for himself and Andrea, then heated some water in a kettle. He would have hot chocolate for the kids. It was getting colder outside.

An hour later he decided he needed a drink. He wondered if he should use the agency vehicle to drive to the liquor store. To hell with it. Without putting on his coat, he walked to the car.

He got a six-pack and drove through the snow back to their home. The outline of a sedan was in front of the house. Tears of joy came to his eyes. They're home! Relieved, he eased the car through the snow and into the driveway. Then he saw the emergency lights mounted on the top of the vehicle. A sheriff's car! There's been an accident, he realized. They're hurt! Dead! He bolted out of the car. The deputy sheriff had just turned away from the front door. "My family!" Jeff screamed. "Are they okay?"

"Are you Mr. Vinton?"

"Yes! What's wrong?"

"I presume your family's okay, Mr. Vinton, but we'd better go inside."

"You're sure they're okay?"

"Yeah," he said.

"Oh, great! Come on in then. Christ, I was scared. And it's cold out here."

The deputy sheriff followed Jeff into the house.

"I'm sorry I yelled at you. My family, they're not home. I'm concerned."

"You wanna sit down, Mr. Vinton?"

"Sure. What are you doing here, anyway?"

"I've been ordered by the court to serve these papers. They're for you."

"Am I being sued?"

"Yes. Here they are."

"Thanks," Jeff said, perplexed. The stark heading on the cover page immediately caught his attention: VINTON vs. VINTON.

"What is this?" he shouted, tears coming to his eyes, then flowing down his face.

"Didn't you know?"

Jeff was unable to respond.

"I went through this a year ago," the deputy said. "It's hell, but you'd better see an attorney. It's a wham-bang process in this state. There's nothing you can do about it."

"Where is she? I've got to talk to her!"

"I don't know."

Jeff was losing his ability to think, to cope. A numbness began to overcome him, but it did not dull the emotional pain. "I've got to see her!" he sobbed.

"I'm sorry. Are you okay?"

Jeff was immobilized. Then the noise was intolerable, the area directly before him hazy. He heard someone shout, followed by the staccato sound of the M60 pumping bullets into the green darkness below. He had difficulty breathing. His foot was on firm matter, but in a sickening way. It wasn't really solid. His foot was touching the black body bag. One more step. One more step on these goddamned bags. He just needed the energy to make one more step. But he could not move. He was in complete turmoil. Powerless. Impotent. He slumped to his hands and knees. A tall uniformed man was standing over him. His stomach muscles retched. Vomit spewed forth.

The deputy just shook his head. He turned toward the door then looked again at Jeff. "Better get a lawyer, pal."

Sometime later the stench of his vomit forced Jeff to get back on his feet. He opened a can of beer, gulped its contents, opened a window. The cold air was refreshing. He took off his suit coat and let it fall to the floor, then his shirt. He finished the beer, opened another, and walked to the bathroom where he grabbed a towel to wipe up his vomit.

Jeff couldn't stabilize. He looked in the medicine cabinet for some sleeping pills. There were none. He went to the bedroom to lie down. The bed smelled of her. He went to the living room couch, quietly crying. At four o'clock the next morning he rose and showered, made some coffee. He turned on the radio, but his sobbing increased after a few seconds of the soft music. He turned it off. At six-thirty a picture came on the television, then the anthem, the news, weather, commodity prices. It was a normal morning for the rest of the world. Everything was as if nothing had happened. He thought of Andrea, of little Ned, of the big kids. He cried some more. He called Gwen at eight o'clock. She asked what was wrong. Too ashamed to tell her, he said he was ill, that he wouldn't be in.

He began to fantasize. She had made a mistake, a terrible mistake! She'll change her mind! Why is she divorcing me anyway? What have I done? He went to the living room and picked up the divorce petition. Some of his vomit had dried on the cover sheet. He turned the pages until he came to the name of the legal firm. Her lawyer's name, Harold Carr, Esq., was at the bottom. Her lawyer? For Christ's sake, she's my wife. Why does she need a lawyer?

After getting the firm's number from information, he dialed the office. "Mr. Carr, please."

"I'm sorry. Mr. Carr is in court this morning. He should be back by ten."

"Okay. Ask him to call ..." The line went dead. Jeff felt powerless. He began crying again, then dressed. He made sure that all of the cigarette butts in the ashtrays were out and filled his coffee cup. A few minutes later, after brushing the snow from the agency car, he drove out of his way to avoid Flatwater. Two hours later he arrived at the building of office suites where her attorney worked. Entering, he told the receptionist he had to see Mr. Carr.

"Of course. May I tell him your name?"

"Vinton." A tear fell from his cheek.

"Please wait here." When she returned she asked, "Mr. Jeffrey C. Vinton?"

"Yes."

"Mr. Carr is unable to see you. He advises you to immediately retain counsel. Good day, Mr. Vinton."

"I want to know where my family is." Tears were flowing down his face.

"Your lawyer will assist you, sir. Good day!"

Jeff stood in front of her for a few minutes. She ignored him. He walked out of the office, down the hallway, saw a public restroom. He entered and relieved his built-up nasal pressure then splashed water on his face. His eyes were bloodshot. A rash had developed on his

367

forehead. He walked down the corridor lined with doors and frosted windows. On one was printed HENRY MUELLER ATTORNEY AT LAW. He walked in. He was with Mueller minutes later.

The lawyer quickly assessed Jeff's condition. "You look like you need some coffee."

"Yeah."

"I'll get us some."

Moments later he looked at Jeff again. "DWI?"

Jeff sipped his coffee. "No." He reached into his pocket and drew out the crumpled papers.

"These look soiled."

"I'm sorry."

"No problem." He glanced at the petition. "It's boilerplate, but let me look through it."

Jeff sipped his coffee

"I assume you don't want the divorce."

Jeff looked up, tears flowing down his face. Divorce? Divorce was anathema to him. Marriage and family were sacred. Families are forever. "No. I love her. We just had a baby. No." He saw Mueller for the first time. Old. Balding. He looked gentle.

"Well, you'd better prepare yourself, Mr. Vinton. I can't do anything to stop it." Mueller paused. "Unless there's a lot of property to divide, I can't delay it."

"Don't I have anything to say about it?"

"No.

"I have no rights?"

"Not to save your marriage, your family."

"Are you serious?"

"I'm afraid so."

"You mean if I commit a crime I have the full power of the Constitution behind me, but there's nothing I can do to save my family?"

Mueller shook his head. "I haven't heard it put that way, but no. You must understand. That which was probably never a consideration to you is soon to be a judicial mandate. What you evidently saw as impossible is now inevitable."

"Jesus Christ!"

"Have you slapped your wife around a bit?"

Jeff looked up, surprised. "No. Why?"

"It says here you're violent."

Jeff couldn't understand what was happening.

"Anyway, the judge has restrained you from seeing your wife or children. And you are to vacate your home."

"Why?"

"The judge has so ordered. It's the law."

"If I don't?"

"You'll be in contempt of court. That means a fine or imprisonment."

Jeff was unable to grasp this. His head was spinning. "Can you find out where my family is? I want to talk to them, to see them."

"Not if she doesn't want you to. The court has restrained you."

Jeff began crying again. This time he couldn't stop.

Mueller only looked at him. He could offer no encouragement. Nothing. Finally he asked, "Do you have a drinking problem?"

"No."

"Are you sure?"

"Yeah."

"Then I want you to do exactly as I say. First, go and have a couple of drinks. Have the bartender put some authority into them. Then go eat a big lunch. Then go see a movie. I want you to get your mind off this for a while. There's nothing you can do. Come back about four o'clock. In the meantime, I'll try to get some information."

Jeff followed the lawyer's instructions. He took the elevator to the street and walked into the cold air. He went several blocks until he saw a bar. He entered, sat on a bar stool, and ordered a drink.

Thirty minutes and three drinks later, he left. He was thankful for the numbness the alcohol afforded him. He had an early lunch then walked the streets until the cinema opened at one o'clock. At four o'clock he was sitting before Mueller.

"Your family - soon to be your ex-family - is okay," Mueller assured him. "They're home. Your wife doesn't want to see you. She showed the police the restraining order and will have you arrested. She'll put your clothing in suitcases and have them on the front porch tonight. Pick them up at precisely eight o'clock. She says she will need the car, to buy groceries, take the kids to the doctor, those sorts of things."

"I need the car to get to work."

"Where are you staying?"

"Nowhere. I mean I don't know."

"She says you can stay at the hotel in Flatwater."

Out of self-pity tears flowed again. "I can't believe she's doing this."

Mueller looked at Jeff with some sympathy. "We human beings have too many emotions, care too deeply, make too many commitments. We're the most vulnerable of God's creatures." Then he asked, "There isn't much property, huh?"

"No."

"I assumed not. It's on the docket for next week."

"So soon?"

"Yeah," the lawyer affirmed.

"There's nothing I can do to stop it?"

"No. Nothing."

"But my family!"

Mueller shook his head. "Forget it! You don't have a family."

Stunned, Jeff stared straight ahead for a few minutes. "I'm scheduled to go on a business trip. I'll cancel it."

"Why? You don't have to be in court. I can handle it for you. Where are you supposed to be?"

"In Washington."

"D.C.? What for?"

"Nothing important. I'll cancel it."

Mueller thought for a moment. "No matter what I do, she'll get your child. He's only an infant. And the other two, they're not yours anyway. You've no claim to them. Plus she'll get whatever property you've amassed. The court will give her that. So there's really no reason for you to be around. Why don't you get out of town? Go to Washington and have a good time."

Jeff just looked at Mueller.

"And I'll need a check from you in the amount of seven hundred dollars."

"What for?"

"A hundred for the cost of her filing the petition, a hundred for her attorney, and five hundred for child support."

"Why do I have to pay her attorney and the filing charges?"

"It's the law."

"I don't have it."

"Well, eventually you'll have to pay. Plus my fees, plus her attorney's fees."

"Christ, I think we're in debt real bad."

"You think? You mean you don't know?"

"No. Andrea insisted on handling our finances."

"I'll check to see how indebted you are. How much do you have?"

"About twenty dollars. I don't know how much is in the bank."

"The way this is unfolding, I suspect the account has been closed. She's probably opened a new account with the money in her name."

"Is that legal?"

"Yes." Mueller questioned him. "Why does she hate you so much?"

"I don't know. I didn't know she did."

***

"How many nights?" the motel clerk asked.

"Tonight and tomorrow."

"Cash or credit card?"

"I'll use my credit card."

"Okay. Let me have it. I'll run it through for you."

"Sure."

Once in the room, Jeff laid on the bed. He couldn't understand what was happening. And he was exhausted. His mind was still active, terribly restless. And his body felt strange. Numb. Nauseous. His stomach felt hollow, was cramping up. He began crying again, then he somehow fell asleep. An hour later he awoke. But nothing had changed. No! Everything had changed.

He went to the dresser. There was some stationery in the drawer. He wrote a note to Gwen, telling her he had an agency car, that he wasn't feeling well, that he would nonetheless go to Washington. He appointed Dave the acting director in his absence. He asked her to leave his travel check and airline tickets on his desk so he could pick them up tomorrow night. He told her not to contact him under any circumstances.

After dropping the note off at his office, he began driving toward his home. He pulled into a truck stop. His fatigue was overwhelming. He ordered some coffee and a hamburger. He looked at his watch. Six fifty. He was ten minutes from home. He drank the hot coffee, rubbing the rash on his forehead. This would be his first chance to see Andrea since she had left him at work yesterday morning. He would ask what he had done wrong. He would find out what the difficulty was. He would reason with her. Find out what the hell had happened. There's no reason for a divorce, no reason for this! He couldn't eat, but he had more coffee.

Driving down the highway, he noted his high beams reflecting off the snow. The low-pressure system had moved a bit east. The sky was still cloudy, the wind still from the southwest. The temperature was slowly rising even though the sun had set hours before. It would have been a pleasant evening. But the highway to his home was too familiar. Even the goddamned highway caused him pain.

He drove into the small community that had been their home. Tears flowed from his cheeks, onto his coat. He couldn't stop crying. He saw the headlights of a car behind him. He would reason with her. Maybe he hadn't been strong enough. He tried to stop crying, afraid it would reinforce her perception of his weakness. He drove down the street and parked before his house. It was dark except for the light over the front door where some suitcases had been placed. He saw that the car behind him had stopped, too. He turned off his car lights. The driver behind him did the same. He got out of the agency car and looked behind him. It was a police car. The officer remained in it.

Jeff walked to their home, stepped around the five suitcases and to the door. He twisted the doorknob. It was locked. All the drapes and shades were drawn. He rapped at the door. No one came. But the police officer had gotten out of his car and was walking toward Jeff. Jeff knocked harder at the door. The police officer was coming up the sidewalk. Jeff yelled, "Andrea, open the door!"

The officer tapped his shoulder. "Are you Vinton?"

"Yes," Jeff said.

"Are you aware of the restraining order?"

"Yes," Jeff repeated.

"Then pick up your suitcases and get the hell out of here before I arrest your ass."

"But this is my home."

"Goddammit, I heard what you've done to your wife and kids. If you want to beat up on someone, try me."

Jeff was unable to respond.

"You punks are all the same. Abuse your kids, beat up on your wives. But you're not man enough to fight a man. Move punk, or you're under arrest."

Like the walking wounded, Jeff carried three of the suitcases to the agency car and returned for the other two, the officer watching his every step. It was as if a bullet had hit him in the brain. Only he hadn't died yet. He wasn't even comatose. He could still function in a physical sense, but he knew he was clinically dead. He had died twenty-four hours ago.

He drove off, away from his home, away from his family.

CHAPTER THIRTY-THREE

Bill Sergent's secretary brought in the morning mail, smiling pleasantly as she handed it to him. At least this guy shows up in the morning, she thought. And he doesn't come back from lunch tipsy from martinis. Maybe this place might get going again. She waited while he looked over the mail. He was close to the governor, and that propinquity sure as hell couldn't hurt, she surmised. But, like Greg Allen, he doesn't have any staff. She recalled that during Dawson's administration as many as fifteen staff members worked in this office. But at this point this place is lucky to have him, she allowed.

"Anything important?" she asked.

"I don't know," Bill said. "Look at this."

The correspondence had the letterhead of the Health and Welfare Committee. It addressed the confirmation process for Sergent's appointment as director of the Department of Integrated Human Services. She scanned the letter. "Don't worry. It's their constitutional mandate, but they don't take it seriously."

"What do you mean?"

"How many of Elam's appointees failed to receive confirmation?" she asked.

Bill thought for a moment. "I can't think of any."

"Right. Mr. Allen didn't even need to go to a hearing. A senator came by the office and asked a few questions. He wasn't with Mr. Allen for more than ten minutes. The appointment was confirmed a week later."

"How did Allen feel about that?"

"Oh, he was relieved, of course."

"Do you suppose my appointment will be confirmed the same way?"

"I'm sure it will be."

Sergent fell into thought. His secretary remained by his desk. Then he asked, "Do you know anyone on that committee?"

"No. But a friend of mine lives with Senator John Dalmann who's on the committee.

"Is he a good friend?"

She smiled. "Yeah, she's a pretty good friend."

Bill smiled. "Forgive my naïveté. We may need a favor of her."

"Shouldn't be a problem. What's the favor?"

"Let me think it through. Okay?"

"Sure. We got a week before they'll come to see you."

"Oh, just a week?"

"About."

The short timeframe caused Sergent some concern. "Anything else?" he asked the secretary.

"Yes. One of the CAP directors was picked up by a state trooper - for DWI."

"Which one?"

"John Rediger. He's with the CAP way out west."

"Yeah. I know the name."

"The arrest record says Rediger threatened to have the trooper fired. He got abusive and told the officer he has friends high up in the government."

"Who'd he mean?"

"Greg Allen, I suppose. They're pretty close. Greg must have traveled out there a dozen times."

"I'd better advise the governor to tell Allen to stay the hell out of it," Sergent thought out loud.

"Anything else?" she asked.

"Yeah. Can you arrange a luncheon with your friend tomorrow?"

"Which friend?"

"The one living with the senator."

"I think so. Let me check."

"Good."

***

The secretary entered Sergent's office at two thirty the next afternoon. "Well, I did what you asked."

"Tell me about it."

"Well, after we ate, we had a few drinks. Then I said I'd better leave my car and walk back to the office so I wouldn't be picked up. I

375

chatted about the new alcohol safety program, the increase in arrests."

"You developed it just like that, huh?"

"Yes."

"Good. Go on."

"I pretended to be tipsier than I was. I mentioned that Nancy Hoffman, the director of DMV, had her license suspended. I said it was awkward for a person with that kind of driving record to head up DMV."

Sergent nodded.

"My friend said she hadn't seen it in the papers. I told her it had happened three months before her appointment. Then I mentioned the senate's sloppy work in its confirmation responsibilities."

"And then you dropped the subject."

"Yes. Just like you told me."

"Great. Thanks so much."

She was perplexed. She had followed Bill's instructions. She believed she deserved an explanation. "Why don't you like Ms. Hoffman?"

Bill looked up, surprised. "I do. She's a great gal."

"But then why ..."

"I've got a lot to do in the next few days. I'd better get to it."

Recognizing the obvious dismissal, she rose to leave.

Bill looked to her before she reached the door. "And thanks."

That didn't help. She had been used, and she knew she had jeopardized Nancy Hoffman's reputation, perhaps her job. She felt crummy.

She was busy for the next few days typing a speech that Sergent was going to make. Her boss possessed a flair for the spoken word. His phrases were compact and direct, his use of parallel structure effective. He was reaching for perfection. And throughout the speech was an undercurrent depicting the malaise in government. She recognized some of the phrases the governor had used. "... good people and good programs are often frustrated by bad mechanisms, by bad structure ..." Good clean language; not the inflated rhetoric that Allen had used so unsuccessfully.

Still, something was obviously missing from the final draft of Sergent's speech. She wondered who the hell this would be delivered to.

Another letter came from the chairman of the Committee on Health and Welfare. The letter directed Sergent to appear before the full committee at ten o'clock the following Monday morning. The full committee, she thought, not just a perfunctory visit from a committee member. Jesus Christ! Alarmed at this and the short time notice, she took the letter to Bill.

He read it, reached into his desk drawer, and took out several sheets of paper. "Please incorporate this at the beginning of my remarks," he said.

She returned to her desk and began typing:

"Mr. Chairman, distinguished Committee Members, my name is William P. Sergent. I understand my name has been presented to this Committee as director-designate of the Department of Integrated Human Services. I am honored to have received this appointment, and am pleased to be before this Committee. With the Chairman's kind permission, I would like to make a few introductory statements prior to receiving inquiries from the members.

"Initially, I would like to state that I view the legislative responsibilities of program oversight and appointee confirmation to be among your most critical.

"I consider myself privileged to be the subject of your confirmation duties and will welcome any scrutiny afforded my department should you honor me with confirmation.

"The matter of human services is a difficult element of government. The necessary programs that serve those without power, without prestige, without access to governmental policy have never been politically popular. Legislators and executives have too long given slight attention to these critical programs. Yet, the programs consume large amounts of the public sector's efforts and dollars. I am pleased to note that our Governor and this Committee are not satisfied to do that which is politically expedient, but indeed are willing to...

She kept typing. She realized he had contrived his appearance before the committee, and therefore was one shrewd sonofabitch. But why had he done this, she wondered?

**

The hearing room was filled when Sergent arrived. The statehouse pundits who had predicted this large turnout for the confirmation of the director of DIHS based it on two factors. First, this was to be the first full hearing given a director-designate in recent memory. It was, in fact, a legislative event. Second, there was an aura of mystery around Bill Sergent.

Those bureaucrats working in human services had heard his name from the early days of the administration. He was going to change their departments and was therefore the focal point of their conjectures and second-guessing. He was described as insensitive, uncaring, ill-advised; a PR man who dealt in the dishonest packaging and marketing of imperfect products, but an individual who was a formidable factor because of his association with the governor.

The word had quickly gotten around bureaucratic circles that Greg Allen was at best a joke, at worst a waste of taxpayers' money. The bureaucrats relaxed, secure in their knowledge that Allen was a buffoon. But now the architect of the reorganization plan had been appointed to implement that abstract plan. Concerns for their own futures prompted a large turnout of bureaucrats for this hearing.

The chairman conferred with Vice Chairman Hammond one last time, then seated himself and gaveled the hearing to order. The lobbyists and bureaucrats were slow to end their conversations, slow to move to their chairs.

"This hearing will come to order!" The chairman rapped the gavel several times. After he surveyed the hearing room, after the crowd had quieted, he spoke into the microphone. "This committee shall convene for the purpose of receiving testimony related to the confirmation of Mr. William P. Sergent as the director of the Department of Integrated Human Services. This committee has been advised by the Office of the Governor of the appointment of Mr. Sergent, and consistent with our constitutional authority and responsibility, I, noting that a quorum exists, call this hearing to order. As the first witness, I invite Mr. Sergent, the director-designate, to be seated before this committee. Is Mr. Sergent present?" The chairman was looking squarely at Bill as he asked the question.

Bill rose and walked to the table before the senators. He seated himself and adjusted the microphone.

"Is the director-designate willing to be sworn in?"

"I am, Mr. Chairman."

"Please rise and raise your right hand. Do you swear that the testimony you are to present to this committee to be the truth, the whole truth, and nothing but the truth, so help you God?"

"I do," Sergent swore.

"You may begin your prepared statement, Mr. Sergent."

"Thank you, Mr. Chairman. Mr. Chairman, distinguished committee members, my name is..."

Sergent spoke from his prepared remarks for a full twenty minutes. He had tailored his comments to indicate his enthusiastic support of consolidating all human services within one department, yet never did he say anything that be construed as disloyalty to his governor.

He sensed the interest of the senators in his comments and contempt from the bureaucrats behind him. First he felt their eyes boring into the back of his head. After a few minutes, however, he felt their antagonism dissipating, as if they began to understand what he was proposing. They even applauded a few times during the latter part of his remarks. When Sergent referred to a chart showing that nine federal nutrition programs were administered by eight different state agencies, he observed the initial surprise among the senators, then their awkward laughter moments later. When he completed his remarks, he sensed that some of the bureaucrats were supportive. He was not so sure about the committee members. He looked to the chairman and awaited the first question.

The senators were simply not prepared. Never in the few times that the committee had held confirmation hearings had a director-designate appeared with such an erudite yet understandable presentation. Finally Jake Hammond spoke. "Thank you, Mr. Sergent. What you have presented to this committee represents a broad and sweeping revamping of state government. Were your comments cleared by the governor?" He smiled at Bill as he awaited his response.

Sergent responded tersely to Hammond. "It has been my experience that the governor affords his appointees administrative flexibility."

"Is that your answer?" Hammond shot back.

"Yes, sir."

"Is the governor quite aware of this flexibility he has afforded his appointees?"

"Of course."

"I see," Hammond said, sitting back.

Senator Laura Philippi was next. "Mr. Sergent, is it your understanding that the reorganization effort is ongoing?"

"Yes, ma'am, consistent with the governor's timetable."

"And what is that timetable?"

"One requiring more than a year but to be accomplished with deliberate but prudent speed."

"Just about how fast is that?"

"The framework is there. It's just a matter of administrative and legislative action."

John Dalmann, the three-term senator from the Fourteenth District, first looked to Hammond and then cleared his throat. "This committee has tabled the reorganization bill," he said to Sergent. "Surely you are aware of that."

"Yes, sir."

"Then what in tarnation are you talking about?"

"That the governor and I realize that there were compelling, sound, and relevant reasons for the bill's initial submission and that these elements remain outstanding. That the remedy the bill offers continues to be relevant."

"This bill no longer offers anything," Dalmann countered. "It once did. It doesn't anymore. The bill is dead. But I wish to step away from the bill for just a second and ask you a very direct question. Is it your belief that the current structure of programs and services is faulty?"

"Generally speaking, yes. I thought that was the common perception," Sergent responded.

"The only common perception around here is the acknowledgment of your insatiable quest for power," Dalmann said sternly. "It wasn't good enough for you to be the governor's administrative assistant. No, young man, you had to contrive a super department, then posture yourself to assume the reins of that department. You, sir, have ill-served your governor, and your appointment is an insult to this committee." After he spoke he glanced at Hammond who benignly stared straight ahead.

Sergent stared back at Dalmann but could only manage a weak reply. "The senator is sadly and totally mistaken." He sat back, bewildered. He tried to understand where the undercurrent was and where it was taking him and who the hell was controlling the water gate.

It became obvious that his tactic to publicly press the governor to again support the reorganization bill had completely backfired. It had been a blunder. He had tried to use intrigue to achieve a goal that was no longer possible. His subtlety had failed. And the control factor had been deftly taken away from him. Hell, Sergent accurately reflected, he had never been the operative factor; only the fool.

"The senator has spoken unkindly to you, Mr. Sergent," Hammond said. "On behalf of this committee, I wish to apologize."

Sergent looked at Hammond but said nothing.

In a more mellow voice, Dalmann said, "I may have spoken a bit harshly, but opportunists get up my dander."

Sergent's dismay was obvious. "Senator, I assure you I was perfectly happy with my former job. I did not seek this position, and I was surprised when I was appointed. With the current configuration of state government, and with the climate that I'm witnessing, it appears to be an impossible job. It is true, nonetheless, that there may be opportunities. It is untrue that I am an opportunist."

"Is there something terribly unhealthy about the so-called 'climate' in this hearing room, Mr. Sergent?" Dalmann asked. A few chuckles surfaced from the audience.

Sergent became flushed. His voice was uneven. He became angry, too angry. "There is, Senator, a distinct and obvious miasma of mediocrity emanating from the entire human services provision system. In my few minutes before this committee, I have learned the origins of much of that malaise."

The hearing room was silent for just a few moments, then it erupted in pandemonium. The chairman rapped his gavel several times. It failed to quiet the clamor of the bureaucrats and lobbyists. Now nearly all of the committee members were attempting to be recognized. The cacophony of voices behind him and the committee members shouting before him upset Sergent's sense of balance. He felt dizzy, nauseous.

"Mr. Chairman. Mr. Chairman ..."

The chairman was unable to restore order. The government workers refused to shut up. Most of the senators were clamoring for a chance to be recognized, to gain the floor. Except for Jake Hammond. He was sitting back in his chair with a certain sense of contentment. "Malaise," he thought. "Miasma of mediocrity." Great stuff! Then he recalled how he had criticized the National Guard commander. A colonel, wasn't it? He couldn't remember. What was it he said? "Not even a modicum of mediocrity." "Miasma of mediocrity" was much better. He would have to remember that one. "Miasma of mediocrity." He wrote the expression on his pad.

Hot damn, he thought.

***

Governor Elam was expressionless as he turned off the speaker in his office. He had heard enough of the committee hearing.

Three days later, during its morning meeting, the committee voted 8-2 against the confirmation of William P. Sergent as director of the Department of Integrated Human Services. Senator Jake Hammond voted "present."

Elam called Sergent to his office that afternoon. "I'm sorry, Bill," he said.

"Wasn't your fault. It was my fault. The whole damned thing."

"What do you mean, the whole thing?" Elam asked.

"Nothing. Just that I blew it."

"Yeah."

Silence interrupted their conversation. Then Elam asked, "Well, what are you going to do now, Bill?"

"What do you mean?"

"Do you have another job lined up?"

"No. I thought ..." Sergent now realized his predicament. "No, I haven't. I'm ... I'm finished in state government, huh?"

Elam sadly shook his head, agreeing. "Do use me as a reference, won't you?"

"Sure."

***

Moments later, after Sergent had left, Hammond came in from the adjacent office, a broad grin on his face. "You know, those confirmation hearings are a lot of fun. The committee should have them more often." He winked at Elam. "Now let's break out that Napoleon brandy, Bobby-boy."

"Why not?" Elam agreed, going to the liquor cabinet.

CHAPTER THIRTY-FOUR

The aircraft had climbed steeply then banked left after taking off from Jackson City. Jeff Vinton had a window seat in the back of the main cabin. The two other seats in that row were unoccupied, and he felt lucky to be alone. The sky grew lighter as he stared out the window, then it turned blue seconds later as the plane rose above the cloud cover. Jeff put on the sunglasses he had purchased at the airport. His eyes were still red, the flesh around them still puffy from the tears that continued to fall. The sunglasses hid those signs of his sorrow from the flight attendant when she brought him coffee and a piece of pastry. The aircraft would touch down briefly at Lambert, then fly nonstop to National Airport in Washington, D.C. Jeff placed his seat in the reclining position and tried to sleep.

The five mismatched pieces of luggage were now in the belly of the aircraft. He no choice but to bring all of them with him and had no idea what Andrea had put in them. He would sort out the contents at the hotel. He hoped that Andrea had laundered his clothing.

It was a good thing he had cashed his travel advance last night because he had needed the money to pay his motel bill after the clerk had told him his credit card was over the limit. He was dumbfounded. What the hell had she been buying? After paying his bill, he had ninety fewer dollars for the two weeks in Washington.

Gwen had been concerned when he had called and told her to have someone pick up the agency car at the airport. Don't worry, he told her. Everything was fine.

What was little Ned doing now? He really hadn't had the time to get to know his son. How the hell do you get to know an infant? Would he ever get to know him? Did he have any control over where his son would live? Who he would live with? How he would live? Would he be consulted? Consulted? It was his son! Jesus Christ!

And how would Andrea live? And with whom? Could he face the man Andrea would choose next? When she died, who would she rest beside? And why was she doing this? What had he done to cause this? What the hell was going on?

The aircraft leveled off at twenty thousand feet. Jeff felt momentarily detached from his predicament. He stretched his legs. He thought of Andrea, her soft eyes, her high cheekbones, her demure yet substantial smile. He wanted to ask her one simple question: "Why?" He wanted to shout it. But she was too far away. He could not reach her – or touch her.

He thought of the gaping hole in the paratrooper's chest. He had wanted to touch him, too, to restore life to that lifeless mass just as he now wanted to restore life to his marriage. But everything was untouchable, he realized, once life had departed.

His mind lingered on the concept of death and its finality. Suicide? Death? It was an option. But was it viable? He thought for a few moments, considering this contrived convolution. Yes, he decided. It was viable. He dozed for a few minutes. His tears awoke him. He raised his hand, rubbing the tears into his skin, into the flesh of his face. What was he doing on this goddamned aircraft? He felt trapped within it. He had the urgent need to rid himself of it. He should be trying to see Andrea!

The sheriff.

To call Andrea!

An unlisted telephone number by now.

To touch Andrea!

Too far. Can't reach her.

To write Andrea!

Yes. That was it, he decided. He would write her.

Jeff fell asleep minutes before the aircraft began its descent into St. Louis. He awoke as the cabin pressure changed. He hadn't gotten much sleep since Andrea had dropped him off at his office; the last time he had seen her. He was exhausted, but his mind couldn't rest. There was no reason for his predicament. He remembered the reasons the ADC mothers told him. He hadn't done any of those things. If only he could let her get into his mind. If he could just speak to her. Let her know how much he still loved her. And maybe he could get into her mind. Make some sense of things. He looked out the window after the plane landed, watching the snow fall.

Some passengers had gotten off. More were now boarding. The two seats next to him were occupied. Jeff readjusted his sunglasses and faced the window. He pretended to sleep to discourage the inevitable and inane chatter that occurs between airline passengers. He stayed that way until the plane landed at National Airport.

Jeff watched the cab driver load his mismatched luggage. He wished Andrea had given him his own luggage. This stuff must have been Ned's and Joyce's. Jesus Christ, he thought.

Jeff watched the meter in the cab, wondering when they would reach his destination. He recognized a few of the landmarks from the airport, but now they were traveling northeast along the beltway. "Just where is Gaithersburg?" he finally asked.

"You don't know?" the cabbie replied. He was an Iraqi or an Iranian or something.

"No, I don't."

"It's up in the Maryland countryside."

"Oh."

Later, Jeff carried the suitcases to his room and began opening them. He stopped. It was too painful. He walked to the cocktail lounge. He signed the bar bill in an alcoholic haze four hours later. He did not remember the amount.

***

Using his gavel, Fr. Dunn called the emergency meeting of the Community Action Program's board of directors to order. Gwen soberly called the roll then advised the chair that a quorum was present.

Fr. Dunn announced that the requisite number of directors had requested this meeting and thus, in accordance with the bylaws, the meeting was in order. He then stated the meeting's purpose: to discuss the status of the agency's executive director.

He called for discussion. No one spoke. "Dammit, I would think those directors who requested this meeting would let the rest of us know what it's all about," Fr. Dunn admonished.

After a brief silence, a woman's voice from the far end of the table said, "Come on, Father, we all know what's going on."

Fr. Dunn sighed. "Okay, for the record, why don't you inform us."

Ruth Chaney had made the error of speaking first. Now she had to follow up. "Through sundry means – you can't keep secrets in these hills – we know Jeff is undergoing considerable personal duress. We're fearful that his judgment will be impaired because of these severe troubles. The reason we requested this special meeting is our concern for the well-being of the agency."

It was clear that Chaney, who represented Montgomery County, had said what the others were thinking. She sat back.

No one spoke.

Ruth felt the need to keep the discussion flowing. "Some time ago I went through a divorce. I was immobilized for months. In fact, it was over a year before I could cope with it."

Another member of the board spoke up. "We can't have a director who's incapacitated. We've made too much progress in these past months. We can't regress."

"So what do you recommend?" the chair asked.

Again no one spoke.

Jack Geis from Johnson County joined in. "Let's face some facts. This agency is located on an Indian reservation surrounded by farming communities that are among the poorest in the state. We've never done a good job serving the poor, although that's been the agency's purpose and mandate. These folks need an effective agency, one they haven't had until very recently. And thanks to Jeff, we've made considerable progress."

"Yes," Fr. Dunn concurred. "We owe him a lot."

"But he could undo all the good he's done," Chaney persisted.

"And pigs might fly, but we don't know that," the chair retorted. "Let's find out if all this undoing you speak of is really gonna happen."

"This ain't personal," Chaney snapped back. "It's business. He may not be able to run this place if he is suffering from extreme depression."

"You're suggesting a temporary leave of absence?" the chair asked.

"Maybe longer than temporary," said a muffled voice from down the table.

"I can't believe I heard that," Fr. Dunn said.

"It represents the point of view some of us think is necessary."

Realizing things were approaching an irrational consensus, the chair looked for a voice supporting Jeff. Most of the directors looked down, not wanting to be called on. None spoke.

"I can't believe this is happening. We're all just sitting around, unwilling to defend our director," Fr. Dunn observed. "Maybe that's because he's done nothing wrong and doesn't need defending," the Jesuit continued. "And yet, there's an unwholesome undercurrent here I don't understand. What the hell has Jeff done to deserve this?" demanded Fr. Dunn, his eyes going from director to director.

"Wait a minute, Father," said Harold Jameson from Caldwell County. "We all like Jeff. We all appreciate what he's done. It's out of respect for him that we don't want these positive things undone."

The meeting went on for two more hours. At its conclusion, a motion was made and passed. It was Chairman Dunn's chore to inform Jeff of the board's decision.

***

"... during this two-week period, we – you and I – will deal with the following training modules. The first two-day period we'll examine the authorizing legislation. We'll examine testimony given at hearings before the congressional committees and try to determine not only what the law says, but delve into the intent of the law. What were the congressmen and senators thinking as they deliberated ..."

Jeff tried to remember when he and Andrea had last made love. He could not. Huge blocks of memory were gone.

"... we'll examine the demonstration programs upon which Congress patterned the community action agencies. We'll discover the dichotomy operative during this period of deliberation. Should the CAPs become politically active? Or should they serve as clearinghouses for services, or even one-stop marketplaces for programs? A large number of congressmen wanted the CAPs to examine the existing power structures within the communities and confront those structures. We'll attempt to make judgments in regard to their actual intent ..."

Jeff had no idea how much money Andrea had when she filed for divorce. It couldn't have been much. How were they eating? Of course they always bought most of their groceries right after payday. Still, what if little Ned needed medical care?

"... we'll help you inventory those existing programs in your communities. When you leave here you will know which federal assistance programs will meet which needs of the poor. Now, no matter where you live, these programs exist. You might have to travel a hundred miles in a rural area to get to the local office, but they exist and the programs are there to help the poor ...”

Jeff suddenly felt guilty. He should have left some of his travel advance with Andrea in case of an emergency.

“... now who are the poor? Well, there’s the working poor and the nonworking poor. Let’s take the nonworking poor first. Who are they? Well, generally, they are the aged, the blind, the disabled, the dependent children and their custodians. The nonworking poor are more easily organized for community action. Why? Because they’ve got time on their hands. That’s why! Amazingly, the aging is one group that community organizers ignore. Yet the aging are becoming politically active. You’ve heard of the Gray Panthers ...”

Jeff was daydreaming about Andrea; her blonde hair, her sipping coffee on a Sunday morning, her getting breakfast on the table...

“... so these adverse economic factors cause dad some problems. He’s out of work, no money coming in, low self-esteem. This situation is a hotbed for child and spousal abuse, for incest, for street drug use, for alcohol abuse. He slaps mom around a bit, beats her up. He fondles his daughter, or forces her to sexually submit to him. He’s usually drunk. But, man, that don’t matter ...”

Just what the hell is their financial situation? He remembered the phone calls from the credit departments. His credit card was two hundred dollars over the limit. He had tried to find out how deeply in debt they were.

“... to protect herself, her kids, mom’s got to get out of the house. Where does she go? No money! A broken-down car. No nearby relatives. Where does mom take the kiddies? How does she manage this? ...”

This is all a bunch of nonsense. Andrea will snap out of it! She just needs some time. Everything will be okay!

“... by now, dad’s got this other little cutie on the string. He could care less about mom and the kids. Now this cutie has moved in. Why not? Mom and the kids were forced out ...”

It was at this moment that Jeff decided he would be magnanimous. He would forgive her. But he would warn her: Never again!

That defense mechanism served Jeff well. He ignored his own reality for the next few days and went dumbly on with his life. He attended all of the training sessions and actively participated. One afternoon, when the instructors listed programs available to the victims of runaway fathers, Jeff surprised them by identifying several more. In the evenings Jeff joined the trainees in the lounge. He joined in their discussions, their jokes, their laughter. One evening Jeff thwarted the advances of an attractive director from Kentucky. He did so by speaking of his wife and children. She gracefully accepted his situation and moved on to a director from Idaho. Jeff resented the idea that she was on the make while wearing a wedding band and ignoring his. It did not sit well with his sense of propriety.

Days passed. Jeff blissfully shut out his real world and escaped into the training environment. But then on Thursday he was told he had received an emergency call. The message read: "Call Mr. Mueller, ASAP."

Minutes later in his room he made the call. "Mr. Mueller? This is Jeff Vinton."

"Oh, yes, Mr. Vinton. Thanks for returning my call."

"She withdrew, didn't she?" Jeff asked hopefully. "She withdrew the petition!"

"No. I'm sorry, Jeff. That's not the reason I called." Mueller paused. "I want you to know we go to court tomorrow afternoon at four o'clock."

"We go to court," Jeff repeated flatly.

"I negotiated the best deal I could. Now it's just a matter of the court approving it. Of course they always do. But let me go through the details to get your approval. It's not good, but it's what we got. After you okay it, and I advise you to do so, I'll use the power of attorney you granted me to sign on your behalf. That way, you won't have to come back."

The sham of his escape was over. The ugly reality and the sickening feeling returned along with the tears and the shock of what was happening to him. He was speechless. No thought would formulate in his mind. Finally he asked, "Did I give you that authority?"

"Hell yes you gave me that authority. We discussed it for twenty minutes which, incidentally, cost you eighty dollars. For Christ's sake,

Vinton, get hold of yourself."

Jeff was unable to do that. Instead, he replaced the telephone in its cradle, sat on the bed, and wept. Mueller called back, but Jeff let the phone ring. He made a call two hours later. After several delays, he was told it was possible. Depart Dulles at 7:00 a.m. A half-hour layover in St. Louis, an hour layover in Tulsa, arrival Jackson City at two thirty.

"Book me."

The drab Jackson City airport only deepened his depression. The afternoon's court action would strike profoundly at the most basic of his tenets: Family. Marriage. They were about to be severed by an arbitrary, perfunctory action of the court: The inviolable to be routinely violated.

His family was no longer a private matter. It was to be put on public display, the records bureaucratically categorized and housed with all the other decrees, dutifully maintained in the court's depositary. "...that the plaintiff is predisposed to violence..." Jesus Christ, he thought.

He placed his luggage in a forty-eight hour locker, then got into a Holiday Inn courtesy van that happened to be parked outside the terminal.

The Holiday Inn was on the outskirts of town. He could catch a city bus downtown. He looked at his fellow passengers in the van, especially a couple about the age of himself and Andrea. Jeff was angered that they were happy and in love; that he was en route to witness the death of his marriage, the dissolution of his family. He remembered resenting the laughter of a couple on the airplane. Christ, he thought, I'm cracking up. But the world was no longer nice. It had taken on a distinct ugliness. It had become cruel and heartless. He looked at the couple again. He resented their sitting so closely together and holding hands. He wanted to strike them.

Jeff allowed the other passengers to get off the van before he did. He lingered outside the motel for a moment and then walked through the crowded lobby to the coffee shop. Minutes later, after gulping down his coffee, he stepped outside. The bus arrived within minutes.

He was standing outside the courthouse twenty minutes later. The sun was low, hidden by the gray sky. Light snow was falling. Darkness was approaching. It was an ugly afternoon. He entered the building and went to the Domestic Affairs Court. Each step depleted his reservoir of self-discipline. Tears filled his eyes. He wished he were going to court for some other reason: armed robbery, murder, treason. But it was for the termination of his marriage and family. Would he ever see little Ned again? He remembered the predicament of Andrea's first husband who hadn't been able to see his children. Why should he be any different?

Walking down the corridor, he noted the ubiquitous, easily identifiable bureaucrats – employees of the court. He saw several women in the company of men who he presumed were their attorneys. He looked into the courtroom hoping to see Andrea. She wasn't there. He leaned up against a wall. He felt crummy. His whole life, all he had worked for was being shattered. How can one person destroy a family? Shouldn't a mutual willingness be required?

He saw Andrea. She was accompanied by a man who Jeff assumed was her attorney. What was his name? Jeff couldn't remember.

He walked toward her.

She saw him approaching out of her peripheral vision. Then, for a moment, their eyes locked together. Tears flowed from Jeff's soul.

Andrea looked away, then stared blindly ahead.

"I love you," Jeff said loudly, approaching her.

Andrea didn't say anything. She kept walking.

"I love our children!"

She ignored him.

Jeff stood in front of the door to the courtroom, his face wet with tears. "I don't want a divorce. I love you!"

Andrea looked at Jeff. Her jaw tightened. He noted her teeth's jagged appearance for the very first time. Her face was dark and contorted. A coldness flowed from her. Jeff was amazed at how effectively she had hidden this facet of her personality from him. "That's tough," she said. "That's really tough!"

Then Jeff felt a hand on his shoulder. He turned. It was Mueller.

"For Christ's sake, Jeff, step aside! There's a restraining order against you. For Christ's sake!"

Like the demise of many entities, this one didn't take long. The days that preceded the event had already exacted their immeasurable toll. And the pain that would follow this administrative death could not be calculated. Jeff knew it would not soon abate.

Andrea took the witness stand and identified herself. She stated her place of residence, stated the marriage had been irretrievably and irrevocably broken. The judge, cloaked in his black robe, ignored Jeff's sobs. He declared the marriage dissolved. It took less than five minutes.

The judge granted Jeff visitation rights to little Ned. Then he rose and returned to his chambers. It was his last divorce proceeding for the day.

It was over. In this instance the bureaucracy had worked well. Vinton's marriage was no more, his family divided. The bureaucrats had easily accomplished this trivial, this insignificant, this ugly bit of business. Jeff rose and left the courtroom, placing in his breast pocket a thick envelope Mueller had given him.

He was numb, walking in a daze on the long sidewalk through the falling snow. He barely heard the voice calling his name. Then the voice was louder. Jeff turned. It was Fr. Dunn, the CAP's board chairman. Vinton stopped. No tears fell from his eyes. There was no expression. It was like that time when the CO got knocked off and the exec had been evacuated with a head wound and the battalion XO had told Jeff to take charge of the company. It was up in II Corps. Six days of ongoing, intensive combat. Thirty percent causalities. Yet the XO's order was so matter-of-fact.

"Hey, Vinton, I've got to see you," Fr. Dunn said again. "Are you all right?"

"Yeah."

"They called me from Washington. Told me you had left. And I've been following your legal difficulties in the *Court Reporter.* And..."

"What's that," Jeff asked, not really caring.

"Just a limited-circulation newspaper. For lawyers, bill collectors, slumlords. Anyway, we've got to talk."

"Okay."

"When?"

"Now."

"You sure you're okay?"

"Sure."

They walked to the chairman's car. "You want a drink or something?"

"No."

They were silent while driving down the highway. They ignored the evening news story that that Governor Robert T. Elam had indicated interest in the Third Congressional District seat. Neither of them was interested. They arrived at the rectory twenty minutes later. The snowstorm intensified as the northeast wind became strong and persistent. They entered the Jesuit's quarters. Jeff stared out the living room window, watching the snow fall, while Fr. Dunn made coffee.

"Let's have a seat," he said as he handed Jeff a cup.

"Sure."

"Jeff, you've only been here a short time, but you've brought the agency a long way."

Jeff looked at the priest, saying nothing.

"The board of directors is very concerned about you."

Jeff sipped his coffee.

"What I'm saying is a tribute to you."

Jeff placed the cup back on the saucer.

"And the staff you've recruited, especially Dave and George. Right now, they're critical to the agency."

Jeff nodded.

"But the board can't let the agency regress. It's too important to too many people."

"Right," Jeff said.

"I've seen what divorce can do to people. It can absolutely immobilize them."

Jeff nodded. He was in no position to argue the point.

"It's been difficult, hasn't it? The divorce, I mean."

A tear rolled down Jeff's check. He wiped it away.

"We need a person to sustain the progress you've made, the growth of the agency."

"Yeah."

"I can see you're in no shape."

Jeff sighed, lit a cigarette.

"You used an agency vehicle for personal use. You left a seminar before its completion. We could outright fire you."

"What do you want from me?"

"The board has directed me to grant you two months termination pay. Then you can apply for unemployment insurance if you haven't found work."

"You're firing me."

The priest placed his hand over his forehead. "How about we agree that your resignation is in the agency's best interests?"

Jeff was unable to think clearly. Nothing mattered anymore anyway. "Okay," he said.

"It's best, Jeff."

"Sure." Jeff looked down at the floor, then asked, "Could you give me a ride to a motel?"

"Of course. But there is something else."

"Oh?"

"The staff has kept me advised of Mrs. Vinton's relationship with the agency. She applied for ADC, MA, food stamps, and the WIC program. She took and then quit a CETA job. She's applied for unemployment and disability insurance at the same time. She's really screwed up, Jeff."

Jeff resented what he was saying about his wife. Then he remembered she wasn't.

"And, Jeff, she's seeking an abortion through the local family planning unit. Isn't that a helluva name for such an abattoir?" He looked squarely at Jeff. "I suppose you know how I feel about the killings of these innocents."

Jeff said nothing. The numbness, the shock was protecting him, his mental balance. But he couldn't stop the tears, the sobbing. He didn't know Andrea was pregnant again. Now, his unborn child was to be butchered by his wife and an abortionist. He could only stare blindly at nothingness.

Fr. Dunn looked at him. "I'm sorry. I shouldn't have mentioned all this."

"Got any bourbon?" Jeff asked.

"Yes, of course. May I get you a drink?"

Jeff nodded. "Just neat, please."

Jeff finished the two ounces of bourbon the priest had poured. "I suppose you've something for me to sign?"

The chairman lowered his head. "I'll get it."

Jeff signed his resignation. Then he said, "I'd better be going."

"Sure. And here's your termination check. Now, where are you staying?"

"I don't know. My luggage is at the airport. But anywhere in Jackson City is okay."

"Of course."

Jeff checked into a motel after they retrieved his luggage, and he thanked Fr. Dunn for the ride. The chairman told Jeff to call him any time. Then, awkwardly, he thanked Jeff for his work. They shook hands.

The act of leaving Jeff alone at a cheap motel room during his time of extreme despair stood in stark contrast to everything the priest believed in. But to offer comfort and sympathy to someone you had just fired didn't make sense either. The poor guy has lost his family, now his job. He's left with little or nothing to hold on to. What a goddamned lousy thing I've done, the priest thought. It wouldn't have been quite so bad if Jeff had been a sonofabitch, but to do this to a decent human being was unconscionable.

The governing board could have called Jeff in, assessed his situation, then either kept him on or fired him. Instead, they washed their hands of any personal or collective accountability or involvement. They made and passed a motion for immediate dismissal, then had the chairman do the dirty work – the guy who had spoken against and then voted against the damned motion. Christ!

Well, to hell with the board, to hell with the agency, to hell with it all. Fr. Dunn felt crummy and, for the first time in his life, he felt amoral.

Tears fell from his face.

***

Jeff stretched out on the bed. He opened the thick envelope Mueller had given him. On the first page was a list of outstanding debts. Jeff's eyes traveled down the list. There were five oil companies, then the department stores, the credit union, medical and dental offices. Then a list of sundry bills, including one from a photographer's studio. Jeff wondered what that was about. And so many more, all past due, all requiring payments. Then the total amount. It was far more than Jeff had imagined. The last sentence read: "These are your obligations under the terms of the decree."

"Jesus Christ!" He turned to the next page.

Here was listed the total amount owed the two attorneys, the monthly support payments. Jeff read the last paragraph of Mueller's letter. "The support payments are incorporated in the court's decree and are exempt from any bankruptcy petition you may make. Other items of indebtedness may be subject to provisions of federal bankruptcy laws. May I suggest you contact me at your earliest opportunity? Now that I am fully aware of your level of indebtedness, I can petition the court to..."

Jeff turned to the last pages, the decree. He noted that Mueller had exercised his power of attorney by signing for him. Tears falling, Jeff reviewed the terms of the divorce. He reflected for a moment. It is, I suppose, a realistic settlement. Andrea hasn't much of an education, she isn't working, has no resume.

Then the full import of his situation struck him.

He had been thrust from his home, barred from seeing his family, subjected to a divorce he didn't want, and would probably never see his son again.

Several things occurred to Jeff the next morning as he sat sipping coffee at a café.

He would have to get an apartment. He couldn't see his friends – at least for a while. He couldn't handle that. He should leave the area, apply for a job somewhere west of here; where Andrea's presence couldn't haunt him so much.

Jeff then reviewed his professional achievements.

His military service had been honorable, but it hadn't been an honorable venture in which he was involved, that Vietnam business. The public's perception had changed, had soured, had turned against the war. It was now conventional wisdom that all who had been there were space cadets, murderers, and probably mentally unsound. His military record probably wouldn't help him very much.

But in Harney County he had done well by making welfare programs work. He had gotten assistance for the aged, the blind, the disabled, and dependent children. He had helped to feed the old, the lame, and the kids. And he'd helped to house and clothe them. He had used his administrative skills to get the job done – there as well as in Flatwater. He possessed good administrative skills. Damn good administrative skills! He had been a successful advocate for those without access, without power, without a voice. He had placed the poor on welfare so that they might experience a little dignity within their drab lives. This was truly God's work. He thought of Dee and her kids, of Donny, of Lisa and her children, and all the other kids. He had made life better for a hell of a lot of people, he thought smugly.

Then he recalled an expression from his tour in Vietnam: "It don't mean nothin'!"

And he was struck by a terrible irony. Now little Ned, his own son, was a dependent child. On welfare. He had become a bureaucratic number among all the other bureaucratic numbers, with all the other dependent children. Little Ned was a beneficiary of the WIC program and the food stamp program and the medical assistance program and the...

Jesus Christ! Little Ned! His son!

Jeff wiped the tears from his face and sipped the last of his coffee. He had advocated for these programs. But he always thought his family was immune, somehow above, somehow superior to those programs' purposes.

Jesus Christ, he lamented. It was almost a prayer – but for what?

He checked out of the motel and awkwardly walked with his suitcases to the bus depot. He was bound for the capital city two hours later.

Jeff was troubled throughout the entire trip, suffering from a deep philosophical dilemma. Andrea had used the welfare system, the system he had advocated, as a means to achieve divorce.

Then the vast ramifications of what he had professionally done, what he had philosophically stood for, totally and devastatingly impacted him.

Had he, by advocating for the poor, by instituting new programs, by making these programs readily and easily accessible...

Had he, all this time, been facilitating the dissolution of families?

Jesus Christ!

CHAPTER THIRTY-FIVE

Jeff Vinton found himself passing the Plainsmen Hotel while aimlessly walking the capital city's streets. The pain recurred. He remembered the long trip from Union. It was so long ago: Andrea's relentless pain, the doctors' inconclusive findings.

Those were not good times, but they were better than these times. Jeff became sad when he reminisced too much about that part of his life. Tears were forming now.

He thought of the hotel's lounge. He had gotten a drink there. He remembered its darkened ambience. It would be a good place to ensconce himself to get through this oncoming bout of sadness. He passed through the hotel's lobby to the lounge and took a seat at the bar. He ordered a beer and surveyed the place. Then he remembered the loud voice, the boisterous laughter, the two women, and his first encounter with Greg Allen.

The place was nearly empty, only one guy sitting at the end of the bar. The bartender brought his beer. "Haven't seen you before. You from around here?"

"I'm kinda passing thru." Jeff sipped his beer.

The bartender mindlessly wiped away the wet ring caused by Jeff's glass. "I'm Joe."

"Hi, Joe. You know, I was in here once before, a long time ago. I remember some folks seemed to be getting ready for a ménage a trois."

"Oh yeah. That could have been Senator Allen – before he became a senator."

"How is the senator?" Jeff's interest heightened.

"I don't talk much about my customers. Not my style. See the guy at the end of the bar? He used to work with Allen." Joe looked down the bar. "Hey, Bill. This guy wants to talk with you."

Sergent didn't look up. He still hadn't gotten over his fall from grace or the summary dismissal of his plan. What a waste! He stared at his drink. "What about?"

Jeff picked up his beer and walked over to him. "My name's Jeff Vinton."

Sergent looked up, his forehead creased with curiosity. "Why do I know your name?"

"Don't know," Jeff replied.

"You from around here?"

"No. I used to live in Union, then Flatwater. But that was a long time ago."

"Oh yeah." Sergent looked hard at him. "Now I know why I know your name. How's things?"

"Not so good."

"Why not?"

"Long story," Jeff replied

"Lot of that going around."

Sergent's face looked tired and drawn, but Jeff recognized him from the many news photographs. "You were the governor's AA, weren't you?"

"A long time ago."

"What happened?"

Sergent again stared at his drink. "A lot of not-so-good things. Long story."

"A lot of that going around."

Sergent nodded.

Both were silent. Sergent looked away from Jeff, wanting to be alone.

Jeff finished his beer, looked at Sergent. "Try to remember," he said, recalling another place, another time. "It don't mean nothin'."

Sergent nodded. "Don't mean nothin'."

***

The months passed slowly and painfully. The healing benefit of time hadn't taken hold. And now Jeff had to endure this cold and rainy autumn alone. Even the winds from the south were chilling and conspiratorial, the oncoming grip of winter all too apparent.

Snow was mixing with rain as Jeff left the aging building where he had taken a one-room apartment in a rundown neighborhood. He lit a cigarette before securing the top button of his sun-faded army fatigue jacket. He had ripped off his nametag, the 173rd Brigade and U.S.

Army patches. The points of his collar that had been protected from the tropical sun by his lieutenant's bars were especially prominent.

He had thought of himself as a winner. He realized he was not. He had been an officer and a gentleman. Now he was unemployed, nearly bankrupt, a bum. He stopped dressing in his business suits, shirts with buttoned-down collars, Windsor-knotted ties. The weekly trips to the employment office were not encouraging. There were no jobs. The nation was in an economic recession. Jeff's individual plight seemed to reflect the overall depressed state of mind.

He went to a bank to cash his unemployment check. His rent was forty dollars a week. That left $103.00 for everything else. It was not what he had expected from life, but he was getting by. He even managed to buy – and register – an old Dodge from an elderly woman who needed the cash more than she needed the car.

He returned to his apartment. There was nothing to do but to do nothing. Little Ned would soon be two years old. Jeff had bought a stuffed giraffe for him but didn't know where to send it. Andrea had been moving around since the divorce. Jeff thought of calling the district court to get her most recent address, but that would be a long-distance call. Besides, the bureaucrat wouldn't tell him. She'd just ask why he hadn't made the full child support payments these past months. Jeff tried to remember what little Ned looked like. He couldn't. He tried to nap.

He was awakened about an hour later by the pounding on his door. It was the landlady telling him he had a call. He walked to the end of the corridor and picked up the telephone. "This is Jeff."

"It's me, Jeff."

Her voice overpowered him. "Where are you? Where's little Ned? Is he okay? Are you okay?"

"You're behind in your support payments."

"I'm sorry. I haven't been able to find work."

"We need the money." Her voice was soft, just as before.

"There are no jobs around here."

"Then go where they are."

Jeff didn't respond. Tears were forming. Moments of silence ensued.

"I can do you a favor," she said.

"Don't," Jeff said flatly.

"Just listen. It makes sense. The guy I'm with, he wants to marry me. His divorce will be final in about three weeks."

"Congratulations," Jeff said bitterly.

"He wants to adopt my children."

"Not little Ned," Jeff said desperately, tears again freely flowing. "He's my son."

"My lawyer says you've abandoned him. He can make a case for it. You're not paying child support, I mean."

"I'm sending what I can. I don't have that much."

"Don't you see, if you'll just give up little Ned, you won't have to pay any more support." She paused. "Will you relinquish your parental rights to Ned? It's in his best interest. That's the only reason I ask."

"Go to hell!" He jammed down the telephone, returned to his room, put on his fatigue jacket, and walked out into the rain. He walked a mile before he realized how badly he needed a drink. He walked into the first bar he saw.

***

Jeff paused before the door. The goddamned welfare office, he thought. I've come full circle. He considered the possibility that the staff would recognize his name. Andrea's and little Ned's names would undoubtedly be on the state welfare files somewhere.

He was still ashamed that he was divorced. So what? he asked himself. Everyone is divorced these days. Nonetheless, he released his grip on the door. He was already late. What difference would a few more minutes make? He stepped back outside. It was blustery. The strong wind in his face was opposing his every step. Continuing to resist this mindless force, he questioned himself. He was going nowhere, just aimlessly walking. Why not, he thought, walk with the wind? Why not join the forces of the universe, be in concert with them, flow easily with them? Why continue to oppose these things? Jeff walked on, into the wind.

Unknowingly, he had walked three blocks toward the city's business district. The wind was keeping his eyes dry, but he nevertheless avoided eye contact with those he encountered. He hungered for a cigarette. Reaching into his shirt pocket, he drew one out and looked for a sheltered area to light it.

A recessed doorway was immediately ahead. He stepped into the wide entrance and saw that it led to a photographer's studio. He knew that because a framed photograph rested on an easel inside a display window. A spotlight illuminated the photograph of a smiling couple and their three children. The husband and wife were beaming, obviously filled with joy.

Jeff turned away from the photograph. He carefully replaced the cigarette in the pack and stepped back onto the sidewalk. This time he walked with the wind.

He patted down his disheveled hair as he reentered the lobby he had left a few minutes before. He looked for a restroom but couldn't find one, then looked at his reflection in the plate glass window. Satisfied, he entered the office, walking to the receptionist. "I've an appointment with Mrs. Edelmann. My name's Vinton."

"Her office is third on the left down that hallway." She turned in her chair, pointing to the corridor. "She's pissed because you're late."

Jeff thanked the receptionist and walked to Mrs. Edelmann's office. He knocked on her door.

"Yeah, what is it?" The voice was not unfriendly.

He opened the door and entered. "I'm Jeff Vinton."

"You're late, but come in."

"Thank you."

"Sit down."

"Thanks."

"I can't believe you're here."

She was a stern-looking woman. She reminded Jeff of Agnes Moore.

"How's that?" he asked.

"Well, you were a welfare director, I see."

"Yes, that's right."

"An officer in the army. Decorated. Then most recently, a CAP director."

"That's right."

"And now you're here."

"Yeah."

"Hard times?"

"Hard times," he affirmed.

"Well, I can't offer you much."

"I really want the job."

"Okay. If I hire you, you'll be an intake worker; the first to see the clients. You'll have to assess their needs and refer them to the proper caseworkers. You know, decide if it's an ADC case or food stamps or general assistance. You know."

"Yes. I know."

"We normally don't get applicants with your experience."

"I suppose not."

"You cleared Civil Service. Do you want the job with the pay I can offer?"

"Yes."

"Report tomorrow morning. Eight o'clock sharp."

"Thank you."

Jeff thanked the receptionist as he left and walked with the wind to his back. Sidestepping a man lying near the door, he went in and climbed the stairs to the third floor. He entered his apartment, then got a beer from the Styrofoam cooler, turned on the TV, and laid on the bed. He was beginning to feel a bit better about himself.

He put on a brown business suit the following morning. He looked at himself in the mirror. The suit hung loosely on him because of the weight he had lost. It was wrinkled from being in the suitcase. So was his white shirt. But the striped tie looked presentable even if it didn't cinch as snugly around his neck as he would have liked. It would have to do for his first day of work.

He did not, however, want be seen leaving this shabby place in a suit, so he put his suit coat in a paper bag and put on his fatigue jacket. He changed in the men's room of a drug store where, at the lunch counter, he had eggs and toast with coffee. He walked into the welfare office at six minutes after eight.

"You're late again," Mrs. Edelmann greeted him. "Come to my office."

Jeff followed her. She sat behind her desk. "Our biggest problem is these goddamned runaway pappies. They get bored with their wife, sick of their kids. They find a new filly and disappear. Then mom's stuck with a bunch of kids and no money. You got the picture?"

Jeff nodded.

"Help these poor gals out, Jeff. They're really hurting! Brokenhearted, no money, no job, a house full of kids."

"I'll try."

"Good! Now let me show you to your desk."

Two hours later, Jeff had seen ten clients. Two couples came in because the husbands had been laid off and they wanted to know if they could get any help. Three others, included a disabled woman, needed food stamps. The other three were ADC applicants. Jeff had dealt with each of them compassionately. He had made the appropriate referrals with a courtesy unusual to the office.

Then his eleventh client presented herself. She was leggy, thin, blonde, attractive. She had high cheekbones.

Jeff rose as she stood before him. "Please sit down."

"Thanks." After situating herself, she asked, "Your name is...?

She's got class, Jeff thought, watching her cross her long legs. "I'm Jeff. Your name?" He reached for an intake form.

"Jacki Higgins. That's Jacki with an 'I.' "

"Marital status?"

"Divorced."

"Your first?"

"My third."

"Oh."

"Yeah."

"Kids?"

"Four."

"What happened?"

"What do you mean?"

"To your marriage."

"You mean the last one?"

"Yeah."

"Oh, I just had to find myself. You know, get some space."

Pain engulfed Jeff, but he didn't change his expression, his tone of voice.

"Did you?"

"Not yet," she laughed.

"Will you?"

"Hey, what is this? Are you my goddamned psychoanalyst?" she retorted.

Jeff ignored her questions. "You getting any support?"

"Yeah."

"How much?"

"Two hundred a month. For the last one."

"Own your home?"

"Yeah. Well, buying."

"Any of your former husbands seeing their kids?"

"That's none of your business."

"You're right. How may I help you?"

"I want some public assistance," she said, emphasizing "public."

"You getting any support from your first two husbands?"

"No."

"Why not?"

"Oh, the court relieved them of their support obligations."

"Why?"

"Because the kids didn't want to see them."

"Oh?"

"Yeah."

"Both times?"

"Yeah."

"How old were the kids when this happened?"

"Oh, they were little."

"I see. How'd their fathers take it, not seeing their children?"

Jeff sensed her glance at his left hand, noticing the absence of a wedding band.

"Is that question on your form?"

"No, it's not."

She was becoming angry. "Then, goddammit, don't ask it."

Jeff did not respond.

Jacki, with unbridled hostility, spoke again. "I want ADC, MA, WIC, and food stamps. And I'm entitled to them!" She stared at him and nearly spat her next words. "You should have punched my ticket by now! I don't have time to hang around this place. Just refer me to a damned caseworker, you goddamned chauvinist."

Jeff sat back in his chair. Returning her stare, he spoke gently. "Of course. Let me just review some things. Let's see, you've just divorced your third husband, and now you're seeking assistance. Do I have all this correct?"

"You got it, babe!"

Moments of silence elapsed.

Jeff spoke again. "You do realize, don't you, that you may be a little confused?"

"What are you talking about? Is this the goddamned welfare office or ain't it?"

Jeff spoke slowly, deliberately. "What I mean is, I believe you may have me confused with someone who actually gives a shit."

With that, Jeff rose and walked out of the office. Jacki watched him leave with a blank, stunned expression.

***

Hours later, Jeff had traveled two hundred and eighty miles; but he did not know to where. When he finally stopped to get a beer, the sun had reached its nadir, lying softly on the flat horizon of the High Plains.

He was very thirsty.

...And I let me go
Where ill winds blow
Now here, now there
Harried and sped
Even as a dead
Leaf, anywhere.

Autumn Song
Paul Verlaine